Right Next Door

Ivy Duncan

First paperback edition September 2024

Edited by Amy Snyder

ISBN: 979-8-9899850-1-2

Author's Instagram: author_ivy_duncan

Other Books by Ivy Duncan

Five Years and 2,000 Miles

Trigger warnings

Mentions of depression, self-harm, and past suicide attempts.

Chapter One

Ren's new bedroom was small. The bed took up most of the space, with just enough room to shove a nightstand in the corner and a dresser by the door. He didn't want to think about how many times he'd break his toes on the furniture when trying to navigate the cramped room. When he'd first arrived, he considered not using a dresser to avoid such injuries, but one glance in the tiny closet put these thoughts to rest. Given his abundance of clothing, the dresser was a necessary addition.

To top the whole room off, the walls were that ugly apartment eggshell color, and the ceiling was an unflattering popcorn texture.

It was all his though, so he didn't care. His own space. Not like the freshman dorm room that was 50 percent his—well, more like 75 percent. His roommate, Noah, had been content with a quarter of the room.

Ren couldn't remember the last time he'd had a space of his own where he'd felt comfortable. Over the summer, he'd stayed in a room at his grandma's house, but that was more of a guest room he'd occupied for a few months. She'd tried to make it feel like home, but he'd always kept the space too tidy to be relaxing. He hadn't wanted her to regret allowing him to stay.

Even at his dad's, he felt far from comfortable. His room there seemed as if it belonged to someone else. A younger version of himself. It made him feel like an intruder.

But this? A room that was his in an apartment he shared with his best friend? Ren could get used to this.

"Hey." *Speaking of his best friend.*

Hale stood in the doorway, looking around as if there was much to see. There wasn't.

"What's up?"

"You're still not done?" Hale could have sounded annoyed—they'd moved in three days ago, and his boxes had been empty since before bed on the first night—but he seemed amused instead. "Want a hand?"

Thankful, Ren turned back to the boxes stacked on his bed. "You couldn't have asked earlier?" he joked as Hale joined him in the tiny room, standing close enough that their shoulders touched.

"I wasn't here." Hale reached out to pull a box closer. When he looked into it, his brows furrowed. It was still full. "What have you been doing all afternoon?"

Ren ignored the question. "Where were you earlier?"

Hale's blue eyes lifted from the mess on the bed to regard him. His cheeks were red. The response he gave failed to explain the expression. "I went to the store."

"The store," Ren echoed. "What happened at the store?"

"Nothing." Hale laughed at the look that came across Ren's face. "Really. Nothing happened at the store. When I was getting back—"

Hale was interrupted by a thump on the other side of Ren's bedroom wall, coming from the apartment next door. It was a sound Ren knew he would have to get used to—a normal aspect of cheap apartment living—though it was the first time he'd heard anything coming from the other apartment.

"What the fuck?" Ren said. "It's been silent over there so far."

"Yeah," said Hale. "We have new neighbors." His voice was light, as if on the verge of giggling. Curious, Ren fixed his roommate with an expectant look, waiting for an explanation. "They're freshmen. I met one of them in the elevator. He's super cute."

It was easy to pique Ren's interest. "*Cute* cute?"

Laughing, Hale nodded. Clearly, he was smitten. "Yes. *Very* cute."

"You should go for it, then," Ren said, bumping their shoulders together.

"Oh." Hale reached into the box, withdrew a shirt, and started folding it. "Nah, I don't think …" he trailed off with a shake of his head.

It wasn't difficult to tell that Hale was feeling self-conscious. He was beautiful, with his sky-colored eyes and light brown hair, features elegant in a way Ren would kill for. Hale had gained some weight since their freshman year, giving him the curves Ren desperately wanted, but Hale hated his own body. His self-deprecation was hard for Ren to watch, though there was nothing he could say to make Hale see himself the way Ren did.

Still, that didn't mean he'd let this whole thing with their neighbor go. "Well, maybe I should go say hello," Ren suggested, intent on talking Hale up to the guy next door.

"You should," said Hale, pulling another shirt from the box. He looked less exuberant than he had a moment before, but not upset. "You'd probably hit it off. You're good at talking to men."

As Ren watched, Hale folded another shirt. "You know I'm going to undo that and put it in the closet, right?"

Hale tossed the fabric down onto the bed. "Find me hangers. I'll do it for you."

With a huff of annoyance that was entirely for show, Ren combed through the other boxes, the topic of their neighbor forgotten for the time being.

Ren went next door after dinner while Hale was in the shower. It would be a quick exchange, he told himself. He'd say hello, talk about how amazing Hale was, and gauge the neighbor's reaction, then return to his own apartment before his friend even realized he was gone.

After he knocked, it was a minute before the door opened. Ren was immediately captivated by the man before him. He was tall, leading Ren to tilt his head back to meet his hazel eyes, and his hair was a muted shade of red. Right then, it was ruffled, giving him a wild sort of appearance Ren very much enjoyed. He had on a pair of gray sweatpants and was covered in a sheen of sweat. Exactly Ren's type.

Damn it, Hale, he thought, gritting his teeth. *You're lucky I love you so much.*

"Hi," Ren greeted, letting none of his interest show in his voice. "I'm your neighbor."

"Ah," was the only thing the man said as he eyed Ren up and down. He looked unimpressed. The reaction almost made Ren frown, but it didn't matter whether this guy liked him; he just had to like Hale. "Hello. How can I help you?"

"I thought I would come introduce myself."

Nodding, the man pushed his hand through his hair, disheveling it further. "I see. Well, you haven't done that yet."

"Done what?" Ren asked, dazed. *Hale, you are so lucky.*

"Introduced yourself."

"Oh! Right. That's why I'm here. I'm Ren." He held his hand out to shake.

The other man looked at it for a moment, then made a gesture Ren didn't understand and revealed, "Miles."

"That's your name?" Ren asked, not because he was stupid but because he felt awkward tucking his un-shook hand into his pocket and wanted to cover the action with words. Miles made a face. "You don't have to answer that. I got it."

"Right," said Miles, throwing a glance over his shoulder.

"Well, anyway, I was just curious if you remember running into—"

The other man cut him off. "Could I get back to what I was doing?"

Stunned, Ren fell silent. "Oh. Sure?" The second the words were out, the door shut in his face.

Ren didn't move right away, replaying the interaction in his head. Maybe he had interrupted something, but it wasn't like he was demanding much time. As Ren saw it, Miles should have been thankful for a break. He'd obviously been working hard, or he wouldn't have been sweating. There was no reason to be rude.

Ren stomped back to his own apartment. "What's cute about *that*?"

Chapter Two

Senior Year

Hale brought it up when Ren was getting ready for a date.

Actually, Hale brought it up *because* Ren was getting ready for a date.

"What are you doing?" he'd asked when Ren walked into his room, going straight to the closet. They weren't the same size, but they were close enough that they could fit into some of each other's clothing. Ren was more likely to take advantage of this fact than Hale, preferring many options for his outfits.

He had missed having access to Hale's closet over the summer, so he'd worn only his best friend's clothing for the two days he'd been back.

"I have a date with that guy from the bar," Ren said, pulling a mint-green shirt off its hanger and holding it up in front of the mirror. Typically, he stuck to darker colors, preferring how they looked with his black hair and pale skin, but he wanted to try something different. "What about this?"

He turned to Hale, shirt still held up. Hale was frowning. "What is it?" Ren asked, dropping his arm. "No good?"

"You always look good. That's not the problem."

"There's a problem?" Ren sat beside his roommate on the bed. "What's going on?"

Hale smiled. "Nothing. Don't sound so worried. I was just going to ask if you wanted to get a drink tonight and talk." He sounded normal, but there was something about his expression that kept Ren on the bed.

"Talk?" he echoed. "Talk about what?"

Hale's cheeks were pink. "It's not a big deal, I just—" He cut himself off. "How late is your date supposed to go? Would you get a drink with me after?"

"I can cancel," Ren was quick to offer. It wasn't an important date. He'd met the guy the night before, and he agreed to get dinner with him only because it seemed to be the next step after kissing the guy for ten consecutive minutes. "It's not a big deal. Just another bar boy. It's not like it's gonna go anywhere."

Still, Hale shook his head. "No need to cancel. What about brunch tomorrow?"

"Can't you just tell me now?"

"I'd really like to discuss it later."

They kept eye contact, challenging the other to back down. When it became clear Hale wouldn't budge, Ren dropped against the mattress. "You know I'm not a patient person."

"Yes, I know." Hale patted Ren's leg.

Scoffing, Ren rolled onto his side toward him. "I can meet you after my date," he said. "We're having dinner at five thirty, so I'm guessing we'll finish by seven if you want to meet at the bar then."

Hale lay down as well. "Is that okay? I don't want you to rush because of me."

"I'll let him know when he picks me up that I can't stay super long so he won't think I'm ditching him if things go well," Ren assured. "It won't be a problem."

This ended up being a lie. Making plans with Hale following his date was indeed a problem for Ren, not because he didn't want to leave when the time came but because he found himself unable to focus on anything his date was saying. All he could think about was what Hale had to tell him.

Thankfully, Ren didn't need to pay much attention. He'd participated very little in the initial conversation. His date, Derek, was more than happy to talk about himself.

About thirty minutes into their meal, Derek reached out to brush Ren's hand. The touch made Ren aware that he had been absently pulling at the leather cuff around his left wrist, and he stopped the anxious action.

"Are you alright?" asked Derek. "Is it not good?"

"What?" Ren lowered his gaze to his untouched plate. "Oh. No. It's very good." He slipped his hand free and brought it back to his fork. "Sorry."

Derek's eyes narrowed. Clearly, Ren's well-being was not important enough to pry over, because after a few seconds, he returned to talking about himself. With a sigh, Ren squeezed his fingers tight around his fork and willed himself to pay attention. He wasn't interested in anything being said, but he hoped listening would keep him from thinking about Hale.

It was a failure, though he found himself temporarily distracted when Derek asked him for advice regarding his ex-girlfriend. If it had been any other night, Ren probably would have left, but it wasn't as if he was being a suitable date either, so he bit his tongue and offered a few words of counsel.

By the time Derek was dropping him off at the bar, Ren wondered weathered he was more desperate to meet up with Hale or be done with yet another failed attempt at romance. Still, when Derek pulled up to the curb outside the familiar brick building and leaned over to kiss him, Ren stayed.

It wasn't a big deal. At this point in his life, he'd kissed enough people for it to hold little significance, and he'd learned the night before that Derek was good at kissing. *He'd probably practiced with his ex-girlfriend.*

When they parted, Derek kept his hand on the back of Ren's neck. "You really have to go? You don't want to come back to my apartment with me?"

Ren pulled back until the hand slipped away. "I promised my friend I'd meet him," he reminded. It was easier than saying he had no desire to go back to Derek's apartment.

Derek looked at him for a moment longer—searching for any sign that he'd cave with more pressure—before leaning back in his seat. His confusion was familiar. Ren didn't address it.

"I'll see you around," Ren offered as his goodbye, making sure not to imply that he was hoping for a second date. If Derek called him, they could discuss it, but he wasn't about to inflate the ego of someone who was just playing him.

He climbed out of the car and shut the door. As Derek drove away, Ren waved, mumbling, "Waste of my fucking time" under his breath.

I just want to be happy, he thought, dropping his hand when the car was out of sight. *Is that too much to ask?*

A familiar and irritating voice interrupted his moment of self-pity to ask what was wrong.

It wasn't surprising he was there—Miles worked part-time at the bar most weekends—but Ren had been hoping to avoid him. His lips pulled down when he turned to Miles. They'd never warmed to each other over the years.

"Didn't you have a good time?" Miles asked. The look on his face suggested he didn't care about the answer. Ren suspected he was just asking to be annoying.

"I had a good time," he lied, not wanting Miles to know he had once again wasted a night on someone who didn't really want him. "Thanks for asking."

His hazel eyes narrowed, but Miles said nothing more. Instead, he gazed down the sidewalk. Ren hated it when Miles spoke to him, but he hated it even more when Miles ignored him. "Not that it's any of your business," he mumbled as he moved toward the bar's entrance.

Unphased, Miles followed him inside.

The bar had quite a few people there for seven p.m., but he knew where to look for Hale. His friend was not as outgoing as he was, and Hale's ideal bar experience was not as exciting as Ren's. When the bar was busy, Hale sat at the back, as far as he could get from the speakers blaring music. Since Jonah's was the bar they frequented most often—close enough to their apartment to walk—Ren knew where to go.

He got only halfway there before his feet stopped. Hale was not alone. Seated in the booth beside him was Logan, the other occupant of the apartment next door. It was a strange sight, Hale and Logan together, but they seemed to enjoy each other's company.

Ren turned. As expected, Miles was still beside him. "Are you here to meet Logan?"

"Yeah." Miles didn't look away from the booth ahead of them. "You're here for Hale?"

Nodding, Ren glanced back at the two men. Whatever Logan was saying was making Hale laugh, his hand reaching out to settle on Logan's arm. Logan seemed pleased.

He was handsome, a black man with deep brown eyes and a smile that had made Ren look twice the first time he'd seen it.

It wasn't often Logan smiled at him. Ren gave neither Logan nor Miles a reason to share such an expression with him. Hale was the same, or so Ren thought, but he couldn't help questioning it as he watched them together.

"What are they doing?"

"Don't know," Miles responded, moving forward again. Frowning, Ren followed him.

Miles stopped at the end of Hale and Logan's table, leaving enough room for Ren to stand beside him.

Hale's eyebrows shot up when he noticed them. "Did you come together?"

Such a ridiculous question did not deserve a response. "What's going on?" Ren demanded.

Hale ignored him. "How did your date go? I was talking to Noah earlier, and he said the guy was cute."

This was doubtful. Their friend Noah was too worried that Ren would tease him for him to admit that another man was attractive. Ren narrowed his eyes.

Finally picking up on his irritation, Hale frowned. "Oh, sorry. What did you ask?"

Chill as ever, Miles slid into the free side of the booth, pressing against the wall to make room for Ren. Ren didn't like that Miles had concluded that the four of them were supposed to meet. He remained standing.

After looking at the space beside Miles and then back at his roommate, Ren asked "Why are they here?"

"Ah." Hale's smile was nervous. "Well, you see, that's what I wanted to talk to you about." He looked at the booth's only empty space. "Please sit down."

"Why?"

No answer was given. Hale glanced at Logan. In response, Logan settled a hand over Hale's on the table. Shocked, Ren took a seat.

Nothing happened for at least a minute. Hale continued to stare at Logan, eyes wide and glassy. It was a look Ren knew well. His best friend directed it at him sometimes, when he was uncomfortable and wanted Ren to save him. Logan seemed aware of the glance because his thumb moved over Hale's knuckles, though his gaze remained on Miles.

Ren didn't know where to look. All he knew was that schooling his expression was unnecessary, since no one was looking back at him.

It came then—the truth—and even though he should have been expecting it given the circumstances, he wasn't.

"We're dating," Logan announced.

How? Since when? For what reason? Why, Hale? Why? Ren wanted to ask, to *demand*, that his best friend answer his many questions, but before a single syllable could leave his mouth, the sound of Miles laughing cut him off.

Startled, Ren shot a side-eye to Miles. It wasn't often he heard Miles laugh. This didn't seem like the right situation for it.

"Well, congratulations," Miles bid, reaching out his fist for a bump from Logan. Hale cracked a small smile, his eyes slipping back to Ren.

Ren wasn't sure what kind of face he was making. He wished he could be happy for his friend, but he was far too confused to achieve that.

Hale and Logan are dating. My best friend is dating someone I hate. My best friend is dating someone and didn't tell me about it. My best friend has feelings for Logan and he didn't tell me …

Did Hale have feelings for Logan?

After only a minute of watching the couple, Ren could tell that their feelings were mutual. Even though Hale looked nervous, he smiled every time Logan reached out to comfort him, eyes glinting with a fondness that differed from the kind Ren received. Hale liked Logan. Ren wondered whether it was a recent development. Two years ago, when they'd all moved to their building, Logan had actually been the neighbor whom Hale had taken interest in, but Hale never mentioned that attraction again after Ren voiced his distaste for Miles.

Just when Ren felt that watching the couple was becoming too much, Hale reached out to touch his arm. Ren missed the context of this action and stared down at the fingers with a frown.

"Ren," Hale said softly. "Let's go."

"What?" It was the best he could manage after spending the past twenty minutes zoned out.

Logan explained, "I was saying that maybe it would be best for the two of you to talk alone."

This didn't meet Ren's expectations, and he felt the question *Aren't you supposed to be taking him from me?* on the tip of his tongue. Ren didn't ask, knowing the look Hale would give him, full of sadness and guilt and maybe even disappointment.

"Okay," Ren said. He nodded, just in case they hadn't heard him over the sounds of the bar.

He slid out of the booth. As Hale did the same, Logan said, "Ren, I promise, I'm not stealing him from you."

Before he could respond, Hale wrapped a hand around his wrist and guided him away. "Do you want to stay for a drink?" he asked. "We could even go to a different bar." Ren shook his head. "Alright."

Hale was too slow in turning away to hide his disappointment.

As they walked to their apartment, they didn't speak. Multiple times, Ren considered what he could say, unhappy about feeling so tense around his favorite person, but each time he thought about Hale and Logan, he was speechless.

"*I'm not stealing him from you,*" Logan had said, and maybe that wasn't his intention, but he'd already caused this awkwardness between them. What if it led to their friendship falling apart? Then, Hale would turn to Logan instead of him, and wasn't that pretty much stealing? Either way, Ren would lose Hale.

"Hey, why don't you tell me about your date?" Hale suggested.

Ren's heart ached at the break of routine. Usually, he would return home from a date and crawl into bed beside Hale, gossiping about whomever he'd spent his evening with. It didn't seem like the kind of night they'd do that, but Hale asking about it now rid them of the opportunity to.

After swallowing heavily in an attempt to loosen the tightness in his throat, Ren managed, "It was fine." He was planning on leaving it at that before a glance out of the corner of his eye revealed Hale's pained expression. "He was a nice guy, but he only talked about himself and wasn't really interested in me."

"Oh no," Hale said, smiling at his cooperation. "That's impossible. Are you going to give him another chance?"

Ren shook his head. "He probably heard the rumors and thought I'd be easy. Besides, you know me. I'll have another date secured for next weekend in no time."

It was the excessive dating that had given Ren the label of *easy* in the first place, though it wasn't true. He didn't sleep with just anyone—he'd gone all the way with only two people—and the lack of action often disappointed his dates. The reason he dated so much was in hopes that he would find the companionship he craved, so men's reactions to the absence of sex helped him weed them out.

Hale hummed. When he spoke again, hesitance was clear in his voice. "Hey, about Logan and me—"

"I don't want to talk about it," Ren interrupted before he could stop himself.

Hale looked back at him sadly. "Are you really that angry with me?"

"I'm not angry with you. It's going to take some time to get used to, is all. I need to process the information I have before you give me more."

There was a pause, and then Ren felt fingers grasp his own. "Alright."

They were silent the rest of their walk.

Chapter Three

The first week of the semester was uneventful. Ren was taking three English classes for his major and a simple math course for a needed credit, and his only homework was to read part of a novel he already knew well. Given any other circumstance, the free time would have been much appreciated, but Hale was also an English major and had a similar workload. At first, Ren thought this might be good. Maybe he and Hale could take the time to figure things out, just the two of them.

Hale seemed to have a different plan for handling the situation.

It was as if Logan had moved in with them. If Hale was in their apartment, his boyfriend was with him.

The first few days of this weren't awful. Ren didn't mind hiding in his bedroom when he didn't have class, reading, playing games on his phone, or taking naps whenever he felt like it. Every couple hours, Hale would check in on him, always with a hopeful expression as he asked Ren to join them. Every time, Ren refused, turning away because he couldn't handle the dejected expression on Hale's face. He didn't need to see it to feel guilty.

Still, he couldn't bring himself to go out there yet. He'd told Hale he needed time to adjust, and instead of respecting that, his best friend forced him into exposure therapy.

By the fourth day, Ren was sick of it. When he opened his eyes to the sound of Hale's laughter in the living room, he wished he could sleep until everything was back to normal between them.

Thankfully, Ren had plans before class that morning, so he wouldn't have to listen to the couple for long.

As he did first thing every morning, Ren rolled toward his nightstand and took a pill from a tinted orange bottle. Then, because a glance at his phone revealed it was almost nine and he knew that Noah would be annoyed if he was more than ten minutes late, Ren climbed out of bed and went to his closet.

By the time he left his bedroom, he had a text from Noah asking where he was. He responded with *I'm leaving now* as he went to the bathroom to brush his teeth, paying no mind to the pair on the couch.

He was still brushing when Hale poked his head into the room, mouth stretched into a grin.

"Hi! Are you having breakfast with us? Logan was talking about making pancakes."

Ren shook his head and ducked to spit in the sink. "I'm meeting Noah for breakfast."

Hale's gaze dropped. "Okay. Tell him I said hello."

"Sure," Ren agreed, rinsing his toothbrush. "You could come with us." *Without Logan* went unspoken.

Most of the time, Hale acted normal. His pestering Ren to come out of his bedroom was normal. During the two classes they shared, Hale leaned over to talk and steal his pens like normal. Hale sticking his head into the bathroom to encourage Ren to eat breakfast with him before class was normal.

But if things were normal, Hale would have accepted Ren's offer to join him and Noah. Instead, he shook his head and backed up, making room for Ren to leave the bathroom.

"Next time."

Noah watched Ren eat his breakfast sandwich with raised eyebrows. When Ren snapped, "*What?*" his friend smiled.

"Nothing. I've just never seen someone eat so aggressively before. I take it things aren't any better?"

Ren didn't dignify this with a response. He just glared and took another angry bite of food.

"It's almost been a week, Ren. Are you ready to admit you might be overreacting?"

"Do you understand how blindsided I was?" Ren shot back, talking around a mouthful of breakfast sandwich. When Noah rolled his eyes, he swallowed. "What?"

"You shouldn't have been." Noah pulled a hash brown in half and ate it. "You're dense as shit. It's been obvious for years that Logan and Hale were interested in each other."

Ren dropped his sandwich back into the yellow plastic boat. "No, they have not! You're saying you weren't at all surprised when he told you?"

"Not really. Though, he told me before they went on their first date, so they weren't technically a couple at that point."

Ren leaned down to take a long sip of his iced coffee. "What's with that?" he mumbled around the straw. "How come he told you about it before me?"

There was a moment of silence, and when Noah broke it, it wasn't to answer the question. "You know, I think they're happy together."

With a noise of distress, Ren pushed away his food and folded himself across the table, his head cushioned on his crossed arms. "I know."

"You don't have to sound so miserable about it," Noah scolded, patting the top of his head. "You look like a sad puppy."

"I'm not sad. Really. It's just—" Ren huffed. "Why him? You know? Why did he have to date someone I don't like?"

Noah hummed, his green eyes lowered. "Do you really dislike him?" he asked. "I mean … I know you hate Miles, but it feels like you just dismissed Logan because you don't like his best friend."

"What person in their right mind would have *that* as their best friend?" Ren could not keep the disgust from his voice.

It earned him a laugh. "You are *such* a bitch."

"Yeah? *And?* You've known this for three years and we're still friends."

"Why do you think I didn't want to live with you again after freshman year?" Noah shot back.

"We totally would have lived together again if I didn't want to live with Hale and you didn't want to live with Jules," Ren defended. "We were great roommates."

They really were. Noah was so low maintenance, it was a good fit for Ren. The school had randomly paired them—people with similar majors or minors got put together to give them something to talk about—and it hadn't taken long for them to get out of the awkward my-roommate-is-a-stranger stage.

"You were bossy," grumbled Noah.

Ren shot him a knowing look. "Yeah, and you had your homework done for every single class, didn't you? Your grades have only gone down since you started living with Jules."

"This is true. I'll give you credit for that." Noah raised his hand to check his watch. "You're bad at keeping track of time, though. We should get going so we're not late."

After one last bite of his sandwich, Ren rose from his seat. "You think we're gonna have any homework today?"

"It's creative writing." Noah grabbed both of their backpacks and put one over each shoulder. "If anything's assigned, we'll have a few weeks to complete it. Don't worry. You'll still have plenty of time to wallow in sadness."

Ren took another sip of his drink, following Noah as he weaved around the tables toward the door. Sitting at one of them was Derek, along with a pretty girl he was obviously interested in. When their eyes met, Ren winked, unconcerned. They hadn't spoken since Ren got dropped off at the bar after their date. He was neither surprised nor disappointed by this.

"Hey," Noah began, slowing so they were walking side by side. "Want to go out with us again this weekend?"

Ren didn't need to think about it. "I'm willing to do anything that gets me away from my apartment."

***

As he walked home after class, Ren thought about what Noah had said to him before they parted ways.

"Tell Hale how you feel. You know he'll listen to you."

Of course, Ren knew this. That wasn't why he was hesitant.

Why should I tell him anything when he clearly feels he doesn't have to tell me things? It was petty and stupid, and Ren knew that way of thinking wasn't productive, but he couldn't stop being frustrated over it.

Still, when he returned to the apartment, he didn't go straight to his room. Instead, after responding to Hale's greeting with one of his own, he sank down on the couch beside his best friend, nodding to Logan on the other side of him in hello. There was a pause in which Hale looked at him, shocked, before he beamed.

They were watching a popular sitcom everyone had seen before, and because of that, they allowed themselves to get distracted. Hale and Logan got lost in each other, and Ren watched them. He couldn't help but notice every time they touched. The actions seemed familiar, like they were used to doing them. Clearly they'd passed the initial awkward phase of their relationship.

Isn't it a little soon? Ren realized he didn't know how long Hale and Logan had been together. They had both stayed in their apartments over the summer, so it could have happened at any time over the past three months. *How long has he been hiding this from me?*

Bothered, Ren abruptly rose.

"Where are you going?" Hale asked.

Ren stopped on his way to the balcony to grab his cigarettes and lighter from his room. The pack was mostly full. He'd cut back over the summer—this was typical for his breaks, as he still lived with his grandmother and the smoke made her cough—and was hoping to keep up with it this time around. Something told him he was going to fail.

"Gonna smoke," he answered, slipping outside before Hale could respond.

It was a moment of instant regret. The second he closed the door behind himself, a camera shutter sounded. Miles was out on his own balcony, seated in a plastic green chair. Held up to his face was his camera. His eyes squinted as he gazed out across the parking lot through the lens.

Do I go back inside? Ren considered, but the idea of returning to the couch wasn't appealing. Thankfully, it didn't seem like Miles was going to pay him any attention, so Ren let his fingers slip from the doorknob and took a seat on the concrete.

He removed a cigarette from the carton and pinched it between his lips as he lit the end. *"Filthy habit,"* his brother had accused after finding a pack in Ren's room back when he was in high school. *"It'll kill you, eventually."*

"Why do you care?"

It was the memory that vexed him, but his brother wasn't there and Miles was, so he snapped, "What are you even taking pictures of?"

Miles didn't react to his voice. "The parking lot."

"Why?" Ren demanded, looking over the boring pavement for something eye-catching enough to warrant snapping a photo. Miles shrugged. It was infuriating.

"I'm bored," he offered with a sigh, picking up on Ren's not-subtle annoyance. "Trying different things."

Ren took a huff at his cigarette, hard enough that the nicotine made his throat burn. He was taking his irritation out on Miles, but their relationship had always been like this. Ever since Miles had been rude to him the day of their meeting, Ren determined that Miles could serve as a sort of outlet and he wouldn't have to feel guilty about it.

"Can't you *try things* inside? I'm angsting here and you're bothering me."

Miles lowered his camera. He didn't go inside, but he stopped taking pictures. Content with this compromise, Ren closed his eyes and rested his head against the glass door.

It didn't take him long to pick up on the sound of Hale and Logan laughing inside. The noise was far less welcome than even Miles's camera, and Ren bared it for only a minute before putting his cigarette out on the cement. Right away, his fingers itched for another. "I can't fucking stand this," he complained.

"I'm not even doing anything—"

"I'm not talking about *you*," Ren snapped. "I'm talking about *them*! They're around *all the time* and it's driving me crazy."

"They're there all the time because of you," Miles pointed out, as if Ren couldn't have figured this out on his own already. "They're trying to get you used to seeing them together so you can stop *angsting*."

"Yeah, and it's annoying the shit out of me," Ren grumbled. "And why are they harassing only me? What about you? Don't you need to adjust as well?"

The answer Miles gave was flat. "No. Because I'm not throwing a tantrum like a four-year-old."

"Fuck you."

"Why would I need to adjust? They're happy, and I'm glad my best friend found someone who makes him feel that way. I'm not just going to dismiss their relationship out of pettiness."

Ren was silent. He knew he deserved to be called out, but Miles being the one to do it was frustrating. "That's not it, though," he protested, his voice softer than it had been earlier. "Maybe I'm just a little irked, but I could easily get over that. What bothers me is that he didn't tell me about it sooner. I'm his best friend. I tell him *everything*. How come I had to wait so long to find out he has a boyfriend? Why didn't he even tell me he was interested in Logan?"

"Probably because he knows you and expected you'd be difficult."

Ren considered what would have happened if Hale had been open with him the whole time. He would have been less angry, though he had enough self-awareness to know he would have tried to talk Hale out of dating Logan before they got together.

"Look," Miles continued. "I understand you being upset over him not telling you. It bothers me somewhat that Logan didn't tell me until now either, though I suspect that's because if they'd told me before you, you'd be even more of a pain in the ass. Regardless, why don't you be a bigger person and try to be understanding? Then, the next time something like this comes around, he won't hesitate to tell you."

Ren shuffled his feet against the concrete. "I am making an effort," he grumbled weakly, thinking of the ten minutes he'd spent on the couch. There wasn't a response, so he assumed Miles wasn't convinced. "I am, but it's hard, okay? There are things I can't help but consider. What if he takes Hale away from me?"

Miles shook his head. "You're the one putting distance between the two of you."

It was the truth, and Ren closed his eyes at the sound of it. "Why do you care what I do?"

"First off, you're the one who brought it up," Miles pointed out. "Second, you acting like this stresses Hale out, which stresses Logan out, and unlike you, I actually care about the emotional well-being of my best friend." The accusation made Ren wince. "Also," this was spoken more softly, "I'm home alone all the time … it gets kind of lonely."

Ren wondered whether it was worth it to defend himself. After a moment, he realized there was nothing he could say to refute Miles's accusation, because it was true. Lately, he'd been ignoring Hale's well-being.

He pressed his forehead against his knees. "Why don't you get a girlfriend or something?" he said. "You'll be less lonely then."

Miles sighed loudly enough that Ren glanced at him out of curiosity. "No thanks." His voice was thick with exhaustion. "You date enough for the both of us."

"I hate you," Ren told him right before Miles slipped inside and closed the door.

That night, while Hale was in the shower, Ren leaned against the back of the couch beside where Logan was sitting. "Hey."

His approach must have been quiet, because Logan jumped before turning his face up toward him.

"Are you scared of me?" Ren asked.

Logan smiled, as if the mere idea of this was amusing. The expression reminded Ren of how attractive he was. It made him feel proud of Hale, who deserved nothing less. "You're the one who's been avoiding me," Logan pointed out.

Ren huffed.

"Scared isn't the right word," Logan said. "Cautious. I don't want to do anything to make you dislike me more than you already do."

Abashed, Ren stared ahead at the television screen, unable to meet Logan's gaze. "I don't dislike you." From the corner of his eye, he could see Logan's eyebrows raise. "We should talk. Would you like to get coffee with me sometime?"

Logan gazed at Ren with a bewildered expression. "I figured I should get to know you if you'll be living with us," Ren added.

Breaking into a wide grin, Logan said, "I would love to."

Chapter Four

The following night, Ren found himself at his favorite Chinese restaurant with his best friend's boyfriend. Logan had chosen the place, and Ren suspected Hale had something to do with it.

So Hale knows? While he and Hale hadn't spoken, he'd suspected Logan would share their plans with him. Ren liked this; he didn't want Hale dating someone who went out to meals with other men and hid it.

"You're sure this is okay?" Ren asked, settling into the booth. On the ride over, he'd planned on asking this, but Logan had inquired about his day, and he'd gotten distracted venting about class.

"Is what okay?" Logan grabbed a menu from the napkin holder and slid it across the table to Ren before grabbing another.

He's a gentleman too, Ren mentally added to the list of Logan's qualities he was compiling. He realized after his conversation with Noah the day before that he knew nothing about Logan and was attempting to gather information before judging him too harshly.

So far, Logan had been quite pleasant. This was good, even if it made Ren feel more guilty.

"Well, it's a Friday night and we're getting dinner," Ren said, looking over the menu as if he didn't order the same thing every time. "I thought Fridays would be date night."

"Before the semester began, every night was date night, so he was fine giving me up for the occasion."

It reminded Ren he knew very little about Hale and Logan's

relationship. Instead of getting upset like he had been, he decided he could try to change that. "Hey…" he began, lowering his menu. "Would you mind telling me a bit about you two?"

"What do you want to know?"

"Whatever you're comfortable telling me, really. I know you must have explained things to Miles and me the night you told us you were dating, but I couldn't focus."

He was expecting Logan to look exasperated with him—it was his own fault that he knew nothing, so why should Logan have to repeat himself—but he just nodded and closed his menu. "I don't mind talking about it again. Is there anything particular you're curious about?"

Ren considered it. There was a lot—when they started dating, where they went on their first date, who had asked who out—so he suggested, "Let's start at the beginning."

Logan's face lit up. It was cute how happy he was to get to talk about Hale.

Ren thought his best friend deserved no less.

Hale and Logan started dating about halfway through the summer after Logan asked Hale out to dinner. According to Logan, he'd been thinking about asking Hale out for years by that point, ever since they first met. With both of them lonely over the summer and their roommates gone, Logan had a chance to get close enough to Hale that asking him out didn't seem random.

Logan hadn't been talking long before Ren came to realize that Logan was completely in love. It made Ren's heart hurt, craving for someone to feel that way about him, but he pushed the feelings away and asked Logan about their first date. Seeming more than willing, Logan continued on with the tale of his and Hale's relationship.

★★★

When they'd both finished their meals and fought over who would pay—Logan won and slipped his debit card to the server with a triumphant grin—Logan looked at him with hope. "So, am I worthy of dating your best friend?"

Ren sipped the last few swallows of iced tea through his straw. "Almost," he said. "Just one question … why *Miles* as a best friend? Like … come on. Can't you reconsider?"

Logan laughed. "Miles is a good guy. You just don't know him very well."

This was the answer Ren had been expecting. "Well, other than that, I suppose you're alright." Ren smiled at Logan's pleased expression. "Just don't hurt him, okay? I'll seriously kill you if you do."

As he took back his debit card and receipt from the server, Logan nodded. "I've had a huge crush on him since I was eighteen. I'm not planning on ruining this."

"Good." There was one thing left for Ren to do. "I'm really sorry about how I've treated you these past few days. I really hope you don't think anything less of Hale for having a friend like me."

Logan stared at him with parted lips. Ren knew what he was thinking.

People often thought Ren's opinion of himself was very high, that he refused to apologize because it would be acknowledging his imperfections. Those people couldn't be more wrong. Ren's feelings toward himself bordered on hatred, and he often avoided admitting fault because he saw no purpose. People apologized so others knew they felt remorse and could be forgiven, and Ren didn't really care about forgiveness. What was one more person's dislike toward him when he couldn't even like himself?

It was different when it concerned Hale, though. If Hale ever came to hate him, Ren didn't know what he'd do.

Having recovered from his surprise, Logan cleared his throat. "Thanks for apologizing, but you don't have to. At least, not to me." Ren's expression must have given away his nerves because Logan's smile was gentle. "Come on," he urged, sliding out of the booth. "Hale's waiting."

***

When they got back to Ren's apartment, Ren expected Logan to follow him inside. Instead, when Ren stopped outside of the door to fumble with his keys, Logan continued to his own place.

"You know Hale should be here. He only has his night class on Monday and Wednesday," Ren said.

"Yeah. He is. I'll come by tomorrow. I think I should give you guys some time alone."

The relief that washed over Ren was unexpected. He couldn't remember the last time it had been just him and Hale in the apartment. The thought of it made something in his chest ache as he remembered how badly he missed his best friend.

I'm not stealing him from you, Logan had said the day they revealed the relationship. Ren could finally believe this.

"Thank you," he offered sincerely. Logan's eyes widened, and Ren wondered how bad Logan's perception of him was. He didn't ask, just raised his hand to wave, thanked Logan for dinner once again, and slipped into the apartment.

Hale was sitting on the couch, a novel open on his lap so he could pretend to read it, eyes focused on the television. At the sound of the door, he looked up.

"I'm such a dick," Ren blurted out.

Hale's gaze flicked away. "Uh …?"

"I mean," Ren continued, kicking off his shoes, "*I'm sorry* for being such a dick."

Grinning, Hale abandoned his novel on the couch. He came up to Ren and placed his hands on his shoulders, leaning forward to press warm lips against his cheek. "It's okay," he said when he pulled back. "I still love you."

Ren reached to hug Hale as Hale reached to hug him.

"I'm sorry for not telling you sooner," Hale said, speaking low. "I was nervous when I shouldn't have been." He pulled back, even though Ren didn't feel quite ready for that. His next words consoled him. "I bought stuff for root beer floats."

They did something they should have done earlier in the week. They pressed together on the couch under the same blanket, both with coffee mugs filled to the brim with ice cream and root beer. A quart of ice cream stayed close on the coffee table so they could add more when they ate what was already in their cups. Then they talked.

They talked all about Hale and Logan's relationship and Ren's feelings on the matter. There was a lot to discuss, and it took two refills of ice cream for each of them before Ren asked, "You still a virgin?"

Hale made a distressed noise. He bumped his shoulder against Ren's, causing some of the root beer from his mug to splash onto his forearm. With a whine, Ren lifted his arm to his mouth and licked up the spill.

"Come on," Hale said, his voice like a scolding. "We haven't been dating that long."

Smiling into the rim of his cup, Ren mumbled, "He's too hot not to jump."

Hale gave a breathy laugh. It was a sound Ren knew, one Hale would make when they folded over a magazine and Ren said something crude about an attractive man. It was always someone unattainable, some actor or model who they'd never meet, so it felt out of context. For the first time, Hale made that noise for someone who wasn't a dream to him.

"I know, right?" he said. Ren watched as Hale took another sip of his float and licked the froth from his lips. "Why is he even with me?"

"Because you're beautiful."

As usual, Hale's cheeks pinked, and he waved a dismissive hand, not really believing him. "*Your opinion is skewed,*" Hale explained once, when Ren demanded to know why Hale always brushed him off like that. It was an ongoing battle that Ren was determined to win. He thought this made Logan his ally.

"If you were in my situation," Hale continued, as if Ren hadn't even spoken, "you wouldn't have had sex with him yet either. You only have sex with people who are in love with you."

This was the biggest rule Ren held himself to. *Don't sleep with anyone who doesn't love you.* It was a precaution, a way to keep himself from getting hurt again.

The first time Ren had sex, he was fifteen, a sophomore in high school. It had been his childhood best friend, Rhett, who confessed first, allowing Ren to admit his feelings as well. They dated for only a short while.

After a few weeks, they'd decided to take the most adult step they could think of. The morning after, Ren's father had discovered the two of them in bed together. While sheets covered them, they were still obviously naked, a condom wrapper on the floor telling the story of what they'd done.

Rhett, terrified of his parents finding out—Ren's father didn't care about either of them enough to tell on them, so it was a pointless worry— had ended things almost immediately. *"Don't think about it too much,"* he had said to a shocked Ren. *"I was just curious. Think of it as an experiment. I never expected it to go this far."*

Lies. Ren knew it. The two of them had been the best of friends; it wasn't something you messed with for the sake of *experiments*.

As he grew up, Ren came to understand that while Rhett had been lying to him, he hadn't actually loved Ren. If he had, he wouldn't have left, or at the very least he wouldn't have lied.

And so, Ren wouldn't give himself to someone who didn't truly love him ever again. The consequences hurt far too much.

Ren had slept with only one person since—Julian, close friend and current roommate of Noah—and Ren knew Julian had been in love with him. They'd dated for six months a year and a half ago, parting after Ren came to terms with the fact that Jules loved him and Ren couldn't love him back.

Saying any of these thoughts aloud would take them off topic, so he didn't voice them. Instead, he said, "If you think he isn't in love with you, you're stupid. You can tell by how he says your name."

Hale slapped a hand down onto Ren's knee, the action one of dismissal. "So!" His voice came out loud. "Let's talk about something else. What happened with that guy you went on a date with … Derek, I think his name was."

It was. Hale was good with details. It saved him time when writing essays.

"Eh. It didn't work out," Ren dismissed, taking a loud slurp of his drink. He wasn't upset about it, and he waved his hand around to communicate this when he caught Hale's eyes still on him. Though Hale nodded in understanding, he reached out to grab Ren's fingers.

"That's okay," he said in a voice that carried a mother-like comfort as he patted Ren's hand. "Don't rush. It'll happen."

The way he spoke, without a single doubt, made Ren sigh. He leaned his head against Hale's shoulder. "I never want to fight with you again," he mumbled, smiling when the shoulder beneath his head jumped with little chuckles.

"Okay," Hale agreed, as if it was as easy as that, as if Ren wasn't difficult. "Let's not."

Chapter Five

Ren smiled at himself in the mirror, then slapped his cheeks when it felt fake.

The morning had been rough, his mind refusing to let his body get out of bed, forcing him to lie there for an extra hour in a numb state until Hale knocked on his door and invited him to breakfast. Once he'd gotten out of bed, it was better, but there was still the looming feeling of emptiness that snuck up on him when he wasn't distracting himself with something else.

Ren would not let it ruin his night. He had plans to go out with Noah and was looking forward to it.

After rubbing his sore cheeks, Ren checked his outfit in the mirror again. He was wearing women's clothing—high-waisted black shorts with three buttons in the front and a flowy white shirt—but he looked good in it. He often dressed this way when going out. While it wasn't what he felt most like himself in, it gave him confidence in a way men's clothing didn't.

Leaning forward, he met his own brown eyes. "Eyeliner," he decided. Then, louder, he called out, "Hale!"

"Yeah?"

Ren ripped his door open, grabbing the felt-tip eyeliner pen from on top of his dresser as he left his room.

"Can you do my eyeliner?" he asked, making his way to the couch where Hale and Logan were sitting. The question made Logan's eyebrows raise. "What? You've seen me out at the bar before."

"I didn't know Hale put the eyeliner on you."

Ren handed the pen to Hale and sat on the couch to his right. "He has a steadier hand than me."

Hale rose and stood in front of him, close enough that Ren's knees touched his legs. With amusement clear on his face, he gazed down at Ren.

"What?" Ren asked, dropping his chin to his chest to check his outfit again.

"Nothing," Hale said. There was a pop as he removed the cap of the pen. "Noah is going to tell you to change when he gets here."

Widening his eyes in a way he knew made him look innocent, Ren asked, "What's wrong with what I'm wearing?"

It drew a laugh from Logan. Proud of himself, Ren smiled. Hale paused, eyeliner pencil raised, then shook his head. He grabbed Ren's chin, tilting his head backward. Ren closed his eyes.

"I look cute as shit," he said as he felt the first touch of the pen.

"You do," Hale confirmed. "You also look like someone Noah is going to need to take care of all night."

"Sounds like Noah's problem."

When Hale huffed out a chuckle, Ren felt his breath against his face.

The pen lifted from his left eyelid. "I like it when you pull your hair up," Hale said. "I can see your face better. "

Ren's hair wasn't exactly long, but it was long enough to get annoying, falling in his eyes at inconvenient times and tickling the back of his neck. It wasn't a big enough problem yet to cut it, but to avoid irritation he often pulled the front back into the world's smallest ponytail on nights he went out.

He cracked open his eyes. The skin of his left eyelid felt damp, and he closed them again, hoping he hadn't messed up Hale's work. "You're okay," Hale assured without Ren having to ask. "Here." Hale blew across his face. When he was done, he said, "This is what you get for buying cheap makeup."

Ren blinked his eyes open. "It's not worth splurging for something I'm just going to cry off by the end of the night." He closed his eyes again, waiting for the touch of the pen on his other eyelid. It didn't come. "What are you doing?"

"Did you take your medication this morning?"

The question didn't surprise him. On nights Ren was going out, Hale often checked to make sure he had taken his antidepressant. The days after drinking were rough, and they bordered on unmanageable if he skipped his medication. They had learned this the hard way their freshman year when Ren thought it was best to not take his pill because of its negative side effects when mixed with alcohol. Now, he compromised and drank less so he could still take his prescription. "Yep," he said in a cheery voice. "I'm good to go."

They were silent as Hale did his second eye, blowing on the skin to help it dry faster. When Ren felt him move away, he opened his eyes. "Thanks," he offered, leaning back as Hale went to return the pen to his room. "Did he do a good job?" Ren asked Logan.

"Yes?" Logan sounded unsure. "Hey, is that uncomfortable?"

"The eyeliner? No."

"Ah, no. Sorry. I meant …" Raising a hand, Logan pointed to his own neck as if he didn't know the word. Still, he ended up saying it. "Choker."

Ren thought of the smooth ring of leather around his throat. It matched the thick leather cuffs he wore on each wrist, though those were far more worn from everyday use.

He raised a hand to hook a finger under the choker, pulling it tight against the back of his neck. "This? It doesn't bother me, but maybe that's because I like things around my neck." He dropped an eye in a wink and sunk his teeth into his lip to keep from laughing at Logan's reaction.

A hand gently pulled at Ren's hair, forcing his head back so he was staring up at Hale. "If I didn't know you any better, I'd say you were trying to flirt with my boyfriend," he accused. His expression was playfully stern.

Scoffing, Ren lifted his head. "Oh please. I'm not an idiot. I know there's no room for me, and I'm not the least bit bothered by it. Also, I would never do that to you."

Hale's hands settled onto Ren's shoulders. "What shoes are you going to wear?" The subject change confirmed his lack of concern with Ren's teasing.

"Hmm." Lifting his legs, Ren looked down at his socked feet. "My white sneakers?"

"Don't wear white shoes to the bar," Hale said, taking a seat beside Ren. "Borrow my black ones."

"Okay." Ren stared ahead at the television screen. He could feel it creeping up on him, the numbness that had kept him in bed that morning. Somehow, Hale must have sensed it as well, because he bumped his shoulder into Ren's, jostling him from his trance.

"You alright?"

Laughing because Hale always knew, Ren hugged his friend tight around the waist. "I'm perfect," he said. To keep this true, he had to get moving. After a quick kiss to Hale's cheek, Ren stood. "I'm just tired, is all."

"You don't have to go out," Hale said. "Stay in with us." As he said this, he placed a hand on Logan's arm.

"Nah." Ren looked at the space between the couple. "I'm not that tired. Besides, you two need alone time to do coupley things."

There was a knock at the door then, so Ren didn't have time to appreciate the blush spreading across Hale's cheeks.

Noah was out in the hall, dressed like a typical straight man. Ren didn't feel bad for judging, because it was clear he wasn't the only one doing so. After looking him up and down twice, Noah pointed toward Ren's bedroom. "No."

"Yes." Ren left the doorway. "I'm almost ready. Give me a second."

Dramatic as always, Noah covered his face with his hands and groaned into his palms. Once his point had gotten across, he dropped his hands and looked to Hale in betrayal. "Why'd you let him put that on?"

Ren was crouched by the shoe rack so he couldn't see Hale, but his voice told Ren he was amused. "He didn't ask me for permission. Also, I'm not his parent."

Ren moved back to Noah, placing a hand on his friend's shoulder to steady himself as he pulled on Hale's shoes. "Noah, don't be embarrassed," he said. "You'd look bad beside me no matter what you were wearing. The gap between the effort we put in will be beneficial to you. People will just assume you look bad because you're next to me and not because of that ugly polo."

After pulling the second shoe up over his heel, Ren dropped his foot to the ground and smiled up at Noah. Noah's expression was blank. "I know you're a man, but punching you would be too similar to punching a woman, and I just can't."

Shaking his head, Ren let his hand slip from Noah's arm. "Alright, let's head out. I want to get to Rita's before they're all out of wap." As usual, the plan was to pregame with—and steal alcohol from—Noah's friends before hitting the bars.

"You're going to Rita's?" Hale asked. "Will that be okay?"

Noah's friend Rita didn't like Ren. It had to do with Julian, her boyfriend, being Ren's ex.

"She's the only one with a house this year," Noah explained. "She knows Ren's coming with me, so it should be fine. I'll keep an eye on him."

"On *me*?" This didn't seem fair. "What do you think I'm gonna do? *She's* the one with a problem."

Ignoring him, Noah asked, "Do you have your wallet?" Following the question, he stared down at Ren's shorts, probably noting the smooth fabric suggested empty pockets.

"Do I look like someone who's going to be buying their own drinks?" Ren demanded, raising an eyebrow. On the couch, Logan huffed out a laugh. "Besides, we're going to pregame, so I can just drink there."

As Ren ushered Noah out the door, eager to begin the night before his weird mood could get the best of him, Hale called, "Please bring him back alive!"

It was cold outside when they left the bar, but the air felt good on Ren's hot skin. Noah was somewhere behind him, calling out to him from the sidewalk. Paying no mind, Ren wandered down the middle of the street with his head tilted back to see the stars. It wasn't dark enough to appreciate the view, though he kept looking, waiting to be moved.

Emptiness.

When do I get to stop feeling like this?

"Ren!" It was louder this time, a little more panicked. Ren lowered his head.

A car had turned onto the street ahead of him, only a block away and quickly approaching. Before it even occurred to him to move out of the way, a hand clamped around his forearm, pulling him out of the street. "What the fuck are you doing?!" snapped his rescuer.

Ren stumbled over the curb, hands grabbing the shirt of the person in front of him so he didn't fall. Curious, he looked up at Miles's face. For a moment, he didn't react, the word *warm* echoing in his head as he stayed pressed to the other man's chest. He thought of Miles's words and pulled away.

"What the fuck are *you* doing?" Ren shot back, slapping away Miles's helping hand when he once again stumbled on the curb. "Who told you you could touch me?"

"Thank you!" called Noah. Ren watched his friend jog over to them, raising an unimpressed eyebrow when he stopped beside them and bent over, panting. When he straightened after a long moment, he looked at Ren and said, "I'm going to murder you."

"Woah." This came from outside their circle of three, and Ren turned to see who had spoken. The movement caused a brief bout of dizziness.

Four people were standing in a group a few feet away. Ren recognized one of them, a brunette girl he'd seen with Miles around campus often. He'd watched them from afar, amused by the obvious way the girl—her name was Clary, if he remembered correctly—was desperate for Miles's attention. Before pulling Ren out of the street, Miles must have been with them.

"Everything alright over here?" It was the guy who had spoken before. He was Asian and had bleached blond hair, the color almost yellow under the lighting from the streetlamps. Ren thought he was cute.

Noah's hand reached out toward Ren. "We're okay," he said. When his fingers brushed Ren's arm, Ren jerked away, bumping against Miles. To catch him, Miles's hands settled on his hips.

The look on Clary's face amused him enough that he didn't pull away, allowing Miles to continue to steady him. The girl glared.

Noah continued. "Ren's hammered and stupid and won't listen to me. I'm trying to take him home so I can go to bed, but he doesn't want to."

Another guy from Miles's group laughed. He was cute too, though Ren assumed that had more to do with his coloring than him being attractive. His dark hair was a perfect contrast to his piercing green eyes. Ren wondered whether his hair was naturally that color or if, like his friend, he dyed it. In their current lighting, everything looked artificial. "How much have you had to drink?" he asked Ren, who held up his thumb and forefinger as if to say only a little. It was a lie, and it must have looked like one, because the man laughed again.

The hand on Ren's left hip tightened, just enough that Ren thought the action might be unconscious. "I can take him off your hands if you'd like," suggested Miles.

Ren was expecting Noah to ignore the offer. Curious, he looked at his friend, who stared back at him and Miles with raised eyebrows. "You don't need to do that."

"It's fine," Miles assured. "I just got done with my shift and ran into these guys, but I'm kind of beat so I wouldn't mind going home. He can come with me. You go get some rest."

It occurred to Ren that this was something Noah might agree to. "I don't want to go with you," he protested, squirming out of Miles's grasp.

"I thought you said you'd come out with us for a while," Clary voiced, acting as if Ren hadn't spoken.

"Next time," said Miles.

"Hey!" Ren snapped, frustrated. "Noah." When he turned, Noah was already a few feet away.

"Thanks man," he said to Miles before fleeing. Ren watched him go, his jaw slack.

Behind him, he could hear the group trying to convince Miles to go out. "He can just come with us," one guy said.

When Noah was a dot in the distance, Ren turned back around.

Clary was scowling at the suggestion to bring Ren along. To fuel the fire, Ren chimed in, "Yeah, let's do that." Hanging out with Miles and his friends was one of the last things he wanted to do, but he preferred it to returning home for the night.

Of course, Miles disagreed. "I think I should get him home," he said. "I'm too tired to be fun, anyway. I'll see you guys later."

It was a clear dismissal. Miles's friends left with no more encouraging, bidding them both goodbye before continuing the way Ren had come from.

"Did you make me ruin your night so you'd have another excuse to hate me?" Ren asked.

Miles made a face. "You didn't ruin my night." He looked after his friends for a moment before sighing and cocking his head to the side. "Let's go."

"I don't want to go home yet," Ren said, not moving even as Miles walked away. On nights like this, when Ren felt that familiar weight, he would cry if not distracted. It was late, almost one a.m., and Hale was surely asleep already. If he returned to his apartment, there would be nothing to take his mind off the emptiness. "Miles!" Miles didn't react to his call, so Ren chased after him, catching up quickly. When he looked up at Miles, he was struck again by Miles's height. "I want ice cream. Will you take me to get ice cream?"

"No."

"*Miles.*" Ren pulled on his arm. "Please. I want ice cream and I'm *cold.*"

"If you're cold, you shouldn't eat ice cream," Miles pointed out. Ren pouted. With a sigh, Miles slipped off his jacket and draped it over Ren's shoulders. "I'd be cold too if I was dressed like that."

He continued walking, once again leaving Ren behind. Surprised by the act of kindness, Ren stared after him for a moment. The jacket was warm and smelled pleasantly of laundry detergent.

Ren caught up to him again, tucking his nose into the jacket's collar. "I look good," he mumbled. "Are you going to buy me ice cream?"

Miles didn't respond right away. Ren gazed at the stars. "I'll buy you ice cream as long as you eat something else as well."

"Like French fries?" Ren asked hopefully.

Hazel eyes regarded him with interest.

There was a fast-food place a few blocks down, and Miles brought him there. He told Ren to take a seat while he ordered, and then joined him a few minutes later with a large order of fries and a caramel sundae.

Ren took the ice cream first, offering the sincerest "Thank you," he'd ever given to Miles. With a grunt of acknowledgment, Miles sank into the seat across from him.

They sat in silence for a handful of minutes, Ren eating his sundae and Miles watching with his head propped up on his hand.

Miles spoke only when Ren dribbled caramel down the front of his shirt. "You're like a little kid," he said. It came off as more of an observation than a scolding.

"Well, it's better than being like an adult." Ren scrubbed at his shirt before determining it a lost cause. When he raised his head to meet Miles's eyes, Miles looked back, his expression warm for a reason Ren couldn't think of. It wasn't something he wished to dwell on.

"You worked tonight?" Ren asked.

"Yeah."

"At Jonah's?"

"That's where I work."

Ren licked his spoon clean. "Is bartending fun? I think it would be fun."

"You just think that because you'd flirt with everyone."

"Are you judging me?" Ren snapped.

"No."

Ren eyed him suspiciously, but gave up and ate a French fry.

"You have a huge hickey," Miles observed.

When Ren raised his hand to his neck, he expected to feel the leather of his choker. His fingers met only skin, and he recalled the removal of the accessory before receiving the mark Miles was referring to. Proud, he turned his head to better display his neck. "That's because someone kissed me tonight!"

"That guy you went on a date with?" Miles asked, sounding more interested than Ren had been expecting.

With a shake of his head, Ren dipped a French fry in his ice cream and ate it. "Nah, he was boring. This is a new guy. We met tonight at the bar."

"Good for you." It sounded dry and uncaring.

"You're the one who asked," Ren grumbled, scooping out the last big spoonful of ice cream and pressing it past his lips. Mouth full, he asked, "Are you going to date that Clary girl?"

Miles's brows furrowed. "That's not her name."

"Really?"

An amused huff left him. "What's it matter who I date? Why do you care?"

"I don't," Ren said, beginning to pick more consistently at the French fries. "I just don't like her."

Miles sighed. "I'm not interested in Clarisse."

Not looking up at him, Ren nodded. He didn't want to continue the conversation, afraid it would get weird if they ventured further into each other's love lives. They fell silent once more.

He was just eating the tiny French fries out of the bottom of the bag when Miles broke the silence to ask, "Are you alright?"

Curious, Ren raised his chin. "Peachy."

Miles seemed skeptical.

"Why? Do I not look alright?"

"It looks like your eyeliner ran a little."

Ren scrubbed at his eyes. Right. He'd cried in the bathroom at the bar. "I don't know what you're talking about," he said anyway. "I'm perfectly fine."

"Okay." Miles didn't sound as if he believed him. Ren both hated and appreciated him for it. "Why don't you want to go home, then?"

Ren crumpled the bag the fries had been in. Why would Miles ask such a question? It made it sound as if he cared. "I just don't. Home is where the night ends."

"Exactly. You seem tired."

There was nothing Ren could say to counter this. Miles seemed to take his silence as acceptance, because he rose from his chair. "I don't want to," Ren said, looking up at him.

The other man offered Ren his hand. *Why?* Ren wanted to ask, but he feared the answer would be pity. Begrudgingly, he was pulled to his feet.

They didn't speak. Miles led him through the dark living room, pausing only to gesture at the open door of Ren's bedroom to confirm it was his. Inside, Miles pressed on his shoulders until Ren sat on the bed. He helped Ren out of his coat, and then crouched by his feet to remove his shoes for him.

Ren wanted to know why he was being so nice. It was too quiet to ask, so instead he climbed beneath his covers when Miles pulled them back. "Sleep," Miles said as he draped the blankets over Ren.

When he left, Ren's door closed behind him with a barely audible *click*.

Ren didn't sleep.

The tears came, and he looked up at the ceiling and wondered whether existence was this hard for everyone.

Chapter Six

The next morning, Ren woke up to Hale petting his hair. His body was warm, the covers tucked around him, and he wished he hadn't woken up. Everything felt pleasant, but he wasn't happy or content. Sleep was better than this.

"How are you feeling?" Hale asked.

"I'm okay." Ren rolled over, hugging Hale around the waist and pressing his face into his stomach. The hand in his hair continued to move, ruffling the strands in comfort.

It wasn't abnormal for Hale to coddle Ren the day after he got drunk, knowing the effect alcohol had on him.

"Want to come eat some breakfast?" Hale's hand slipped down to rub over his shoulder blades. "There's bacon and pancakes and I could make some French toast if you'd like. Miles and Logan are here, so if you're uncomfortable, I can bring food to your room."

"Why are they here?"

"Miles told Logan you had a rough night. They thought it'd be nice to provide breakfast."

Ren thought of Miles the night before, kneeling to help Ren slip off his shoes. "That's fine," he grumbled, lifting his head and squinting into the light. "What time is it?"

"Almost ten." Hale twisted toward Ren's nightstand to get his prescription bottle. Ren sat up, pulling his hair out of the messy ponytail he'd slept in and taking the chalky white pill Hale offered him.

"Thanks." Hale got up while Ren began undressing, lifting his hips so he didn't have to leave the warm bed to remove his shorts. Without a word, Hale gathered the clothes and provided him with a clean pair of sweatpants and a T-shirt. Once he'd pulled them on, Ren tucked the covers around himself again.

"Do you want to stay in here?" asked Hale. Ren shook his head. "Want to bring the blanket with you?" Another shake. "Want to take a shower?"

Ren nodded. "After I eat." He pushed the covers off, but Hale stopped him from getting up.

"Wait." He had brought a damp washcloth with him, and he used it to scrub at Ren's eyelids. "Your eyeliner is all over."

"Thank you," Ren said again, this time for helping him take care of the simple tasks that seemed unbearable when he was in this kind of mood. He almost repeated his gratitude a third time, because a part of him had worried Hale wouldn't have time this anymore after getting a boyfriend.

"Don't worry about it."

They left the bedroom, Ren trailing behind his roommate. By the time he reached the small dining table, Hale was already fixing a plate for him by the stove. Ren sank into the chair across from Miles, trying to ignore his stare. It made him feel self-conscious.

"What?" he demanded, sounding more tired than feisty.

Miles's eyebrows drew together.

As the four of them ate, Ren remained silent, speaking only when someone addressed him and always in short answers. He could tell it was throwing Logan and Miles off. They peeked over at him increasingly as the meal continued. By the time Ren was leaning back from his plate, food only half eaten, both men were trying to watch him subtlety.

"Done already?" asked Hale, frowning at Ren's plate. "Aren't you going to be hungry later?"

"Maybe, but I'm not hungry now." Nodding, Hale reached over to gather his dishes and carried them to the sink.

"Um ..." Logan began. He sounded uncomfortable. "How do you feel this morning? I mean ... Miles said you had a lot to drink last night. Are you hung over?"

"I'm fine. I have a bit of a headache." Both Logan and Miles were staring at him now with skeptical expressions. Ren wondered what their faces would look like if he just up and announced *I'm not acting like this because I'm hung over, I'm acting like this because I'm depressed.* "I'm going to go take a shower," he said instead, standing from his chair.

Still facing the sink, Hale offered, "I'll bring you a towel and a change of clothes in a minute."

A stab of shame punctured Ren's chest, the feeling welcome since it was something other than indifference. It meant the day wouldn't be as awful as it could be.

"I can grab it," he mumbled. "Thanks."

Hale shut off the faucet. "You sure?"

Ren felt like a child. It made him hate himself. "Yeah," he confirmed, and Hale must have detected something in Ren's voice because his eyebrows pulled together. That too made Ren feel bad. He wanted to know if there was a way to navigate life that didn't make him feel awful, and he reminded himself that every day wasn't like this.

He felt Hale's hands on his face before he even realized he'd closed his eyes. "Come on," his best friend said, taking his hand. "One thing at a time."

There was a fresh towel and clean pair of briefs on the toilet seat when Ren finished his shower. He dried his body slowly before wrapping the towel around his shoulders and hugging himself. *I could just stay here*, he thought. *No one expects anything from me when I'm in here. No one expects me to be not empty.*

As usual, when he had these sorts of thoughts, discomfort accompanied them. It was far easier to slip into emptiness and stay like that until his mind was ready to focus on emotions, but he still preferred to be forced out of the trance before he fell too deeply in.

Ren grabbed his leather bracelets from where he'd discarded them on the vanity and put them on one at a time. The feeling of them around his wrists was a comfort. "Okay," he muttered to himself. "Underwear, pants, shirt." Mindlessly, he followed his own instructions. "The rest of the day will be better." He forced himself to look at his reflection in the mirror.

In a disconnected sort of way, he observed the shadows under his eyes and the red mark a guy whose name he didn't remember had sucked into his skin the night before. He felt as if he were looking at someone else.

"I should stop drinking," he said, watching his own mouth move. It was pointless to say. Ren knew drinking had a direct hand in making him feel this miserable, and even if he'd always regret it the day after, there was just something about being drunk that pulled him back in every time someone invited him out.

With a forced smile at himself in the mirror and a sigh at the failed attempt, Ren pulled open the door to the bathroom. The thought of returning to his room to sleep the day away was a temptation, but Hale twisted on the couch to look at him, his expression hopeful. Once again, Ren fought to present a smile. It must have been painful looking, but it was worth it because Hale beamed. Ren's smile felt less fake.

"Come watch a movie with us!" Hale invited, patting the spot next to him. Ren let his gaze wander over to it, and then further to where Miles was sitting. Their eyes met. It wasn't a big couch and Logan was on it as well. If he sat, they'd all be pressed together.

Still, Ren went over to them, stepping over Miles's legs to sit between him and Hale. As predicted, one of his shoulders pressed into Hale's and the other into Miles's. All Ren could think was how warm it was when Hale pulled a blanket over him.

They were watching a movie on the Syfy channel, something with a complex plot involving aliens. It wasn't Ren's kind of movie, but he found enjoyment in it then, liking how distracting it was to figure out what the hell was going on. About forty minutes into it, Hale moved his attention from the hushed conversation he was having with his boyfriend to ask, "Do you like this?"

Ren made a noise in the back of his throat and sunk farther down on the couch until the blanket tickled his lower eyelashes. "I'm confused," he said, which wasn't really an answer. "Why are they bringing explosives? Didn't the last crew get wiped out because the alien-thing was explosive-proof?"

Clearly, Hale hadn't been paying close attention to the film, because his expression went blank. To Ren's right, Miles cleared his throat.

Preparing to be annoyed by whatever he would say, Ren glared at him. He'd been avoiding looking at Miles. The way they were sitting put Miles in the sunlight shining in through the windows. The light was kind to him, making his hair appear bright orange and his skin flawless. Ren hated how hot he thought Miles was. "They're bringing the explosives to blow it up from the inside."

Ren turned to more fully regard him.

Hazel eyes widened. "What?

"You've seen this stupid movie before, haven't you?"

Miles appeared offended. "You're the one invested enough to ask questions," he grumbled, leaning so there was distance between them. Ren opened his mouth to speak again, but all that left him was a breathless laugh. Seeming almost as surprised as Ren felt, Miles's lips twitched as he fought a smile. "You're laughing at me now?"

"You're embarrassed," Ren accused. "That means you know it's bad."

"I like this movie."

Shaking his head, Ren turned back to the television. He'd missed a lot of content during the past two minutes, though he didn't mind. If he got confused, he was sure Miles could explain whatever he needed to know.

Noah arrived about twenty minutes later, when the characters on the screen were discussing how to get the dangerous predator to consume explosives. He let himself in without knocking, alarming only Miles and Logan with his sudden entrance. Hale and Ren both knew to expect him on days after Ren drank. Ever since freshman year, the three of them gathered at these times, since Hale and Noah wanted to be there for Ren. It was sweet, and while Ren always insisted they didn't need to, he took comfort in their presence.

"Yo," Noah greeted, pausing at the sight of the four of them huddled together. "You look cozy." He shut the door behind himself and toed off his shoes.

He approached from the back of the couch, reaching over Ren's head to drop a small red box with a familiar chocolate company logo on his lap as he passed. "I got you chocolate-covered toffee to apologize for ditching you last night. You should share with Miles as thanks for taking care of you."

"You don't have to apologize," Ren assured. "I would have ditched me too." He opened the box, removed one of the rectangular candies, and bit into it. It crunched under his teeth. From the corner of his eye, he could see Miles looking at him, so he extended the box toward him.

"Aw, come on," Noah chided as he dropped onto the chair. "If you were really that bad, I'd stop asking you to come out with us."

Ren snorted softly, earning a surprised glance from Noah. "The reason you don't stop inviting me to go out with you is because you're afraid of me kicking your ass."

Any regular day this would have led to bickering about whether Ren could beat up Noah, but Noah just stared at him for a moment longer and then directed a smile toward the television. "You're in a good mood today. Is it because of the new friend you made last night?"

Ren assumed Noah was referring to the guy he had kissed, so when Hale asked, "New friend?" he raised his hand to point out his hickey.

"He and Rita were getting along," Noah elaborated. The memories that came back to Ren made him groan, and he dropped his hand upon realizing that the words along with his action made it seem as if he was implying Rita had been the one to give him the mark.

Hale didn't seem as distressed. "That's great! I always thought you two would get along if you were more open-minded. You're very similar."

"That's why Julian dated them both," said Noah.

"Wait," Logan chimed in, leaning around his boyfriend to look at Ren. "You dated Julian Readbocker?"

"Yeah," Ren answered. "Sophomore year."

"Can I ask who broke up with who?"

It wasn't a strange question for people to ask, and it had been long enough since their breakup that Ren no longer minded talking about it, but he frowned anyway. "It was a mutual agreement."

"They both took it super hard," Noah chimed in. "It was a rough month after that."

The reason Ren and Julian had broken up had been Ren's fault, though Julian never blamed him for it. They'd been together for six months when Ren realized he couldn't think of Julian as anything other than a friend. It wasn't fair to Julian, who deserved to be loved, so they'd broken up before anything had the chance to go bad between them.

It had been difficult. After spending so much time together, Ren viewed Julian as a best friend, and he struggled to get over the loss of their relationship and the feeling that he'd thrown something good away.

"Yeah," he said. "As far as breakups go, it was clean, but I don't think either of us wanted it to be over." He could feel Miles's eyes on the side of his face and turned to meet his gaze. As they held eye contact, Ren thought of Miles the night before, watching him from the other side of the table at the fast-food restaurant.

Why does he look at me like that? Ren wondered, feeling both self-conscious and defensive.

"Are you two alright now?" Miles asked.

Shrugging, Ren looked back toward the TV. The volume had been turned down during their conversation, so the main character's mouth opened in an inaudible scream. "We're fine. I'd consider us friends, but we're not as close as we used to be, and we wouldn't ever go out to do something just the two of us."

This was a lot of talking for him on one of his bad days, and he felt the need for a break. He dropped the open box of toffee in Miles's lap and rose from his seat. The blanket fell to the floor.

"Where are you going?" Hale asked, reaching out to grasp his wrist. "If you don't want to talk about Julian, we can stop."

"I don't care that we're talking about Jules," Ren said, shaking his wrist free. "I just want to smoke."

Noah slapped his hands down on the arms of the chair. "I'll come out with you," he offered, making a move to stand.

"No need." Ren stepped over Miles's legs and paused by the chair, pressing his hand into the top of Noah's head so he didn't get up. "I'm fine. Really fine. I won't burn my fingers." This was why he didn't smoke when his depression was bad, prone to zoning out until the heat got at his fingertips.

Noah gazed up at him, green eyes framed by his thick lashes. They were wasted on a man who thought sweatpants were appropriate everyday attire. "I'll keep you company."

Now Ren yanked his hair until Noah hissed and slapped at his wrist. "I don't want your company. You annoy me."

"What's with you?" Noah demanded, sounding more amused than offended. "I came over to distract you from misery, but you're just as mean as normal."

"Yeah, yeah." He went to his bedroom to grab the pack of cigarettes and lighter off his dresser. The weight of the carton told him he'd need to buy more soon.

As an afterthought, he swiped his cell phone off his nightstand.

Out on the balcony, after lighting his cigarette, he checked his phone for the first time that day. There were a lot of pointless social media notifications that he ignored, as well as two unread text messages.

One was from Noah earlier that morning, asking how he was. The second was from an unknown number.

Hey, it's Sawyer from the bar last night. Wanna get together some time?

Ren didn't respond. Instead, he slipped his phone into the pocket of his sweatpants and leaned against the railing of the balcony, exhaling smoke when his lungs ached.

There wasn't much that he thought about, but thanks to the group of guys inside, he wasn't quite empty, and he didn't burn his fingers.

Chapter Seven

On Monday, Ren ran into Miles in the hall on his way to his 8:30 class.

It wasn't unusual for them to see each other in the mornings. They typically stayed silent and then went their separate ways, but as they waited side by side in front of the elevator that morning, Miles spoke.

"How are you feeling?"

"What?" Ren asked, sharp because that's just how he was on weekday mornings.

The elevator opened and Miles stepped inside first, holding his free hand against the door so it wouldn't close on Ren. In his other hand, he was holding a bagel. "You just seemed kind of off yesterday. I wanted to make sure you were feeling better."

"I'm fine," Ren dismissed, stepping into the elevator and crossing his arms. Miles pressed the button for the first floor.

"Would you like a bagel?"

Ren's stomach almost rumbled at the thought. He'd skipped breakfast in favor of lying in bed for a couple of extra minutes. "Excuse me?"

Miles's hand stretched out toward him in offering.

"Why would you give me that? Isn't it your breakfast?"

"No," Miles said. It very much seemed like a lie. Ren gave a light scoff. "Hey, it isn't. I was going to give it to Clarisse."

"Give me that," Ren snapped, taking the bagel from him as the doors parted. Miles seemed all too pleased.

***

When Ren took his seat beside Noah in math, his friend zeroed in on the bagel. "Where'd you get that? Can I have some?"

"Screw off."

Noah huffed. "So that's how we're going to start our day together, is it?"

Pulling apart the bagel, Ren hummed at the amount of cream cheese between the halves. "I know you, and I know you never miss breakfast in the morning. It is not my fault your stomach is a bottomless pit, but I haven't eaten." Ren slipped his arms free from the straps of his backpack.

With a laugh, Noah propped his elbow up on the table and rested his chin on his palm. "I know you too, and you usually end up skipping breakfast because you're too concerned about your appearance." Noah's green eyes flicked down to what he was wearing, raising an eyebrow at his dark shirt and red flannel. "Are you really not going to share with me?"

Defeated, Ren extended the bagel toward his friend, who leaned forward to take a bite.

"Thanks," Noah said, speaking with his mouth full. "Where'd you get it, though? Did Hale get up early to make sure you ate?"

More mindful of manners, Ren waited until he swallowed to speak. "I ran into Miles in the hall and he gave it to me."

Noah's eyebrows raised. "That's interesting. Did something happen between you two on Saturday night?"

Ren paused, teeth pressed into the bagel, about to take his next bite. He thought of Miles on Saturday, slipping his coat around Ren's shoulders as they walked outside. Before responding, Ren took his bite, chewed, and swallowed. "Nothing happened. He wasn't horribly irritating, which was unexpected."

"Ah, come on. He's not such a bad guy," Noah claimed, receiving a dry look from Ren. "You're eating the food the man gave you for free, probably because he was worried about you."

Ren didn't like this. "He's not worried about me," he protested, starting on the second half of the bagel. At the front of the room, their professor asked them all to quiet down. Ren lowered his voice. "The bagel was for someone else."

"And yet you're the one eating it."

Huffing, Ren reached over to grab Noah's cup of coffee from the table, taking only a sip so he didn't burn his tongue. "I don't want his pity."

"Give that back."

Ren did.

"I don't think he pities you, and you shouldn't be upset with him for being worried," Noah continued. "Anyone would be worried after seeing you yesterday."

"You're not worried."

"That's because I've been around on those days for the past three years, and I know that compared with your worst, yesterday was a good day."

As he licked the leftover cream cheese off his fingers, Ren sunk lower in his seat.

"How are you feeling today?" Noah asked. His low voice suggested they were talking about something important.

"I'm fine. Back to my exceptional self. You know I bounce back quickly."

Noah's lips curled up. "That's what I told Rita."

At the sound of Julian's girlfriend's name, Ren grimaced. "*Rita?*" he echoed. "Why were you talking to Rita about me?"

Their professor scolded them then, inviting them to leave if they couldn't be quiet. They put the conversation on hold until the end of the class.

Rita stayed in the back of Ren's mind, so he was prepared to pick up where they'd left off once their professor dismissed them.

"So, what did you tell Rita about me?" he asked as he followed Noah out of the room. Any other day, they would have parted ways outside the classroom, but Noah had borrowed a novel from Ren that he needed for class. He knew he'd never get it back unless he went to Noah's room himself.

"Nothing bad. Rita, Jules, Luca, and I went out to dinner last night, and she asked me how you were feeling, so I told her you'd be fine by today." Noah snorted at the face Ren made. "Of course she'd ask about you. She was with you when you cried at the bar."

"That's horrible."

Laughing, Noah reached back and grabbed Ren's arm, pulling him out of the way as a herd of underclassman pushed past them. "You say it's so horrible and yet every time you drink, you get drunk enough to cry."

"I do not." In Ren's back pocket, his phone buzzed. He reached for it, expecting it to be a request from Hale to bring food back to the apartment with him. "It's just every time I drink with *you*," he said, failing to point out that most of the time he drank, it was with Noah.

"Are you telling me I make you sad?"

Distraction prevented Ren from answering right away. The text wasn't from Hale, but Sawyer, the guy from the bar. *How are you this morning?*

Ren chewed his lip and typed out a quick response. They'd texted back and forth a few times the night before, the conversation coming easily. Sawyer seemed like a nice guy. Guys he met at the bar rarely reached out to chat, so Ren thought maybe Sawyer was actually trying to get to know him.

When he raised his head, Noah was watching him. "I'm not saying you make me sad, no," Ren dismissed, returning his phone to his pocket. "I'm telling you, I know I can get you to take care of me."

Noah glanced ahead as they approached the exit. "Speaking of going out, how about you, me, Hale, and Logan go out the weekend after Hale's birthday?"

Right. That was coming up. "It's next Wednesday, isn't it?"

"Yeah," Noah said, holding the door open for Ren.

He really treats me like I'm a woman, Ren noted.

"You two doing your thing?" Noah asked.

Their *thing* was an uneventful evening for just Ren and Hale. On Hale's birthday, Ren would make dinner for them—on Ren's, it was the other way around—and after eating, they'd make a cake and consume as much as they could manage.

The first time they'd done this was during their freshman year. Ren was in the dorm kitchen at ten p.m. making a pizza for himself when Hale, who he barely knew at that point, wandered downstairs with a box of cake mix and a bag full of ingredients. They'd shared, just enjoying each other's company for the first time, and planned to do something similar for Ren's birthday during second semester.

It was a tradition now, and every year Hale's birthday came around, Ren felt as if they were also celebrating the anniversary of their friendship.

"We are!" Ren said. "I think drinks that weekend would be fun. I'll mention it to Hale when I get back to the apartment."

"Great."

Ren's phone buzzed again. The message this time read: *I'm glad. You feeling up for dinner this weekend?*

Laughing, Ren showed Noah the screen. Noah seemed unimpressed. "Well, of course he's going to take you out. How could he not after marking his territory?" At this, Noah flicked Ren in the neck where his hickey was.

Ren paid the teasing no mind and responded to the text.

When they got to Noah's dorm, Julian was there, sitting on the futon with his computer in his lap. He raised his head to look at them as they entered, eyebrows lifting at the sight of Ren.

"Hey."

He was wearing his reading glasses, and the thin frames reminded Ren of when he'd climb into Julian's lap and whisper something suggestive at the sight of them. That time had passed, so instead, Ren nodded in greeting and looked at Noah's desk.

"Get searching," Ren instructed.

As Noah groaned and dropped his backpack on the ground dramatically, Ren went to sit beside Julian on the futon.

"How are you?" Jules asked, watching Ren from the corner of his eye. *How are you feeling after Saturday,* Ren translated.

"I'm all good," he dismissed, waving a hand.

"He's got a date with that guy!" Noah chimed in. "The one who gave him the hickey."

"Hey!" Ren snapped. "Keep looking!"

Julian seemed amused. "That's great."

Unable to make eye contact with his ex-boyfriend as they discussed a potential relationship, Ren stared straight ahead at the door. "It's too soon for that. Probably won't go anywhere. Just a bit of fun."

Julian shrugged and said nothing else about it. Ren was thankful. Jules knew him well enough to know he was always hopeful the newest guy would be the one so he could stop searching for happiness and experience it instead.

"How's Luca?" Ren asked to change the subject. "Noah said you guys got dinner last night. I was shocked Luca took a break on a school night."

Luca, like Noah, knew Julian from before college. He was Julian's best friend, but it was hard to tell, since Luca was rarely around, too busy studying for med school or law school or one of those hard things. Also, according to Noah, Luca seemed to be in love with Julian, though, weirdly enough, it wasn't a big deal. They didn't talk about it or pay it any mind, and Luca seemed unbothered by Julian's relationships.

"Luca is Luca," Julian said. "He's overworked, though somehow not exhausted or stressed. It's amazing."

"And terrifying."

Julian chucked. "He's misunderstood, I think."

"Here it is!" Noah exclaimed, holding the desired novel high over his head. "I was worried I'd left it at home, but I remembered packing it for move in." He tossed the book at Ren. "I also highlighted important passages you may need."

The novel was required for the English class Ren had at noon, which Noah had taken the year before. As Ren flipped through the pages, he thought for the first time that maybe it had been a good thing they weren't taking it together. "Ah, that's great. Thanks."

Noah seemed proud of himself.

"You're going back to your room?" Julian asked. "If you want to hang out for a bit, you can come get lunch with us at eleven."

Ren shook his head and stood. "Nah. Hale is probably waiting for me back at the apartment. We usually eat together." He waved the book at Noah. "I'll see you at two thirty."

"Yeah," Noah said. "If you see Miles, be sure to thank him for the breakfast."

Ren bid his very last goodbye with his middle finger.

In his apartment, Ren found Hale, Logan, and Miles seated at the small kitchen table with an open box of pizza. He paused, taking in the sight. "It's ten in the morning. What are you doing?"

"Eating pizza!" Hale answered, taking a bite of the slice he had folded in his hand.

"Want some?" Logan asked. "We got an extra large."

Ren left his backpack by the door and went to join them. The only seat available was the one beside Miles, so he sunk into it with a grumble. "The sight of you in this apartment is getting too familiar."

Miles removed a slice from the box with his free hand and offered it to him. "Well, I saw they ordered pizza, and I was hungry."

Ren accepted the slice with a quiet "Thank you."

"You can't blame me for being hungry. You're the one who ate my breakfast, after all."

Jaw dropping, Ren hit Miles on the shoulder. "I *asked* if that was yours!"

"Well, I lied."

Ren didn't know what was more annoying—how proud Miles seemed of himself or that Miles had known Ren would take the bagel if he told him it was for Clarisse. With a huff, Ren turned to his pizza. He wasn't hungry—after all, he had eaten Miles's breakfast—but he took a bite for the flavor.

"Ah, Hale," Ren began when he finished chewing, grabbing a napkin from the center of the table to wipe his mouth. "Noah asked if you and

Logan wanted to go to the bar the weekend after next to celebrate your birthday." Ren glanced at Miles. "You can come too."

Miles made a face, his eyes flicking across the table to Hale.

"Ah, well, I was hoping we could go on a trip that weekend … the four of us," Hale said, his expression hopeful.

"By the four of us, you mean—"

It was Logan who explained. "The four of *us*." He gestured around the table. "It'll be fun."

His displeasure must have been obvious, because Hale said, "*Come on,*" and reached across the table to take his free hand. "I thought we could book a cabin by Lake Michigan for a Friday and Saturday night and hang out."

The idea of spending a weekend with Miles made him want to wrinkle his nose, but it was what Hale wanted, and Ren more than owed his best friend. With a groan, he leaned forward and rested his forehead against their clasped hands. "I love you so much," he said.

Hale gave his hands a squeeze. "I'll call to book a place tomorrow."

Chapter Eight

On Friday, Ren took a seat next to Logan at the bar in Jonah's. He wasn't there to see him—he was there for a date with Sawyer—but when he'd spotted Logan, he thought it would be strange not to say hello. Miles was there as well, on the other side of the bar. It wasn't surprising to see him working, but Ren had been hoping he'd have off.

"Ah, hey!" Logan greeted with a smile. "What are you doing here?"

"Date," Ren said. "What about you?"

Logan nodded toward Miles. "Just visiting."

Ren looked at the bartender. Miles always seemed tall, but when Ren was sitting, the distance was almost ridiculous. "I suppose you'd get lonely without Logan, huh?"

Miles's smile was cocky. "Nah. I get hit on quite a bit."

Ren scowled at that idea. He turned to Logan, choosing to ignore the brag. "Hey, you want to come over on Hale's birthday for dinner and cake?"

Logan raised his drink to take a sip. It must have been soda—Logan was only twenty, and Ren doubted Miles served alcohol to underage customers. "Hale said he couldn't do anything that night. Said it was a tradition for the two of you."

"Ah, he just said that for my sake. He'll be happier if you're there too, so I'm okay with it."

This seemed to please Logan. "Yeah, then. I'd love to come."

"Great. I'll text you the time. Don't tell Hale you're coming. It'll be a surprise." Ren glanced at Miles. "You can come too. Wouldn't want you to be lonely in your apartment by yourself." Logan chucked.

"No need to worry about me," Miles dismissed. "It's next Wednesday, right? I already have plans with Clarisse."

Ren wrinkled his nose. He didn't want to feel curious, but he *did*, and before he could stop his tongue, he echoed, "Plans with Clarisse?"

"We have the first photography exhibition coming up, and my work will be displayed, so we're helping set up that night."

Sometimes, Ren forgot Miles was a photography major. He didn't give off the *artsy* vibe Ren associated with photographers. He was curious if Miles was any good at it, though he must be if his work would be featured in an exhibition. The year before, Ren had dated a photography major for a couple weeks, and he recalled the man complaining about how difficult it was to get work displayed in the school's exhibitions when you weren't a senior.

Ren noticed Sawyer then, standing by the door, his gaze roaming the bar for him. It was Ren's first time seeing Sawyer since the previous weekend, and it was a relief that Ren still found him cute. Sometimes, alcohol clouded his judgement and he made choices he wouldn't have sober. "It looks like I'll be taking my leave," he said as the blond man approached.

He rose from the stool just as Sawyer stopped at his side. "Hey."

Smiling, Sawyer wrapped an arm around Ren's waist. "How are you?"

"I'm good. Looking forward to our date. You want to order something to drink before we take a seat?"

Sawyer nodded and gave Miles his attention. "I'll get a rum and coke and ..." He dropped his gaze to Ren. "What do you want?"

"Vodka cranberry."

Miles nodded but didn't move. "You're a junior, right?" he asked. "Could I see your ID?"

Seeming amused, Sawyer removed his wallet from his back pocket and thumbed out his license. "Sure thing. I'm old for our grade."

"Oh, so's he," Logan chimed in, nodding toward Miles. "When's your birthday?"

Miles answered for Sawyer as he handed his ID back. "He's August."

"And when is yours?" Sawyer asked. Sensing tension, Ren glanced between the two guys. Birthdays seemed like a stupid thing to get competitive over.

"July," Miles said, turning to fix their drinks.

Sawyer made a face, then looked down at Ren. "So," he began. When Ren glanced up at him, he noted Miles was taller. "When'd you get here?"

"Not long ago," Ren said. "I didn't wait long. It worked out well. Logan—you know Logan, right?—he's dating my best friend, Hale, and I had to talk to him about plans for Hale's birthday coming up."

"Oh? You having a party?" It was such a frat boy thing to say that Ren had to fight a grimace.

Before he could respond, Miles placed two glasses on the counter. The sound was louder than Ren thought it ought to be. He glared at Miles, but Miles wasn't looking at him. "How would you like to pay?"

"Start a tab," Sawyer instructed, handing over his credit card as he looked down at Ren. "Come on. Let's find a more private place to talk."

"Yeah. Let's."

As Sawyer led him to the booths along the side of the room, Ren swore he could feel Miles's gaze on his back, but when he took a seat and glanced in his direction, Miles wasn't looking. Ren thought maybe he'd imagined it.

Just after eleven, Ren told Sawyer he should head home. He was having a good time—Sawyer was funny and cute, and when he asked Ren about himself, he seemed interested in the answers—but it was a Friday, and by eleven he just wanted to fall into bed. Like a good date, Sawyer offered to walk him home.

To Ren, walking him home meant to the apartment building, so it surprised him when they arrived and Sawyer insisted on accompanying him to his door. "I won't get attacked in my own apartment building," Ren assured. Sawyer followed him inside anyway.

Outside his apartment, Ren paused. It had been a nice date, and most nice dates ended in kisses, so he didn't go inside yet. "Thanks for tonight," he said.

When Sawyer kissed Ren, it wasn't what he had been expecting. The entire night, Sawyer had been a gentleman, respecting Ren's distance at the bar and linking their fingers on the way home.

There was nothing gentle about his kiss. It was bruising, not in the romantic way Ren had read about in novels and even experienced himself a few times, but in an uncomfortable way that made him think, *Ouch.*

Maybe the alcohol had affected Ren's memory, but he was sure their kiss the night at the bar hadn't been like this.

Roughly, Sawyer parted his lips, tongue seeking his out. Ren's hands clamped down on the blond's shoulders, a noise of surprise leaving his throat as Sawyer pressed him back against his door.

What is even happening?

Sawyer pulled away and looked down at him, blue eyes half lidded seductively. His mouth parted to speak, lips red from the force of his kiss, but before anything beyond the word *"can"* left him, the sound of a throat clearing cut him off.

They both turned to Miles, who was watching with a deadpan expression. Sawyer seemed confused.

"He's my neighbor," Ren said, using Miles's presence as an excuse to push Sawyer back. "It is getting late. You'd better go."

For a moment, Sawyer didn't move. It seemed he was expecting Ren to change his mind. When he didn't, he nodded and backed away. "Yeah, okay. I'll text you tomorrow." He left, passing Miles without even glancing at him.

Ren regarded his neighbor with raised eyebrows, daring him to say something. With a grimace, Miles continued toward his door. "Well, that's something I never wanted to see."

Scoffing, Ren removed his key from his pocket. "I'm sure you'll get over it." He fumbled to unlock the door. "Hey, aren't you done a little early? It's not even midnight. Get fired for neglecting customers for your girlfriend?" He was referring to Clarisse, who Ren had seen stop by during

Miles's shift.

Miles kept his eyes down as he unlocked his door. "No. I was just covering half of someone's shift tonight."

Nothing was said about Clarisse being his girlfriend, and Ren felt another prick of annoyance. "Whatever," he grumbled, finally getting the key to turn in the lock and pushing open the door.

The apartment was quiet—Hale most likely asleep already—and Ren slipped through the living room, stopping in the door to his bedroom to grab his pack of cigarettes.

It was chilly out on the balcony, but he had gotten used to it from the walk back, so the cold didn't shock him. Still, after lighting his cigarette, he shoved his left hand into his pocket for warmth.

As he exhaled smoke through sore lips, Ren thought of Sawyer and questioned what kind of person kissed someone like that after a first date, and whether Miles had interrupted them because he could tell Ren hadn't enjoyed it.

Chapter Nine

On the night of Hale's birthday, Ren tried not to feel lonely.

Hale was happy, so he was happy, but he missed his friend's presence in the kitchen with him as he cooked. Instead, this year, Hale and Logan sat together on the couch while Ren made the preparations in silence, chiming into the conversation only when they included him.

Still, he didn't regret inviting Logan over. It improved the quality of Hale's birthday, if his smile was any sign.

They look so happy together, Ren thought, watching Logan push Hale's hair off his forehead. Ren looked away, a familiar pang stinging in his chest. *I want that.*

"Dinner's ready," Ren announced, mixing the spaghetti with the Alfredo sauce he'd prepared. "Come eat."

He'd set up three place settings, and Hale dragged him to the side of the table with two, leaving Logan across from them. "Thanks for making dinner," Hale offered.

"Yeah, thank you," Logan bid as well, taking his seat and leaning forward to look into the large serving bowl of pasta. "It looks great. I didn't know you could cook."

"Ah, I can't really." Ren watched as Hale served them all, starting with Logan and then moving to Ren, leaving himself for last. "I just found a recipe online. Sorry, there's no salad or anything. Vegetables are expensive, and I only make money during the summer."

Hale finished filling his own plate. "Salad is overrated."

"You don't work between semesters?" Logan asked.

"Nah. I could get a job, I guess, but my dad covers my tuition and sends me money for the apartment every month." As he spoke about his father, he kept his eyes down. It wasn't a topic he liked to discuss, and he hoped they didn't stay on it for long.

Of course Hale knew this, and he steered the conversation away. "This is delicious! Both of you, try it."

They did, and Ren was pleased to note that Hale was right. It was quite good. "Good recipe," Ren credited, already gathering his second bite.

"I doubt it'd taste like this if I made it," Logan claimed. "It's very good. Miles would love it."

Ren hated that his curiosity piqued at this. "Really?"

Nodding, Logan wiped his mouth with his napkin. "Yeah. He's rather passionate about cheesy pasta."

"Well, he could have come for dinner. I invited him."

"You invited Miles?" Hale asked, shocked enough to speak through a mouth full of food. His skin flushed, and he raised a hand to cover his mouth. Once he'd swallowed, he spoke again, "Sorry." Logan seemed far more charmed than put out with the temporary lack of table manners.

"It would have been weird not to invite him. He was there when I asked Logan."

"He couldn't make it?" asked Hale.

"The art exhibition is a week from Saturday and they're doing some of the setup tonight, so he couldn't," Logan explained.

Right, Ren thought. *He's with Clarisse.*

"Oh!" Hale sounded delighted. "That's right. He was told last Thursday he was getting space, wasn't he? That's a big deal for a junior. Is he excited?"

"He *is*, but I think it's also stressing him out quite a bit, so he's been in a bad mood."

Not wanting to seem too interested, Ren brought his attention to his food and resumed eating. Hale paused, fork hitting his glass plate with a little *clink*. "Well, we should go support him. He'd be okay with that, right?"

"I think he'd like that."

It fell silent, and Ren realized that was because they were staring at him, waiting for his response. "Oh. Me too?"

"Yeah!" Hale said. "Come on. It'll be fun, and you love art."

Ren considered it. Going to a photography exhibition could be a waste of a Saturday—Sawyer asked about taking him out again, and Saturdays were suitable days for dates—but he couldn't deny that he was curious to see Miles's photos.

"Alright," he agreed. "I'll go, but if you all get dinner afterward, you can't force me to come."

"Of course not. I already feel like I'm forcing you to come to the cabin with us this weekend."

Ren was quick to shake his head, not wanting Hale to feel guilty. "You're not forcing me. If I didn't want to go, I wouldn't. What's the place you reserved like?"

"Oh, I forgot to send you the link …" Hale trailed off as he unlocked his cell phone, navigating for a moment before handing it over to Ren. "Look through the pictures. It's super cute, and it's right on the lake. There's a fireplace down by the water, so I thought we could get stuff for s'mores."

"Sweet." Ren flipped through the pictures. "How much do I owe you?"

Hale made a noise that was hard to decipher, and Ren waited for his friend to swallow his bite of food. "You don't owe me anything. My parents are covering it as my birthday present."

"I'll have to reach out to your mom to thank her."

"Can I do that?" Logan asked.

With a pat to his boyfriend's hand on the table, Hale said, "No, you cannot."

Ren knew Hale's family wanted to meet Logan, and Logan wanted to meet Hale's family, but Hale had chosen to keep them apart for the time being. "*My mother obsesses, and my cousins are a lot*" was the excuse he'd given Ren when he asked about it earlier.

"When can I, then?" Logan asked. "After six months? A year? I'd like to meet the people who are important to you."

This was sweet, and Ren would have taken satisfaction in Hale's blush any other day, but he'd finished going through the photos and realized something startling. "Hey." He scrolled back through the pictures. "Are there only two bedrooms?"

"Yeah," Hale confirmed. Ren made a face that Logan laughed at.

"Don't worry. Miles will sleep on the couch, so you'll have a room for yourself."

Ren handed the phone back to Hale. "I can live with that. So, you two are sharing a room? Are you sure you're ready for that step?"

He was just teasing, but only Logan could laugh it off. Hale's cheeks flushed an incredible shade of red. "Let's talk about something else," he said. "Ren, have you finished reading that novel for Advanced English Lit?"

Ren groaned, but since it was Hale's birthday, he had to accept the subject change.

Hale and Logan apparently were ready for the step of sharing a bed, because after finishing their slices of freshly baked cake, they bid him goodnight and went to Hale's room together. Ren remained at the table for a couple of minutes, gathering courage.

Logan had said Miles was in a bad mood and that he'd like the pasta. There were more than enough leftovers, and maybe he skipped dinner to help set up ...

He's probably back home now, right? It's been a few hours. How long does it take to set up an art show?

What if he already ate? If I skipped dinner for something, I'd still eat right after... But what if he hasn't?

And so Ren left the apartment with a glass container of pasta and a paper plate holding a large slice of chocolate cake. He had to knock on the apartment door with his foot, too scared of spilling to balance everything on one hand. There was a pause long enough for Ren to doubt himself, and then Miles opened the door and squinted down at him.

He was wearing a pair of plaid pajama bottoms and a white shirt. Behind him, the apartment was dark. "What are you doing?" he asked.

"Were you sleeping?"

"It's eleven. What's up?"

Ren thrust the piece of cake out toward Miles. "There was extra." He also extended the pasta. "And these are leftovers for you to eat whenever … Logan said you'd like it."

At first, Miles didn't move, staring down at him. He then flicked on the lights and took the pasta from Ren. "Come in."

"What?" Ren watched Miles back as he went to the kitchen.

"I can't eat that entire piece of cake by myself," Miles said, putting the leftovers in the fridge and grabbing two forks, which he held up when he turned back to Ren. "Come on."

Ren stepped inside, glancing around as he did. The apartment was weird. The layout was just like his and Hale's, but everything else was different. He found himself intrigued by the stereotypical *male* setup of the place. There was no couch, just a futon with sheets on it—*Who slept there?*—and lawn chairs for additional seating. The television was absurdly large, and multiple gaming consoles were tucked beneath it. He didn't want to know what the bedrooms looked like.

"It's no wonder Logan spends so much time at our apartment," Ren said, closing the door and trying not to think about how they were alone.

To his surprise, Miles laughed. "Come on," he urged again, nodding his head toward the balcony. "Let's sit outside. It's nice out."

Ren followed Miles outside. They sat side by side, their backs against the glass door.

For the first minute of eating, they were silent. Ren wondered how things had turned out like this. He didn't know why he'd cared that Miles might have been hungry or in need of something to lift his bad mood, or why he hadn't refused when Miles invited him inside.

"Did you make this yourself?" Miles asked.

Ren startled at the sound of his voice, reaching out to steady the plate of cake balanced on his legs. It was a bad idea to put it there, since Miles's fingers brushed his leg every time he steadied the plate to grab a bite. Neither of them said anything about it.

Why are we like this?

He cleared his throat, wishing he had water to wash down the rich dessert. "Logan and Hale helped."

Chuckling, Miles shook his head. "I'm amazed Logan didn't ruin it."

Logan had been good help, though clumsy, so Ren hummed and took another bite of cake.

"Thanks, though. It's good. I needed this."

He hated the blossom of warmth in his chest and did his best to ignore it. "How did setting up go?"

"Fine." Miles sighed. "I'm going to be sore tomorrow, but I'm very strong, you know."

Eyes rolling, Ren mumbled, "Shut up."

Miles licked his fork clean.

Ren thought he should stop eating cake. His stomach felt weird.

"Hey," he began, and Miles's eyebrows raised. "What do you take pictures of?"

"Why?"

"I'm curious," Ren admitted. Before Miles could get any wrong ideas, he added, "We were talking about your exhibition over dinner, and I was just wondering what kind of photos you took that got you in as a junior."

Miles didn't respond right away, eating the last few bites of cake. When he finished, he laid his fork down beside Ren's. "I took pictures of people's expressions," he said, looking out across the parking lot. "Ones I wanted to look at more than once because they were interesting. There doesn't have to be a deep meaning behind it."

Ren liked that, and he thought he ought to think that way more often. It now felt acceptable to dismiss his concerns over why he'd come to see Miles.

There's no deep meaning, it's just what I felt like doing.

Still, he forced his gaze away from Miles when he considered what it would be like to kiss him. That seemed like it would be far too big of an offense to dismiss.

Chapter Ten

"Do you think they're doing this on purpose?" Ren asked Miles, breaking the silence that had been stretching between them for well over twenty minutes now.

It was Friday, and earlier that day he, Miles, Logan and Hale had driven the short distance to the cabin where they'd spend the weekend. Ren had been looking forward to lying on the beach until dinner, but Hale had suggested they all go into town. Since it was his birthday trip, it was only fair, and so Ren found himself walking down a quaint Main Street lined with shops.

Miles jerked at Ren's voice, looking down at him with an expression that suggested he'd forgotten he was there. He recovered quickly, before Ren could get annoyed. "Doing what on purpose?"

Ren gestured ahead of them to where Hale and Logan were, far enough away that he was suspecting they'd forgotten he and Miles were with them. "That. Leaving us alone together."

"Like, you mean, are they trying to set us up?"

Ren glared, because no, that's not what he'd meant.

This seemed to amuse Miles because the corner of his mouth quirked up. "No, I don't think it was on purpose. Look at them. They're in their own little world." Reaching up, Miles pulled his baseball cap down so the visor shaded his face. "Besides, they didn't leave us alone together as much as they just left. Either of us could go off on our own."

"Then why don't you?" Ren asked, squinting against the sun and wishing he too had brought a hat.

The response didn't come right away, so Ren observed Miles in silence. He looked good, wearing a black baseball cap that did little to contain his copper curls and a navy hoodie. *He's barely doing anything and is still attractive.* Ren looked down at his own striped button-down and considered how long he'd spent in front of the mirror that morning.

"I," Miles began, gathering Ren's attention once more, "am perfectly content."

They walked awhile longer, watching as Hale and Logan got farther and farther away. Once Ren gave up on catching up with them, he began to observe his surroundings, looking for places to stop. He didn't want the trip into town to only consist of strolling with Miles.

It didn't take long for him to spot a boutique up the street. He grabbed Miles's arm as they passed, pulling him off their course. "I want to look at clothes," he said.

"Why are you taking me with you?" asked Miles, though he made no move to pull his arm out of Ren's grasp.

They went to the back of the store. "You said you were content with me." He dropped Miles's arm, giving him the option to leave.

"That's not what I said." Still, Miles remained at Ren's side when they stopped in front of a shelf of hats. "You want a baseball cap?"

"I didn't think it'd be this sunny out." He grabbed a black hat with a light-yellow embroidered pineapple on the front and sidestepped to stand in front of a mirror.

When Ren put the hat on, their gazes met in the reflection. "I don't know," Ren said, reaching up to touch the hat. "It doesn't match my outfit."

After a brief examination, Miles nodded. "You look fine."

Displeased, Ren took off the hat and pushed past Miles to return it to the shelf. "I don't want to look fine." He went to look at other things.

Miles trailed behind. "You're not getting one now? Is it because of me?"

It was, though Ren didn't want to admit it. "I have a lot of hats like that at home. Buying a new one would be a waste of money—" As he said this, he felt something light drop on his head. He began to turn back to Miles, but stopped when he caught sight of himself in a mirror. Beside him, Miles seemed quite proud of himself, as if the tan bucket hat he'd placed on Ren was the epitome of fashion. "Why …?" he trailed off, reaching up to touch the rim of the hat.

"I like that one," Miles said. "I've never seen you wear one like it before, either."

Ren considered admitting this was because he wasn't fond of bucket hats, but the words got caught in his throat like glue. He glanced back at himself in the mirror. It would do its job of keeping the sun off his face, and the light color looked good with his dark hair.

He didn't give Miles much, just a mumbled "I suppose it's not awful." Regardless, Miles grinned.

There was a short pier by the beach, and when Ren was tired of walking, they went to stand at the end of it. It had been a while since they'd last spoken, so Miles surprised him when he suddenly said, "I wish I'd brought my camera along."

"You left it at the apartment?" He didn't look at Miles as he spoke, distracted by the waves.

"No. At the cabin."

Ren leaned against the boardwalk's wooden railing, crossing his arms over the top of it. "What do you like so much about taking pictures?"

A response didn't come, and after a minute of silence, Ren peeked at Miles from the corner of his eye. The other man was looking back. "What?" Ren demanded, feeling defensive.

"Pictures," Miles began after a pause, "don't lie. You take a picture of something, and it shows you exactly how it looked."

"Do you have trust issues?"

A laugh left Miles as if it were startled out of him. "I don't think so. No one has hurt me enough for that."

"How lucky." Then, to change the subject, he asked, "Are you ready for your exhibition?"

"I think so. I'm nervous about the feedback, but everything is ready to go."

Ren considered mentioning his plans to attend but kept it to himself.

He was prepared for them to fall silent once again, so Miles's question caught him off guard. "You're an English major, right? What do you want to do when you graduate?"

"I—" Ren began, cutting off when Miles's gaze met his. "You've never shown interest in this before. Why are you asking now?"

Miles shrugged. "You asked something about me, so I thought I could ask something about you."

This seemed fair, and it wasn't information Ren minded sharing. "I want to write novels," he admitted, lifting his head and stretching his arms out past the railing. "I'll need a job doing something else first, so I've been looking into publishing and editing companies. My hope is to get a full-time job by next semester, since I have only one class left to complete my degree."

"Wow." The way Miles spoke made it seem like it was impressive, though Ren didn't feel a sense of accomplishment over anything. "What would you write about in your novel?"

"Just the usual stuff." Ren leaned hard against the railing, pressing himself onto his toes so he could bend over it and look down at the water. He placed one hand on his head, assuring his new hat didn't fall off. His balance felt fine, but Miles still reached out to steady him.

"I'm fine," he said. The hand on his side didn't waiver, so he backed up.

"You looked like you could fall." Miles's hand slipped away to remove his phone from his pocket. "You should be more careful…"

Intrigued, because Miles had yet to check his phone since they'd given up on following Hale and Logan, Ren leaned forward. "What?" he asked. Then, unable to help himself, "Something from Clarisse?"

Miles had no reaction to this other than his eyebrows drawing together. "Logan and Hale want us to meet them for dinner. I routed us, and the restaurant is only a few minutes away.”

“I’m surprised they’re not ditching us to eat together.”

“I’m sure they considered it, but they both know you don’t want to spend any more time alone with me than you have to.” Miles returned his phone to his pocket. “I think I know where we’re going. Let’s go.”

As he followed Miles down the pier, Ren chewed his lip. *What about you?* he wanted to ask. *Why do you say it as if spending time together only bothers me?*

Chapter Eleven

In the early hours of the morning, Ren lay in bed staring at the ceiling, wondering what had woken him. Had it been a sound? A gust of wind loud enough that in his sleeping state he'd interpreted it as a threat?

He could tell himself that some outside intervention had disturbed his sleep all he wanted, but the pounding of his heart was familiar, as was the wet feeling of sweat at the base of his neck. *Nightmare.*

In the plethora of unpleasant things his past held, there was only one person he still had nightmares about, so even though he didn't remember the dream, he thought of his brother, anyway. No pleasant thoughts came to mind—he didn't think he had any pleasant experiences with his brother—and it made falling back asleep impossible.

He sat up and checked the digital clock on the nightstand. It was only two a.m.

Usually, he'd remain in bed awake until it was time to get up for the day, but the lake was close enough to hear from the cabin's front porch, and he hoped it would soothe him enough that he'd be able to fall back asleep.

When he pushed the blanket off his bare legs, he shivered. He'd brought shorts to sleep in, overlooking the fact that it'd be colder by the water than it was back at the apartment.

Far too tempted by the sound of the waves and the idea of a cigarette, Ren left the bedroom.

Floorboards creaked beneath his feet as he made his way down the stairs despite his best attempts to keep silent. The sound wouldn't disturb Hale and Logan in their bedroom, but Miles was in the living room.

When he spotted Miles's face lit from the light of his phone as he stretched out across the couch, Ren realized his concern was irrelevant. Miles's head turned at Ren's arrival. "What are you doing?"

"Smoking," Ren said, casually as if was a normal thing to wake up to do in the dead of night.

He grabbed his cigarettes and lighter from where he'd left them on the coffee table and unlocked the door to the porch. The cold reached him before he could even open the storm door, and he soon discovered that the outside was worse. The screens around the porch were perfect to keep away bugs, but they did little to fight the lake breeze.

On the porch was a large wooden dining table, and he took a seat at the bench alongside it, folding the checkered tablecloth under the table so it rested on his thighs like a blanket. He withdrew a cigarette from the carton and pinched it between his lips as he fumbled with his lighter. Once it was lit, he took a deep inhale and kept it in his chest. Holding the lighter steady, he passed his fingers over the flame, hoping it would warm him more than it did.

The storm door opened, and Miles stepped out onto the porch, a blanket folded over one of his arms. Ren burned his fingers and coughed up the smoke from his lungs.

They watched each other as Miles approached. Once he was close enough, he dropped the blanket down onto the table. "For you," he offered. Ren was expecting him to leave, but he rounded the table and slid down the bench to sit at Ren's side. "I thought you'd be cold."

"I am," Ren confirmed. He used his free hand to pull the blanket over his bare legs. "What about you?"

"I run warm." Miles's eyes lowered to look at the cigarette. Reminded of its presence, Ren took another inhale. "Are you alright?"

The question gave Ren pause, not because he didn't know the answer but because he hadn't been expecting Miles to ask it. He waited until the need to exhale burned his throat before responding. "Why do you ask?"

They were sitting close enough that when Miles shrugged, he felt it against his own shoulder. "I thought you looked sad."

Ren wasn't sad. At most, the memories disturbed him and it bothered him that even after all this time, his brother's past actions could still make him lose sleep. "Bad dream," he admitted, taking another huff of his cigarette.

"About?"

Miles didn't seem to have any concerns about boundaries. Eyes narrowed, Ren turned to him. Unwavering, Miles stared back.

Nothing about the expression was the least bit persuasive, but Ren gave in anyway. "My childhood."

Miles didn't ask for further clarification.

He didn't need to. Ren explained all on his own.

After one last inhale on the end of the cigarette, he put it out on the back of his hand. Miles hissed as if he were the one being burned. Ren paid no mind to the red-hot pain. "I have an older brother," Ren continued, dropping the dead cigarette to the tablecloth once he was sure it wouldn't start a fire. "He hates me. When we were growing up, he was horrible. Sometimes I think about it and can't sleep."

Ren brushed his thumb over the irritated skin on his hand. In the morning, Hale would see it and scold him.

Miles's hand entered his field of vision, fingers stretching out toward Ren's before he halted and made a fist. It was only a second before the fingers on the table uncurled and Miles cleared his throat. "Why would your brother hate you? Is it because you're gay?"

A laugh startled out of Ren's throat. "No." Leaning forward, he crossed his arms on the table and used them as a cushion for his head. He felt calmer than he had before, the cold air and the sounds of the water lapping at the unseen beach having the desired effect. "It doesn't help, but he's always hated me, even before I knew I liked boys." He closed his eyes. A response never came, so the only thing that reached his ears was the wind and the waves.

It'd been so long since he'd last talked to someone about his brother.

His close friends knew about it, as did Julian, but none of them ever brought it up unless Ren did, and Ren *never* brought it up in an attempt to forget. He never did, though, and he could admit that maybe ignoring his problems wasn't the best way to solve them.

"He blames me," Ren said. Once again, he received no answer. Curious, he cracked his eyes open. Miles was watching him, his expression troubled.

Oh boy, Ren thought, amused. *He's realized he stepped on a land mine.*

"Aren't you going to ask what for?"

Miles's throat bobbed with a heavy swallow. "I don't think you'd tell me even if I asked." He didn't sound so sure of himself, probably startled by how much Ren had shared of himself already.

"Clearly," Ren began, "I'm in a sharing mood."

Ren waited for an answer. It took long enough that he felt himself drifting off to sleep when Miles's words reached him. "You don't have to tell me if you don't want to …" he trailed off, took a deep breath, then asked what Ren was expecting.

"My mother died in childbirth," Ren admitted. He yawned, sleep pulling at him. "He lost his mother and getting me as a brother was little consolation."

If Miles had a response, he didn't get to hear it. As soon as the words left him, it was like a weight had been lifted, and his consciousness slipped away.

Chapter Twelve

It was the sun that woke Ren next, shining through the window onto his face. Groaning, he turned his back to the light. The clock told him it was eight thirty. He yawned, listening for any sound that would suggest his travel partners were awake.

When none reached him, he rolled out of bed. The day before, he'd felt ambitious while packing homework, but he was grateful to have something to do while he waited for the others to wake.

He slipped into clothes for the day—a simple pair of tan shorts and a white shirt he covered with a light flannel—took his pill, and ventured downstairs.

In the living room, he found Miles stretched across the couch, his long legs propped up on the armrest. Ren paused, their conversation in the early morning returning to him. He wasn't hung up on having told Miles something personal about himself. Instead, he kept thinking about how he'd gotten back upstairs and whether Miles had carried him.

He continued to the door, unlocking it and slipping out onto the porch. His cigarettes and lighter were on the table where he'd left them, and he considered lighting one, but the fresh air felt too good for it to be more than a fleeting thought.

He only got twenty minutes of work in before Miles joined him outside. His fingers paused on the keyboard.

Miles wasn't there for very long. He stopped beside the table for only a second to place a warm mug of coffee beside Ren's laptop. Before he could ask Miles why, Miles was leaving the porch to venture down by the water, hands fiddling with the camera strapped around his neck.

Perplexed but grateful, Ren resumed writing his paper.

Thirty minutes later, when Miles returned, Ren's mug was empty, and he was two pages into his second draft. "Thanks for the coffee," he said before Miles could disappear inside.

"You're welcome." His voice was soft. "Do you want a refill?"

"I'm alright," Ren said, turning away when his face felt warm. "If I drink too much caffeine, I'll get jittery." The sound of the door opening reached him. When he looked over, it was swinging shut. "Alright then," he mumbled, unsure of what he'd been expecting.

After having to put up with Ren the night before, it wasn't like Miles would want to spend time with him. They didn't have anything to talk about, so of course he would stay inside while he waited for Hale and Logan to wake up—

The door opened again, and Miles reemerged, this time with his own mug and a laptop. He noticed Ren's stare and paused. "Can I sit out here with you? I want to edit the photos I took."

"You can do what you want." Ren focused on his laptop, moving his fingers over the keys but not pressing any. He felt hyperaware of Miles, tensing when he took a seat on the bench across from Ren.

What the fuck? Pull yourself together. It's Miles, for fuck's sake.

"How's your hand?"

Ren frowned. "My hand?" He thought back to the night before. "Oh." Turning his palm down, he looked at the circular red mark burned into his skin. "It's fine. Only hurts when something touches it."

Miles nodded, then immersed himself in his work.

It wasn't fair, Ren thought. He could no longer focus.

"Let's go for a walk," Hale said, tugging on the small ponytail he'd made when he'd pulled Ren's hair back from around his face. "We can walk down the beach."

Ren groaned. "It's hot."

"We can't stay inside all day," Hale said. "It's a waste of a trip."

"I wouldn't mind going for a walk," Logan chimed in, smiling when Ren shot him a less than pleased look.

"Me too," said Miles.

Hale's hands rested on Ren's shoulders. "Then it's settled! We'll go for a walk."

Hale retrieved both his and Ren's shoes from the mat by the door. "*I* have to go too?" Ren asked, refusing to take the shoes. Not accepting the protest, Hale dropped them on the floor by Ren's feet and took a seat beside him on the couch.

"You shouldn't just stay here by yourself. Also, it's my birthday and you love me."

"It's not your birthday anymore," Ren grumbled, but Hale had won and they both knew it. "Does it feel good to have me wrapped around your finger?"

Hale's smile shifted into something sheepish. "Kinda," he admitted. "It's not like I use it to make you do anything bad, right? Walks are good for you, and you should take better care of yourself." He grasped Ren's hand, turning it over to look at the back. "I don't like it when you hurt yourself. Why'd you do it?" His fingers wandered up to wrap around Ren's wrist, the leather band there preventing him from touching skin.

Ren could feel both Miles and Logan watching them, Hale's attempt to not appear upset failing. Guilt pricked at him, and he lowered his gaze. "Sorry," he offered. "It was stupid. I didn't have anywhere to put out my cigarette, so I did it without thinking."

"You promise?" Hale asked, quietly enough that Ren was the only one to hear.

He linked his pinky with Hale's and squeezed. "I'm sorry," he said again. "You're right. I should take better care of myself. I'll come for a walk."

With a smile, Hale slipped his hand from Ren's and stood. "Put your shoes on, then. We'll be waiting down by the beach." We, in this case, seemed to refer to himself and Logan, because Miles remained seated in the chair as the couple left hand in hand.

"Is that a common occurrence?" Miles asked as Ren slipped into his shoes. "You hurting yourself?"

Ren stood. "Why would you ask me that?"

Rising from the chair, Miles shrugged. "You don't have to answer if you don't want, and if you tell me I'm crossing a line, I'll leave it be." As he spoke, he removed his camera from the black bag on the coffee table.

Miles was crossing a line, and he knew he could refuse to answer, but as he had the night before, he didn't hate the idea of talking about himself. He'd written it off as the exhaustion loosening his lips, though that didn't seem to be the case. "I'll answer if you agree to answer a question for me as well."

Miles's eyebrows raised. "I'll tell you anything you want to know."

"It's not a common occurrence," Ren said, glancing toward the door to the porch. Beyond it, he faintly picked up on the sound of Hale's laughter. "It used to be, which is why Hale's sensitive to it, but I'm okay now." Miles had no reaction to this confession. It was as if he was expecting as much from Ren. Annoyed, Ren spat out, "Anyway, my past actions aren't important. I want to know how I got to bed last night."

"Oh, that." Miles waved a hand. "I carried you. You're not very heavy and you seemed cold. Sorry for touching you without asking."

Ren wanted to yell at him. He wanted to demand why Miles was like that, why he'd say things that made it seem like the only reason their relationship was tense was because of Ren, like he wanted things to be different but Ren was keeping him at a distance. He wanted to ask Miles why he always looked at him like that, with an expression that tricked him into thinking he could tell him anything and it would all be fine.

Then Ren wanted to yell at himself, because he'd been paying close-enough attention to realize all of this.

He opened his mouth to snap something that would only momentarily make him feel better, but Hale's voice interrupted. "Come on, you guys! We're going to leave without you."

"Let's go," Miles said. "I'm sure you don't want to get stuck walking just the two of us."

Logan and Hale did little to keep them all together, wandering farther away with each minute, just as they had the day before in town.

Ren and Miles didn't stay together this time. Ren walked a handful of feet ahead, listening to the sound of the camera shutter behind him as he thought about the past twenty-four hours.

Sawyer had messaged him about getting together again. His stupid brother had disrupted his sleep. In a moment of weakness, he'd told Miles about his mother and burned himself. Miles had carried him to bed and brought him coffee in the morning. Noah had posted a picture of himself, Julian, and Rita on social media, and Ren had thought of the time when he'd been the one to make Jules smile like that, and then he had been angry at himself. Hale had seen his burn and gotten upset. Miles asked yet another personal question he had no business asking, and Ren responded with the truth, anyway.

He felt as if he was all over the fucking place and pulling himself together had never been his strong suit.

Ren turned, mouth open so he could take it out on Miles as he often did. The shutter of Miles's camera went off, and Ren's words froze in his throat when he realized it was pointed at him. He could feel his expression softening into something confused. The shutter went off again, and Miles lowered the camera. "Sorry," he offered, but he looked at the screen of his camera right away to examine the photo.

Had Miles always been like this? They'd spent little time together in the past, so maybe Ren just hadn't realized how bold he could be. He asked.

"Pretty much," Miles said after a pause. "It just feels different to you because you've finally started paying attention to me. Would you like to see the picture? I'll delete it if you want me to."

His face warm, Ren turned back around. "Do what you want with it." He took a step forward, planning on leaving Miles and his camera behind, but he didn't get far before he spotted Hale and Logan ahead of them. They'd stopped to talk, far enough away that Ren couldn't hear what they were saying, but it made Hale smile and Logan laugh before ducking down to kiss him.

He'd never seen Hale kiss someone before. His best friend was reserved about such things, and the last thing Ren wanted to do was interrupt. As he pushed down an envy he wished he didn't feel, Ren faced the other direction. Miles was closer to him now, and he closed more of the distance with his long legs. Stopping beside Ren, he lifted his camera to take a picture of their friends down the beach.

Ren's hand shot out to grip Miles's arm. "They deserve privacy."

"They're kissing outside."

"Kissing is a private thing."

"Don't you kiss random people at bars all the time?"

With a huff, Ren walked away. What he meant when he said kissing was private was that it was private when Hale was doing it, but he no longer felt like explaining this to Miles after that comment.

Not seeming to understand that Ren was trying to put distance between them, Miles followed. "It's a good picture, though. It could make a good anniversary gift. Even if it is private, it'll be something they'll want to remember."

Without Ren asking, Miles held his camera out in front of him. Curiosity got the best of him, and Ren looked at the photo on the tiny screen. It was beautiful with the water and cloudless blue sky, the two forms on the beach in the right half of the frame, unrecognizable, though obviously joined in passion. Ren offered no praise, refusing to give Miles the benefit of the doubt even when he deserved it.

They walked side by side in silence for a handful of minutes in the opposite direction of their friends. Ren doubted the couple even noticed their absence.

Periodically, Miles would huff and rub at his shoulder. It was something Ren hadn't noticed him doing earlier, and he was going to pretend not to hear him, but it went on long enough that it became the only thing he could focus on. "What's wrong with you?"

"What?"

"You sound distressed."

"Ah." Miles raised his hand to rub at the back of his neck. "Yeah. The couch was a little short for me, so I didn't sleep great. I woke up with a knot in my neck."

Ignore him. He's fine. It doesn't matter. He'll be okay for one more night …

But Ren couldn't ignore Miles like he used to. He'd spent too much time around him. He knew him a little too well and was a little too interested. "The bed is big enough for the both of us," Ren announced, looking down at his shoes and then back up again when he realized this made him seem nervous.

Miles stared, his expression incredulous. He opened his mouth, then paused. He cleared his throat. "Is this some kind of trick?"

It annoyed Ren how he said this. It made it sound as if he'd offered to do something bigger than share a mattress. "It's not," he snapped. "There's just enough room for you, and I don't mind sharing as long as you don't touch me."

"That won't be a problem. Thanks."

They continued down the beach. Ren dwelled on why he'd offered to share his sleeping space with a man who required far more room than he did. He hoped Hale and Logan didn't say anything about it.

"Hey."

Miles was a few feet ahead of him, looking down at something blue in his hand. "What is it?" Ren approached, but before he could get close enough to make out the object, Miles curled his fingers into a fist and extended it out toward Ren.

"For you."

When Ren reached out, Miles dropped something smooth into his palm. It was a piece of sea glass, deep blue and rounded at the edges. It was pretty, Ren thought, turning it over and lifting it up so the sunlight shone through it. When he looked down, he noticed Miles was once again moving along the edge of the water, away from him.

Not wanting to be left behind, Ren curled his fingers around the glass and quickened his pace to catch up.

What a weird way to say thank you, he thought.

Chapter Thirteen

The stretch of beach near the cabin had a sandy firepit, and the four of them sat around it after dinner. It was a chilly evening, and Ren was more than content to slip on a hoodie and let the flames warm his legs. They didn't have any chairs to sit on, but the sand was warm from the evening sun.

Ren felt good in a way he often didn't, in a normal underwhelming way. Everything felt okay.

He still had the sea glass Miles had found earlier. It was too pretty to return to the beach, and he drew it from his pocket to look at how the light from the fire shone through it.

"What is that?" Hale asked, straightening from his lean into Logan's side. "I noticed you playing with it earlier, too."

For a moment, Ren didn't move, the smooth piece of glass still held out in front of him, pinched between his thumb and forefinger. He didn't want to show it to Hale, didn't want his best friend to want it because Ren loved him enough to give him anything.

He handed it over anyway. "Sea glass," he said. Then, "Ginger found it."

Logan huffed in amusement, but Miles seemed unconcerned. When Ren risked a quick glance in his direction, his expression told Ren he also felt happy. He looked at the water like there was something beautiful there, something more than the darkening sky and blue waves fading together in the distance. Ren wished he could see it too.

He's pretty, he thought.

"It's pretty," Hale said, and Ren felt as if his thoughts had been read. Hale smiled knowingly. "The stone."

Ren accepted the glass when Hale passed it back to him. "It is."

In the sand beside his hip, his cell phone buzzed. His screen must have been visible to Hale, because he asked, "How's Sawyer?"

"Fine," Ren said, checking the message with little interest. "Doing dumb frat boy stuff."

"He's a frat boy?" Logan inquired. Hale leaned into him again, and he suddenly seemed less interested in Ren.

"He is."

"Do they make gay frat boys?" Miles asked. His gaze on the water didn't waiver, but clearly he was paying attention.

Shrugging, Ren removed his cigarettes from his pocket. The pack was almost empty now, and he flirted with the idea of not replacing it. "Apparently." He thumbed a cigarette out of the carton. "We haven't spoken much about his sexuality. He's probably bi." Leaning forward, Ren light his cigarette in the fire, grimacing at the heat as he did.

"Doesn't that hurt?" Logan asked as Ren drew his hand back.

"It hurts today." Ren brought the cigarette to his mouth but didn't smoke yet. "Pain is relative."

No one seemed to have anything to say about this. Ren smoked.

Miles broke the silence. "Smoking's not good for you."

To his surprise, Ren didn't feel all that annoyed by the statement. "I know."

"He's been trying to quit for a while," Hale chimed in.

"I'm not very good at it," Ren said. "I've been trying to quit for as long as I've been smoking."

It was Logan who gave in to his curiosity. "When did you start?"

"High school." Ren didn't feel proud of the surprise on Logan's face. Only people with good home lives reacted like that.

"Didn't your parents care?"

When Ren laughed, Hale looked at him with sympathy. "I doubt my dad even noticed. We aren't close."

Logan seemed troubled, but he thankfully didn't ask Ren about his mother.

The bedroom was still empty when Ren returned from his shower, so he went in search of Miles. He told himself that if Miles took the couch instead of the bed, it wasn't his problem, but he didn't want Miles to do that out of consideration for him.

He found Miles draping a blanket out across the couch. "Aren't you going to be uncomfortable?" he asked. Startled, Miles turned, the blanket slipping from his hands.

"Oh, hey. You're done in the shower."

This seemed both obvious and not the point. "Are you sleeping down here?"

"I just thought it was easiest."

"For who?" Ren asked. "If you're trying to be considerate, you can stop."

"Don't say it like it's a bad thing."

"That's not what I meant," Ren said. "I mean, in this situation, it's unnecessary. I don't care if you sleep in the bed next to me, and I already know you won't do anything to me, so I'm not uncomfortable or anything."

Miles stared. "You trust me?"

Ren crossed his arms. "Not to assault me, yeah. The bar's still super low, so don't feel flattered."

A laugh left Miles. It was a delightful sound, and Ren felt he didn't deserve to hear it. "Alright then. Yeah, if you really don't mind, I'll take the other half of the bed. I'll be there after I shower."

Ren hurried back upstairs to the bedroom.

Why did I do that? He stood at the end of the bed and stared down at the rumpled sheets. The night before, he'd slept in the center, stretched out since the space was only his to use.

When he climbed into bed, he told himself he wasn't waiting for Miles to join him.

Ten minutes later, Miles made his appearance, wearing only a pair of pajama pants and a towel thrown around his shoulders. Ren had been distracting himself with a phone call to Sawyer, but the sight of Miles distracted him from his distraction—or maybe they canceled out, because he'd called Sawyer to take his mind off of Miles in the first place.

Miles, oblivious, crouched by his side of the bed to plug in his phone charger.

"We should hang out again," Sawyer said into Ren's ear. "Wanna come to my room and watch a movie sometime?"

Only half listening, as Ren often did in the presence of attractive shirtless men, he said, "Let's do that." Then he dismissed himself from the conversation. As soon as the call ended, he told Miles to put on a shirt.

Miles folded back the covers. "I get hot," he said, slipping onto the bed beside Ren. "Are you uncomfortable?"

"No," Ren shot back. "I'm not. That's not it … You wore a shirt last night."

"Yeah." Miles settled back against the pillows, then pulled the blankets up to his chin, covering his bare chest. He blinked up at Ren with those hazel eyes. "Last night, I only had one blanket. I was cold."

Neither of them spoke for a long moment. Sighing, Ren mumbled out an irritated "Fine," and lay down as well. "I guess I'll turn off the lamp."

As Ren stretched his arm out to do so, Miles asked, "You sleep with your bracelets on?"

Ren paused, then continued searching under the shade. "I do. They're from Hale."

"So you wear them all the time? Aren't they uncomfortable?"

Him and his damn questions.

Ren switched the lamp off. "They were at first, but I'm used to it now."

There was a pause. "Was the person on the phone your boyfriend?"

There was no reason for Miles to ask that question. "No," Ren said.

He rolled onto his side, his back to Miles. "I mean, it was Sawyer, but he's not my boyfriend. We're just casually seeing each other."

Another pause. Ren didn't let this one fool him. He was expecting Miles to ask another question, so it didn't surprise him when he did. "Can I ask you something?"

Amused, Ren huffed. "Now you ask?" This wasn't the answer Miles was looking for, and after a minute, Ren had to try again. "You can, but I might not answer."

"I'm just curious about what happened between you and Julian."

"*What?*" Ren sat up to glare down at the man in bed beside him. Even with the lights off, he could pick out Miles's eyes. They were round, as if it shocked him that this was the question Ren considered to be *too far*.

"It's just …" Miles sighed. He pushed himself up on one elbow. The motion was accompanied by the rustling of sheets, and Ren was relieved the darkness prevented him from seeing Miles's exposed chest. "It seems strange to me. I didn't realize he was the one you'd dated your sophomore year until that day after you got drunk. You guys are still friends, aren't you?"

Ren frowned. "How'd you know I was dating someone sophomore year?"

"Your room shares a wall with our living room, and it's *thin*."

Horrified by what was being implied, Ren opened his mouth to ask, *Why didn't you tell me?* He realized that would be stupid. Back then, Ren would have reacted far worse to this information than he was now. "So you'd *listen?*" he spat out.

"No!" The word came out loud. A distressed groan followed it. "I mean, sometimes I couldn't help but hear, but I wouldn't like, stick around. You know what? Never mind. I'm sorry for asking. I shouldn't have brought it up."

Ren supposed it was good that Miles revoked the question right then. He didn't want to admit it, but he had been considering answering. Why not, after he'd already told him about his mother?

It bothered him a little, though.

Is he not making me answer because he's sorry, or does he not want to know anymore? Does he not care? Have I bored him enough that he's no longer curious about me?

It wasn't long before the sound of Miles's steady breathing reached him, and Ren realized he was the only one still thinking about it.

When he woke up the next morning, Miles was still asleep beside him. He'd stretched out some and rolled onto his stomach, but true to his word, he was nowhere near touching Ren.

After untangling himself from the sheets, Ren took his medication and went downstairs to see whether Hale and Logan were awake.

He could hear them moving around in the kitchen before he could see them, the sound of running water accompanied by the familiar sizzle of bacon in a hot pan. When he got to the base of the stairs, he paused. Logan was at the stove, though his attention was on Hale standing beside him instead of their cooking breakfast.

They were talking about something Ren couldn't hear, their voices drowned out by the frying bacon, but it had Hale's eyes averted and his cheeks flushed an impressive color. Logan laughed, then reached out to grab Hale's waist, pulling him closer so he could hug him while tending to the stove. Ren could no longer see Hale's expression, though he saw him raise his hands and knew he was covering his face.

"Good morning," Ren announced, making his presence known.

Hale didn't leave the cage of Logan's arms, but he dropped his hands and leaned around him so Ren could see him again. "Morning," he chimed back, even more sunny than usual.

Something must have happened last night, Ren realized. He was glad he'd encouraged Miles to sleep upstairs, away from the other bedroom.

"Breakfast is almost done," Logan announced. "Want to wake Miles up?"

Sighing, because Ren had been hoping this wouldn't be his job, he went back upstairs.

Miles had stretched across the mattress, taking up the space Ren had vacated. For only a moment, Ren allowed himself to appreciate the sight, eyes raking over the other man's bare back, lingering on the dusting of freckles he discovered across Miles's shoulders. He looked peaceful, expression relaxed and lips parted. Red hair splayed across his forehead, indicating he'd tossed and turned throughout the night. If he had, Ren hadn't awoken. He'd slept well.

Reaching out, he shook Miles's shoulder. Nothing happened.

"Miles." His voice sounded loud in the quiet room, but there was no reaction. Ren shook harder.

Apparently, the man could sleep like the dead, because Miles didn't even so much as stir as Ren took the next few minutes trying to wake him. Eventually, he announced, "This is fucking ridiculous," and hit Miles repeatedly with a pillow until the man groaned.

"Talk about a rude awakening."

This irritated Ren, because he hadn't needed to come wake Miles. "I'm going to eat all your bacon."

Hazel eyes cracked open. At first, Miles just studied him, as if his tired brain needed longer to process that he was there. Then he said, "I don't like bacon."

"What the hell is wrong with you?" Ren left without waiting to see if Miles would join them.

"I did my best," he told Logan when eyebrows raised in question as he returned alone.

Miles's difficulties getting out of bed must not have been a surprise to his roommate, because Logan smiled and shook his head. Ren went to help Hale set the dining table.

"Give me those," he instructed, taking the forks out of Hale's hand. His best friend's eyes followed the silverware, but he didn't look at Ren. *Something totally happened.* "How'd you sleep?"

Hale's cheeks flushed. "Fine."

Not doing anything with the silverware he'd taken, Ren trailed after him. "Just fine?"

After placing the last knife alongside a plate, Hale took the forks back from him. He was blushing harder now, but he met Ren's gaze. "Why don't you brew the coffee if you want to be helpful?" His blue eyes shifted then to look over Ren's shoulder. "Miles, would you help him?"

Apparently, the temptation of breakfast was enough to rouse the younger man, because there he was in all his glory, hair still unkept and eyes tired. He'd put a shirt on before joining them. Ren had mixed feelings about it.

"I can do it myself," Ren protested.

The look on Hale's face was both loving and amused. "Last week you brewed hot water."

Ren scoffed, insulted, and he hurried over to join Miles at the coffeepot, eager to prove himself. "Make room," he said, bumping his shoulder hard into Miles to get him to take a step to the side. "You don't need to help me."

"Okay." Miles placed his hands on the counter but didn't leave his side. "What are you doing?"

"I'll watch," Miles insisted, reaching out to grab the unopened bag of coffee beans and holding them out. "Here you go."

Feeling all kinds of frustrated because it was morning, he hadn't had coffee, Hale was teasing him, and just *Miles,* Ren snatched the bag and tugged at the top. "You know, I don't appreciate—"

The bag ripped from the harsh treatment. Coffee beans flew everywhere.

From the corner of his eye, Ren could see Logan pause in front of the stove. The sound of metal on metal ceased as Hale took a break from placing the silverware. Miles stared down at the floor. Ren curled his fingers into a fist around the half-empty bag.

"That's not where those go," Miles announced.

"I know that!" Angered, Ren thrust the bag in Miles's direction. "Just do it yourself."

It was Hale and Logan who laughed at him. Miles only smiled and accepted the bag. "How about you get water?" he suggested. "I can do the rest."

Ren watched Miles pour the remaining beans from the bag into the coffee grinder.

Without complaint, though visibly irritated, Ren got the water.

The weekend had taken its toll on Ren, and he collapsed onto the couch as soon as they were back in their apartment, bags abandoned on the floor of the living room. Hale laughed, placing a hand on the top of his head as he passed to go to his bedroom, more considerate of where to leave his belongings. "You sound exhausted."

"Well, yeah," Ren agreed, folding his arms under his head to use as a cushion. "I had to interact with Miles a lot this weekend. It wears me out." The words didn't sound as sincere as usual.

"Oh, come on."

Ren wondered whether Hale had heard his hesitance, or if he was just saying it because he felt he should now that he was dating Miles's best friend. He returned to lean over the couch and pinch Ren's leg. "You two seemed almost friendly this weekend."

Ren jerked away from the fingers. "We're not friends."

From the corner of his eye, he could see Hale's hand hovering over his knee. His body felt tense, but it eased some at the sound of his friend's soft voice asking, "Are you okay?"

"Yeah. Sorry. I'm just a little annoyed with myself. I didn't mean to take it out on you." When Hale's gaze remained persistent, Ren sat up. He hugged his legs to his chest.

"What's up?" Hale asked, sitting in the now open space beside him.

Ren rested his forehead on his knees, hiding his face. "It's just …" He first thought of Miles on Hale's birthday, his steady presence beside him as they shared a slice of cake. Then he thought of Miles at the cabin, walking with him on the beach and sitting beside him on the porch in the dead of night, in bed next to him, asking questions in a room so dark they could barely see each other. "He makes me feel—"

The word he was about to use was *safe*, and he huffed at the ridiculousness of it. "It's *Miles*. I don't like him. He's annoying, but I feel like I'm always on the verge of letting my guard down around him." Tilting his head just enough to peek at Hale over his knees, he admitted, "I told him about my mom."

"Oh." Hale reached for Ren's hand, lacing their fingers together. "Ren … yeah, you've hated Miles for two years, but you didn't really know him all that time, and you were so convinced he was a bad person that you lashed out before he had the chance to show you differently. Miles isn't a bad guy, and there's nothing wrong with changing your opinion of him after getting to know him better."

Ren closed his eyes. "He asks me questions about things that I don't want to talk about, but I think it's okay if it's him. It scares me." He almost felt stupid for saying it, though when he opened his eyes, he noticed Hale was looking at him without judgment.

He knew Ren's issues with trusting people better than anyone, knew of the ways he'd been burned before from doing just that. "Well," Hale began, squeezing Ren's hand. "Do what's best for you. If you're comfortable letting Miles know you better and want to tell him more, do that. If you need time to think about it, take time. There's no rush for anything."

The words relaxed Ren some. He felt less pressure to figure everything out, knowing Hale supported him taking time to get his thoughts in order.

"I'll take some time and think about it. Thanks."

"Of course." Hale slipped his hand out of Ren's and rose from the couch.

Immediately, Ren reached for him. While he'd been spending his weekend either with Miles or thinking about Miles, Hale had been off with Logan. They hadn't gotten to spend much time together, just the two of them. "Where are you going?"

"I was going to unpack," Hale admitted, responsible as usual. "You should too. Once we're done, we can go get something to eat."

"Just you and me?"

Hale smiled. "If that's what you want, yeah. I was thinking we might invite Noah, but he doesn't have to know."

Ren considered this, then dropped the grip he had on Hale's shirt. "Invite Noah, too." As Hale made his way to his bedroom, Ren watched him over the back of the couch. "I'm sure he's going to want to hear about what happened between you and Logan last night as well."

Hale's feet faltered.

Chapter Fourteen

On Wednesday, Ren's noon class finished early. This was rare, and usually he would celebrate with a nap before his 2:20 p.m. class, but he had lunch plans with Noah, so Ren went to wait outside the art hall. For some reason, Noah had chosen to sign up for a pottery course that semester.

It would be a few more minutes until Noah joined him, so Ren took a seat on a bench near the building's door and lit a cigarette. He'd forgotten his pack of cigarettes up at the cabin and his motivation to get another hadn't kicked in until early that morning, so the burn of nicotine brought him even more relief than usual. He was just beginning to hope that Noah would take his time so he could enjoy the cigarette all the way to the end when he noticed two people leaving the building.

Ren hoped they wouldn't stop to speak to him, but Miles was already looking at him in interest. Beside him, Clarisse appeared perplexed. It didn't take long for her eyes to find Ren as well, and her face twisted into something unpleasant. She reached out toward Miles, and Ren thought, *Yes, keep him away from me* and *Don't touch him* at the same time.

He wondered why he cared.

He wondered whether Miles would forget about his presence if Clarisse asked him to.

He wondered whether Clarisse knew that he and Miles had shared a bed this past weekend and how she felt about it if she did.

Clarisse's hand never reached Miles, because he changed direction to approach the bench. Ren realized he'd been holding in a large lungful of smoke and coughed it out. By the time he composed himself, Miles was standing before him, with Clarisse on her way to join them.

When neither of them said anything, Ren raised his eyebrows. "What's up?"

"Are you waiting for someone?" asked Miles.

It seemed like a good time to tell Miles it wasn't any of his business, but that seemed aggressive and he wasn't in the mood. "Noah has class here. We're getting lunch, so I'm waiting for him to be done." He took a pull at his cigarette.

Clarisse crossed her arms, her displeasure clear in her posture.

"Do you have something to say to me? You seem upset," Ren said.

"I don't like smoking," she said. "It's gross."

Unconcerned, he shrugged. This wasn't anything unknown, and it hadn't been enough to stop him before.

She looked at Miles. "Don't you agree?"

Now, this intrigued Ren. Miles had never seemed to mind his smoking before, saying nothing about it other than the occasional "It's not good for you."

Miles's expression was impossible to read, his eyes squinted as if he was facing the sun—he was not—and lips curled up at the corners in a pleasant sort of smile. Ren stared back at him, the cigarette pinched between his forefinger and middle finger, burning itself away. Before speaking, Miles's smile widened. "You should quit if you can."

He said the last three words slowly, applying emphasis Ren was certain was intentional. *If you can.* That, paired with the proud look on Clarisse's face, as if she'd just gotten Miles to say something bad about him—which she had *not*—pissed Ren off.

Huffing, he got up from the bench and walked the few steps over to the metal garbage can. He ground his cigarette out on it, then removed the new pack from his pocket and tossed it in the bin. The regret he felt was almost instant, and he tried not to let it show as he turned back to the art students. "I quit then," he said.

As he went back to his seat, he took pleasure in Clarisse's obvious annoyance but ground his teeth at the small smile Miles wore.

Thankfully, Noah interrupted the moment. "Wow" was the first thing he said. "How is everyone?"

Clarisse gave Noah a look that made his expression shift to confusion. It was Miles who answered. "Ren quit smoking."

"Oh? I've been telling you to ever since we met. When'd you do that?"

"Like thirty seconds ago," Ren grumbled. It was no surprise when Noah laughed at him, but Ren kicked his friend in the shin anyway. "Shut up."

"That's not going to stick," Noah said, bending down to rub at his leg. "It never does, even when it's not a hasty decision."

Ren glared. "How am I ever going to quit if you don't have any faith in me?"

"You're far more likely to stick with it if I don't have faith in you."

This was very true. He now felt the need to prove all of them wrong and show he could get by without smoking. "Fuck you. You're buying me lunch."

Unconcerned, Noah turned to Miles and Clarisse. "What are you guys doing? Want to join us?"

Ren would have kicked Noah again if he wasn't busy watching Miles's reaction, horrified that the man seemed to think this was a good idea. His mouth opened, probably to agree, and for the first time Ren was thankful for Clarisse's input. She placed a hand on Miles's arm and said, "We have somewhere we need to be."

Miles looked at her, then nodded. "Next time," he told Noah, gaze flicking down to Ren for just a second.

"Sounds good, man," Noah assured.

With a brief "See you later," Miles let Clarisse pull him away.

As he watched them go, Ren was unable to ignore how good the two of them looked together. If Miles ended up dating her, their pictures together would be striking.

They should get married in the fall, Ren thought. *She'd look beautiful with red or orange flowers, and fall leaves would be a suitable backdrop for Miles's hair.*

"Hey." It was Noah's turn to kick him, though his foot was far less heavy than Ren's had been. "What are you thinking about?"

"Why would you ask them to join? We're going to eat in your room."

"Oh, right." Noah took a step back as Ren stood, holding out a hand for his backpack, which Ren handed over. "Well, we could have changed our plans if they wanted to come." As Noah hiked Ren's backpack over his free shoulder, he started toward the dorms.

Ren trailed a pace behind. "I don't *want* to eat with them."

"*Really?*" The sarcasm was thick.

Noah didn't understand the problem. Ren wasn't annoyed with him for inviting them because he didn't want to spend time with Miles. He felt *scared*, because what if he spent more time with Miles and gave more of himself away before even deciding that was the right choice?

Ren quickened his pace so he could elbow Noah. His friend laughed, unharmed.

When they got to Noah's dorm, Julian was sitting on the futon. Noah had said nothing about him being there, but he'd bought an extra sandwich for lunch, so it didn't surprise Ren.

"Hey," Julian greeted, glancing up at him from his laptop and then almost immediately to Noah. They never looked at each other for too long anymore. "Oh! You got me food. You didn't have to."

Ren shut the door. The futon wasn't big enough for the three of them, so he hesitated, unsure of where to sit.

"Well, I figured you wouldn't have anything to eat since Luca canceled on you," Noah said as he gestured toward the futon for Ren, pulling out his desk chair for himself.

Ren took the seat next to Julian. "You and Luca had plans?"

"Ah yeah, well, you know how it goes." Julian unwrapped his sandwich. Ren watched. Sometimes Julian dressed like some kind of young historian or librarian, all rumpled button-down shirts and glasses with thin frames and large lenses. It was cute, but it made Ren remember too many of their date nights in the past. "He says we can hang out, but then he's just too busy to make time. He's been volunteering at the courthouse to have something to put on his law school applications."

"Well, that's what you get for choosing a nerd as your best friend."

It made Julian laugh, though he also sounded exhausted. The situation with Luca was weird. Noah swore Luca loved Julian, and Ren could see why he thought so. Luca seemed grumpy around everyone but Julian, and the only time Ren had seen Luca smile, it had been directed at Jules.

It would go nowhere. Julian was incapable of seeing Luca as anything more than a friend. Ren thought it might be why Julian had been so understanding with Ren breaking up with him for a similar reason.

Noah once said he thought Luca would love Julian forever, but Ren didn't think that was true. Luca was just too busy to find someone new.

"Hey, Jules, guess what?" asked Noah. Jules lifted his head, raising his hand to lick mayo off his thumb. "Ren quit smoking."

Ren scoffed.

"Oh? That's great." His genuine happiness made Ren more annoyed with Noah. "How are you feeling?"

Noah laughed but said no more, leaving Ren to explain, "Well, it's only been about fifteen minutes. Noah's just being an ass because he thinks I can't do it."

"Well, I think you're capable of it," Jules claimed. "How'd you decide to quit?"

Ren pouted down at his sandwich, worried his reasoning would lead Julian's faith in him to waiver. "I got pissed off."

"By Miles?" Noah asked.

"And Clarisse," Ren said without thinking.

Both men seemed shocked. "Did you ..." Noah began, trailing off in an annoying way. "You just diverted some of the blame *away* from Miles? What's wrong with you? Are you feeling okay? Do you need to smoke a cigarette?"

"*Shut up*," Ren snapped. He took the first bite of his sandwich angrily.

"They both made me mad, okay? Clarisse said smoking is gross and tried to get Miles to agree and he didn't, but he said I should stop *if* I could and it kind of felt like he implied I couldn't and that annoyed me, so now I'm doing it."

"Wow." Noah put his half-eaten sandwich down on his lap and leaned forward. His eyes were bright, and Ren glared back at him, knowing whatever he said next would make him even more angry. "You really care what he thinks of you now, don't you? Before, you would have just told him to fuck off, but now you're trying to *change* for the better because he suggested it?"

Ren didn't know what to say to this. His jaw went slack.

Noah's gaze turned mischievous, which was never good. "Did something happen during your weekend away? I heard from Hale that the two of you shared a bed."

Now Julian looked curious too. "You shared a bed?"

Ren groaned and covered his face with his hands. "Why is Hale telling people that? Ugh, nothing happened. It's just … lately, not only on the trip, we've been interacting more."

"And?" Noah prompted.

For a moment, Ren gathered his thoughts. He wasn't sure what to say about Miles or how he felt about him now that they'd gotten to know each other better. "He's not awful," Ren admitted. He exhaled in vexation. "Do you think I ever gave Miles a chance?" It was a selfish question, since he was only asking in hopes of making himself feel better. He felt guilty at the possibility that he's been dismissing Miles this whole time when he was turning out to be not so bad.

Now Julian was laughing along with Noah. This stung a little. Julian didn't laugh at him often.

"Besides the minute in which you checked him out the first time?" Noah asked. "No. I don't think you gave him a chance."

Julian had stopped, but Noah laughed at his expense for a little while longer before adding, "He's a good guy. I'm not surprised you like him now that you've gotten to know him for Hale's sake."

"I don't *like* him," Ren protested. In his pocket, his phone buzzed, and he shifted to free it from his pants. "I can tolerate him."

Noah snorted. "Yeah, that's *real* convincing."

This was annoying, so Ren ignored it, focusing instead on the text he'd received. It was Sawyer, confirming their plans for the evening. After he finished his classes for the day, Ren was going over to his dorm for the first time to watch a movie.

"Who is it?" Noah asked, voice muffled as his mouth was full of food.

"Mind your own business." Ren spoke without venom, and he caved when Noah frowned. "Sawyer."

"That's the guy you're seeing, right?" asked Julian. "How's it going?"

Shrugging, Ren put his phone down and brought his attention back to his food. "It's fine." He thought of the aggressive kiss after their first date. "He's not bad. I had a good time on our date, mostly."

Julian made a face. Before Ren could ask why, Noah summed it up with a simple accusation. "Your standards are so pathetically low."

"There's nothing wrong with giving people a chance," Ren defended, though he wished he had chosen different words, because when Noah locked eyes with him, Ren knew he was thinking about Miles and how inconsistent Ren was with *chances*.

Ren went to Sawyer's room right after class. It was a standard, tiny dorm room with bunked beds, a futon, and a small TV. Ren allowed himself a few moments to take it all in before turning to Sawyer and asking, "Where's your roommate?"

"I sent him out for the evening." Sawyer gestured toward the futon. "Wanna take a seat? I'll get the TV going."

Ren sat as instructed, folding his hands in his lap as he waited. "What are we watching?"

"Um ..." Sawyer joined Ren on the futon, remote in hand. "Whatever you want. What movies do you like?" He made a face. "Romantic comedies?"

Romantic comedies were more Hale's thing, and Ren suspected Sawyer only asked because he didn't understand gay men. "You realize I'm not a woman, right?"

Shocked, Sawyer's head swiveled to look at him.

"I have a dick," Ren added. Sawyer's gaze dropped, and then he turned away. His cheeks were pink.

"I know that," he said. "Sorry. I didn't mean to suggest I thought otherwise."

Ren laughed. "I'm not offended. I don't mind romantic comedies. I just prefer action movies. You know, most women don't only like romantic comedies either."

"Sadie does," Sawyer claimed, seemingly without thinking because the *oh shit* was easy to read in his expression.

Eyebrows raising, Ren leaned back. "And Sadie is …?"

"My sister," Sawyer spat out.

It was obviously a lie. "Am I supposed to believe that?"

Sawyer's expression became sheepish. "Ah." He rubbed the back of his neck. "Sorry. She's actually my ex-girlfriend … I thought it might have been too soon for us to bring up our exes."

But it's not too soon to lie, Ren thought. "When did you two break up? It must have been recent if you still slip up and mention her."

Sawyer nodded. In his hand, he fiddled with the remote. "It was pretty recent, yeah … I don't want you to think that you're just a rebound. I mean, that night at the bar, maybe I was just looking for someone to take my mind off it, but after meeting you, I really started to like you."

Ren wasn't sure whether he should believe this, but he didn't think it mattered. It wasn't like they were serious. If he found out Sawyer was lying, then there was nothing stopping Ren from moving on to explore different options whenever he pleased.

He reached out to grab the remote. "You like superhero movies?" he asked, already navigating through the streaming app pulled up on the television.

"Love 'em." Sawyer continued to watch him.

"Sweet." Ren played the first superhero movie he came across. "Let's watch this one then."

They were ten minutes into the movie when Sawyer cleared his throat. "We cool?"

Ren didn't even turn away from the screen. "Why wouldn't we be?"

This was answer enough, because Sawyer draped his arm along Ren's shoulders and seemed to finally relax.

Sawyer must have liked the movie, because he waited until the very end to kiss Ren. This was fine—Ren didn't mind being kissed—but after only a minute, it became clear that Sawyer was trying to sleep with him. This wasn't something Ren was interested in. He had his rules, and he intended to follow them.

The question was how to get out of it. One of Sawyer's hands was in his hair, the other beneath his shirt, pressed into his back. His tongue was in Ren's mouth, licking at him, and Ren let a little noise of surprise escape from his throat when he felt teeth on his lower lip. It was far more enjoyable than their last kiss, and he considered staying like that for a while, but Sawyer's phone rang and it seemed like a fine opportunity to get away.

As Sawyer checked his phone, dismissing the call, Ren stood.

"Oh." Sawyer frowned up at him. "I'm sorry, it was just a buddy of mine. You don't have to go. I'll call him back later."

Ren waved a hand. "It's fine." He straightened his collar, hoping he didn't look too much like someone who'd recently made out on a futon. "There's a novel I have to read by Friday for class, so I should get going, anyway." This wasn't an accurate statement—he had already finished reading the novel—but it seemed easier than the truth. "I'll see you later?"

"Yeah," Sawyer said, frowning. "I'll text you."

"Sweet." Ren let himself out, then leaned against the closed door for a long moment, thinking. Sawyer wanted to sleep with him. He considered telling Sawyer his rules about sex the next time they met. It would be an awkward conversation, and Ren had been hoping to avoid it for as long as possible.

Confident in his ability to evade, he decided discussing it wasn't necessary at this point in the relationship.

Chapter Fifteen

The photography exhibition was Saturday evening, so Ren got to laze around for most of the day before Hale knocked on the door to his bedroom and told him it was time to get ready.

He wasn't feeling the need to stand out at all—he was hoping Miles wouldn't notice he was there—so Ren dressed in all black. It seemed to surprise Hale, but his friend only smiled and said, "You look nice."

Logan was waiting in the hallway. He greeted them, his grin widening when Hale pressed onto his toes to give him a kiss in hello. "Thanks for coming with me. Both of you," he said as they walked to the elevator. "Miles's will be busy, so it'll be nice having company."

"He's not able to hang out with you while you're there?" asked Ren. He was trailing behind the couple, the hallway too cramped for the three of them to walk side by side.

"I don't think so. He said he'll have some free time, but for most of it he'll be networking. It's super important in his major since there's no guarantee there'll be jobs available around graduation," Logan explained.

This made sense, and it was something Ren could sympathize with as he was struggling to find jobs to apply for. "Will Clarisse be there too?"

Hale glanced back at him.

"What? I'm just trying to prepare myself."

Logan laughed. "I don't think her work is being displayed, though she helped set up, so maybe. I imagine she'll make an appearance to support Miles, even if it's not. I'm not positive, though. She and I aren't close."

When they reached the elevator, Hale pressed the button. "Really?" he asked, turning his face up to his boyfriend. "I thought you all knew each other from before."

"We do." When the doors opened, Logan stepped in first, pulling Hale behind him by their linked hands. "Still, she's always been much closer to Miles than to me. They've known each other since they were little. Their parents are friends, so they've always been together."

For a moment, Ren considered not saying the words he was thinking, but by the time the elevator doors opened to the first floor, he'd settled on a *fuck it* mentality. "She has a crush on him, right? Has it always been like that?"

Logan sighed. "I'm not surprised even you noticed. Yeah. It's always been like that. At least, for as long as I've known them. It's not worth thinking about. Miles is adamant he sees her as a sister."

Ren wasn't sure how he felt about Logan adding this bit. He hoped it wasn't for his sake.

To avoid giving the impression he cared, Ren let the subject drop.

When they arrived, Logan and Hale went to find Miles, so Ren wandered around on his own.

He enjoyed viewing art. It was one of the few nice things he'd done with his father while growing up, and every time he found himself in a gallery or art museum, it was a little easier to convince himself his childhood wasn't horrible. It would only take a glance at his wrists or a text message from his brother to remind him he wasn't so lucky, but Ren didn't mind wearing long sleeves and muting his phone to savor the feelings of remembered happiness.

He didn't know why his father took him to see art. Every few months, the small gallery in his hometown would have a showing of local photographers' work, and they would go together. They never talked about the outings or planned ahead. When the gallery would send a brochure to their house, notifying them of the upcoming exhibition, whoever got the mail first would pin it to the fridge with a magnet for the other to see, and the night of, they'd meet in front of the door.

There were a few things weird about those evenings. The first was that his brother didn't come along. Ren had always wondered whether this was intentional, or whether he'd just never understood the ritual and missed out. The second thing was that his father knew the staff at the gallery somehow, and they'd always greeted them warmly when they arrived. Ren had never asked about either of these things, too afraid that his father wouldn't answer when he did.

Ren walked through the school's exhibition thinking about those evenings with his father. He wasn't being very attentive, his eyes roaming over the students' work, looking for something that caught his attention. Ren preferred to look at photos of landscapes, but he supposed it made sense that this exhibition didn't have many of those. Most college kids didn't have the time to drive all over the state to find pretty places to take pictures. Instead, photos of flowers, and people's pets, food, and interesting campus architecture covered the walls. They were enjoyable to look at, but nothing made his feet falter with a desire to observe just a little longer.

He didn't stop until he got to the back wall. Only three photographers had their work displayed there. The first person had chosen a theme that had something to do with light, all their photos capturing different rays and shadows. The second person's theme was about shoes.

It was the third student's work that gave him pause, because Ren was standing before a picture of himself. The black-and-white photo was of his own profile, a cigarette held to his lips with a relaxed hand. He didn't recall the photo being taken, but his expression in it explained that. He looked distant, not fully there. *Empty.*

It shocked him. He knew the expression well, had seen it countless times reflected in the mirror on his bad days. He didn't like this expression of his, but he didn't mind that someone else paid enough attention to him to catch it.

Curious, Ren glanced around at the other photos. There was one of Hale and Logan together, both of them smiling, Hale's gaze lowered in shyness while Logan looked straight at him. One of Clarisse, her brown hair pulled back, mouth open in laughter. There was a middle-aged woman Ren didn't recognize, though some of her features were familiar. A child crying. Another picture of Logan, this one with a hand raised to his forehead as if he was rubbing it in frustration. The last photo was of the guy with dyed hair that Miles had been going to the bar with, his face twisted into something like pain, though he looked amused at the same time.

They were all in black-and-white, all beautiful in their own way.

Ren's gaze returned to the picture of himself.

"I'm sorry." The apology came from his left, and Ren turned. Miles stared back at him. "Ren, I ..."

Wondering what kind of expression he was making to cause that reaction, Ren raised a hand to touch his cheeks. They were dry. "Why are you saying sorry?"

"Because you look sad," Miles said, which made sense because Ren kind of wanted to cry. He shook his head.

"Not sad." He turned back to the photo. After a long moment, he felt Miles's arm against his as he moved to stand beside him.

"I should still apologize," Miles said. "I didn't have your permission to take your picture, or to use it for this kind of thing. I didn't think you'd ever find out, if I'm being honest. I didn't know you'd be here."

"How did you decide to use this picture?"

A slight shift in weight pressed Miles's arm against his shoulder more. Still, neither of them moved. They were speaking softly, and Ren felt the lack of distance was necessary for the sort of moment they were having.

"Well ... my theme was emotion, and my professor thought that picture of you captures it particularly well. She asked if you'd consider modeling for some of the portrait shooting in class, but I said no."

This was the first Ren was hearing of this. "Why?"

"Because you're interesting to photograph."

"No. I mean, why did you say no?"

Miles frowned. "Do you want to?"

Ren considered it, then shook his head. "Not really."

"Then there's no problem, is there?"

A part of Ren wanted to pry. A larger part felt he wasn't ready to.

Instead, he looked at the picture of himself and thought about how Miles made him feel. Once again, Miles had ventured into unfamiliar territory. Ren strangely didn't feel panicked. As he gazed at himself, framed on the wall, he was reminded that emptiness was just another part of himself, and Miles had seen it and thought something of it other than disgust or pity.

Ren swallowed, expecting his throat to feel tight. It didn't. "You asked me about what happened with me and Jules, right?"

Miles was watching him now. Ren could feel it, but he didn't look back. "I did," Miles agreed after a long pause.

"He loved me," Ren admitted. "We had a great time together, and he loved me like I've always wanted someone to love me, but I … I just couldn't."

"Couldn't?"

"Couldn't love him back," Ren said. He turned toward Miles but didn't look at him. "I don't know why I couldn't. He's a fantastic guy. I just wasn't able to see him as anything other than a friend, no matter how hard I tried. And I tried. For those six months, I tried *so hard*, but it wasn't fair to him to keep going on like that, so we broke up." Not yet ready to meet his gaze, Ren stared at the suit Miles was wearing. "And now he loves someone else the way he loved me."

It took Miles a couple of seconds to respond. "Why are you telling me this?"

"I don't know," Ren said. "I think I just want to." He glanced up, meeting Miles's eyes. "You scare me sometimes. With your questions."

"I just want to know more about you."

Neither of them said anything after that, both turning back to the wall of photos. Ren was sure their focus was more on each other than what was in front of them.

It wasn't long before Hale and Logan found them. Miles had just shifted beside him when Logan's familiar voice said, "There you are."

With a small gasp, Miles jerked away. Curious, Ren glanced at their friends, but both Hale and Logan were smiling at Miles in a way that told Ren he had missed something.

"We've been looking for you, but I see Ren found you first," Hale said after a minute of them all staring at each other.

"I've been busy," Miles said.

Hale hugged Ren's arm, looking over his shoulder at all the pictures on the wall. "I'm up there! Ren, you are too!"

"I noticed."

Hale took his time viewing the rest of the photos. "You're quite good at this, aren't you?" he said to Miles.

Miles grimaced, and Logan laughed, placing a hand on his roommate's shoulder. "He is, yeah."

Distressed by the compliments, Miles looked at Ren, who pressed his lips together to hide a smile.

"This thing wraps up in about twenty minutes, doesn't it?" Hale asked. "Do you have to stay and help pack up afterward?"

"Um …" Miles pulled his eyes from Ren. "No. I don't. We're doing that during class next week. Why?"

Hale propped an elbow on Ren's shoulder, leaning into him. "Well, I was thinking we could get dinner after this."

It didn't surprise Ren when they all turned to him for confirmation. He recalled the day Hale invited him to the exhibition, when his friend told him he could turn down any offers of dinner if he pleased.

Only Ren didn't want to turn down the offer. He nodded in agreement and was faced with three expressions of surprise. "You sure you're free?" Hale asked, giving him an easy out. "You and Sawyer don't have plans or anything?"

Over Hale's shoulder, Ren peeked at Miles. He was already looking back, his expression open. Ren saw hope there. "We don't," he dismissed. "I'll come to dinner."

Chapter Sixteen

Ren, Hale, and Noah had plans to get a drink.

They were supposed to meet at Johan's by seven, so it annoyed Ren when he arrived ten minutes late and neither of his friends were present. Hale's tardiness was to be expected—he was being dropped off after a date—but Noah was always so strict about being punctual, it was strange for him not to be on time.

Ren went to wait at the bar, watching Miles work as he approached. He was making a drink, nodding along to what the girl on the other side of the bar was saying to him. It was when Ren took a seat that Miles's eyes flicked in his direction, probably just marking him down as another customer before realizing who it was. His hands paused.

Miles finished making the drink and said something to the girl as he handed it to her. It must have been a dismissal, because he approached Ren then. "What'll you have?"

"Whiskey sour," Ren requested.

"Got it. Be back in a second." He left to make the drink.

They had spoken little since Miles's exhibition, just a few times in passing, but things between them felt better. Ren wasn't nervous to be asked questions he couldn't handle, and Miles wasn't tiptoeing around him to avoid pissing him off.

We're almost friends, Ren thought.

"Busy night?" he asked when Miles returned, a glass with a thin lemon slice on the rim in hand.

As he slid it across the bar, Miles shrugged. "It's a Saturday, but it's still early. It hasn't been bad so far."

Ren took a sip of his drink and hummed. "It's great. Thanks." He handed his credit card over. "Could you start a tab?"

"Sure." When Miles took his card, their fingers brushed. At the contact, Ren glanced up, but Miles's eyes remained down. "You have a date tonight?"

This wasn't what Ren had been expecting him to say. "I ... no. Hale and Noah are supposed to be meeting me, but they're late."

"Ah. I thought he and Logan go out on Saturdays."

Nodding, Ren took another sip of his drink, puckering a little at the sourness on his tongue. "Yeah, Logan's dropping him off. I'm not sure where Noah is."

"Right here." The stool to his left creaked as Noah took a seat. "Sorry I'm late."

Ren was prepared to give Noah shit for it, but his eyes widened at the sight of his friend's pale face and red-rimmed eyes. "Oh my god, what happened to you?"

Miles laughed at the scowl that came across Noah's face. "Nothing," Noah said. "I just drank too much last night, so I feel awful." His gaze settled on Miles. "Hi again."

"You want water?" Miles asked, amused.

"That would be amazing."

Annoyed by the familiarity, Ren flicked his gaze between the two of them. "What the actual fuck?" he hissed at Noah once Miles was out of hearing distance. "You two are like friends now?"

Noah looked at him like he was crazy. "What the hell is wrong with you?" he asked, tone a little harsh for Noah. When Ren flinched, he seemed regretful. "Shit, sorry. I just feel terrible, and I don't know why you're mad at me."

"I'm not mad." Ren stared down at his drink.

Sighing, Noah leaned on his stool so his elbow pressed against Ren's arm. "I didn't mean to snap at you."

Ren nodded in acknowledgment, still not looking at him.

"You know how to make me feel like I kicked a puppy, don't you?"

Liking that he had this effect, Ren smiled.

"Ah." Relief was clear in Noah's voice. "There we go."

Miles returned for just long enough to deliver Noah's water before being called to the opposite end of the bar. "Really, though. I thought the two of you were getting along. Why are you pissy about me talking to him? You jealous?"

"*What?*"

"Don't worry. Even if I'm friendly with Miles, you're still going to be my favorite."

Noah had the wrong idea, but his understanding was far more simple than Ren's true feelings, so he let it go. "He and I are fine," Ren said. "He's just not as horrible as I originally thought."

"I'm proud of you for admitting that."

"Admitting what?" asked Hale, taking the seat on Ren's other side. Ren couldn't help but notice his friend's mouth was red, and he wondered how long he and Logan had kissed in the car before he came in.

"That Miles is a good person," Noah filled in.

"That is *not* what I said," Ren set straight. "Shut up. Hale, don't listen to him. He's still drunk from last night."

Hale gazed past Ren to Noah, his lips curled up in a pleasant smile.

A *tsk* came from over Ren's shoulder, showing Noah's displeasure, but he didn't bother to acknowledge it. Instead, he took another sip of his drink, licked the lemon flavor off his lips, and asked Hale how his date had gone.

The expression on Hale's face shifted into something fond. "Ah, it was good. It's always good."

It was so sweet, Ren needed to take another swallow of his drink to wash it down with sour. "What did you guys do?"

"Just dinner and a movie."

Noah whistled. "He takes you to the movies when it's not discount night? Now that's true love."

At this, Hale appeared incredibly pleased. It occurred to Ren that he didn't know whether Hale and Logan were at the point of exchanging *I love yous*, even though the feelings were clearly there for both of them.

"Have either of you said it yet?" he asked, glancing at his almost empty drink and then down the bar to Miles. "I love you?"

"No," Hale said. "Neither of us have. I don't know how to bring it up."

Miles noticed Hale's presence and started toward them.

"So you want to say it?" Noah deducted.

"I want to say it," Hale admitted. "It's just … saying it for the first time is kind of nerve-wracking. You only get to say it first once."

When close enough, Miles greeted Hale with a friendly "Hey, how was date night?"

Hale, who hadn't seen him coming, jerked on his stool. "Oh gosh," he said, gazing up at Miles with large eyes and then glancing at Ren.

He had no problem reading the question there. *Did he hear me?* Ren didn't see why it mattered if Miles had heard Hale admit to loving Logan, but he shook his head to reassure his friend.

"Date night was good," Hale answered. "Thanks for asking."

Nodding, Miles's attention moved to Ren's glass. "You drank that fast. Another one?"

"Could I have a vodka cranberry and a rum and coke for Hale? You can put both on the tab."

"You don't have to do that," Hale assured with a frown. Ren was pretty sure the expression wasn't because of Ren paying for him, but he trusted Hale to not bring it up when Miles was around. "I brought money for myself."

Ren drained his glass, waving his free hand dismissively. "Let me get it. You rarely drink, so I never get to buy you any."

With the matter of payment settled, Miles went to make their drinks.

"You opened a tab?" Hale asked. "Are you planning on drinking a lot?"

Lately, Ren had been feeling good, and he hadn't felt the need to distract himself with alcohol. "I did, and I'm not," he said, reaching out to pat Hale's hand. "I'll take a break after this one."

"That's what I said last night," Noah grumbled. He began to complain about the night before, though he didn't get far into his rant before another interruption cut him off. This time, there was no one else who was supposed to be joining them, so Ren jumped at the feeling of arms coming to rest over his shoulders from behind. He turned his head up and then huffed at the sight. *"Jason."*

Noah groaned. "Dude," he said to the man behind Ren. "Fuck off. I do not want to see your face right now. Why do you look so composed?"

Everyone knew Jason. He was most definitely the most extroverted person Ren had met on campus over the years, frequently spending his weekends socializing at bars. Freshman year, he had ended up Hale's roommate—he was an English minor, if Ren remembered correctly, though he and Hale were so different despite their shared interest in studies, them being paired together still felt like a joke.

Ren liked Jason. He was funny and smart and easy to talk to. Incredibly pretty as well, with dark hair and eyes alike, tan skin and dimples when he smiled. At one point, Ren might have even considered dating him, though all possibility of this had gone out the window once he realized Jason flirted that much with *everyone* and preferred not to be tied down by a single partner.

"You're hung over?" Jason asked Noah, hands raising to tilt Ren's head down so he was no longer looking at him, then settling his chin against his hair. Having a lack of understanding of personal space was something Jason was known for, so Ren didn't pay it any mind. "I didn't drink that much last night."

As the two men bickered, Ren rolled his eyes at Hale.

"Your drinks," Miles interrupted, putting the two glasses down on the counter.

Noah and Jason fell silent.

"Thank you," Hale offered.

"Oooo," Jason voiced, moving so his chin was on Ren's shoulder instead. "What'd you get?"

"None of your damn business," Ren retorted, grinning when Jason whistled and pulled back from him.

"Can I have what he's having?" Jason asked Miles.

When Ren glanced up, he noticed Miles's expression twisted with distaste. Given how often Jason appeared at the bar, Ren figured that Miles must be familiar with Jason, and Ren wondered what could have happened between them in the past.

Miles nodded. "I'll be right back."

"Well, *he's* in a shit mood," Jason said. He went to sit on the other side of Hale.

"You're having something to drink?" Noah asked, sounding miserable.

The words went ignored. Jason's attention was now on his old roommate. "What have you been up to, cupcake? I don't think I've seen you since last year."

Hale laughed, taking a sip of his drink. On the other side of Ren, Noah made a gagging noise. Ren wasn't sure whether this was in response to Jason's use of the word *cupcake* or whether he felt sick enough to throw up. "I've been busy," Hale said.

"With?"

Judging by the blush across Hale's cheeks, he wasn't going to be able to say it, so Ren leaned into his side and explained, "He's got a boyfriend now."

"You're kidding," Jason said. Hale shook his head, his face an incredible shade of red. "Who?"

"Um, Logan Wallace?" It sounded more like a question. "I don't know if you know—"

Jason cut in. "The hot one?"

Hale covered his face with his hands.

"No shit?" said Jason. "Well, good for you. I'm proud. If you ever get sick of him, you know where to find me."

It was bad timing on Miles's part that he returned then, and he immediately looked even more displeased. Jason didn't seem to realize. He held his hand out for his drink. "Thanks, babe. I'll even tip you 'cause you're cute." He slapped a handful of bills down on the bar. With a blank expression, Miles took them and left.

The four of them watched him go. "I think he hates you," said Noah.

"Nah, he's usually not like that," Jason claimed. "Maybe he got up on the wrong side of the bed." Whatever it was, he didn't seem bothered, because he grinned and looked to Ren. "What about you then? Still single?"

Ren shook his head. "I've been seeing someone."

Jason made a grossed-out noise that was followed by a good-natured smile. "You guys and all your commitment. Well, I guess I'll be having fun without you two." He stood. "Noah, I'm not interested in you, so I was never planning to have fun with you anyway. I'll see you guys later."

"Fucker," Noah grumbled as Jason wandered off.

"I take it you two ran into each other last night?" Ren asked, facing him for the first time since Jason had sat beside Hale. Somehow, Noah looked even more pale. "Are you seriously alright?"

Noah shook his head. "No, sorry, I feel like shit. And we did run into each other last night. He came to say hi to Julian, but he was with some girl so he didn't stay long." He sipped at his water, then cleared his throat. "How are things going with the guy you're seeing?"

"They're fine," Ren admitted. "We text every day and get meals in the cafeteria when we have time … I don't know. It's something to do, I guess."

"Have you slept with him?"

Shocked, Hale choked on his drink, and Ren offered him a few pats to the back.

"No. I doubt we'll sleep together." Ren thought of Sawyer kissing him on the futon in his dorm room. "I think he wants to, but I'm going to keep telling him no."

"And if he doesn't take it well, then he's not worth your time," Hale said.

"Yeah, yeah." Ren took a sip of his drink. Miles always made a tart vodka-cranberry, which Ren rather enjoyed. "I know. You don't have to tell me. I've *more* than learned my lesson about guys who just want to screw me."

It wasn't uncommon for men to approach Ren for that specific reason, and he felt he'd done a good job of weeding them out so far.

"Really, though. I think Sawyer's a good guy. I'm just not sure if we have enough chemistry to make it work."

Chuckling, Noah took another sip of his water. "I love you, Ren. But I have to say, you're not the best judge of character."

While this was true, he didn't like it when people straight out said he wasn't good at something, and he narrowed his eyes. To his horror, Hale laughed and added, "Yeah. I mean, you thought Miles was an asshole for years, and he's one of the most laid-back and helpful people I know. He took care of you when you were drunk and he carried you to bed when you fell asleep on the porch that night at the cabin."

Embarrassed, Ren turned to his roommate. "How do you know about that?"

"He mentioned it."

Ren looked to where Miles was gathering empty glasses from the counter. "Why would he—"

"There you go again," Noah grumbled. When Ren turned to him, Noah was leaning heavily against the bar, face now white. "Focusing on the unimportant things so you can overlook something else."

Ren felt annoyed with both of them. "Why am I being attacked right now?"

"We're not—"

"I need to throw up," Noah announced, getting up from his seat and rushing toward the back of the bar.

"I expected that," Ren told Hale, shifting to get his phone out of his back pocket. "I'm going to text Julian to come get him in his car. I can't believe he's ruining our night out like this."

For the first time in over a year, Ren sent Julian a text message. Hale must have been watching, because he waited until Ren pressed send to say, "You know we weren't attacking you, right? You've just always been critical of the little things with Miles, and I thought you were finally self-aware enough for me to call it out."

The words made Ren laugh. "I know you weren't intending it, but that was totally a burn."

"Was it?"

"It's not like I'm mad or anything about him telling you he carried me to bed. I guess I just don't see how it could have come up unless he wanted to talk about it, and if he wanted to talk about it, I'm assuming he brought it up to complain."

"Not at all. I don't think he would have told me if I hadn't asked. I was asking him about that night because you burned yourself and he slipped up. It's my fault."

"Nothing's ever your fault, Hale."

Smiling, Hale patted his arm. "I wish that were true." He took a sip at the rim of his glass, eyes on Ren's phone as it lit up with a message from Julian saying he was on his way. "Once Julian gets Noah, do you want to hang out here just the two of us, or should we go back to the apartment?"

Ren shot a look in Miles's direction, then glanced away just as quickly. "Let's hang out at the apartment. It's gonna get busy here soon anyway."

They finished their drinks as they waited for Noah.

Miles must have been paying attention, because as soon as their glasses were empty, he approached. Ren eyed him, curious if he was in the same poor mood Jason had brought out of him, but Miles seemed perfectly pleasant. "You want anything else?"

"We're going to be leaving soon," said Hale.

"Noah's throwing up as we speak," Ren added.

Miles grimaced. "Well," he began, taking the empty glasses. "He was plastered last night, so it's no surprise he doesn't feel good."

"You were working?" asked Hale.

"I do most Friday and Saturdays, these days."

"Aww, when do you go on dates?" Ren teased. Immediately, he wished he hadn't, since they both turned to him with matching startled expressions. "What? It was just a joke."

"I don't go on dates," Miles said. "I'll be back with your card. One second."

Noah returned as Miles left. Some of the color had returned to his face, though the skin under his eyes was still dark with exhaustion. "We're leaving," Ren told Noah. "Miles is just closing my tab."

"I'm fine," Noah grumbled, taking a large drink of water.

"Well, I already told Julian to come."

A groan left Noah. "Why would you do that? He already spent most of last night taking care of me."

"I didn't want to watch you throw up on the side of the road." Ren's phone buzzed. "Jules is here. Noah, you don't have to wait for us."

Noah opened his mouth to respond, but Miles brought Ren's card and receipt. "You just need to sign," he instructed, pulling a pen out of his apron.

After writing out a generous tip, Ren signed and bid, "See you around."

The three of them left together, stopping by the door to rifle through the coatrack for their jackets. Noah was still complaining about Ren's decision to call his roommate, but as soon as they were outside, he went to Julian's car without a word and climbed into the passenger seat. Rolling his eyes, Ren grabbed Hale's wrist and pulled him over to the car parked on the street, checking for traffic before going to stand by the driver's side window.

Julian rolled it down and grinned at them. "Thanks for coming," Ren told him. "He got sick in the bar."

"I told him to reschedule with you guys, but he said you'd try to cut his dick off if he did that," Julian said, making Hale laugh. "Get in. I'll give you guys a ride, too."

"Oh." Ren tried to avoid getting in Julian's car when he could. It didn't make him uncomfortable or anything, he just had a lot of memories in there that had become bittersweet. "We're okay." He looked back at Hale, who nodded in agreement. "We don't live very far, and I want to smoke on the walk back."

Julian smirked. "I thought you quit."

"*Damn*," Ren swore. This was happening often, the habit of smoking for so long making it difficult to forget. "I *have* quit, by the way. I haven't even cheated yet."

"Good for you," Julian praised. "Come on and get in. Even if you don't live far, it's getting cold out."

Hale tugged on Ren's arm—an unspoken question. *Is that okay?*

Ren's answering nod was to both of them. "You win." He pulled open the back door and gestured for Hale to get in before him. "Thanks."

To his surprise, he didn't spend the car ride thinking about his and Julian's past. His mind was still on the man back at the bar for a reason he couldn't explain.

Chapter Seventeen

Ren was cutting through the parking lot when Miles exited his car. When they spotted each other, Ren's feet stopped, his first instinct to wait.

It was only when Miles raised his eyebrows that Ren felt silly and continued toward the door.

"Hey!" Miles called. From the corner of his eye, Ren could see him weaving through the parked cars more quickly. He was only a few feet behind when Ren unlocked the door. He considered shutting it before Miles caught up, but he held it open anyway.

"Thanks."

"Yeah," Ren said, not looking at him as he pressed the elevator button. "Where are you coming from?"

"Craft store." Miles raised the plastic bag in his hand. "Every year I make my mom a scrapbook of the pictures I've taken, so I bought stuff for that."

His cheeks were pink. *Cute.*

Miles cleared his throat. "What about you? What were you up to?"

"Sawyer and I got dinner," Ren said. The elevator doors opened.

They both stepped inside, and Ren pressed the button to their floor.

"Ah. The boyfriend."

"He's not my boyfriend."

"You've got commitment issues or something?"

Annoyed, Ren *tsk*ed. It had been a while since Miles last said something that pissed him off.

"Ah," Miles said. "I didn't mean … I just meant that you two have been doing this thing for a while. When does it become official?"

Still looking away, Ren grumbled, "What's it matter to you?"

Miles didn't respond until the doors had opened. "I'm just making conversation."

The atmosphere had been ruined by Ren's poor attitude. He didn't want to leave it like that, but before he could think of what to say to fix it, Miles was already inside his apartment.

"So stupid," Ren mumbled to himself, unlocking his door. It was such a silly thing to say, *What's it matter to you?* It made it seem as if Ren expected Miles to care about his love life, as if he hoped that Miles would be upset by his relationship with Sawyer.

Ren slipped into the dark apartment, closing the door softly in case Hale was already asleep. He had just hung up his keys and was reaching for the light switch when he heard a noise.

It was just a soft creak, the sound of mattress springs, and he closed his eyes to listen harder.

After a moment of squeaking, Ren realized what he was listening to, and his eyes flew open. As quiet as he could manage, Ren grabbed his keys and slipped into the hall.

"Oh my god. What do I do?" He wanted to laugh. *I have to text Noah.*

As he freed his phone from his coat pocket, Miles emerged from his own apartment. Ren recalled Miles telling him how thin the walls were. Hale and Logan must have gotten louder.

Miles spotted him. "Did I just hear what I think I did?"

"The sound of your best friend taking my best friend's virginity?" Ren couldn't help it. He laughed. It was such an unexpected situation, and the look on Miles's face wasn't making it any less funny.

Once Ren started laughing, he couldn't stop. It seemed like Miles wanted to join him, but instead, Miles closed the distance between them and slipped a hand over Ren's mouth, blocking the sound. "Hey!" Miles said, speaking low. He was grinning. "They might hear you. The walls are *thin*! If they weren't, I wouldn't be scarred for life."

Ren reached up to grasp Miles's wrist, pulling his hand away. "What do we do?"

"I *don't* want to be here when they finish," Miles said.

Intrigued, Ren glanced at the door. "Why? Do you think we'd be able to hear it from here?"

This startled a laugh out of Miles. "What? No. I mean, can you imagine the look on Hale's face when he sees Logan out and the two of us are just sitting here waiting for them? He'd be horrified, and then Logan would never get laid again and resent me."

"So? What do we do?"

Miles was thinking, staring down the hall over Ren's shoulder. After a minute, he said something unexpected. "Want to go somewhere with me?"

Ren was sitting in the passenger seat of Miles's car, glancing around at everything while trying not to be too obvious about it. It was a typical boy car, an old sedan with empty cans in all the cup holders and a back seat filled with shopping bags and old receipts. "Don't look back there," Miles said when he noticed Ren's interest. "I haven't had time to clean."

In the dim light of sunset, Ren took a long moment to watch Miles's cheeks flush, and then he turned in his chair to look between the seats. He grabbed a receipt. "Just over a year ago, you bought a twenty-pack of lime green balloons. So you haven't had the chance to clean your car in over a year?"

"What guy my age cleans their car more than once every two years?" Miles asked, turning into the parking lot of the local drive through ice-cream shop. The choice of location pleasantly surprised Ren.

"I wouldn't know. I've never had a car." Ren reclined his seat slightly when Miles pulled up to the end of the drive-thru line. "Ice cream, huh?"

"You like ice cream, right? That night you were drunk, all you wanted was a sundae."

"I like ice cream," Ren confirmed, pleased Miles remembered something so insignificant about him.

They were silent for a handful of seconds, and Ren began jabbing the buttons on the radio. "It doesn't work," Miles told him. The line advanced by one, and Miles pulled forward a few feet. "Car's too old. There are CDs in the glove box, if you're interested."

"*CDs,*" Ren echoed mockingly while searching for them anyway. It wasn't hard; when Miles said there were CDs in the glove box, he meant the *only* thing in the glove box was CDs. "Why do you have all these?"

"I told you, the radio doesn't work." This wasn't the answer Ren was looking for, and he fixed Miles with a blank stare. Miles grabbed one of the CD cases and flipped it over so Ren could see the back. There was a small faded sticker that designated the price as fifty cents. "I like to listen to music, but I'm not particular, so I just pick a couple up at the thrift store every time I go."

Interested, Ren flipped through the CDs. "How do you choose which ones to get?"

Miles pulled the car forward again. "It's not deep or anything. Most of the time, I just choose what looks good. Depending on who I go with, I sometimes let them choose an album or two for me."

"Does Logan?"

"Yeah." Miles glanced over at Ren and seemed surprised that he was looking back. "Logan seems to think it's funny to make me buy a bunch of old jazz albums. It's not my favorite, and he knows I listen to everything at least once."

Ren continued to stare. The sun was mostly down, the car lit with the fluorescent lights from the parking lot. It wasn't the most flattering. Nevertheless, Miles looked good.

"What are you listening to now?" Ren asked.

Miles reached out to press a few buttons. Sound filled the vehicle. It was a song Ren didn't recognize.

Miles ordered and paid, protesting when Ren tried to get out his own card. "I brought you here," he said, turning in his seat to hand Ren his caramel sundae before accepting his plain vanilla cone from the woman in the window.

"Well ..." Ren looked at the red spoon in his clear plastic bowl. "Thank you."

As if this was embarrassing, Miles just grunted in acknowledgment.

He pulled his car into a parking spot under a street lamp. "You okay if we sit for a while?" he asked, licking his cone before a drip could run down the side.

Swallowing heavily, Ren took his own first bite. It was cold and sweet on his tongue. "I don't mind. Might as well give them time to bask in the afterglow."

As Miles laughed, Ren withdrew his phone from his pocket. "What are you doing?" Miles asked.

"I want to take a picture."

"Why?"

Ren held his sundae out and took a photo. "*You're* asking me why I want to take a picture? Isn't the desire to take pictures something you understand?" He examined the photo he had taken.

"Can I see your photos?" Miles asked.

Alarmed by the request, Ren pulled his phone into his chest. He considered handing it over and letting Miles go through his camera roll freely, but Ren rarely deleted photos, so this seemed dangerous. "What? No. You'll just critique me."

Miles chuckled and licked at his ice-cream cone. "I won't," he said. "I think it's interesting to look at the pictures other people have taken. Gives me a peek at how they see things."

After a long moment of consideration, Ren held his hand out toward Miles. "Give me your phone." Miles obeyed. "What's your passcode?" Without hesitation, Miles told him. "Aren't you worried I'm going to look through *your* photos now?"

"No." Miles shook his head, then took a full bite out of his ice cream, shattering the illusion Ren had in the back of his mind. He thought he might be in a car with a psychopath. "I wouldn't have asked to see your pictures if I wasn't willing to share my own. Look at whatever you want."

Tempted, Ren paused in his navigation of Miles's phone. "Don't you have anything embarrassing? Like, at least a folder of nudes that were sent to you? You're cute. There's got to be some girls shooting their shot."

Miles appeared baffled. *"Nudes?"* He stared out the windshield. "I thought you weren't supposed to save those."

Laughing, Ren shook his head and brought his attention back to the cell phone. His sundae was melting in its bowl, chilling his right hand as it did, so he set it on the dashboard. "Your apps are all fucked up," he announced, scrolling through them until he located the one he'd been searching for. After requesting to follow himself on it, he handed the phone back to Miles.

"This is you? I didn't realize you had an account," Miles said as Ren went into his own phone to accept the request. There was a moment of lag, and then his profile became visible on Miles's screen.

"There you go," Ren said. "You can see those photos."

"Oh." Miles, who had somehow consumed his ice cream at an alarming rate, peeled the wrapper off the cone, eyes not leaving the screen. Ren took another bite of his sundae.

For a few minutes, they listened to the CD in silence, Miles navigating through his pictures with interest. The longer he went not saying anything, the more the nerves in Ren's stomach twisted until it was unbearable. Lots of people had seen those photos before, but he'd never considered someone looking at them the way Miles did, his attention unwavering.

"This makes me uncomfortable."

Miles lowered his phone. "Really? I don't have to see."

"That's not the problem," Ren grumbled. Even he didn't know what the problem was. "Just ... I don't know. Keep talking so it's less embarrassing for me."

"You're embarrassed?" When Ren didn't respond, Miles raised the phone again. "Well, you shouldn't be. I like your pictures." He swiped through a few more, then turned the phone in his hand so Ren could see what he was looking at. The photo was from about a year ago of himself and Noah. "I forgot your hair used to be this short."

Ren pinched a strand of hair between his fingers. *It's getting to the point of too long*, he thought. "Maybe I should cut it again. It's been a while."

"Do you prefer it short?" Miles scrolled past the photo.

"Not really. I don't prefer it like this either, though. Probably somewhere in between." He grabbed his spoon again. By now, his ice cream was a soupy mess. "Noah says I look like a girl when it's this long, and I don't want to look like a girl."

"You don't look feminine, I think," Miles said. "Looks good either way … Is this the day you moved into the apartment?"

Ren checked the photo Miles was referring to. He and Hale were lying in Hale's bed on their stomachs, smiling at the phone Ren had propped up on the dresser. The comment attached to the picture was some cheesy line about how happy he was to live with his best friend.

"Yeah," Ren confirmed. He ate another spoonful of ice cream, careful not to let the liquid spill over his spoon onto his jacket. When he'd licked the utensil clean, he added, "You see, I was living with Noah in the dorms the year before that, and as you can imagine, the apartment and Hale were a real step up."

Chuckling, Miles shook his head. "Was this the day we met?"

The question was unexpected, since their initial meeting wasn't something they spoke of often. "No," Ren said. "If it was the day we met, I would be angrier in that picture, since you were such an asshole to me."

"And Hale would look starstruck after meeting the love of his life."

This made Ren smile. "Who would have thought they would be banging two years later?"

Grimacing, Miles lowered his cell phone, the screen having gone dark. "You don't have to put it like that."

Miles stared out the windshield. Ren finished his ice cream. This time, the silence wasn't unbearable, but Ren still broke it. "I'm envious of them."

"For fucking?"

"No, idiot." He considered it further. "Well, maybe just a bit for that, but I really mean I'm jealous of how happy they are together."

The CD ended, and Miles reached out to eject it. "You're not happy with Sawyer?"

Shrugging, Ren gazed out the window at the empty parking lot. "I don't know. He's fine, and I guess things are going good. It's just … it's not the same. What Hale and Logan have is more real."

"Yeah," Miles agreed. "I know what you mean. It must be nice to find the right person."

Ren shifted in his seat. "What about you and Clarisse?" he proposed. "You two are together a lot. Couldn't she be your right person?"

"No, I don't think so," Miles said without pause. "Clarisse and I have known each other since we were children, you know. Our parents are friends from college, so we've grown up together. Our moms like to joke about us getting married someday, but I've never thought of her that way."

Does she know that? Ren wanted to ask, but it was none of his business. *None* of this was his business. "I see," he said. "Well … maybe we just have to keep looking."

"Yeah," Miles said, his gaze lowering. "Maybe."

Chapter Eighteen

When Ren woke up on Tuesday, he found Miles asleep on the couch. He didn't wake him right away, too startled at first to do anything but stand and stare. Miles looked handsome as he slept, his hair pushed back off his forehead so his peaceful expression was on display.

If only he wasn't so bothersome, Ren thought as he reached out to give Miles's shoulder a shake.

Hazel eyes cracked open.

"What the fuck are you doing?" Ren asked.

Miles groaned and rubbed his eyes. "Sorry." He sat up, and Ren couldn't help but think the way Miles's hair stuck up at the back of his head was cute. "I haven't been here all night. They woke me up at like two a.m. and I wanted to sleep more, so I stole Hale's keys and snuck over."

"Woke you up?" Ren asked. "You mean—"

"They did that thing they discovered," Miles confirmed. "Really, I'm shocked. They knew I was in the next room."

Ren laughed and went to the kitchen. He felt a little self-conscious in his cotton shorts and a loose T-shirt, but he figured Miles didn't care. "Aww, come on. It's sweet. They can't keep their hands off each other."

"*Sweet?*" Miles sounded as if he disagreed.

"You want some coffee?" Ren asked.

"That'd be great. Do you need help?"

"Fuck off." Still, Ren smiled at the sound of Miles's laughter when his back was turned. "I suppose I should make enough for all of us. And maybe

I should make something for breakfast while I'm at it. You think they'll be up soon?"

Miles scoffed. "They were up pretty late, so I don't know."

Not satisfied by this answer, Ren hovered in front of the cabinet with the pots and pans. He thought it would be weird to make breakfast for just him and Miles.

"I'll text Logan, and if they're not up by the time you're done, I'll go get them," Miles said.

"Great." Ren removed two pans from the cupboard, one for eggs and bacon, and the other for pancakes. After a minute—Ren prepared the coffee and set it to brew—Miles joined him in the kitchen. "I don't need your help."

"It's fine," Miles said. "I know you don't *need* help, but I want to help. What are we making?"

Ren chewed his lip and considered telling Miles to leave him alone. Instead, he said, "Pancakes, eggs, and bacon, since that's all we have."

"I'll start mixing the batter."

Nodding, Ren got him the box of mix from the pantry. "Thanks," he said. Miles's eyebrows raised. "Shut up."

Smiling, Miles accepted the box.

It went surprisingly well. Ren had been prepared for the two of them to struggle in the small kitchen, but they were rarely in each other's way. He'd first thought it was just coincidence, though he realized that Miles was just watching him closely enough to know when to move.

It made him feel strange, but he supposed it worked to his benefit.

Miles finished the eggs and bacon first and leaned against the counter by the stove as he waited for Ren. "So," he began, breaking the comfortable silence they'd fallen into. "You really quit smoking?"

"What?"

"I mean … you were trying to quit, right?"

Ren frowned as he flipped a pancake poorly. "Why are you asking me this?"

"I'm just curious," Miles began, "… about how far your spite goes."

With a scoff, Ren shook his head. "I didn't quit for spite. Spite just quickened the process, you could say. And I really quit. I haven't had a cigarette since that day, though I've wanted one more than once."

"Good for you," Miles praised. Ren wrinkled his nose and Miles laughed. "What?"

"We've been spending *way* too much time together." The pancakes on the griddle were finished, and he transferred them to the top of the plated pancake stack. "You saying that didn't even piss me off that much."

"We have been seeing each other more," Miles said. "Not sure I'd use the phrase *too much*, though."

Ren didn't know what to say to this. He spooned more pancake mix onto the griddle. The front door opened.

"Smells good," Hale announced, coming to the stove to hug Ren around the waist. "I am very sorry," he told Miles.

Miles shrugged. "It's alright. Luckily, you have a comfortable couch … I'd just prefer a little heads-up next time."

"Deal," said Logan as he closed the door to the apartment. "It does smell good in here. Bacon, eggs, and what else?"

"Pancakes," Ren answered. "They're almost done, so take a seat."

Hale's arms slipped from around his waist. "Do you need help with anything?"

"I got it," Miles said before Ren could respond. "Sit. I'll bring stuff to the table." With a smile at Ren that looked mischievous, Hale went to join Logan at the dining table.

Eyebrows raising, Ren directed his attention to Miles. Miles was looking back at him, but before Ren could say anything, his eyes drifted down to the stove. "You should take those off or we won't be able to eat them."

The pancakes on the griddle were smoking. "Fuck!" Ren tried to remedy the situation while doing his best to hide a smile at the sound of Miles's laughter.

***

When Ren finished class at noon, he went to the library instead of back to his apartment. He wasn't sure whether Miles and Logan had left, and while he didn't mind them being there—Hale was happy when they were around—he knew himself well enough to know he'd get distracted if they were, and he had homework to get done.

A couple hours into writing a paper, he got a text from Hale inviting him to an early dinner.

Ren: *Just us?*

Hale: *Logan and Miles too.*

Ren considered it.

Ren: *I'm good. Have seen enough of Miles lately.*

The thought of going to work in the empty apartment occurred to him, but he was already in a good headspace, so he stayed at the library until he was done with his first draft. As he packed away his things, he thought of inviting Noah over while Hale was gone, but recalled his friend mentioning plans with Julian.

Ren returned home alone. It was quiet in the apartment, and he threw his keys down on the table just to the hear the sound. He thought of all of them sitting there that morning, talking like a group of friends, and shook his head.

"Who would have thought …" he mumbled, taking a seat on the couch with a huff. He remembered how Miles had looked right after waking up, and closed his eyes. "Who would have—" The sound of his cell phone ringing cut him off.

Hale, he thought. It wasn't unusual for him to call while out to eat to see if Ren wanted anything off the menu.

With this in mind, he answered. "I don't want anything. Just bring your cute self home."

There was a long pause. "Um … I don't think I'm who you were expecting. Sorry."

He didn't need to check the caller ID. He knew his father's voice, even though it wasn't often they spoke over the phone. Or at all, for that matter. "Dad… sorry. I thought you were my roommate."

"It's alright."

For a long couple of seconds, neither of them spoke. It was awkward. "Why are you calling me? Is everything alright with Grandma?"

His father sighed. "Yes, technically. Nothing is *wrong*, but we moved her into a nursing home this afternoon and I thought you should know."

Ren wasn't sure what to say. The decision didn't surprise him. His grandmother was old, and after living with her during his breaks, he realized what this meant. Still, he was hoping it would be put off at least until he graduated.

"What about me?" he asked, unable to stop himself from sounding panicked.

"Well …" His father cleared his throat. "I guess you're just going to have to come home over break."

This wasn't what Ren wanted to hear. "I can stay here," he offered. He hadn't already planned on doing that because Hale wouldn't be there and he didn't want to stay in the apartment for over a month without him, but it was better than going home.

His dad sighed as if Ren's words caused him great stress. "No. You should come home. Your brother and I haven't seen you in quite a while. It'll be nice to catch up."

Nice to catch up? Ren bit his lip, hard. He could feel himself getting more upset. Just the idea of spending time under the same roof as his brother had his stomach turning.

"Why?"

"Why?" his father echoed. "Well, we miss you around here."

No, you don't, he wanted to say. He knew there was no way his brother missed him, and it was doubtful his father thought about him enough for it to get to that point. "I'll think about it," he offered. "That's the best I can give you right now, okay? I'm hanging up." He didn't want his father to pry further.

After he ended the call, Ren shut his phone down and tossed it to the end of the couch. He hoped he'd be able to put the conversation in the back of his mind and withdraw it only when he absolutely had to deal with it later, but he could already feel the anxiety setting in.

He thought about that house. Thought about how painfully quiet it was, and how careful he had to be to avoid his awkward father, who couldn't even bring himself to look at Ren, and his older brother, who couldn't keep himself from glaring with disgust.

His brother wouldn't hurt him anymore. He hadn't since Ren's incident in high school after his heartbreak, but he would make it known that he didn't like Ren's presence.

It would be manageable, Ren thought. It didn't feel true. Nothing would physically happen to him in that house, but he feared the emotional toll would be too much to bear. It was sometimes difficult to keep himself together in the apartment with Hale, where he was happiest. He didn't know how he would even survive in the place that reminded him so much of the past that he was trying to get away from.

His entire body felt as if it were being pricked with needles. He couldn't calm down.

He thought about snapping himself out of it with some sort of pain, but imagined how Hale would look at him if he ever found out.

It was a while before Hale returned, and when he did, Ren was still sitting there, staring ahead at the dark television. Logan and Miles were behind him in the doorway. Ren could hear their laughter, and he tried to act like normal.

"Hey!" Hale greeted. Ren released a shaky breath and tried to smile. "Hey," Hale said again, this time with concern. He reached out to hang his keys by the door without looking and ended up dropping them on the floor. He didn't go back for them.

Ren stared down at his hands on his lap as Hale approached, disappointed with himself for being like this. Hale kneeled on the floor in front of him, leaning his chest against Ren's knees to look up at his face. "What's wrong?"

Letting out a long breath of air—his lungs ached, he realized then, and he tried to remember the last time he'd inhaled—Ren closed his eyes. He felt Hale's touch on his wrists, fingers slipping under the leather bands just a little, searching. Ren shook his head. "I didn't," he choked out before sucking in a sharp breath. When he opened his eyes, Hale dropped his head down onto Ren's hands, shoulders heaving with a sigh of relief.

When Ren cried, it wasn't because of what his father had said, or because he hated himself for easily spiraling into mental instability. It was because Hale cared about him so much when he didn't deserve it.

Look at how much pain I cause him. Look at how much I make him worry.

"I'm sorry," Ren said, raising a hand to scrub at his eyes. "I'm fine, I'm fine." He let out a weak laugh, and Hale looked up at him. "Really. I'm happy I'm crying. Before you came home, I just felt numb."

Hale brought his hands to Ren's face, thumbs brushing over his wet cheeks. "What happened?"

A strangled noise left his throat. "Dad …" When he blinked, his eyelashes felt wet. "He called and asked me to come home over break … The thought of being in that house again just—"

"I know," Hale interrupted, probably sensing he'd cry harder if he finished the sentence. He rose to take a seat on the couch beside Ren. From over Hale's shoulder, Ren noticed that Logan and Miles were no longer in the doorway.

God, he thought, closing his eyes. *I must look so pathetic.*

"We'll figure it out, okay? You can stay here, or come home with me. Don't panic. If you don't want to go home, you don't have to. Alright?"

Ren wasn't sure whether he believed it. His father paid for all his expenses at school, and Ren thought it was only fair he did what he requested. Still, he nodded and dropped his head onto Hale's shoulder. "Sorry for freaking out."

"You didn't freak out," Hale assured, slipping a hand behind his shoulders. "And it's okay."

"Miles and Logan were going to come over?"

There was a pause. "We were going to watch a movie."

"Oh." Ren lifted his head and pulled the collar of his shirt up to rub his cheeks dry. "You can go get them. I'll just hang out in my room."

Hale caught his wrist. "Let's just spend time the two of us tonight," he said.

Ren could have cried again. But he didn't. Instead, he took a deep breath and nodded his head. "Thank you," he offered. Guilt tried to eat at him.

You're ruining his night.

But he wasn't. He knew Hale didn't blame him. His friend just wanted him to feel better, so he didn't protest as Hale pulled a blanket over them and put something they both enjoyed on the television.

For the time being, Ren was going to let himself believe Hale was right and they'd figure it out.

Chapter Nineteen

Writing often made Ren feel better, so when he still felt drained from his conversation with his father days later, he went to the library with his laptop again. He had to work on a short story for class, and he had stressed enough over the prompt that he felt prepared to put his thoughts into words.

The prompt was too unspecific to be simple: *Write about something bittersweet.*

Noah said he was going to write about the taste of his favorite iced coffee. This was to be expected. At first, Ren had thought Noah was lazy in his writing, always choosing to write about *things* rather than situations, but he'd edited enough of Noah's work to know his friend enjoyed writing pretty descriptions that made his view of the world very clear.

Ren liked to write about situations. He liked stories, and he was planning on telling one in this assignment.

He began by introducing his characters and their relationships with each other. It was easy to get lost in it, easy to pretend he was describing his own life. No longer was he sitting in the library trying to forget.

After a page and a half of typing, Ren allowed his hands to rest. He reflected on what he'd written so far. It was only the first draft, so in no way did it need to be perfect, but he still wanted to be thoughtful in his composition.

So next—he began, though before he could string together an idea, he felt a hand settle on his shoulder. The touch didn't alarm him—it was far too gentle for that—and he looked up to see who was interrupting his creative process.

Miles was gazing down at him.

"What do you want?" Ren asked, not unkindly.

The last he'd seen of Miles was Tuesday, when Miles returned from dinner with Hale and Logan. Ren wondered whether Miles was going to ask why he'd been upset that night. Far more personal question had been asked by him before.

"I have something for you," said Miles. Unsure of what to expect, Ren watched as Miles slipped off his backpack and put it on the table. After a long moment of rifling through it, he pulled out a sucker. The wrapper was pink. Strawberry flavored. "Here."

Ren took it, confused. "What the fuck?"

With a short laugh, Miles picked up the backpack and pulled the strap over his shoulder. "It's for smoking withdrawals, or whatever," he said. Almost immediately, Ren's fingers itched for a cigarette. He'd gotten to the point in quitting where he'd stopped thinking about smoking so often, but every time he heard someone talk about it or got a whiff of the smell, it felt unbearable.

Ren unwrapped the sucker and popped it into his mouth so his lips were busy. "Thanks, I guess."

Nodding, Miles rubbed at the back of his neck. "So, how's it going?"

Unsure of what exactly he was getting at, Ren narrowed his eyes.

Miles elaborated, "I meant, how's quitting smoking going? Not …"

"Not?" The attempt to steer clear of the subject of his mental health was amusing.

"Not … not how things are going with you."

Ren laughed around the sucker before pulling it from his mouth. "Now, that's funny. Really though, chill out. Quitting smoking is going fine, and I'm fine as well. You don't have to act weird or anything."

Miles gave an unexpected smile. "What are you working on?" he asked, taking the seat across from Ren. Beneath the table, their feet brushed, so Ren tucked his legs under his chair.

"I'm writing a short story."

"For fun?"

It made Ren chuckle. "I don't have much time to do things for fun between homework and job applications."

"Senior year is hard, huh?"

"Just you wait."

A sigh left Miles. "What's your short story about?"

"We're supposed to write about something bittersweet."

"And?" Miles prompted. "What's your bittersweet?"

Ren considered lying but didn't see the point. "I'm going to write about two people who love each other." He had to look away from Miles's intense gaze.

"Love?" Miles sounded perplexed. "You think love is bittersweet?"

"Sometimes it can be." The story was going to be about the right person at the wrong time, about finding genuine love but not being able to make it work. Bitter as goodbyes were, sweet as love.

"Interesting." Something about the way he said the word told Ren more was coming, and he forced himself to meet those hazel eyes. "Have you ever been in love?"

Why is he like this? He had to wonder something similar about himself as well, because when Miles looked at him with such focus, Ren couldn't help but tell him whatever he wanted to know.

"I thought I was at one point, but looking back, maybe not. I was very young." He thought of high school and his old best friend. Their time together wasn't something he reminisced about often. It always left a sour taste in his mouth, but this time he could replace it with Miles's strawberry sucker. "Maybe I don't think of it as love anymore because of how it ended. No one wants to imagine love hurts that bad."

The expression Miles wore was difficult to read. Before Ren could ask him what was wrong, Miles asked, "How can you write about love, then?"

"Because this story won't have a happy ending either. Hence bittersweet."

"Let me read it when it's done."

"Absolutely not." Ren was used to shooting down people's requests to read his writing. It was often too personal for him to share. He worried that with this short story, his desire to be loved and wanted would show through at a level that would be impossible for Miles to miss.

"Why not?"

"Something about vulnerability," Ren said. "I'd feel like I was giving you something of myself that I couldn't take back."

Miles stretched out his arm. At first, Ren thought he was reaching for his hand, but then he wrapped his fingers around the discarded sucker wrapper. "Is that such a bad thing?" he asked. It was a stupid question, so Ren deadpanned. "I'm just saying, as far as people go, I'm a safe bet for you to be vulnerable with. I mean, I won't use it against you."

"I'm not so sure," Ren snapped. The look Miles gave him suggested he knew that wasn't how Ren really felt. It was a true judgment, and Ren relaxed a little because of it. He'd long since realized that Miles didn't want to hurt him. Miles was safe. "I've already given you enough. I've told you things about myself that I never thought I'd share again. What more do you want from me?"

As if he hadn't realized he'd asked Ren personal questions in the past and received responses to them, Miles looked surprised. It didn't sit right with Ren. It made him feel as if Miles didn't see any of the things he'd shared so far as important. "I'm not letting you read this," he said again, his voice firm.

"Alright," Miles accepted. "Well, if you change your mind, let me know. I'd love to read your writing."

Winkling his nose, Ren asked, "Why?"

Miles shrugged and smiled. Ren hated that he thought this was cute. "You've seen my art, so I'd like to see yours."

It didn't take long for Ren to realize he was referring to the picture of him in the gallery and his face grew hot. *Art*, Miles had called it. He'd made him into art.

The sucker had melted against his tongue, leaving behind a wet paper stick. He reached out toward Miles's fist and tapped against his knuckles.

Eyebrows raising, Miles opened his hand and Ren took the wrinkled paper to wrap the stick in.

"Do you think that helped?" Miles asked. "I can bring you more."

"You don't have to," Ren told him, but he didn't deny that it had helped.

"I'll bring you more."

Ren bit his lip. Whatever was happening was familiar to him. He'd gone through it many other times, usually at bars but sometimes in classes if the other person was bold enough. He always responded playfully. This was Miles, though, and Ren didn't know what his weighted gaze meant. It was hard to meet.

"Ren—"

Before Miles could say anything important, Sawyer interrupted. He was loud as usual, dropping his books onto the table beside Ren, the sound echoing in the otherwise quiet room. His arrival made Ren feel relieved.

Sawyer took the seat beside him. "What's going on here?" There was a tense smile on his face.

"Just visiting," Miles said.

"Ah, that's nice." Sawyer pulled his backpack onto his lap and unzipped it. "Well, we're going to be doing homework." The way he said it was more of a dismissal than an invitation.

Miles frowned. "I should get going." He stood and pushed his chair in. Only then did he meet Ren's eyes. "I'll see you later."

"Yeah," Ren said. "Later."

Once he had walked away, Ren turned to Sawyer. "Are you going to sit next to me?"

"That a problem?" asked Sawyer. He was still staring ahead, watching Miles go. His expression was strange. It looked like distaste. Ren wanted to know what Miles had done to deserve such a thing.

"It's not ..." Ren trailed off, following his gaze. He sighed and glanced back at his laptop to turn down the brightness. He hoped that Sawyer wouldn't try to read his writing over his shoulder.

"Ren," Sawyer said, and it sounded so different from the way Miles had spoken it that he didn't react right away. An elbow pressed into his arm.

Humming in acknowledgment, Ren gave Sawyer his attention.

"Should I be worried about him?" The words were teasing, but there was something serious about his expression.

"No." When Ren looked toward the entrance, Miles was just leaving. He paused on his way out to hold the door for someone, and in that moment spared a glance back in Ren's direction. Their eyes met. "We're not even friends. Our best friends are dating."

"Really?"

Miles smiled and raised his hand in a wave. "Really," Ren answered.

Chapter Twenty

When Sawyer told Ren he wanted to take him out on Saturday, Ren was hoping they'd go somewhere to eat, but Sawyer brought him to Jonah's bar instead. Ren didn't mind the bar, but he thought it was about time they go on a dinner date that wasn't in the campus cafeteria.

His disappointment must have shown in his expression, because Sawyer squeezed his hand to get his attention and asked, "Is this alright? I figured this place was okay since we've been here before, and it's the closest bar to your apartment."

"It's fine," Ren assured. "I thought we might get dinner, but this is good, too. I've been stressed lately, so a drink will help me take my mind off it."

This wasn't just something he was saying to reassure Sawyer. It was true. His father's request for him to come home was still weighing on him.

"Is there something going on?"

"No," Ren denied. "I mean, just family stuff, but it'll all work out."

Nodding, Sawyer tugged on Ren's hand to get him moving toward the bar. Ren wasn't surprised to see Miles there. Miles didn't notice the two of them right away—he was pouring liquor into a glass, eyes down so he didn't spill—and Ren hoped he and Sawyer could get situated before Miles noticed them holding hands.

Thankfully, Sawyer dropped his hand when they got to the bar. By this point, Miles had finished with the customer and turned to welcome the newcomers. At the sight of Ren, he smiled and waved. When his eyes slid to take in Sawyer as well, the expression seemed less genuine.

"Your friend works a lot, huh?" asked Sawyer.

"My neighbor?" Ren corrected, taking a seat. "I think he works most weekends. I don't know, though. He's usually here when I come, but I haven't been going to the bars a lot."

As if he wasn't already approaching, Sawyer waved Miles over. "Oh? Why not?"

"I don't know. I just haven't been in the mood to drink." He didn't mention he often felt like shit after.

Miles was in front of them then, so their conversation paused. "Hey," he greeted, addressing Ren only. "How's your writing coming along?"

"It's fine," Ren assured. "Still not going to let you read it."

"Ah." Hazel eyes moved to the man on Ren's left. "Hey, man."

Sawyer nodded in greeting and got straight to the point. "Could we get a Long Island and a …" He trailed off and glanced at Ren, waiting for his order.

"I'll have a whiskey sour."

"And could we get two shots in that?" Sawyer requested, holding out his credit card.

Eyebrows raising, Ren asked, "Are you trying to get me drunk?" His voice was teasing. It made his date smile.

"Oh damn. You realized."

Miles pressed his lips together and accepted the card. "Want me to start a tab?"

"Yes, please." Finished with the bartender, Sawyer swiveled his chair to face Ren.

"Thanks," Ren told Miles, uneased by Sawyer's rude behavior.

Nodding, Miles didn't meet his eyes. "I'll be back in a minute with those."

When he left, Sawyer said, "I don't think he likes me."

"I think he just doesn't know you very well."

"Yeah, maybe."

Something about Sawyer's expression as he watched Miles's back had

Ren saying, "You don't seem to like him all that much either."

Sawyer shrugged. "Yeah, well, I don't know him that well either."

Not satisfied with this response, Ren frowned, but Sawyer was too busy checking his phone to notice.

"Are you waiting to hear from someone?" Ren asked, noticing Sawyer seemed disappointed as he tucked the device back into his pocket.

Sawyer's eyebrows raised. "Why would you think that?"

"You know," Ren started, propping his elbow on the bar and leaning forward against his first. "You've been acting different for a few days now." It was something he first noticed when Sawyer studied with him in the library. Sawyer seemed on edge, fidgeting a lot and checking his phone often. "Is there anything you want to talk about?"

"Different?" Sawyer echoed. His gaze lowered. "Oh. I'm surprised you noticed. I guess you could say I've been a little out of it as well." Ren opened his mouth to reply, but Sawyer was quick to cut in. "Don't worry about it."

When Miles came to drop off their drinks, Sawyer's expression shifted to something more pleasant. "Thank you," he said, taking both glasses and offering Ren his. "Since it seems like we both have a lot going on, I think we should take tonight to let loose. What do you say?"

Miles had slipped a few feet away to wipe up a spill on the bar, but he was still close enough to hear them. At these words, he raised his head.

Their eyes barely met before Ren glanced away. "Why not?" He knocked his glass against Sawyer's before taking the first sip.

Sawyer had taken *let loose* to heart. Over the next two hours, he drank enough to sway in his seat, hands frequently reaching out to latch on to either Ren or the bar to steady himself. He somehow kept up their conversation, even in this state, and Ren found himself fascinated by the alcohol tolerance of a frat boy.

Ren also drank quite a bit before cutting himself off early, not wanting to spend another night crying in the bar's bathroom.

At some point, without Ren asking, Miles had served him water, and he used it to sober up some while Sawyer got drunker. The last thing Ren wanted was for them to get lost on their way home since they were both too pissed to focus on where they were going.

However, Ren wasn't sober enough to dodge Sawyer's kiss when the younger man leaned over to connect their mouths. As soon as Ren realized what was happening, he put his hands on Sawyer's shoulders and pulled away, hoping Miles hadn't seen them. The idea had his cheeks burning, and he resisted glancing in the bartender's direction to check.

"Do you want to get out of here?" asked Sawyer.

It wasn't for the reason Sawyer was implying, but he did want to leave. They could talk about that later, so Ren nodded and pushed Sawyer back an arm's length. "Let me just go to the bathroom." He wiped his mouth with his thumb, slipping off his bar stool.

"I guess I can wait," Sawyer said, hooking a finger in the belt loop of Ren's pants to pull him close and kiss him again. "Be fast."

"Sure." Ren slipped away. As he turned toward the bathroom, he caught Miles's eye. The look from Miles gave Ren pause, his eyes half lidded, jaw tense.

A pleasant shiver made its way up Ren's spine.

He was in the bathroom for only a minute, just long enough to splash water on his face and use the mirror's reflection to fix his appearance. It was perhaps *too* long, because when he left, Miles was at the end of the bar speaking to Sawyer. At first, Ren saw nothing wrong; Sawyer was probably just closing out his tab.

As he got closer, he noticed the tension in both of them, noticed the looks on their faces. They were angry. Only Sawyer's mouth moved, and whatever he was saying seemed to make Miles more enraged.

Ren quickened his pace. When he was close enough, he heard Miles say, "Are you *fucking* serious?"

By then, Sawyer had spotted him and failed to respond. Instead, he forced a smile, as if something strange wasn't happening. "Hey!" he greeted, appearing far too happy in his obvious panic. "Ready to go?"

Ren stopped beside Sawyer's stool. "What's going on here?" He frowned when Sawyer stood and wrapped an arm around his waist, pulling him backward.

"I was just closing the tab," Sawyer said. "We're all good. Let's head back to your place now."

Ren tried to hold his ground, but Sawyer was stronger than him and moved him a few feet. "Hey," Ren protested. "What are you doing?"

"I don't want to be here anymore," Sawyer claimed. With his hold on Ren's waist, he lifted him off his feet.

"What were you talking about?" Ren asked, no longer struggling against the man's hold. It seemed pointless to fight him.

Sawyer stumbled but caught himself in the doorway. "Um, don't worry about it."

"*Seriously?*" Ren spat. "Clearly it wasn't nothing—"

"Ren!" It was Miles. Before he could look, Sawyer got him out of the bar.

Huffing, Ren pushed against Sawyer's shoulder. "Put me down," he demanded. When Sawyer didn't comply, Ren added, "You can't just force me to go places with you. That's practically abduction."

Sawyer paused then. Finally, he set Ren back on his feet. "Sorry. I just—"

"Ren!" Miles had followed them outside. "Hey, wait a minute." When he was close enough, he grabbed Ren's arm and pulled him to his side. "I need to talk to you."

Annoyed with both of them for pulling him around, Ren yanked his arm free from Miles's grasp. "What the fuck is going on?"

Sawyer's mouth opened, but no sound came out.

For a moment longer, Miles glared at the blond man before focusing on Ren. He seemed conflicted, as if there were so many things he had to say and just couldn't choose the words.

He chose wrong. "Don't sleep with him," he blurted out.

By the time Miles realized how this sounded, Ren was already livid. "Excuse me?!"

At the sound of his displeasure, Miles's eyes widened. He held his hands out between them, palms facing Ren. "Wait a minute. That's not how I meant it—"

"I don't give a damn how you meant it," Ren snapped. When Miles reached out farther, Ren slapped his hand's away and took a step backwards toward Sawyer. "What makes you think you have the right to tell me what to do?" He turned toward his date. "Let's go."

Grinning, Sawyer took his hand. "Yeah, let's."

"Ren," Miles tried again. "You don't understand—"

"Fuck you," Ren cut in. "Seriously. Fuck you, and fuck off."

They went back to Ren's apartment, but before he unlocked the door to get into the building, Ren encouraged Sawyer to walk home. "Come on," Sawyer said, reaching out to grab Ren's forearms. "Are you serious? You're sending me home?" He pulled Ren against his chest. "Don't make me leave you."

"We've both been drinking," Ren pointed out. "I think it's for the best that you go home."

"You're going to listen to that prick?" he asked. His fingers found Ren's hips and gripped too tightly. "You're going to do what he says?"

Ren wished he was a better person, wished he wasn't petty enough to be swayed by those words. But they bothered him enough that he led Sawyer into the building.

It must have taken them at least a few minutes to get to Ren's bedroom—it was an older elevator, and Sawyer wasn't walking quickly since he was drunk enough to stumble—though it felt like a matter of seconds. *This is all going so fast.*

When Sawyer made a move to kiss him, Ren stopped him with a hand over his mouth. "I don't have sex with people who don't love me," he said, as both a reminder to himself and a last-ditch effort to get Sawyer to leave.

"I love you," Sawyer lied. It was painfully obvious the words were fake.

Still, it was enough for tipsy Ren to accept.

It'll be fine, he told himself, watching Sawyer pull off his shirt. *We've been together long enough that it's not abnormal for us to have sex.*

The thoughts didn't make him feel any better. After this, he couldn't see Sawyer anymore. He'd feel too bitter about himself when he did. He'd be ashamed for breaking his own simple rule and for being so easily persuaded.

Afterward, Ren felt emotionally numb and wished he felt physically numb. Numbness would be preferable to the pain. It became apparent minutes after they'd removed their clothing that Sawyer had never even bothered to research how to have sex with a man, and he didn't seem to want to learn in the moment. It had been less than pleasant, and Ren had asked multiple times for them to stop for a minute so he could adjust. The plea had fallen on deaf ears.

If he was still trying to make it work with Sawyer, he might have told himself this was because Sawyer was drunk and not himself, but now that he was resigned to it he mumbled the word *"Dick"* with complete sincerity as he slipped out of bed.

The ache was worse when he moved, so he paused for a moment to gather himself. When he felt ready, he would go to the bathroom to take a shower. Before he recovered enough to move, Sawyer's phone buzzed on the floor of his bedroom. It had been doing that frequently—Ren had focused on the sound when Sawyer first pressed into him in hopes it would distract from the discomfort—and he slowly made his way over to the noise.

When he found it, the name *Sadie* was on the screen.

He recognized the name from his and Sawyer's conversation about his ex-girlfriend. It was none of his business, and he knew he should let it go to voice mail. Sawyer could deal with it in the morning.

But something didn't sit right with him, so he answered the call. He said nothing, waiting for her to realize.

"Sawyer?" Her voice came through after a long moment of silence. "I thought you weren't going to pick up. You were out drinking, weren't you?"

"Why are you calling?" asked Ren.

There was another pause. "Oh, sorry." She laughed. "Who am I talking to? I don't know all his friends well enough to pick them out by voice." Her cheery tone was giving Ren a headache.

"Aren't you his ex-girlfriend?"

Her chuckle was now nervous. "Um … I'd say that's up for debate right now."

It was all adding up, but Ren needed the full story. "What's that mean?"

"We're getting back together," she answered, irritated. "I'm coming to see him tomorrow, but we've been talking and we miss each other and we're planning on getting back together."

It was Ren's turn to laugh. It made perfect sense. Sawyer's recent interest in his cell phone and his jitteriness. Why Miles had gotten so angry—he must have found out somehow—and the pressure Sawyer put on Ren to sleep with him. *It was his last chance to try*, Ren realized. "Oh fuck."

"Who is this?" she asked. "Why are you answering Sawyer's phone?"

Ren gazed over his shoulder at the man in bed. Almost immediately after they finished, he'd passed out, the orgasm and alcohol getting to him. "I'm sorry to tell you this," he began, pausing then to consider if he wanted to do this. She deserved to know. "I've been dating your boyfriend."

She was quiet.

"I'm not saying this to be mean. I don't even want him anymore, so I'm not saying it to take him from you. I just think you should know that I slept with him tonight. If I had known about you, I wouldn't have, and you shouldn't make the same mistake," Ren said. He laughed, but his eyes felt hot. "Oh fuck. I am so sorry. I swear I didn't know."

There was a loud sigh, followed by a sniffle. He thought she might be crying. "Are you serious?"

"Yeah," he admitted. Another sniffle. "I am *so* sorry."

"I'm not mad at you," she snapped. Then, "Well, I am, but I know it's not your fault." There was a long minute in which she just breathed into the phone, calming herself. "*Fuck*." He got the impression she didn't swear often, the sound coming out too harsh and unpracticed. "That jackass."

"Yeah."

Neither of them said anything for a long time. At some point, she cried again, and Sawyer began to snore. The call stretched long enough that Ren could barely tolerate the ache from standing, and he wondered how much longer he'd have to endure this, but then she said, "I'm sorry too," and hung up.

Chapter Twenty-One

Getting Sawyer out of the apartment was easy. Ren shook him awake and told him his girlfriend had called, and the man left on his own, pulling on his clothes as he tried to call her back. "What did you tell her?" he asked.

"That you're shitty in bed. Now get the fuck out."

Sawyer left, and any remaining suspicion that he actually had feelings for Ren went with him.

If Ren still smoked, he would right then, but he didn't have any cigarettes, so he went out on the balcony empty-handed.

Miles was on his own balcony, gazing out over the parking lot. At the sound of the door, he turned to Ren.

"What time is it?" Ren asked, not because he cared but because he felt like he had to say something.

Instead of answering, Miles went inside.

Ren noticed his face was wet before he realized he was crying. He couldn't feel it, so there was no emotion he could suppress to stop it. He sank to the ground, sitting with his back against the door.

Maybe he was crying because he felt pathetic. It wasn't because he cared that much about Sawyer, or because he cared about Sawyer's girlfriend either. He felt used and stupid. Stupid for giving in to Sawyer because he had been angry at Miles for telling him what to do. It was embarrassing. Humiliating.

The ache from Sawyer pushing into him wouldn't let him forget.

Desperately, he wanted a cigarette.

There was a knock on the door behind him. He looked over his shoulder, expecting Hale.

It was Miles. Ren didn't move right away. *How did he get in?*

Feeling tense, he turned forward. *I don't want to see him.* There was another knock. Then another. When Ren turned back, Miles gestured for him to move.

With a deep breath, Ren slid so he was no longer blocking the door. Neither of them spoke until Miles had settled beside him. He had the knit blanket that was usually folded over the back of the couch, and he tossed it across Ren's lap. "The door to your apartment was open."

Ren wanted to laugh because Sawyer couldn't even leave correctly. Instead, he sniffled.

"It's two a.m., by the way," Miles said next.

Letting him outside may have been a mistake, Ren realized, but Miles thankfully fell silent after that.

It was Ren who spoke next, minutes later, when he felt he could manage without crying harder. "I know what you're going to say to me."

"I don't think you do."

"You're going to say it's my fault, because I get angry and impulsive and make stupid decisions. It's my fault that people treat me like this." He was saying it about himself, but it was easier to blame the words on Miles.

Beside him, Miles shifted so their arms pressed together. "I wasn't going to say any of that. You shouldn't say it either."

From the corner of his eye, he saw Miles move. He didn't look, so he jerked in surprise when he felt fingers pushing his hair behind his ear. He was going to snap at him, but before he could, Miles held up a wireless earbud.

"What?"

Miles didn't answer. When he reached out again, Ren didn't pull away. Slowly, as if he was worried about hurting him, Miles pressed the earbud into his ear. He put the other in his own.

It took a minute before Miles chose a song and music played.

Somehow, this helped. When Ren cried, this time he felt it.

Even though Miles wasn't looking at him, Ren hid his face against his knees. They listened to a handful of songs without speaking. It was an album Ren wasn't familiar with, but he recognized the singer's voice as someone he'd heard on the radio a few times during throwback weekends. It was soothing, and he began to calm down.

Only once he had stopped crying did Miles speak. "Are you okay?"

It made his eyes water again, and he feared speaking would push him over the edge, so he only shook his head no. When Miles had nothing to say in response, he cleared his throat and forced out, "It hurts." This was only one of many issues, but physical pain was easier for him to discuss than emotional pain.

"You really liked him, then?"

"No." Ren turned his head on his knees. "That's not it. I mean physically. I'm in pain."

Miles hadn't been looking at him to respect his privacy, but his shock must have made him forget this. "Did he—"

"He didn't force himself on me," Ren clarified. He sniffled and wiped his nose with the back of his hand. "I consented and everything. He just didn't know what the fuck he was doing." Ren laughed. "Which makes sense now, I guess, since he's just some straight guy."

"I caught a glimpse of his phone when you were in the bathroom." Miles's gaze was very intense. "Why on earth do you date guys like that?" There was anger in his voice.

"I'm just trying to be happy."

"You're trying to be happy with the wrong people. If you don't like them, don't date them."

This was sound advice, but it was Miles who was giving it, so Ren couldn't just accept it. "Sawyer was … he was fine." The words had Miles narrowing his eyes. "I mean before tonight," Ren corrected. "He was okay."

"Did you really like him?"

Ren thought about it. Sure, he hadn't minded Sawyer's company, though he'd also never been excited about their relationship. Not knowing how to answer, he shrugged.

This must not have been a satisfying response, because Miles shook his head. "Don't give everyone a chance. If you do, people will just keep taking advantage of you."

The need to cry was long gone. Ren just felt tired and sore and frustrated. The song playing in his ear changed, distracting him for a second as he tried to pick up the tune. "Why do you care?" he asked. "Why are you even here right now? Why did you try to warn me? I don't understand why you concern yourself with me. It's not like you have some kind of obligation. We're friendly because of circumstance."

Miles looked conflicted. It was intriguing, and Ren stared back. He wanted to know what Miles was thinking about right then.

It was only when Ren opened his mouth to ask that Miles turned away. His expression became more grave, so Ren was expecting him to say something upsetting.

Instead, he took a deep breath, raised his chin, and announced, "I'm in love with you."

The music in Ren's ear felt very loud. It had to be. He couldn't have heard Miles correctly.

But he knew he had. If he was being honest, he wasn't all that shocked. The second he heard the words, he realized that he'd kind of already knew and just hadn't let himself think about it. What caught him off guard was Miles telling him.

He didn't know what to say. Miles looked back at him, his expression fond. If Ren had been questioning whether he'd heard him correctly, his face right then would have rid him of doubt. He was looking at Ren in the way Ren had always wanted to be looked at.

"I have been for a while now," Miles said.

Ren couldn't speak. His lips parted, but no sound came out. There wasn't enough time to process the confession, or for him to come up with a way to respond.

He'd be lying if he said he'd never thought about it before—it was the *first* thing he'd thought about after meeting Miles—but it was *Miles*.

His silence must have been an answer on its own, because Miles smiled—it was a sad smile—then leaned forward to kiss his forehead and mumble, "Let me know if you need anything." He went back inside.

There was still an earbud playing music into Ren's ear. The song was familiar. It was one he also had on his own playlist, and he wondered whether he'd ever be able to listen to it without thinking about this night, and the man who loved him.

Chapter Twenty-Two

On Monday, Ren didn't go to class. Earlier, when Hale came into his room to convince him to go, Ren told him he didn't feel well. Apparently, it wasn't as easy to buy as he'd hoped, because Hale looked disappointed and said, "It's not that big of a deal, Ren."

Ren hadn't told him about what had happened with Miles. He had told no one, so it was surprising when Hale came home from Logan's and wanted to talk about it. He'd been expecting Miles to regret the confession, so he didn't know why he'd tell Ren's roommate, of all people, if it was something they were going to forget about.

Not wanting to talk about it, he'd rolled over and mumbled, "I'm just not feeling it today."

He didn't feel good. It was probably because he was so nervous about running into Miles on campus that his stomach was in knots.

The next person to enter his room was Noah. It must have been a while later, because he doubted Noah had skipped class to come see him. "Hey," his friend greeted, pausing in the doorway. When Ren remained silent, Noah sighed, kicked off his shoes, and climbed into bed next to him. "Want to tell me what's going on?"

"You haven't heard from Hale?" Ren asked, voice muffled by his pillow.

"I haven't talked to Hale. Why? Are you two fighting?"

"No. Well, I don't think so. Not yet, at least."

"What's going on?"

There were multiple places he could have started. "Sawyer and I broke up."

This didn't shock Noah. "Why were you dating him in the first place?"

"It was easy," Ren admitted. "Dating him was effortless, and at some point I just felt less miserable about my life. I was worried changing the routine would disrupt that. It's stupid."

"I'm pretty sure your life felt less miserable because of Miles," Noah offered, clueless. Ren groaned. "No, but come on. Really, think about it. I know he's not your favorite or anything, but Hale's been busier now that he has a boyfriend, as has Logan, I'd imagine, so you and Miles have this kind of … comradery, right? I mean, from what you've told me, it sounds like the two of you have been getting along well, and he seems to put you in a good mood these days."

Ren didn't want to hear it. "Shut up."

Sighing, Noah patted the back of his head. "Okay, okay. So what happened with Sawyer?"

Even though he didn't want to talk about it, Ren told him everything. When he thought about Sawyer's rough hands on the skin of his thighs, he felt gross. Unclean in a way he never had after sex. When he finished his story, Noah was silent. Ren turned his head on the pillow to look up at him.

"Want me to beat him up?"

Ren laughed. He no longer felt empty. "No." He propped himself up on his elbows, his hair falling across his face to block half his vision. "I told his girlfriend over the phone and ruined his relationship."

Noah was still tense, but he chuckled. "Well, I'm glad you're okay."

"Yeah." Ren settled back down onto his chest, pulling his arms beneath himself. "That's not why I skipped class."

"Oh?"

Biting his lip, Ren considered saying it was because he didn't feel good. Instead, he skipped straight to the reason his stomach was acting up. "Miles told me he loves me."

Noah's eyes widened. "And how do you feel about that?"

"I … I don't really know."

"Have you told Hale?"

Ren scoffed at that.

"Okay, so that's what's going on with you and Hale. What did he have to say about it?"

Sighing, Ren rolled over so he could sit up. "We haven't talked about it all that much. Miles told him, so I didn't get to see his reaction when he first found out, but by the time he spoke to me about it, he was calm. All he said was that I should go for it and that he'd be happy to see me with someone as great as Miles."

"Are you going to?"

The question was expected, but it surprised him how serious Noah sounded. He thought Noah would ask as a joke. Unimpressed, he glared at his friend.

"You give everyone else who asks you out a chance."

"This is different." It was different, without doubt.

Still, Ren wasn't prepared when Noah asked, "Why?"

Ren leaned forward to press his face into Noah's shoulder. "I don't know," he whined, beyond frustrated with the whole situation. He didn't understand why Miles had confessed to him. What if things were weird because of it? Ren was worried they'd be weird. Why'd Miles have to make it weird?

"I don't want to think about it," Ren said, and Noah's shoulders heaved with a sigh. As if to comfort him, Noah raised a hand to pat his head. "Besides," he continued, "Miles hasn't asked me out."

"I thought that was implied when you tell someone you love them." Noah gave his head another pat. "Well, you can't stay in here forever, you know. You're going to have to face him sometime, and knowing you, it's better to do it sooner than later, or you're going to stress about it until you get sick."

Ren's gaze went to his dresser. Where he used to keep his cigarettes was the bucket hat he'd bought on their trip to the lake, the blue piece of sea glass, and Miles's earbud. "I'll go to class tomorrow."

Ren hadn't been sure he'd keep that promise, but the next morning he forced himself out of bed and went to campus. It was all very last minute—he'd decided to go fifteen minutes before his class began—so he'd thrown on an easy outfit before leaving.

He was on edge as he walked there, head tilted down and gaze raised to look at everyone he passed. He hoped that if he saw Miles, he'd be able to look at his feet and pretend to be lost in thought.

Few people passed by him, though. It was because he was so late and most students were already in their lecture halls, but Ren called it luck.

His good fortune ran out ten minutes after his class had ended.

It was his own fault for feeling a sense of comfort at having not run into Miles that morning. He'd told himself it would be fine if he went to the coffee shop to get something to eat. Almost immediately after stepping inside, he made eye contact with Miles. He was sitting at a table with a group of friends, Clarisse to his left.

Ren considered leaving, but his pride wouldn't let him. Swallowing around the knot in his throat, he slid his gaze away and went to the counter to order.

He assumed that would be the extent of it, and he was making a point to stand so his back was to Miles as he waited for his food. This meant he didn't see Miles approach and was startled when he grabbed Ren's elbow. "Oh my god."

Miles frowned. "Did you think I wasn't going to talk to you when you look like that?"

"You're with your friends so I thought—" Ren cut himself off and yanked his elbow free from Miles's grasp. "What do you mean *when I look like this?*"

Hazel eyes held his for a moment longer before flicking down to glance over his body. "You're not dressed like you usually are."

For the first time since leaving his room, Ren reconsidered his appearance. He was wearing a pair of jeans and a gray oversized hoodie with his hair pulled half up. It wasn't how he usually presented himself in public, and he could understand Miles's concern. "Why does it matter how I dress?" Ren asked, feeling self-conscious. "Does it look bad?"

Right after asking, Ren regretted it, thinking that he sounded as if he cared.

Miles must have heard it too, because his expression shifted into something gentler. "It doesn't," he assured. "You look …" He trailed off.

The sound of Ren's name being called at the counter saved him. Ren went to get his breakfast sandwich and coffee. He wondered whether he should try to leave then without saying anything else, but when he turned, he noticed Miles had followed. "What?" Ren asked.

"We should talk."

"Here?" Ren glanced around.

"Sure," Miles said. This was stupid, since they were blocking the counter, so Miles shook his head then. "No. Not here. Let's go outside."

It was cold out, close enough to the end of the year that snow was only weeks away, but Ren liked this idea. He wanted to get away from the prying eyes of Miles's friends. He followed Miles to the entrance, chewing his lip when he held the door open for Ren and guided him through it with a hand against the small of his back. The touch was gentle, and it made Ren feel something other than the ache from last Saturday.

All the tables outside were taken, so they went to sit on a bench. Ren felt himself growing nervous. This was the exact situation he'd been worried about, the reason he'd spent his day in bed yesterday.

From the corner of his eye, he could see Miles watching him, but he stared at his lap instead of looking back. *He's going to ask me to answer him. He's going to want my response, and I'm going to have to turn him down and nothing's going to be the same.*

"Are you alright?" asked Miles.

It wasn't the question Ren had been expecting. "Why wouldn't I be?"

He didn't feel alright, but another part of him—a part he found annoying—thought, *Does he think he has that much of an effect on me?* It was annoying, because Miles clearly *did* have that much effect, and Ren hated he was too proud to accept it.

"Well, I mean … after everything that happened with Sawyer, I was worried about you."

Ren's face felt hot. Of course, Miles hadn't been assuming his confession affected Ren any. Why would he? Ren had been treating him poorly for so long that it probably hadn't even occurred to him Ren could be hung up over it. "I'm fine," he said. "Fuck him. He knows I never want to see him again, and with the way we left things, I doubt he wants to see me, either."

Miles seemed relieved. "I'm glad. He doesn't deserve for you to think about him."

"Is this what you wanted to talk to me about?" Ren asked. "Why are you acting so normal?"

"Normal?"

Ren thought he should be relieved that Miles was going to pretend that it had never happened, but he instead felt irritated. "The last time we saw each other, you told me you loved me."

"So?" Miles asked. "I've loved you for some time now. You knowing hardly changes anything."

Relief washed over him. "Nothing's going to change?"

Miles smiled in a way that made Ren doubt he'd made his relief subtle. "I'm not going to change anything. Are you?" The question was rhetorical. They both knew the answer.

For a long moment, Ren just looked at him. There was a feeling blossoming in his chest, something that was warm but also made him sad. "Why?" he asked.

He thought he'd have to elaborate, but Miles's expression told him he understood. Ren was asking why he was in love with him.

"I'm always so unreasonable toward you."

"I don't know," Miles admitted. "There's just something about you."

It wasn't as specific as Ren had been hoping for, though after hearing that much, he was thankful Miles hadn't told him more. He didn't think he could handle it.

"Thank you," he offered. "I don't know if that's the right thing to say, but I mean it."

Miles squinted at him as if he were the sun. "Sure." His gaze moved back toward the coffee shop. "Alright. Well, now that that's out of the way, I should get back to them. We were in the middle of discussing a photo shoot." He stood.

"Hey, wait." Ren caught his wrist. "Don't go yet." When he was sure Miles would stay, he released him and pulled his backpack off. Last night, he'd put the earbud Miles had left behind in the front pocket of his bag, just in case. He offered it to Miles. "I had it with me in case I ran into you."

"Oh." Miles held out his hand, letting Ren drop the earbud in his palm. "I was sure you were going to run away as soon as you saw me."

Ren's lips curled up. "I was. It was wishful thinking."

Nodding, Miles curled his fingers around the earbud. "Thanks for not doing that."

"I was starving," Ren said, glancing at his wrapped breakfast sandwich on the bench next to him.

Though Miles had said he'd been expecting it, he looked pained by Ren's admittance to wanting to avoid him. He turned, showing Ren his back, but made no move to leave. "We're okay, right?"

"I think we are now," Ren said.

When Miles looked over his shoulder and smiled at him, Ren's heart ached.

Neither of them said goodbye. Miles left just like that, returning inside to be with his friends. Ren watched him get most of the way there until his eyes met Clarisse's in the window. He stood.

As he walked away with his coffee and lukewarm sandwich, he recalled Noah saying Miles made him less miserable, and had to agree.

Chapter Twenty-Three

Ren got a call back for a second interview at a local newspaper, so on Friday they went to the bar to celebrate. It was Hale's idea, and Ren knew his friend wanted to celebrate him, but he thought their going out was less because of that and more because Hale felt bad about their disagreement over Miles. Going to the bar with Ren when it was busy seemed to be his way of making it up to him.

Of course, Hale had also invited Miles to join them for the evening, so maybe he didn't feel too bad.

Ren, Hale, Miles, and Logan, who insisted on tagging along even though he couldn't legally drink, waited outside their building for Noah. They each were bundled in a warm coat, since the temperature seemed desperate to remind them winter was coming.

In his pocket, Ren's phone rang. "I swear to God if that's Noah telling me he's not coming …" He pulled his phone out, and sure enough, Noah's name was on his screen. "That asshole."

To hide his smile, Hale covered his mouth with the back of his hand.

Ren answered the phone. "Where are you?"

"Is it okay if Jules and Rita come?" Noah asked, avoiding the question.

"Why would I care? Where are you?" Infuriating as always, Noah spoke to someone—probably Julian—rather than answering him. "I'm going to kill him," Ren said to the men waiting with him.

Both Hale and Logan laughed. Miles's lips quirked.

"Noah! Come on. I'm getting cold. Where the fuck are you?"

"Maybe you should have worn more clothes," Noah said. "I'm gonna walk over with these guys and meet you there. See you soon." He hung up.

Right then, Ren hated him. "Noah is going to meet us," he told the others, putting his phone into the back pocket of his jeans. "Jules and Rita are coming, so he's going to walk over with them."

Logan's eyebrows shot up. "Your ex-boyfriend and his girlfriend? Is that weird?"

It was Hale who answered. "You would think so, but it's not." His hand was in Logan's, and he used the grip to pull his boyfriend along through the parking lot.

Exchanging a brief glance, Ren and Miles followed.

The two of them had been fine since their talk outside the coffee shop. Every time they'd run into each other since, Miles had acted normal, and Ren had come to accept that nothing was going to change.

At least, outwardly, nothing would change. Already, Ren thought about Miles a lot more than he had before. It was normal, he told himself. Who didn't pay more attention to someone after being confessed to by them?

"Things with Jules and I are fine," Ren elaborated. "They kind of had to be. When we first started dating, Noah said he'd give us his blessing only as long as things wouldn't be weird if we broke up, and mostly, they haven't been. Even Rita doesn't seem to mind me that much these days, which makes things easier."

"You've mellowed some," Hale claimed, and Logan nodded in agreement.

Ren looked at Miles. "Do you think that's true?"

He seemed surprised to have been spoken to. "I'm not sure. From my point of view you have, but I didn't know you that well before the past few months, and you stopped getting so hostile with me after we began to interact regularly."

Ren's eyebrows drew together. He thought of Miles saying he'd loved him for a while now, and considered asking how long that was if he hadn't known him well before now. Instead, he looked ahead at Hale's back and said, "Don't make it sound like I used to beat you up all the time."

This got Miles to laugh, as if the idea of Ren being able to hurt him was funny.

"So," Logan began, glancing back at him. "We're going out to celebrate you getting an interview, right? What's it for?"

The bar wasn't far, so Ren filled the rest of the walk with an explanation of the position. He was just saying, "It's not what I want in the long run, but the pay is okay, and it'll keep me writing," when he spotted Noah standing outside of Jonah's. "How did they beat us here?"

Noah must have been close enough to hear, because he jerked his head up and grinned. His lips moved, and then both Rita and Julian stepped around the corner of the building. They were smiling, hands linked and mouths red, and Ren recalled Julian's enjoyment of kissing while drunk.

"Hi!" Noah greeted, obviously already tipsy. When they got close enough, he threw an arm over Ren's shoulders. "How are you guys? You pregame?"

"No," Ren said. "I'm going broke tonight."

Noah laughed. "I bet you find someone to buy you your drinks within the first hour."

"Nah, I'm not feeling that tonight." He wasn't in the right place to be looking for another boyfriend, and even if he was, it felt insensitive to do so with Miles there. "I want to enjoy time with you guys."

"Aww," Noah voiced, and Ren rolled his eyes.

"Thanks for meeting us," Hale said to Julian and Rita.

Jules grinned. "Yeah, of course. We were planning on going out anyway, and it's always fun with you guys." He looked at Ren. "Congrats, by the way."

"Ah, don't do that," Ren dismissed, waving a hand. "It's just an excuse to drink." It always felt weird talking to Julian when Rita was there, and he spared the man's girlfriend a quick glance. "Um … did Luca not come with you?"

Noah laughed into his ear while Rita cracked a smile. It was she who answered, and Julian wrapped an arm around her waist as she did. "You know how he is."

"He studies Friday nights," Julian added. "On the very rare chance he comes out, it's always on a Saturday."

"I haven't seen him in a while. You should have stressed the importance of celebrating me and brought him along."

The face Julian made was funny, a mix of skepticism and amusement. "First off, I thought you said it wasn't a big deal. Second, Luca still isn't all that fond of you, so I doubt that would sway him."

"Okay!" Noah declared loudly. "Let's talk inside. I can't be the only one drunk! You're all playing catch-up."

The people who knew how intense Noah was about to get—Rita, Julian, Ren, and Hale—all grimaced at the declaration. Miles and Logan smiled cluelessly.

Hale and Logan called quits first. After only an hour and a half, the couple announced they were heading back. By that point, Hale was drunk, but Ren was pretty sure his friend wasn't leaving because of that. He'd been watching the couple pressed together for the last hour, so it was impossible to miss the looks they exchanged. They were probably returning to take advantage of the empty apartment.

They left, but not before Hale took Miles's face in his hands and made him promise to keep an eye on Ren. The two of them locked pinkies.

True to his word, Miles remained at Ren's side. They were at the bar, Ren, Julian, and Rita sitting while Miles and Noah stood. It was a good spot, easy to get drinks whenever they ran out and away from the speaker so they could talk over the music.

Ren was sipping his fifth drink—Miles had asked him to slow down when he'd ordered it, claiming he was not in the mood to clean up vomit later—and laughing at Noah's story about Luca shaming him that afternoon for getting a C on the math exam he neglected to study for when Ren felt someone press against his back.

He tensed, but then relaxed when he heard a familiar voice greet, "Hey kid."

Grinning, he swiveled on his stool. He expected to see Jason—the man lived at the bars on the weekends. "Hello!" he greeted, throwing his arms around Jason's neck, careful not to spill his drink down the back of Jason's shirt. "How are you?"

Jason smiled, dimples and all.

He's so pretty, Ren thought. He was drunk enough that he didn't pull away when Jason's arms wound around his waist.

"I'm great now," he said, his words slurring. Ren laughed at his expense. "How have you been? Still seeing that guy?"

"Nope."

The arms around Ren's waist tightened. "So you're free tonight, then?"

Pressing his lips together, Ren shook his head no. Jason's eyebrows raised. "I'm with Miles."

Ren knew he had given Jason the wrong impression, because his arms dropped from around Ren's waist and he held his hands up as if to show they were no longer touching.

Jason directed his next words at Miles. "Sorry, man. I had no clue."

Miles looked both tense and confused. *Jealously?* Ren wondered.

Jason left his side to go talk to Jules—they were both econ majors and friends for the sake of convenience—and Miles took the place beside him. As if warding away other suitors, he stood close with one arm behind Ren's back, hand resting on the bar. "You're with me?" he asked.

Ren tilted his head back to look up at him. "Am I not?" He kicked a little, letting his foot brush against Miles's leg. "I am going home with you, after all."

Hazel eyes narrowed some. For a moment, Ren thought he was about to get scolded. Instead, Miles let out a sigh and shook his head, lips lifting at the corners. "You're a pain when you're drunk," he accused.

Ren smiled and sipped his drink. "Didn't you know that already?"

"I did." For a moment longer, Miles held his gaze. Then he refocused on the conversation happening in front of them.

When Ren took another sip of his drink, he found it difficult to swallow.

At some point after Ren had left the barstool and began walking around to say hello to people, Miles put his hands on his waist. Every once in a while, Ren would think about it and feel warm, but then he reminded himself that Miles had done this only because he was drunk enough that walking was more like stumbling.

When Miles prevented him from falling and cracking his head on the bar one too many times, he leaned forward to say, "I think it's time to go," into Ren's ear.

This was disappointing, since for the first time in a long while, Ren was fun drunk and not cry-in-the-bathroom drunk.

He was quick to protest. "I can't go back to my apartment. Hale and Logan are there."

It didn't take Miles long to see what Ren was getting at. "Ah." His cheeks grew pink, and Ren didn't know whether it was from that idea or from what he said next. "You can stay at my place."

Ren's eyebrows shot up.

"Don't look at me like that. You know I mean nothing by it. You can take my bed and I'll sleep on the futon."

The offer was sweet, but Ren didn't want to inconvenience him. "You don't have to give up your bed," he said. "I won't crash at your place. Just let me hang out so I don't disturb them."

Miles shook his head. "You should stay over. I'm too tired to keep entertaining you once we get back."

Because of selfishness, for the first time that night Ren considered maybe Miles hadn't enjoyed looking after him. It seemed silly now, but Ren had been thinking Miles wouldn't mind, because it meant they could spend time together, and he loved Ren, so why wouldn't he want to spend time with him. "I'm sorry," he blurted out. "I should have realized this was tiring for you."

Miles's eyebrows drew together. "Of course it was. You shouldn't apologize, though. We're here to celebrate you. I kind of figured this was how the night would go when Hale invited me. I'm not upset."

Ren frowned, but Miles didn't seem annoyed. "Alright," he accepted. "I'll sleep on your futon."

When he said this, Miles nodded, but forty minutes later—because Ren had insisted on saying goodbye to everyone and it had taken them a while to find Jason—when they stumbled into the apartment, Miles guided Ren to one of the bedrooms. He was supporting most of Ren's weight, and when Ren apologized for this, he had dismissed it with a grumbled "It's faster this way, and you don't weigh that much."

Still, when he got Ren onto the mattress, he breathed out a heavy sigh as if the walk back had strained him. For a long moment, they were quiet, both panting. "You drink a lot," Miles accused.

Ren laughed. "Not as much as I used to. I haven't gone out in a while, and I was having a great time. Usually when I drink this much, I end up crying."

With a frown, Miles helped Ren out of his coat and crouched down to pull off his shoes. "Want to brush your teeth?"

The position they were in made Ren think of when Miles did something similar the night he had met Sawyer. Their relationship had changed so much since then. "I don't want to use your toothbrush."

Miles went over to his dresser and pulled open the top drawer. "I have an extra."

"Saving it for a one-night stand?" Ren asked. A T-shirt was thrown at him.

"No. I wasn't saving it for anything. I got it at the dentist last time and I didn't need it."

"Oh." Ren felt stupid for asking. "Yeah, then. Thanks." He held up Miles's shirt. "Um ..."

Miles wouldn't meet his eyes. "You can sleep in that."

Ren thought about taking his shirt off right then to change, about how it would feel to wear something of Miles's. Instead, he dropped the shirt onto the mattress. "I'll brush my teeth first."

He walked to the bathroom on his own, the dizziness manageable as long as he kept his fingertips against the wall. Miles followed to grab him the new toothbrush.

By the time Ren was done, Miles had made a place to sleep on the futon. "I'll sleep out here," Ren offered. "You shouldn't have to give up your bed."

"It's fine." Miles looked up as Ren leaned against the doorframe of the bathroom. "Do you think you're going to get sick?"

"No," Ren said. He wasn't sure if it was a lie. "I just have the spins and it makes my head hurt."

There was a pause, and then Miles closed the distance between them to offer Ren his arm and help him to the bedroom. Once Ren was back on the bed, he mumbled a sheepish "Thank you." Miles slipped away. It looked like he was going to leave, so Ren reached out and grabbed his wrist.

"What?" Miles asked.

There was a better way to phrase this question, but he was too drunk to figure it out, so Ren spat out, "Do you want to date me?"

Miles's expression relaxed into a deadpan. "What?"

"Well, you said that you love me, so I'm asking if you want to date me?"

There was a pause. Then, "You're drunk, Ren."

This was true, but it had nothing to do with what he was talking about. It took him a few seconds to realize why Miles had said it. Feeling embarrassed by the misunderstanding, Ren shook his head. "I'm not asking *will you date me*, I'm asking if you *want* to?"

Miles's expression didn't change. "I mean …" His gaze slid away before focusing back again. He seemed determined. "Yeah, but you dislike me, so it doesn't matter what I want."

"I don't dislike you," Ren was quick to deny. "I did, but not anymore. I think you're annoying as shit sometimes, but I don't not like you." At this, Miles's eyebrows raised. "I think you're an idiot."

A laugh was startled from the taller man's throat. "Oh gee. Thanks." He coaxed Ren back against the pillows, as if he were a child.

"Don't you want to know why I think that?" Ren asked.

"Why you think I'm an idiot? No. I can think of a handful of reasons. You've been telling me for three years now."

Annoyed, because Miles was trying to shut down their conversation, Ren huffed. "See! Annoying. Why can't you just—"

"Why do I have to ask you to be mean to me?" Miles asked. "You know how I feel, so I don't want to hear it. If you're already going to say it to me, just do it. When have you ever needed permission before?"

Ren dropped his hand from Miles's wrist. "I think you're an idiot because you're in love with me," Ren told him, voice quiet since he felt scolded. "People in their right minds aren't interested in me. That's why all my relationships are how they are." Miles didn't respond. He didn't leave either, even though Ren would have let him go. "I'm not good, Miles. Save yourself the pain and fall in love with someone who deserves it, because I certainly don't."

Ren was going to continue, but the sudden look of sadness on the other man's face had his voice freezing in his throat. He waited, curious to see what Miles had to say. Instead of speaking, Miles reached out and brushed a hand across Ren's forehead, sweeping his hair back.

The room was quiet, so Miles's soft instruction of "Sleep, Ren" sounded loud.

When he left, Ren didn't sleep. The look Miles had shown him and the scent of him on the sheets were enough to keep him awake.

Chapter Twenty-Four

When Ren got to class on Tuesday, Noah told him he looked like a boy.

He laughed at this. The night before, he'd gotten his hair cut. It was shorter than it had been in years, but he was quite happy with it. After what happened with Sawyer, he caught himself looking in the mirror often, wondering if his longer hair had somehow made it easier for Sawyer. The man liked women, and maybe Ren's hair had helped Sawyer see him as more feminine.

"I *am* a boy," Ren pointed out, dropping his backpack into the free seat beside his usual chair. "Do you like it?"

"I do!" Noah confirmed. "You look good. What drove this decision?"

Ren shrugged. "I thought it was time for a change, you know?" Before taking a seat, he removed his coat and draped it over the back of his chair. Immediately, Noah reached out to tap his bare wrist. Of course he had noticed. When Ren came out of his bedroom that morning without the leather cuffs on, Hale had noticed right away as well. Noah seemed far more chill about it. "Ah, yeah. I don't think I'm gonna wear them anymore. I don't think I need to."

"Yeah?"

Ren nodded. "I don't feel I need to hide the scars since they're mostly gone, and I haven't felt the urge to hurt myself. I mean, it's not like my depression has gone away or anything, but I think I've been dealing with it long enough to manage better."

"That's great." Noah smiled. "You seem happier."

"I think I have been. Ever since the whole thing with Sawyer, I've been thinking about self-worth and everything that happened in the past that I blamed myself for. I don't want to be thankful for Sawyer, but I think what happened with him helped me to get to this point."

"You think Sawyer has more to do with this than Miles telling you he loves you?"

This made Ren frown. Sure, Miles confessing affected things, but he wouldn't give it that much credit. "You think this is because of Miles?"

As if to say he didn't want to get into it, Noah shook his head. "What's with you guys, though? You seemed close at the bar on Saturday. Is there something going on?"

"No," Ren assured. "Don't look at me like that. I'm serious. He's just a friend. It's flattering that he sees me that way, but he doesn't expect anything from me because of it, and I appreciate that."

"Has Hale been bothering you about it?"

Sighing, Ren removed his laptop from his backpack. "Not really, but he's made how he feels clear."

"That's for sure. From what I get from him, he thinks it would be fun for the four of you to go out on double dates."

"How's that any different from what we've been doing this whole time? It's not like the four of us never go to dinner. Why do Miles and I need to be dating for that?"

Noah shrugged. "Beats me. Maybe he thinks you'll enjoy it more if you're dating."

"Not if I'm forcing myself to date him for Hale's sake," Ren grumbled. At this, Noah made a face. "What?"

"Nothing," Noah claimed. He was smiling in a stupid way that made it hard for Ren to believe him.

On Ren's way back to the apartment, Sawyer confronted him. Ren had been cutting through the back parking lot of a gas station when his ex climbed out of a car. At first, Ren considered hiding before he was noticed, but

Sawyer's eyes had already found him.

Seeing there was no way to avoid a confrontation, Ren stopped and gave Sawyer a cheeky grin. "You look like you've been doing well." This was sarcasm, since Sawyer had dark circles under his eyes. "Were you able to fix things with your girlfriend? Sadie, I believe her name was?"

"Don't say her name," Sawyer snapped. They were about ten feet apart, but Sawyer closed the distance. "You need to help me fix this."

Ren realized the situation could grow dangerous for him. Slowly, he backed away, wondering if it would be worth the hit to his pride to run. He didn't get the chance to fully consider it, because his back hit someone's chest, and then a hand clamped down on his wrist, pushing up the sleeve of his jacket. The touch felt odd—he was so used to feeling the worn leather on that skin that the roughness of this hand felt as if it burned him.

"Going somewhere?" Sawyer's friend asked, smiling at him unpleasantly. He must have just left the gas station, because he had an unopened soda in the hand not around Ren's wrist.

"Don't touch me," Ren said, trying to pull his arm free. He hissed in pain when the grip tightened and realized fighting against it would just lead to injury.

Panicked, he turned to Sawyer, who came to a stop about a foot away from him. "What do you want from me?"

"You need to fix what you did."

"What *I* did?" Ren asked. The grip on his arm tightened further. "You're hurting me."

"Good," the man holding him said, and Ren felt his eyes get hot. He remembered his brother treating him this way and couldn't believe he was reliving it.

"Look, there's nothing I can do to fix it. You should be honest with her. That's why she's mad in the first place," he advised, the words coming out quickly in his frantic state.

"She's mad because you couldn't keep your mouth shut."

"There wouldn't have been anything for me to tell her if you hadn't made such bad fucking decisions," he shot back. "No one made you date me and pretend to like me so I'd sleep with you. That's not *my* fault."

Sawyer was getting angrier. "I wouldn't have done that if there weren't so many rumors about you being easy. You were just a rebound. It's your own fault for thinking that I could *actually* have feelings for you."

That wasn't fair. "Literally, fuck you," Ren snapped.

Sawyer's hand raised and Ren squeezed his eye shut.

The hit never came. When he opened his eyes, a familiar back blocked his view of Sawyer. "*Miles*," he said, thankful.

Miles turned, and Ren saw he'd caught Sawyer's wrist with his right hand. "I think you should let him go," Miles said to the man holding Ren. To Ren's surprise, he did, taking a quick step away from him. *Being tall must be nice*, he thought.

Finally, Miles lowered his gaze to look at Ren. "You alright?"

"Yeah," Ren confirmed, rubbing at his sore wrist. "Thanks." He looked past Miles to Sawyer, who glared back for a long moment before turning away.

"Let's go," he said to his friend. "Not worth our time."

While Ren watched them walk away, Miles gently took his wrist and examined it. "It's going to bruise," he said.

"I can feel that, yeah." As Sawyer climbed into the passenger seat of the car, Ren met his eyes one last time. "Thank you for coming. I don't know what they were going to do to me."

Miles frowned at the possibilities. "Are you really okay? You look pale."

When he opened his mouth to reassure Miles, he thought of Sawyer's raised hand. "It made me think of something from a long time ago," he admitted. "That's over, though. I'm fine."

Miles's eyes dropped to his wrist. His fingers were gentle on Ren's skin, and once again Ren's eyes felt warm from unshed tears. He knew Miles could see the faint scars on his bare wrists, and he wished he hadn't chosen to take off the leather bands the night before. To hide how close he was to tears, Ren lowered his chin.

"Come on," Miles said. "I'll walk you back to the apartment. You should get ice on that so it doesn't bruise too badly. You have your interview tomorrow, right?"

"I do," Ren confirmed, thankful that Miles hadn't brought up the absence of his usual accessories. He cleared his throat. "I'll just wear a long-sleeved shirt and if they ask, I'll say … something that doesn't make it seem like I do bondage."

This startled a laugh out of Miles. Proud of himself, Ren smiled.

"You don't have to walk me home. I don't think they'll pull over to harass me."

"I'm walking you home," Miles said. His voice told him it was final.

Ren didn't mind. They talked about Ren's hair—Miles said he liked it—and the pictures Miles had been taking. About Ren's hangover the day after they went out and how embarrassed Hale had been when Ren explained the reason he'd stayed over at Miles's that night. It was a short walk, but by the time they got to the apartment, Ren felt it had improved his day.

When he went inside, Miles didn't follow. "What are you doing?" Ren asked.

"I'm not coming in," Miles said. "I still have work to do for class, so I'm going to head back to the studio." Ren frowned, and Miles must have realized what he was thinking, because he added, "Don't worry about it."

"Thanks for walking me back."

Miles nodded and turned toward campus. "Tell Hale I said hi if he's in." He raised his hand to wave.

Ren let the door close between them. He was doing the right thing with Miles, he thought. If it wasn't the right thing, he was sure he wouldn't feel so at ease when they were together. Their current relationship was good, and he didn't want to risk ruining it.

Hale and Logan returned to the apartment as Ren was finishing making himself dinner.

"Oh," Hale said at the sight of him by the stove. "We bought you takeout. I should have let you know."

Ren looked at the bag in Hale's hand and then at the stove. Smiling, he shut off the burner. "Guess I have lunch for tomorrow."

As the couple took seats at the kitchen table and unpacked the food, Ren put the chicken he'd made in the fridge. "I thought it was date night for you guys. Why'd you come home?"

"To bring you food," Hale said. "You have your interview tomorrow, so we thought maybe we could put you in a good mood beforehand."

"Thanks, guys. This does put me in a good mood." Hale handed him one of the plastic takeout containers.

"So," Logan began, "are you nervous about tomorrow?"

Ren nodded. "I am, but I'm pretending like I'm not because it helps me calm down. I hope it works out. I need to find a job close by, since I'll still need a few credits to graduate, but there aren't a lot of opportunities in this area. Also, I still don't have a car, and I'd prefer not to wake up at four in the morning to take the bus to one of the neighboring towns."

Logan looked at Hale. "Do you think you'll be able to find something?"

Both Ren and Hale grimaced. While Ren was having a difficult time finding jobs to apply for, he was looking in journalism, and there was always the possibility for him to move into marketing, social media, or digital content creation if a company liked his writing. Hale was hoping for a job in editing, and had fewer roles available to him.

"I don't want to talk about it," Hale grumbled. "I've been watching for something to come available, but there isn't anything."

"Don't worry," Ren assured. "Once I get a job, I'm going to bully the editor on staff until they quit, and then you can come work with me."

This made Hale laugh, but the concerned wrinkle didn't leave his brow.

"Hale—" Ren was interrupted by his phone vibrating on the counter, distracting him. He looked over his shoulder at it, not moving.

"Are you going to get that?" asked Hale.

Ren sighed and stood, fearing his day was about to get worse. "I still haven't heard from my dad about break, so I get anxious when my phone rings."

Thankfully, it wasn't his father's number on his screen. Still, he didn't answer right away.

"Is it him?" Hale asked.

"No. Unknown number. Has our area code."

"Maybe it's about your interview tomorrow?" Logan suggested.

This was a good guess, so Ren answered the call.

It was not about the interview. It was the police department.

"Is this Ren Cleckner?" a man asked. He sounded tired.

"It is," Ren confirmed. He looked at Hale and Logan with wide eyes, gesturing to try to communicate the situation without words. Ren could tell by both of their expressions that he was failing. "How can I help you, *officer?*"

Their faces almost made him laugh. Hale rose from his chair to come stand beside him, leaning in so he could hear what was being said. Briefly, Ren considered putting the call on speaker, but he didn't know why the officer was calling, and he didn't know if it was something he wanted Logan hearing.

"It seems there has been an incident that somewhat involves you," the officer said. Hale raised his eyebrows.

Ren shook his head, confused. "*Me?*" he asked. "I don't—" He thought of Sawyer and his friend in the parking lot that afternoon. If anyone saw them, it probably looked like he'd been in danger, and he supposed it was possible someone had called the police. "Oh. Is this about what happened this afternoon?"

Hale waved his arms around.

"What happened this afternoon?" the police officer asked.

"Nothing," Ren said.

The man sighed. "Would you be able to come in? We're trying to sort this out, but the men involved aren't talking and we would like to deal with this situation before it escalates."

Escalates?

"The men involved?" he asked. "What do they have to do with me?"

"One seems to be your ex-boyfriend—"

There was a protest in the background. *Sawyer.*

"—and the other is your neighbor."

Chapter Twenty-Five

Ren borrowed Hale's car and tried not to speed to the police station.

He failed.

The station wasn't a large building, so when he stepped inside, he immediately spotted Miles sitting in a plastic chair in front of a metal desk. Only the side of his face was visible from that angle, but it was enough to tell that his chin had dried blood on it.

He wasn't alone. Clarisse and the guy with the bleached blond hair were with him. The guy was sitting, seeming unconcerned as he said something with a grin, while Clarisse stood by Miles's side, her hand resting on his shoulder.

Still looking at them, Ren explained to the woman at the front desk why he was there and was told that he could go back by them.

As he approached, Miles's eyes found him. His expression became a mix of troubled and happy. "So you came," he said when Ren was close enough.

"Of course I came, idiot." He grabbed Miles's chin and jerked his head back to see his face better. From the damage, it was obvious he'd gotten hit at least twice, on his jaw and his nose. Neither looked good. "Did you think I wouldn't come?"

"I don't know anything about my ability to make you come."

"That's not funny."

Miles's lips quirked. "Sorry. You seemed tense."

"I am." He dropped his hands and looked around. "Where is he?"

"Why?"

This was annoying, so Ren continued to search until he spotted Sawyer. He was sitting in what looked like a small conference room with an older man wearing a police uniform. His eyes met Ren's through the glass doors. There was a purple bruise over his left eye, and he seemed to have difficulty opening it. "I'm going to kill him," Ren said, taking a step in that direction.

Before he could go any farther, Miles caught his arm. Ren looked down as the hand slipped to clutch his fingers, passing over the bruises on his wrist.

Getting punched in the face made Miles bold.

Ren wanted to know what expression Miles was making, but his bloodied face made him angry, so he instead looked at Clarisse. She was staring at their clasped hands.

"It's my fault," Miles claimed. "I hit him first."

Sighing, Ren sat in the chair beside him, arm still outstretched to hold Miles's hand. "Why don't you tell me what happened?"

Miles did. Apparently, while Miles was out with his friends at the campus cafeteria, he'd overheard Sawyer talking about Ren. He'd been saying bad things, according to Miles, but he'd just wrote it off as Sawyer being an asshole. It wasn't until Miles overheard Sawyer sharing his plan to wait outside the apartment building that Miles intervened, and it escalated from there.

"They didn't fight for long," Clarisse assured. "I brought someone to stop it right away."

Miles brushed his thumb over Ren's knuckles. "I hope he doesn't press charges. My mom is going to kill me."

"He won't press charges," Ren said. "If he does, I'll detach his dick from his body."

This made Miles chuckle. Across the room, the door to the conference room opened and Sawyer followed the officer out. He didn't look at Ren as he approached and flopped into the seat on the other side of Miles.

"You're Ren Cleckner?" the officer asked.

"I am," he confirmed, slipping his hand from Miles's.

Nodding, the man gestured to the conference room. "Do you mind having a word with me?"

This time, Miles didn't stop him from leaving.

He went into the conference room and took a seat in the chair Sawyer had been occupying. The officer said something to Miles and Sawyer about not speaking to each other, and then he came into the room and closed the door. "Sorry for calling you out so late."

"I'm twenty-one. It's not late," Ren responded, wishing he'd cut to the chase.

"I suppose it's not." The older man took a seat across from him at the table. For a long moment, he fidgeted, and Ren waited impatiently. "So, apparently, Mr. Smits had plans to assault you outside of your apartment, which is why your neighbor intervened. Neither he nor Mr. Smits will tell me how it got to this point, and I think it's best we resolve this whole thing before it escalates."

Before he could stop himself, Ren asked, "Is that your job?"

"Would you prefer I call you back after he assaults you?"

"No. Sorry, I didn't …" he trailed off. "As you said, it's late and I must be tired."

The actual tired person sighed. "I'm sure." Then he looked at Ren expectantly.

Ren sat up straighter in his chair. "I don't know if I can tell you anything useful. It's just some stupid relationship stuff." He glanced at Sawyer through the glass door. "I think the only way to resolve this is for me to speak to Sawyer myself."

"I'm not opposed to that," the officer said. "I'd like to be in the room while you two speak, if that's possible. If he is planning on hurting you, it seems in poor judgment to leave the two of you alone."

This wasn't preferable, but Ren supposed it was a fair concern to have, so he nodded. With a small groan of effort, the officer stood. He opened the door of the conference room and called out to Sawyer. Slowly, Sawyer made his way toward them. Their eyes met for a brief second, but Ren glanced past him to Miles.

It wasn't long before Sawyer blocked his vision. Ren lowered his gaze until he took the seat across from him.

There was a long moment of silence. The officer pulled the door shut again and hovered there. "Are you going to press charges?" Ren asked.

"On the guy who attacked me?" Sawyer asked. "Of course I am. Why wouldn't I?"

"Because you owe me."

Sawyer glared. Staring back, Ren wondered how he'd ever found him attractive enough to date; and he looked *better* with the black eye. "I owe you nothing," Sawyer snapped. "You ruined everything. You told Sadie—"

"I did," Ren confirmed, cutting him off. "I'm not sorry."

As if he couldn't bear to look at him, Sawyer turned away. It was a while before he spoke again, and Ren sat silently, waiting for Sawyer to gather his thoughts. "Why?" All anger was gone from Sawyer's voice. There was only defeat. "Why did you tell her?"

"Because she deserved to know," Ren said. "I did nothing wrong by telling her. If you hadn't fucked up, there would have been nothing to tell her."

Sawyer covered his face with his hands. "I love her."

"Loving someone doesn't give you the right to treat them like shit."

His face still hidden, Sawyer bent forward over the table. Ren felt a little bad for him. This was Sawyer's fault, and he deserved to feel guilty, but Ren had at one point felt a sort of fondness for this man, and watching him be so pathetic didn't make Ren feel better about himself.

"I suppose it's a little my fault that this went as far as it did," Ren granted. "I knew there was something up with you, and I should have tried harder to get you to talk about it, but I was just using you because I was bored and it didn't seem important at the time."

When Sawyer lifted his head to look at him, his eyes were red, but his face was dry.

Ren shot a glance at the officer. "Also," he said, "I can't fully blame you for sleeping with me. I mean … yes, you were manipulating me, and you weren't being honest, but I got angry that night, and even though I knew I shouldn't, I slept with you anyway, so it's not entirely on you."

Apparently, the officer wasn't all that concerned about his safety, because he cleared his throat and told them he'd wait outside the room. Ren wanted to laugh.

"What are you doing?" Sawyer asked him.

"I guess I'm trying to say that I suck too," Ren admitted. "And while I felt pissed at you for using me, I was also using you in my own way."

"Are you … forgiving me?"

Ren considered it. "I don't think so," he said. "I mean, I don't feel like I can forgive someone I'm indifferent to. I don't care about you, so I can't forgive you. Does that make sense? You did a bad thing to me, and now I need to forgive myself for falling for it."

Sawyer frowned. "Aren't you trying to convince me not to press charges? If you take some of the fault on yourself, doesn't that mean I owe you even less?"

"Sure," Ren said. "That makes sense, but that's not what I was getting at. What I'm trying to say is, let's just be done with each other. What happened happened. We both made bad choices, and it's over now. Me talking to your girlfriend isn't going to solve anything. It would probably make things *worse*, so how about we get out of each other's lives? No more stopping me in public to harass me, no more talking shit about me to your friends and planning to assault me. What good is pressing charges going to do? You know you were in the wrong, and it won't make you feel any better about this situation. Let's just let it all go."

Ren could see Sawyer was thinking about it. He let him process, hoping Sawyer could be genuine with him at least once in their relationship.

Sawyer sighed. "Sadie is a really good person."

"You're telling me about your girlfriend?"

"No," Sawyer said. "Well, a little. But my point is, she's a good person, and if I want her back, I have to be a better person as well."

Ren still wasn't sure what he was getting at, but this seemed like a reasonable conclusion to draw, so he nodded.

"I won't press charges," Sawyer finally said. "Just tell him if he ever sees me again to walk the other way."

While Ren was relieved, he bit hard into his lower lip to avoid showing it. He was worried that looking too thankful would make Sawyer take it back just to spite him once more. "I'm sure he won't protest that." Ren glanced toward the officer outside the glass door. "Thank you. I'll tell the officer we're done."

"Wait a minute," Sawyer said before Ren could rise from his seat. "I'm still mad at you. Even now, if I'm being honest, I wish you hadn't told her about yourself, because then she'd be my girlfriend again. Still, I'm sorry for everything that happened between us. It wasn't supposed to go like that."

An apology wasn't something Ren had been expecting, nor was it something he felt he needed, so he cared little for it. What got his attention instead was the last thing Sawyer had said. "How was it supposed to go?"

Sawyer must not have been expecting him to ask questions, because his eyes widened. "It never should have happened. It only did because I got pressure from my friends since they thought it would be good for me after my breakup. I wasn't ever expecting to *date* you, but then ..."

None of this was new. "Then I didn't put out. Why didn't you just give up? You didn't have to date me."

"By the time I realized you weren't just going to sleep with me, we'd already been together for a few weeks, and I didn't mind spending time with you or anything. I thought you were fun, and we had a good time together. I thought I'd already put in that much effort, so why not just see it though? It's ... it's horrible when I say it out loud now, but it got to where it felt like I *had* to sleep with you. Otherwise, I would have dated a man for no reason."

"So this is a toxic masculinity thing," Ren summarized. "You might be bisexual, since most straight guys wouldn't be able to do what you did, but I can say with confidence that you should never have sex with a man again, because you're terrible at it." Sawyer flushed. "Can I ask you one last thing?"

Sawyer made a face. "If it's about sex—"

"It's not," Ren assured. "I wanted to ask why you don't like Miles."

The blond scoffed. "He punched me in the face—"

"Before that," Ren cut in. "You've never liked him, right?" He thought of the few times he'd seen Sawyer interact with Miles and his expression as he had. It was a subtle dislike for sure, but it was there.

"I don't know if you want to hear it from me."

"Talk," Ren demanded.

"He was the only one who posed a real threat."

This almost made Ren chuckle. Miles was far from *threatening*, though, he supposed the man whom Miles had punched wouldn't share this opinion. "What do you mean?"

"I mean, I wanted to sleep with you and he was obviously interested in you. It worried me that you might realize," Sawyer claimed. For a minute, he looked troubled, as if he wasn't sure whether to say something. Then, he leaned forward. "I saw how you looked at each other. There would be no room for me once you noticed it yourself."

"What the fuck does that mean?"

His hands up in defense, Sawyer leaned back in his chair. "I said what I said, and I don't feel like it's my business, so I won't say any more."

It crossed Ren's mind to protest this, but pissing off Sawyer by demanding something probably wasn't the best route to take, given the situation.

They left the conference room together. At the sound of the door opening, Miles raised his head. He looked ridiculous with blood on his mouth, and Ren felt a surge of anger for the man beside him once more.

Do I really like him enough that other people notice? Ren wondered. *What if Miles has noticed?*

"Well?" the officer asked. "Has everything been sorted out?"

Ren and Sawyer shared a glance, and Ren raised his eyebrows, waiting for him to speak. "I guess so," Sawyer said. He pointed at Miles then. "I won't press charges, but I don't want to see your face ever again. Either of you," this last bit included Ren.

"That won't be a problem," Miles agreed.

They were all dismissed.

Mumbling something under his breath about putting ice on his eye, Sawyer left. Across the room, Clarisse fussed over Miles, inviting him back to her place so she could clean his face. Ren felt that there was no place for him in that, so he thanked the tired officer for dealing with them and left.

By the time he was walking into the parking lot, Miles was on his heels. He said nothing, just followed Ren all the way to Hale's car. Ren was expecting him to leave when his presence went unacknowledged, but Miles blocked the driver's side door.

"What?" Ren snapped, hand on the door handle. He had half a mind to open it anyway and slam it against Miles's side, though that felt like kicking him when he was already down.

"Why are you angry?"

"I'm not," Ren denied.

Frowning, Miles gazed past him. Ren glanced over his shoulder and spotted Clarisse and the bleach-blond man hovering in the middle of the parking lot. "You should go with them," Ren told him.

"What did you guys talk about?" Miles asked.

"That's none of your business."

"Ren." Miles reached out to touch the hand on the car door, fingers very gentle for someone who had been brought into a police station for assault. "*Ren.*"

He felt himself wavering.

Clarisse called out to Miles. *Go with her*, Ren thought. It would be easier that way. For both of them.

As he pushed a finger underneath one of Ren's, linking them together, Miles mumbled, "Take me home with you."

Right then, Ren felt it was unbearable to stand there and not kiss him.

He didn't know whether it was the finger linked with his or the words or the gentle way Miles looked at him, fond even with blood on his face from Ren's stupid ex. It was probably all of it. All of it made him feel as if he couldn't stand to not be kissing Miles for a moment longer.

Grasping a handful of the front of Miles's shirt, Ren pulled him down to his level. Their eyes met, and Ren had second thoughts. He kissed him anyway, because even if it was a bad idea, he wanted to.

Miles hadn't been expecting it. He went rigid for a long second before Ren felt him kiss back. His hands moved to hold his waist, barely touching him, so gentle.

Ren thought it would be nice if Miles bruised him.

It was so cold outside, but his mouth against Miles's was warm. He relaxed his jaw, giving Miles permission to kiss him deeply. He tasted like blood. Ren groaned and moved his hands to Miles's face.

The touch, even though it was light, must have hurt, because Miles groaned. Before Ren could pull away and see he was okay, Miles's arms encircled his waist, pulling him up against him.

Ren felt more of him right then than he ever had before.

He would have preferred to take the time to appreciate it, but all he could focus on was Miles's partial hardness pressed against him. All they'd done was kiss, and yet Miles's whole body was reacting to him.

Fuck, Ren thought. *Fuck fuck fuck.*

He couldn't recall if he'd ever had a first kiss that felt like this. Like his lips were on fire and his heart would pound out of his chest. Like it wouldn't be enough, no matter how long it continued.

Ren pulled away and hid his face in the front of Miles's shirt. "Let's go home," he said, voice muffled. He felt Miles press against his hair. "Don't get blood on me."

The body against his shook with laughter. Miles raised his head. "Will you help me take care of my face?"

Ren pulled back to look up at him. "It's only fair."

The smile Miles wore lit up his face.

The feeling of wanting to kiss him surged again, and this time Ren huffed and put his hands on Miles's chest to push him away. "Just get in the car."

Chapter Twenty-Six

Logan and Hale were still in the apartment, sitting together on the couch with Logan's arm around Hale's shoulders. They had probably been kissing, given the color of Hale's mouth. Ren wasn't in the mood to tease.

"What happened?" Logan asked Miles. "Dude, your face."

Ren dropped his keys on the counter and turned to Miles. Their eyes met, and he thought about kissing him in the parking lot and how stupid it was and how nice it would be to do it again.

Neither of them were in the mood to explain the situation, so Ren slipped off his coat and headed toward the bathroom. "Come on," he instructed.

"Miles?" Logan asked.

"Don't worry about it." Miles followed Ren into the bathroom and closed the door.

At the click of the latch, Ren opened his mouth to tell him to take a seat on the toilet lid. Before he could get any words out, Miles ducked to kiss him. Ren allowed it for only a moment. "Sit down," he instructed. "You taste like blood."

Eyes bright, Miles took a seat.

With a wet washcloth in hand, Ren moved to stand before him. There was some distance between them, but Miles pulled him forward to close it, lips curled into a smile. Even with the blood on his mouth and the darkness of fresh bruises, he looked handsome.

As Ren cleaned his face, Miles let his hands wander. They roamed from his hips to his stomach, to the strip of skin above his waistband, and then to the backs of his thighs. The adrenaline from fighting and kissing was making him bold.

When Ren announced he was done and tossed the bloodied washcloth in the sink, Miles pulled him into his lap. "You—" Ren said, but Miles interrupted with his lips.

Ren pushed him away. "You should go back to your apartment and rest," he forced out, knowing it was for the best.

"Why?"

"Miles." Ren sighed. "Maybe you shouldn't concern yourself with me. I mean, look at yourself. The more tangled up with me you get, the worse it's going to be for you. I'm no good."

Confusion was clear on Miles's face as he stared up at him. "What are you talking about?"

"From now on, it's best you don't interfere with my problems."

"No," Miles refused.

"What do you mean, *no*?"

"I mean *no*," Miles repeated. "It is my life. If I want to concern myself with you, I will. I understand that me loving you causes some kind of internal struggle, but that's not my problem, so figure it out yourself and don't tell me what to do. I love you, and I'm going to keep loving you, so shut the fuck up about it and deal with it."

The words made his heart pound. His chest ached with a desire he'd never felt before, and the feeling of their lips not touching became unbearable once more. Desperate, Ren kissed him.

Miles groaned and pulled away. "I thought you wanted me to leave."

"You just told me you would do what you wanted, and you don't want to leave."

"So it's okay?" Miles asked, hazel eyes roaming Ren's face. "You're okay with me kissing and touching you?"

Ren lowered his gaze. "Right now it's fine." It had to be fine. The space between them was uncomfortably large and he would do anything to close it.

"And you won't regret it later?"

It was impossible to know exactly how he would feel about this afterward, but he couldn't imagine regretting something he wanted as badly as this. "I don't think I will. You might," he said, curing his fingers in the fabric of Miles's shirt. Something terrifying occurred to him. "Do you think it'll make it hard for us to be around each other?"

After a moment of thought, Miles said, "Nothing would have to change. I mean … I'm not going to change anything about how I act."

This was a terrible idea. It was far too risky, and he'd hate for the delicate comradery they shared to fall apart because of a single night, but Miles was looking at him so earnestly that it was impossible not to believe him.

"Okay," Ren said.

He brought their lips together again, humming when Miles's hands rested on his hips to gently guide him closer until they were snug against each other. They were a perfect fit, and he melted into the other man.

Miles was good at kissing. The thought made Ren kind of bitter, because it meant Miles had a lot of practice, though he supposed he was the one reaping the benefits, so it wasn't fair for him to get angry. It was clear Ren wasn't the only one enjoying himself. He could feel Miles again, erect and pressing against his zipper.

"Do you want head?"

This intrigued Miles, if the glint in his eyes was any sign. Instead of agreeing, he said, "That depends."

His eyebrows raised and he pressed down a little harder against Miles's lap. "Really?"

Letting out something between a moan and a laugh, Miles gripped Ren's hips tightly. "It depends on how far you're willing to go."

Ren had to bite his lip to keep from laughing. The conversation reminded him too much of the time he'd lost his virginity. "You want to have sex?"

"I'm in love with you, and my adrenaline is still up from getting into my first fight since middle school."

Embarrassed, Ren turned his face away. He considered the proposition. If he was being honest with himself, he wanted to have sex with Miles. It was something he'd thought about before, a guilty fantasy he was sure would never happen because he was set on only sleeping with people who were in love with him, and Miles could never be in love with him.

But he was. Ren believed him when he said he loved him, and even if he didn't, his stupid rule about sex didn't even matter anymore after he'd made an exception for Sawyer.

Letting his forehead rest against Miles, he mumbled, "You can do whatever you want with me. I know you're not taking advantage."

When Miles leaned forward to kiss him, it wasn't the kind of kiss Ren wanted.

No. That was a lie. It was *exactly* the kind of kiss Ren wanted, just not right then. Not with a friend he was going to sleep with once. Not with a person who couldn't give him more of those kisses. Not with Miles.

"Where are your condoms?"

"Um." Ren swallowed around the lump in his throat. "In my bedroom."

"Alright. Should we move—"

Ren didn't even let him finish the sentence. "We can't," he said. "Hale and Logan are out there. There is no way that we get to my bedroom without them harassing us."

"We can just ignore them."

This wasn't an option. "If I see any kind of judgment on Hale's face, I won't be able to do this." He was happy Miles didn't ask something stupid like, *Why do you care?*

Instead, he nodded and said, "Okay."

Ren chewed his lip. "You know, I got tested after sleeping with Sawyer. We had used a condom, but I thought just in case … anyway, I'm clean, so …"

The expression on Miles's face was deadpan. "Have you ever done it without one before?"

Embarrassed, Ren averted his gaze. "With Jules." They'd been dating long enough and were sleeping only with each other, so there had been little risk involved.

Miles had no reaction to this. "I'm going to call Logan," he announced.

"What?"

An arm remained around Ren's waist to steady him as he shifted to free his phone from his pocket. Sure enough, he called Logan. Ren didn't see him dial, but the muffled voice he heard on the other end of the phone was unmistakably his roommate's boyfriend.

"What are you guys doing in there?" asked Logan.

"Can you bring us a condom?"

Ren slapped Miles on the shoulder at the directness. He shrugged, but otherwise ignored the hit.

"Uh …" Logan trailed off and cleared his throat. "You want a condom? For what?"

"I think that's fairly obvious."

There was a pause. "Are you for real?"

"Yeah."

Ren squeezed his eyes shut, expecting Logan to refuse and demand they come out to talk.

With a heavy sigh, Logan said, "Ah shit. Okay. Give me a minute."

Surprised, Ren opened his eyes. "He's seriously going to?"

Miles nodded. "Well, yeah. I have the opportunity to get laid. He's not going to get in the way of that." As he spoke, his hand slipped up the front of Ren's shirt. "I've wanted to do this for a while, you know."

"Please stop talking," Logan said, and Ren would have laughed if the fingers trailing up his stomach did not distract him.

He wanted to tell Miles to stop, terrified he'd make an embarrassing noise that Logan would hear over the phone, but then warm fingers met his left nipple and he realized there was no way he'd protest. A small contented sigh left him, soft enough that he was sure only Miles noticed. Hazel eyes widened, as if he hadn't been sure how Ren would react to the touch.

Holding the phone away from his mouth, Miles leaned forward to connect their lips again, pushing his tongue past Ren's teeth to the inside of his mouth. Groaning, Ren curled his fist in Miles's hair and kissed him back so hard his lips ached. He brought his free hand down between them, fingers searching for a grip around Miles's erection through his pants.

There was a knock on the door right as Ren's hand squeezed. "Don't come in," Miles said, bringing his phone back to his mouth. "Just slide it under the door."

Nothing happened. "Are you sure this is a good idea?" Logan asked.

Ren's eyes met Miles's. Neither of them said anything, waiting and watching the other person to react in a way that showed any doubt. When it didn't happen, Ren pressed a quick kiss to the corner of Miles's mouth and stood to pull off his clothes.

"Yeah," Miles said into the phone, watching Ren. "I think it is."

As the condom slipped under the door, Ren stepped out of his pants. He went to get it.

After thanking Logan, Miles hung up the phone.

"Thanks for that," Ren grumbled, and Miles rose from the toilet. "What are you doing?"

Pulling his shirt over his head, Miles asked, "What do you mean?"

"Why are you standing?" Ren elaborated. "I thought I'd be on top."

Miles made a smug face. "That's not how this is going to work." He undid the front of his pants and took a step forward to close the distance between them. "I've been looking forward to this far too much to just lay back and let you do all the work."

While Ren preferred this, it made him nervous, given his recent history. He grabbed Miles's forearms. "Are you sure you know what you're doing?"

"You want to have sex with me even though you're not sure I know what I'm doing?" There was a laugh in Miles's voice that made Ren feel as if he was being ridiculous. Not amused, Ren looked up at him. Miles hooked his thumbs into the waistband of Ren's briefs on either side of his hips. "I've only had sex with my ex-girlfriend from high school, but I promise I know how to do this."

His gaze lowered to Miles's bare chest. "I don't want to hear about your ex-girlfriend," he grumbled, earning chuckle and a kiss to the top of his head. "It's not that I don't trust you, because I do." He trusted Miles more than he should, Ren felt. "Sawyer was the last person I slept with and I was his first man and it hurt."

"I don't want to hear about your ex-boyfriend."

"*Miles,*" Ren groaned, exasperated.

Cupping his face in his hands, Miles smiled down at him. "I'll be gentle," he promised. "The last thing I want to do is hurt you."

Ren handed over the condom.

He was trying to be quiet, but it was hard. True to his word, Miles was gentle, prepping him with careful fingers and distracting him with kisses and touches whenever Ren tensed. By the time Miles was pushing into him, he was so eager for it that the discomfort didn't even bother him.

"You okay?" Miles asked into his ear before kissing the shell. Ren nodded but tightened his grip on Miles's biceps.

The bathroom was far too small for it to be a comfortable place to have sex. They only made it work because Ren could fit on the vanity beside the sink and Miles's hips were just at the right height. Still, it wasn't an easy position to hold, and Ren had to ignore the discomfort in his back and hang on to Miles so he didn't fall.

"Fuck," Ren moaned, dropping his head against the mirror and pushing his knees even farther apart. "That feels good."

"Yeah?" Miles asked, and Ren cracked his eyes open to look at him. Their gazes met.

It felt good, but also strangely normal.

No. That wasn't the word. It couldn't feel normal, since Ren couldn't remember anything that had felt like this before. Sex with Miles was a new, wonderful feeling.

What he meant was that it felt comfortable. He didn't feel any of the first-time nerves he'd felt with other partners, didn't feel any shame in showing the younger man this side of him for the first time. It felt right, and it terrified him.

The smile that came onto Miles's face was slow and sweet, and Ren's heart throbbed. He wanted to cry right then, so he closed his eyes again and asked, "Are you going to move or not?"

Miles answered with his body.

He started with small moments, just little thrusts of his hips that teased Ren more than stimulated him. It drove him crazy, his body aching for something more. Thankfully, it wasn't long before Miles gave it to him, setting a more fitting rhythm for sex for two non-lovers. Even so, his touches remained tender, fingers gripping Ren's hips and thumbs rubbing into the dip there. He kept his lips alongside Ren's ear to soothe him with sweet nothings.

You're so beautiful.

I love how you sound.

It feels so good.

I love you.

This last one was only said once, and Ren suspected it was a slipup. He was glad he had heard it.

Ren had been expecting Miles to be clumsy. He thought he'd have to give him direction, maybe explain what angle to thrust at to find his prostate, but he found criticism unnecessary. This was good, since he doubted his ability to talk coherently.

It had been a long time since he'd last had good sex—it must have been with Julian, but he couldn't even recall their last time and he had forgotten how easy it was to lose himself in it. He tried to hold back, tensing his muscles to dilute the pleasure when it got too intense and biting his lower lip hard to keep his voice in.

"You're thinking too much," Miles told him once he'd noticed, slipping his thumb between Ren's lips and past his teeth, so closing his mouth was impossible. "Let go."

Ren did. He relaxed everything but his hands on Miles's arms, slumping back against the mirror and closing his eyes so he could focus harder on feeling. His voice was loud, but he was also past the point of feeling embarrassed about it. Miles was making noise as well, soft groans whenever oversensitivity had Ren jerking and tensing around him. Each sound that reached Ren's ears drove him closer to crazy.

Ren's orgasm shouldn't have surprised him. It had been building the entire time, growing closer with each movement, but when it crashed over him, stealing his breath and ability to think, he felt completely unprepared. It felt like it took an entire minute to move through his body. He could do nothing but hold on to Miles and shiver through it.

When he came to his senses enough to notice Miles's tension under his fingertips, he cracked open his eyes.

Already looking back at him, eyes dark and half closed, Miles asked, "Can I…?" he trailed off, but Ren already knew the rest of the question.

"You can keep going," Ren said, wanting it even though he was thoroughly exhausted.

It only took a minute for Miles to finish, and Ren used the time as an opportunity to watch him. He'd been so distracted earlier he hadn't even thought to look, and he was sure he'd be upset with himself later if he couldn't remember Miles's expression twisted with pleasure.

He's so pretty, Ren thought, bringing a hand up to Miles's face. He barely touched him, just brushed a thumb over his clenched jaw, but Miles's eyes snapped open to look at him as he came with a small grunt.

Sighing, Ren reached up farther to get his arm around Miles's neck, pulling him down into his shoulder. They stayed like that for a while, just breathing heavily against each other. Once Miles pulled away, pulled *out*, it'd be over.

"Ren," Miles said into the skin of his shoulder.

"Not yet," Ren said, which probably meant nothing to him if they were thinking different things. This seemed likely, since Miles raised his head to look at him with furrowed eyebrows. Ren kissed him again, all tongue and passion. Groaning, Miles's hands came to the back of Ren's head, fingers tangling in his hair to hold him in place until his lungs screamed for air and they had to part.

"You okay?" Miles asked.

"Yeah."

Miles looked down between them and slipped out of him. That was the most unpleasant feeling of the night, and he wondered whether it was because of the weirdness of it or if he just didn't want Miles to leave.

His warmth moved away. Ren allowed his legs to hang over the edge of the vanity. He felt as if he didn't have any muscles. All he wanted to do right then was curl up under a warm blanket and sleep for the foreseeable future.

That wasn't possible. "Fuck," he said, voice scratchy. "I have my interview tomorrow morning."

Miles nodded. "Do you want to take a shower?"

"I probably should." His displeasure must have been obvious in his voice, because Miles smiled. "Want to shower with me?" Ren asked.

"I wouldn't mind that. I thought you'd kick me out right away."

Ren wanted to tell Miles that he didn't want him to leave, but he said, "I'm too tired for that" instead.

If Miles saw through this, he said nothing about it. He must have had some suspicion of Ren's true feelings, because after their shower, when Ren took his hand and lead him through the empty apartment—he didn't blame Hale and Logan for leaving—he followed.

After Ren had pushed Miles down onto his bed and pulled the covers over him, he climbed in beside him. At first, Miles was tense, so Ren pressed against his side and asked, "Hold me?"

An arm slipped around his waist. "I should have known you'd like to be pampered afterward."

It was very much the truth. "It's so easy to feel lonely after sex," Ren mumbled.

Miles passed a hand over his wet hair.

"Thank you," Ren whispered.

"I think I'm the one who should say that."

There was a misunderstanding. Ren was thanking Miles not for sleeping with him but for making him feel loved in the way he'd craved for so long. The last time he'd felt this way was with Julian, though even that wasn't quite the same, because with Julian, no matter how hard he tried or how much Jules loved him, Ren always felt as if he was with a friend. It wasn't like that with Miles.

I'm so fucked, Ren thought.

Chapter Twenty-Seven

Ren's alarm went off at 7:30, and he reached his left hand out from under the covers to turn it off. Instead of his fingers meeting the wood of his bed table or the cool screen of his cell phone, he felt something warm and alive.

He cracked open his eyes. First, he noticed he was not on his usual side of the bed. This made sense when he woke up enough to realize Miles was beside him.

Groaning, Ren climbed out of bed. He found his phone in the pile of their clothes and shut off the alarm.

His interview was in half an hour, and he had enough time to get ready if he didn't get distracted. Still, he allowed himself a moment to stand at the end of the bed with his head in his hands.

They'd had sex. He and Miles. *Miles.*

Damage control would have to wait until after the interview.

Ren tried to get ready quietly. His outfit for the day was already folded on top of his dresser, so he didn't have to worry about waking Miles with the opening and closing of drawers, but trying to do anything without bumping into things in that room was nearly impossible.

He thought he'd succeeded when he'd finished pulling on his socks and Miles had yet to stir, but when he was about to leave his room, he heard a soft "Ren" come from the bed.

"Oh." He turned. "Sorry. I was trying not to wake you."

"It's fine." Miles sat up. It was too dark to make out anything other than his form. "How are you feeling?"

"I'm fine," he assured. "Just a little sore, but that's normal." He flicked on the light, and Miles squeezed his eyes shut. "I have to go, but tell me if you think my outfit is okay."

Miles rubbed at his eyes. "Ah, that's right." After gazing at Ren for a couple of seconds, he nodded and said, "You look great."

"Thanks." Ren reached for his doorknob again. "Um … we'll talk later, okay? Go back to sleep."

He shut off the light, and Miles dropped onto the mattress with a sigh.

When Ren slipped from his room, Hale and Logan were in the living room. At the sight of them, Ren paused. They both looked over the back of the couch. Logan raised his eyebrows. "Why are you awake?" Ren asked.

"I wanted to wish you good luck," Hale said, rising from the couch. He went to the kitchen and poured coffee into a travel mug. "Noah's outside waiting for you, but I didn't want to go into your room to wake you." He turned then, mug in hand. His curiosity was obvious.

"I don't want to talk about it right now," Ren said before questions could be asked about the night before.

Nodding, Hale stopped in front of him and held out the mug. "Okay then."

Sighing, Ren thanked him and accepted the coffee. "Would you tell Noah I'll be out in a minute? I need to use the bathroom and brush my teeth."

"Sure." Hale smiled. "We'll talk later, then."

It wasn't a question.

The interview went well, and he suspected it was because he was too distracted to let his anxiety get the best of him. Instead of nervously answering questions as he had in previous interviews, he said the first thing that came to mind, because anytime he paused to think too long, the night before came back to him. When he left and shook the hand of his interviewers, they told him they appreciated his confidence.

In the car on the way back to the apartment, Noah pestered him for details. Ren gave him the bare minimum, then fell silent in the passenger seat to think. Miles should be returning from his first class right around the time they got back to the apartment, and Ren needed to be prepared in case they ran into each other.

"You're making me think it didn't go as well as you said it did," Noah accused.

"Huh?"

"You're being quiet."

Ren sighed. "That has nothing to do with the interview. I was quiet on the ride over too."

"No, you weren't."

Right. Ren had Noah ask him interview questions to get in the proper mindset. "Ah," Ren mumbled. Then, because it was Noah and he could tell him anything, he told the truth. "Actually, I slept with Miles last night."

Noah slammed on the brakes.

"Oh my god!" Ren exclaimed as his seat belt choked him. He whipped around in his seat to make sure there was no one behind them. Thankfully, the closest car was blocks away. "What is wrong with you?!"

"Slept with? Like … in the same bed, or …?"

"Drive!" Ren snapped, because the car behind them was still approaching and Noah seemed to have no interest in going anywhere.

"Answer the question."

"Slept together like fucked. He put his dick in me and—"

"Okay!" Noah yelled, and the car jerked forward again. "Okay, I get it. How did that happen? I thought you were adamant about staying friends."

Ren put his head in his hands. "I was, but he … he defended my honor and was all bruised and I wanted to sleep with him, so I did."

Frustrated, Noah rubbed his forehead. "There are lots of stupid things that I really want to do but don't," he said. "I would like to drink some weekdays, but I don't since I know I'll regret it when I'm hung over for class the next day."

"I don't regret it," Ren said.

Noah shook his head. "So, what now? Are you going to date him?"

"I don't think so. We talked about it beforehand, and he said he wouldn't act any differently."

"And you believe him?"

"Yeah … I do. I mean … it's Miles, and I trust him. Nothing changed after he told me how he felt, so how is this any different?"

"Him confessing to you was a one-way thing. *Fucking him* is a two-way thing. It's different. It's something you both decided."

This didn't stress Ren the way Noah was probably expecting. It actually did the opposite. "We decided together. That's how I know it'll be fine." Ren leaned his head against the window and closed his eyes. "I can't regret the thing that made me feel loved for the first time in forever."

For the next few minutes, they were quiet. "You know Hale and I love you," Noah said when they were only blocks from the apartment.

"Yeah," Ren said. "But not like that."

He didn't run into Miles in the hall, so Ren figured he had more time to put his thoughts into words before he had to express them.

It was a false sense of security. When he opened the apartment door, Miles was sitting on the couch alone. He looked up at the sound of Ren entering and smiled, his expression soft.

"Where's Hale?" Ren asked, shutting the door behind himself. "I was expecting him to bombard me with questions as soon as I got home."

"I'm sure he'll do that later," Miles said. "How was your interview?"

Ren tossed his keys onto the dining table and put his hands on his hips. He wasn't sure whether he was supposed to sit on the couch or continue to hover. "It was fine," he said. "Good, I think. I wasn't all there, if you know what I mean, so it's difficult to reflect on."

"Yeah," Miles said. He rose from the couch, and Ren let his eyes roam. At some point, Miles had gone back to his apartment for a change of clothes.

"Did you go to class?"

"Yeah. I came back after. Hale let me in."

Ren nodded. "How does your face feel?" The bruises had settled in, and thankfully they weren't as bad as Ren had anticipated. They shouldn't last longer than a couple of weeks.

The question made Miles laugh. "I feel fine. A little ice and I'll be better in no time."

Ren nodded, unsure of what else to say. Miles approached, stopping close enough that Ren had to tilt his head back to meet his gaze. A hand cupped Ren's jaw. "Miles ..."

At the sound of his name, Miles smiled. "Ren," he said in return, his voice too affectionate for Ren to handle. "Date me."

Ren's first instinct was to accept. He wanted to date Miles. *Really* wanted to.

But the history with his exes gave him pause. He'd already tried to date friends in the past, and both times the relationships hadn't been able to return to normal after they'd ended. Miles was important to him, and he felt he had the potential to become even more so. It wasn't worth the risk.

"Oh," Ren said, feeling as if he could cry. "Miles." He settled his hand on Miles's forearm. "I don't think it's a good idea."

This must have been expected, because Miles nodded. Still, he didn't pull away, and Ren slid his hand up to rest over Miles's hand on his cheek.

"We've been doing so well," Ren continued. "We've only just started to get to know each other, and you already mean more to me than I ever thought you would. I like what we have now. I like that you're a constant in my life, and every time I've given it a shot with someone close to me, it's completely ruined our previous relationship. I just don't ..." He trailed off. "I don't want to lose you."

"Alright."

Ren's expression must have reflected his worry, because Miles sighed and pulled him into a tight embrace.

"Hey, it's okay," he assured. "We're okay. I promise. I just thought, why not shoot my shot one last time, but I get it."

Ren hugged him just as tight, hands clutching the back of Miles's shirt. He didn't want to let go, but it wasn't fair of him to hold on, so he stepped back when he felt Miles pulling away from him.

"I'm gonna go," Miles said. "Hale's in my apartment waiting for me to tell him he can come back. You and I are good, though. Nothing is changing. Alright?"

"Yeah," he agreed weakly. He felt as if he'd done the right thing, though his heart ached as if he'd just broken it. "We're good."

To his surprise, Miles ducked to kiss him quickly, lips warm but brief, gone before he could commit them to memory. "Let me know if you ever change your mind."

Before Ren could answer, the door was closing behind Miles with a *click*.

When Hale returned, Ren was on his knees in the same spot, waiting to be comforted.

Chapter Twenty-Eight

The days following his interview, Ren was in a poor mood.

He blamed the mood on Hale's recent behavior toward him. After coming home and finding Ren on the floor, Hale had held him until Ren was smiling again, and then told him he was making a huge mistake.

It wasn't the support Ren had been looking for, and they'd been arguing about it since. Hale couldn't understand why Ren had rejected Miles, and Ren thought his best friend should respect his decision. It was *his* life.

At this point, Ren didn't even want to be around him anymore, so when Hale started again with the "He's such a good guy, Ren. Just give him a chance" on Friday when Ren returned from class, he decided to leave.

"Just because he's a good guy doesn't mean I have to want to date him," Ren grumbled, feeling like a broken record. He tossed his backpack onto his bed. "I'm going to head to Noah's."

"When are you going to be back? We have dinner with Logan and Miles at five."

Ren huffed out a dry laugh. "Yeah, count me out. A double date with someone I'm *not dating* doesn't sound fun to me."

"That's not what this is."

It was, and Ren desperately wished it wasn't. He didn't blame Miles for asking him out, and the suggestion had more than flattered him, but Ren wished he'd never told Hale about it. He and Miles were fine. They'd seen each other a handful of times since the encounter, and there was nothing weird about the way they acted toward each other. Ren would love nothing more than to go to dinner with them, but he didn't trust Hale not to make it into something it wasn't.

"I'm not doing anything with you guys until you're able to wrap your head around the fact that Miles and I aren't going to be together."

"How come you spend all this time moping about being alone and wanting to be loved, and then someone comes along and offers that to you and you aren't even going to *try*?" Hale scoffed. "Do what you want, but the next time you come to me because you think all guys want from you is your body, I'm going to throw this in your face." Hale went into his room then, shutting his door loudly behind himself.

The sound made Ren wince. He wasn't used to Hale being angry at him, but he also couldn't see a simple way out of their current dilemma that didn't end with him giving in.

When he knocked on Noah's door, Julian answered. They stood staring at each other for a moment. Then Julian smiled. "Hey."

"Hi." Ren leaned to look around him into the room. "Your roommate around? I need to vent."

Julian glanced over his shoulder as if he too was checking for Noah. "He's not here. He and Luca went to the grocery store."

"Okay then. I guess I'll go back home." His reluctance must have been obvious, because Jules reached out and grabbed his wrist.

"Want to come in?" he offered. Ren looked down at Julian's hand as he pulled it away. "I might not offer the same quality of sarcasm as Noah, but I can listen."

It would be ideal to not have to return to his own apartment, but he worried it would be uncomfortable to get advice about the current situation from his ex. "It's about a guy ... I don't know if that'll make it weird."

Julian didn't seem surprised. "I think I can handle it, Ren."

This was convincing enough, so Ren walked past Julian into the small room and lay down on the futon. "You heard a bit about it from Noah, I'm guessing?"

Julian shut the door. "Yeah." He took a seat on the floor next to the futon, facing Ren. "I hope that's okay. I asked how you were doing after your breakup, and he kind of unloaded."

"So, you know everything," Ren translated.

"Pretty much. Are you here because of Miles or Hale?"

Ren scoffed and looked upward. The room had those foam ceiling tiles that reminded him of his high school, so he closed his eyes. "They're not mutually exclusive."

"So, both?"

"Hale, mostly, but yes."

As calmly as he could manage, Ren explained his best friend's frustrating behavior and their most recent argument. As he ranted, Julian remained silent, which was very much appreciated. How well Jules listened was something Ren had forgotten.

"I just feel like he's constantly pushing me, even though he knows I hate that shit," Ren finished.

There was a long pause in which Julian seemed to wait to see if he'd say anything else. He spoke only once it was clear that Ren was done. "There's a reason for him to act that way, right?"

Ren glared. "What?"

"I'm not agreeing with him or anything."

"Good," Ren said. They held eye contact for a little too long, and both looked away. "You're not allowed to agree with someone other than me." He had a weird, fond feeling then when he recalled many past conversations, and he remembered he had at one point felt like this all the time.

Why couldn't I just love him?

"So," Julian continued. "Why do you really not want to date Miles?"

The question was abrupt enough to confuse Ren. "What?"

"I know it's not because you don't have feelings for him," Jules claimed. Ren sat up. "I'm sure Hale knows that as well, which is why he's so frustrated with you."

Ren pulled his knees to his chest and tucked his face against them so he didn't have to look at his ex-boyfriend. "I do like him," he admitted. "He's become important to me. Ever since Hale and Logan got together, our relationship has been changing, and I don't want to lose him by ruining things."

There was a loud sigh. A second later, he felt a hand on his knee. He raised his head, surprised to see that Julian had moved to sit on the futon beside him. "You remember why we broke up, right?"

It was a redundant question. Of course Ren remembered.

"If you turn down everyone you know you have the potential to fall in love with, you're never going to be happy in a relationship. You're going to keep repeating us over and over again."

The words shocked him. It wasn't really what Julian said that caught him off guard but that he had yet to consider this himself. His expression must have been easy to read, because Julian smiled. "The fact that you're afraid to lose him, and that you took that chance with me without a second thought, is exactly why you and I didn't work out."

Ren was halfway through the sandwich he'd picked up from the school deli on his way back to the apartment when he started to cry. He stopped eating, his appetite gone, and sat at the table with his head in his hands. He wished he could turn off his emotions, wished he could control the times in which he felt nothing and make now one of them.

It wasn't a thought he enjoyed having. Instead of sitting there and thinking horrible things, he got up from the table and cleaned.

Ren hated cleaning, and for that reason there was a lot for him to do. He gathered his textbooks and magazines from the coffee table, put away the clean laundry sitting in its bin in his bedroom, and pulled all the appliances off the counters in the kitchen to wipe them down.

He hoped that Hale would see this as an apology when he came home, and then they could finally sit down and have a conversation. After talking with Jules, he accepted that he might have been impatient with Hale, and had failed to explain himself well because of it. He was too defensive going into all of their conversations, and whenever Hale disagreed with him, his frustration over his friend's lack of understanding drove him to remove himself from the conversation rather than try to explain it differently.

When Ren was putting the coffeemaker back in its place, his phone rang. Assuming it was Noah calling to talk to him after hearing he'd stopped by from Julian, he pulled the phone from his back pocket.

The caller ID made him pause. It wasn't Noah. Noah's name in his phone was not the vulgar word he was staring at.

Answering was a bad idea, given how pathetic he already felt, but his curiosity got the best of him. "Why are you calling me?" he asked when he picked up.

There was a pause, then his brother laughed in a way people did when something wasn't actually funny. "I didn't think you'd answer."

Ren didn't respond, waiting for the older man to get to the point.

"Dad wanted me to convince you to come home for break," his brother said once the silence got unbearable.

Ren frowned. He hadn't forgotten about his father's offer for him to come home, though he had been hoping his dad would. His father was good at forgetting about Ren, so why would this be any different? "He wanted you to *convince* me?"

"He wants to see you."

Huffing at the ridiculousness of this, Ren brought his hand to his forehead and leaned back against the kitchen counter. "What the hell are you talking about?"

His brother was quiet for a full minute. Ren tried not to let the silence get to him.

"We're still doing this bit, then?" his brother asked. "Playing the victim all the time? Acting like everyone hates you and would rather you be dead?"

Both the words and his brother's bitter tone made him flinch.

"Fucking get over it, Warren. You're not a kid anymore."

Ren laughed. It was funny to hear the person who had made sure he hated himself say such a thing. "I'm like this because of you, asshole," Ren said. "Because of *both* of you."

"Stop blaming your shitty personality on other people. I'll admit that I wasn't the nicest to you when we were growing up, but you're my younger brother, and everyone treats their younger siblings like that. It's not my fault you were too sensitive to handle it."

"Is that your attempt at an apology?"

"I didn't do anything wrong, so no. Dad actually cares about you, and it's unfair for you to blame your faults on him."

"He *cares* about me?" Ren rolled his eyes. "You sound like an idiot. That man doesn't give a shit about me—"

"If he didn't give a shit about you, you would have been put up for adoption like I wanted."

"Should I thank him? If I was put up for adoption, maybe I would have ended up in a family that actually loved me."

"He loves you as much as he *can*." Ren knew what his brother was implying. *He loves you as much as he can love the person who killed his wife.* They were words he'd heard his brother say enough to know.

"It's not enough," Ren said. "Even if it's all he can give me, it hasn't been enough." His eyes pricked with tears again and he blinked them away. His brother tried to speak, but he cut him off. "No, shut the fuck up." To Ren's surprise, he did, and Ren took the few seconds of silence to gather himself. "Do you know what he said to me after I tried to kill myself?" It felt weird to say the words out loud, since he rarely acknowledged this part of his past. To him, it was shameful and terrifying and the lowest he had ever felt. "He said nothing. Because he didn't care."

"What was he supposed to say to you?"

"*Anything.*"

His brother laughed, and this time he sounded truly amused. "You were beyond reasoning with. I mean, you were already having sex with men by that point."

The words made Ren angry, and he said something he shouldn't have. "My biggest regret in life is that when I tried to end it, I didn't do it at home, because I know that if either of you had found me, you would have just let me die and I wouldn't have to deal with this shit now." It immediately made him feel worse, though there was a small reward in his brother hanging up without saying anything else.

"Fuck," Ren said, throwing his phone toward the table and not reacting as it fell to the floor.

He wasn't planning on moving until he'd calmed down some more, but the sound of keys to his left had him lifting his head. The door pushed open and Hale stepped inside. Miles and Logan were in the hall behind him, but neither of them moved. "How long have you been out there?" Ren demanded, though what he really wanted to ask was, *Did you hear what I said?*

The question were answered when Hale began to cry.

"Hale," Ren began, taking a step toward him. "I—"

"Stop," Hale interrupted. "I don't want to hear it right now."

Ren watched, feeling helpless as his best friend crossed their apartment, dragging Logan behind him by the wrist. They went into Hale's bedroom without another word.

Only now did Miles move into the apartment, his expression concerned. "I'm sorry," Ren said, because right then it seemed like the only thing he could say. He began to cry again, covering his face with his hands. "I'm so sorry. Hale, I—" He cut off, his throat burning as he tried to talk through his tears. "It's been the worst fucking day. I didn't mean it."

He felt Miles's hands on his shoulders, gently pulling him forward into a hug.

"I'm really sorry," Ren said again. "I need to apologize to Hale."

"I think you should give him some time," Miles urged. His hand slid up Ren's back to weave through his hair. "How about we go next door and relax? Give them some space to do the same?"

Ren wanted to refuse. He wanted to insist on staying there until Hale came out of his room and talked to him.

But he'd done enough damage for the day, and one look at Miles's face told him it was for the best. "I just want to go to sleep," Ren told him, lowering his gaze to the wet spot on the front of Miles's shirt.

"Yeah," Miles said. The hand in Ren's hair began to stroke. "We can do that."

Chapter Twenty-Nine

Ren woke up disoriented on Saturday. He was alone in Miles's bed, eyelids heavy from all the crying the night before. As he sat up, he looked at the sheets undisturbed on the other side. Last night, Miles had brought Ren to his apartment and helped him into bed. Miles hadn't joined him, instead sitting on the edge of the mattress until Ren fell asleep, comforted by their linked hands. Ren wondered where he had gone after that.

They hadn't talked about anything Miles had overheard. Ren doubted he would have been able to get the words out in that state, though he would have tried if Miles had asked. The topic would have to be broached now that he had gathered himself. He knew if he wasn't ready, he could say so; Miles would respect his feelings, but it wasn't something Ren wished to hide. Trying to kill himself was part of his past, and now that Miles knew, he wanted a chance to explain why, and to promise that it was something he no longer wanted to do.

After rubbing his eyes thoroughly to wake up, Ren pushed away the covers to get out of bed. Before he could stand, the door to the room cracked open and Miles peeked in. "Oh good," he said when he noticed Ren awake. He kicked the door open farther, revealing a plate with toast, eggs, and bacon. "I made breakfast. Sorry it's not much."

"This is enough," Ren assured as Miles handed him the plate. "Should I eat in the dining room?"

"Nah." Miles sat on the edge of the bed. "Stay there. Breakfast in bed is good for you."

Ren took a bite of toast. "Thank you," he said once he finished chewing. "Not just for the food. I mean … thanks for last night, too."

"I didn't do anything."

"If I had stayed in my apartment, I would have made things worse by pounding on Hale's door all night until he agreed to speak to me. He and I weren't in a good place already, and last night I had decided to talk to him about everything instead of just getting defensive, and I somehow made it worse before getting the chance to."

"Hale's okay," Miles said. "Logan texted me. He was just upset with you last night, but I think you can go over and talk to him now."

The idea made him nervous, and Ren hated it. "I'm kind of pathetic," he said, pausing for a minute to eat some more. "I'm afraid to go over there. He's the most important person in the world to me, and every time I fuck up, I can't help but wonder what to do if he doesn't forgive me."

"He'll forgive you."

"I know that," Ren snapped, feeling impatient. "But what if he *doesn't?*"

"Then you make it up to him somehow."

Ren took another bite of toast. "I'm not all that good at apologies."

"I know this about you."

"What's that supposed to mean?"

Miles gave him an *Are you serious* expression, as if Ren had forgotten about his unreasonable behavior toward him for years because of his pride.

"Kidding," Ren added.

Nodding, Miles turned his face away. "You seem like you feel a lot better."

"I do," Ren confirmed. "I mean, nothing's been resolved, and I still have a lot of shit to figure out, but I think crying and being totally pathetic for an entire night helped. Usually, I just shut down or drink too much and feel like shit the next day."

"That's good." Miles peeked at him from the corner of his eye. "Last night on the phone … who was it?"

Ren finished the toast and moved on to the bacon. "My brother," he admitted. "He called to talk about me going home over break. He still lives with my dad." When Miles said nothing, Ren asked, "Do you want me to tell you about it?"

"Your phone call?"

"That," Ren began, setting the half-eaten plate of food on the TV table Miles had beside his bed, "and what you overheard me say."

Miles looked as if this was unexpected. He didn't give Ren an answer.

It made Ren uncomfortable. "Don't you want to know why I did it? Or how?"

Now Miles appeared horrified. "I don't want to know how."

"That's fine."

"You don't have to tell me anything," Miles assured. "Of course I'm curious about why … I want to know everything about you. But if you're not comfortable—"

"I wouldn't have brought it up if I wasn't comfortable telling you," Ren interrupted. He met Miles's gaze. "I'm not gonna say it isn't difficult for me to talk about, because it is. That was the worst time of my life, and talking about it is just a reminder of how low I can go, but it's in the past, and it's something I need to remember so it never gets that bad again."

Miles hesitated, then reached out to take Ren's hand between his own. They'd held hands until Ren had fallen asleep the night before and he had thought nothing of it then, but now Ren felt hyperaware of the touch. "Please tell me what you're comfortable sharing," said Miles.

It took Ren a moment to gather himself before speaking, the words difficult to find. "You remember what I told you about my mom, right?"

"That she died in childbirth."

"It ruined my relationship with my brother and father, and to avoid making it any worse, I tried my best to do everything right. I got good grades, my teachers liked me, I picked up after myself, and I spent a lot of time away from home so they could do their best to forget about me. It didn't change how my brother treated me, but my father was indifferent toward me, and that was better than cruelty. I've always had depression, but I never wanted to bring it up, so I went unmedicated for longer than I should have."

Miles was watching him intensely enough that Ren found it difficult to look back at him. He still tried to, wanting to monitor his reaction to the story.

"I was close with my best friend," Ren continued. "We met in kindergarten. He knew about everything with my family and was more than happy to give me a place to run away to. We spent all our time together, and as I got a little older and realized I didn't like girls, I started to think of him as more than just a friend."

The look on Miles's face made Ren wonder if he was jealous or just uncomfortable with the topic. "It didn't work out?"

"Obviously not." A bitter chuckle left him. "He and I aren't even friends anymore. It's fine. I don't miss him. Hale's so much better, anyway." There was a sharp prang in his chest when he thought of the night before. "He deserves a lot better than me."

The hands around Ren's tightened. "I don't think that's true," Miles mumbled. "Neither does Hale."

His heart squeezed again, though this time with a pained sort of delight. They were nice words, but he did not feel deserving of them. "Why are you so nice to me?"

"You already know why."

All he could manage was "Ah." Embarrassed, he glanced away.

"Keep telling your story, Ren."

"Right. Well, eventually he confessed to me, and I told him I felt the same way. We were young and stupid and had sex pretty much right away, which would have been fine if my dad hadn't found us in bed together the next morning."

Miles grimaced, as if even imagining the embarrassment was too much for him. The reaction made Ren laugh, lifting his spirits even though he was getting to the hardest part of his story to recount.

"It shocked my dad, obviously, and my best friend wasn't ready to come out to his own family, so he dumped me and removed himself from my life."

"Oh," Miles said. "You were all alone."

There was a thick feeling in Ren's throat. "Yeah," he said. It came out strained, and Miles lifted his head. "I was all alone, and I didn't know what else to do."

"You're not alone now."

"I know," Ren acknowledged. "I *do*. I didn't mean what I said on the phone yesterday. I was just sick of my brother never understanding how it felt for me, and I was trying to make him angry."

"As long as that's all it was."

Ren leaned forward, closing some of the distance between them. "I promise." He twisted his hand in Miles's to link their pinkies. It lasted for only a moment before Miles pulled away.

"You should go talk to Hale," he advised. "You'll feel better once you do."

While Ren was sure that was true, he didn't want to leave yet. Miles stood and took a step away from him, but Ren was quick to catch his wrist. "Wait," he said. "I don't want to go."

"*Ren*." Miles sighed. "It's for the best that you do."

"Why?"

A frustrated noise left Miles. "Because this isn't easy for me. You being here in my bed, wearing my clothes. I almost can't stand it." He was probably expecting Ren to withdraw his hand upon hearing these words, but he didn't.

"Do you want to have sex?" Ren asked.

Hazel eyes widened before Miles let out a dry laugh. "I always want to have sex with you," he said. "Now get out of my bed."

"I don't want to." Ren knew what he was getting himself into, but just like last time, he didn't care.

"*Ren*."

"I'm okay with it if you are," Ren said. "Why don't we do it?"

With a sharp motion, Miles pulled his wrist free. "I don't need a pity fuck." He moved away from the bed.

"That's not what this is. If anything, don't you think in this situation, you'd be the one pitying me?"

"I don't pity you. If anything, I think you're very strong."

Again, tears pricked at Ren's eyes. "That's why I want to have sex with you."

"You're asking me to sleep with you? Me, who's in love with you? You want me to put aside my feelings?" Miles asked.

"I don't want that. You're allowed to feel however you want."

A bitter expression came over Miles's face. "But nothing will come of it."

Ren lowered his gaze to his lap. "I don't know that."

He heard footsteps, and then Miles grabbed his chin and lifted his head to look into his eyes. His expression was a mix of confusion and hope. It was beautiful.

"Nothing will come of it right away," Ren admitted, trying to be transparent because he owed Miles as much. "Afterward, I'm still not going to be ready to date you. I still need time to figure out some things with myself first … but I can't say it'll never happen, or that I haven't considered it and haven't wanted it."

Miles groaned. "Alright."

He ducked to kiss Ren before he could vocalize his surprise. When Miles pulled away, he ripped his shirt over his head as Ren watched with a shacked jaw, shocked he was getting his way. "This is the last time, though. I'm not interested in being your fuck buddy."

"I don't want that either," Ren assured. Surely, such a relationship would cause him to fall in love, and that wasn't how he wanted to go about it. Miles deserved more than that.

Ren wondered whether sex with Miles would always feel this good. He'd written off the intensity of their first time as a fluke, assuming they'd just been so pent up after Miles's fight with Sawyer, but once again, it felt amazing to have Miles push inside him. Ren was beginning to think Miles was just good at it.

He was on his back, arms and legs wrapped around the other man. It made it difficult for Miles to pull too far out of him, so his thrusts were shallow but direct.

"So fucking good," Ren told him, over and over. He wished he could give Miles what he wanted. Wished he could tell him he loved him and wanted to be with him, but he wasn't there yet, and he hoped praise was enough. "Miles—"

"Stop." It was growled right into his ear.

Ren shivered and squeezed and once again said, "*Miles.*"

A hand covered his mouth, and Ren cracked his eyes open. Their gazes locked. He wasn't sure what to expect, but it certainly wasn't Miles breathing out, "I love you so fucking much."

It was what Ren had always wanted to hear, and he closed his eyes so he didn't cry.

He felt so warm and so loved. So safe in Miles's arms that he didn't want to ever leave.

He came hot across his own stomach, triggering Miles's release. The hand over his mouth slipped away as Miles relaxed down onto him and Ren pressed his lips to Miles's shoulder.

"I'm so sorry," Ren said, breaking the silence. With a groan, Miles rolled off him, onto the other side of the bed. Ren couldn't imagine how he felt right then. When they had sex, Ren got to feel loved and Miles got to feel used. "It was unfair of me to ask you to do that."

"It was," Miles agreed. "But I enjoyed myself, and I didn't have to say yes, so don't feel too bad about it." He covered his face with his hands. "Do you at least feel better?"

"I didn't have sex with you to make myself feel better," Ren said, sitting up. "I did it because I wanted to." Using a tissue from the box by Miles's bed, he wiped down his stomach.

Through his fingers, Miles watched. "The next time you want to have sex, find someone else."

Ren raised his eyebrows. "You're cool with that? The last guy I had sex with, you punched in the face."

It made Miles laugh, but he didn't for long. "I have to be cool with it, Ren. That's the position you're putting me in. You have to be okay with me finding someone else too."

It was a fair thing to say, but Ren wasn't cool with that. He said as much, and Miles moved his hand to look at him more directly. "I haven't rejected you yet," said Ren.

"You have."

"Well, I'm taking it back. I want more time to think about it."

Miles sighed. "You're stringing me along."

"Would you prefer I turn you down, even though you have a chance?"

"I won't wait forever."

Nodding, because this seemed more than reasonable, Ren agreed, "Okay."

He didn't say it out loud, but he hoped Miles wouldn't have to wait long.

When Ren returned to his apartment, he went straight to Hale's bedroom. The door was closed, but when he tried the knob, it wasn't locked. He went in without knocking.

Logan and Hale were sitting up in bed together. They fell silent at the sight of him. After a long pause, Logan leaned over to kiss Hale's forehead and climbed out of bed. He smiled at Ren as he passed, calming his nerves just in time for him and Hale to be left alone.

The light was dim, but Ren could still see signs that his friend had been crying. Sighing, he went to take Logan's spot in bed.

He lay down and hugged Hale around his waist, pressing his face into his hip. "I love you."

A hand settled onto the top of his head. "I love you, too. That's why I don't want you to think things like that."

"I don't actually think that," Ren promised. "My brother called to talk about me coming home for break, and he was being difficult, so I said it to make him angry."

Hale's hand slid away, and Ren lifted his head to look up at him. "That you even thought to say that tells me you think things like that sometimes, even if you don't do it seriously."

"I won't anymore."

While Hale didn't seem fully convinced, he nodded.

"I'm sorry I upset you," Ren continued. "Last night, and before that, with Miles. I've been so short with you lately that we haven't been able to have an actual conversation, and it wasn't fair of me to get so upset with you when I haven't clearly explained my feelings."

"I've been unfair to you as well," Hale admitted. "I shouldn't have been pushing you … I just … he loves you so much, Ren. It's what you've always wanted, and you're perfect for each other. I only want what's best for you."

"I know you do." Ren hid his face against Hale's hip. "Jules told me that if I keep turning away people I could fall in love with, I'm never going to have the relationship I want. It's true, but it's scary. I want to find love, but that also puts me in a situation I haven't been in in years, and I can't help but remember how it ended the last time. If I fall in love with Miles, and he decides he doesn't want me, I don't know if I could handle it. I've gone through that once already, and I was so miserable I wanted to die."

Hale moved down the mattress to lie beside him. "I'm really happy you didn't kill yourself," he whispered.

"Me too." Ren closed his eyes. "Do you think you could give me a little more time to figure things out? I think I need to be in a better place before I date again."

"You can have more than a little time," Hale assured. "I'm sorry for pushing you."

The apology was welcome, but Ren shook his head, dismissing it. It was already behind them, and he didn't want to think about fighting with Hale any longer. There were far more important things for him to begin thinking about.

Finally, Ren was going to stop focusing on the past and start considering his future.

Chapter Thirty

The semester was ending in less than a week, and Hale insisted they host a get-together the weekend before finals. It was a small group of people—only Logan, Miles, and Noah joined them—but Ren felt that everyone who needed to be there was.

It was a relaxing day. They watched Christmas movies, drank hot chocolate, and decorated the tiny tree Hale insisted they set up every year, even though neither of them would be there to appreciate it over break. Miles took pictures, Hale and Noah sang Christmas carols, Logan strung lights on the tree, and Ren thought maybe everything was going to be okay.

He was sitting on the couch, smiling as he watched his friends cling to each other and sing off-key, when Miles claimed the seat beside him. Things between them had been tense, but not in the same way they had been before the semester began. The tension now was more charged, and a steady increase in his heartbeat accompanied it whenever they were together. Eyes lingered too long and his palms sweat. It reminded Ren of what falling in love felt like.

"Hi," Ren greeted. "Did you get good pictures?"

"I think so." Miles dropped his gaze to the screen on his camera, so Ren didn't feel too embarrassed about gazing at him openly. He was looking at Miles's bruises from Sawyer—they had faded to look like shadows—and thinking about how they had come from Miles defending him.

Before long, Miles turned his camera toward Ren to show him a picture of himself and Hale close together in front of the Christmas tree.

Ren smiled. "Cute."

"It is," Miles agreed. "You've looked happier lately."

"Have I?"

Miles nodded. "Yeah. I've seen you laughing more, or when I spot you somewhere on campus by yourself, you don't look as distant as you used to."

"Ah. Well, I've been trying to figure my shit out," he said. He considered telling Miles the reason, but it was embarrassing to admit he wanted to be less of a wreck so they could be together, so he decided on a white lie. "You know they hired me for that journalist job, right?"

Miles's expression told him he did not know. "Congrats. That means you're staying in the area, doesn't it?"

"It does," Ren confirmed. "But anyway, since I now have an adult job, I thought I should try handling my problems like an adult. I talked to my doctor and I'm going to stop drinking, and I'm still staying away from cigarettes. I also said I would go to therapy, but I'm struggling with that a bit. It's hard to talk about your problems when you've spent so long avoiding them."

"That's great," Miles praised. "You feel better?"

"I think so."

The way Miles looked at him was too intense, so Ren glanced back to Noah and Hale. His roommate met his eyes and smiled. "It hasn't been that long since I committed to this. There are days when I feel I could use a drink to blow off some steam, but I've refrained so far."

"Well, let me know if I can do anything to help."

Ren bit his lip. Something else that would help him relieve stress came to mind, but it was off the table.

"So, are you starting work right away?" Miles asked.

"I'm waiting to start until after break." Nervously, he twisted his hands in his lap. "I'll be at home."

Immediately, Miles's eyebrows pulled together. "Will you be alright?"

"I think so. I'm going to stay for the holidays and see how it goes. If it's too much, I can always come back here." The troubled expression didn't leave Miles's face. "I'd be lying if I said I wasn't nervous. I'll have to deal with my brother, and I have a very strained relationship with my father, but I haven't been home in years, and I figured it was time."

"I hope it goes well." Almost nervously, Miles glanced away. "Um … could I give you my phone number? You can call me anytime you want to. I mean, if things are tough and you need someone to talk to."

It seemed obvious that Ren would call Hale in that situation, but he still handed Miles his phone. "It's kind of crazy I don't already have your number," Ren said. "Text yourself, so you have mine too."

"Sure." The smile that curled up Miles's lips betrayed his excitement. "I promise I won't annoy you or anything."

"You can sometimes."

Miles's eyebrows raised.

"I wouldn't give you my number if I never expected you to use it."

Finished entering his number, Miles returned his phone. "Oh."

Embarrassed, Ren averted his eyes. "What will you be doing over break?" he asked.

"I'm going to be staying my with my aunt for a while. My parents' anniversary is on the last day of the year, and it's their twenty-fifth, so they'll be taking a vacation, just the two of them."

Ren wished he knew what it was like to have happy parents. "That's sweet."

"Yeah," Miles said. "Christmas without them will be weird, but I'm close with my cousin, so it'll be fun to stay with him."

"Nice." This sounded a little too generic for Ren's liking, so he added, "I always wished I had cousins. Hale is super close to his, and I get jealous."

"It's awesome," Miles claimed. "I don't have siblings, so it's nice having someone around my age in my family. He's a year older than me, but we've always been close." The way he spoke about his family made envy stir in Ren's chest, but he also wanted to hear more. He knew little about Miles.

"Tell me more about your family." It came out like a demand. "Please."

Expression unsure, Miles said. "I can, but why?"

"I can tell when you talk about them how much they mean to you, so I'd like to hear more."

Miles raised his mug of hot chocolate to his lips. "Alright. But only if you'll tell me more about yourself as well."

Ren thought of what to say. Nothing pleasant came to mind. "A lot of things about me aren't fun to talk about."

"There's nothing?" Miles asked. "It doesn't have to be about your family or your past."

It only seemed fair to trade stories about Miles's family with stories about his own. "I could tell you about my grandmother," Ren offered after a pause. "I've been staying with her for the past few years, but she moved into a nursing home recently."

"You have a good relationship?"

"Yeah." He smiled. "She took good care of me. She never treated me any differently, even though she loved my mom."

"Is she your mom's mother?"

Ren shook his head. "No. I never met my mom's parents. They're still alive, but they weren't close with my mom and want nothing to do with my family. The only grandparent I have is my dad's mom. She's been taking care of me since I was in high school. After my attempt, my dad didn't know what to do and sent me to live with her. This will be the first Christmas in years I won't be spending with her."

"Are you going to visit her when you're home?"

It was part of Ren's plan for break, but it occurred to him he was only talking about himself. "I thought you were going to tell me about your family first."

Miles's smile was mischievous, as if he'd redirected the conversation to Ren on purpose. "Fine," he said. "What do you want to know?"

"What will you tell me?"

"Pretty much anything."

Ren turned on the couch to face him, pulling his leg up and tucking it beneath himself. "Tell me anything, then."

What Miles chose didn't matter. As long as it was something about him, Ren wanted to hear it.

When the visitors were getting ready to leave, Ren went into his bedroom to grab the stack of papers from on top of his dresser.

It wasn't a gift, and he hadn't been sure when he printed it whether he would end up giving it to Miles, but it felt right. He went back out into the living room and handed him the stack. When Miles raised his eyebrows, Ren explained, "It's my short story. The one I was writing in the library that you asked if you could read."

"Oh," Miles said, in a way that also implied thank you. "You finished."

"It was for class, so I had to."

Nodding, Miles raised his eyes from the pages. "You're sure you want to give me this?"

Ren recalled what he has said to Miles in the library that day. *"I'd feel like I was giving you something of myself that I couldn't take back."* It felt different now. He'd already given Miles a part of himself, even if Miles hadn't realized it.

"You can have it," Ren confirmed. "Let me know what you think."

"Sure." Miles bit his lip, and Ren thought about what it was like to kiss him. "I don't know if I'll see you this week. I'm going home after I present my final project tomorrow."

"Good luck."

When Miles spoke again, his voice was low, only for Ren's ears. "You can call me whenever, okay? Even if you just want to talk."

The pace of Ren's heart quickened. He felt ridiculous. It was *Miles.* How could so much have changed between them so quickly?

"Okay," he said. "Have a good break, Miles."

"Yeah." He raised a hand to touch Ren's cheek for just a second. "I'll see you in two months."

"See you." The words came out in a long breath. It was embarrassing how affected he sounded but worth it when Miles grinned.

I'm going to fix myself, Ren thought. The promise was meant for both of them, though he didn't say it out loud. *When we see each again, I'm going to make sure I'm in the right place for a relationship.*

Chapter Thirty-One

On the thirtieth of December, Ren was hiding in his childhood bedroom when Hale called.

He answered before the second ring. "Hey. You know you don't have to call me every day, right? I mean, I love talking to you, but I'm really doing okay."

It wasn't a lie. He'd been home for two weeks already, and although things between him and his family were awkward, they weren't as bad as Ren had been preparing himself for. His brother and father mostly ignored his presence, and Ren didn't mind slipping throughout the house silently like a ghost.

"I want to talk to you this often," Hale said. "You might not need an escape from your family, but I do."

Hale had a crazy family. He was his parents' only child, but his aunt lived in the house next door, and Ren knew from countless stories that Hale's cousins were constantly over. Ren would have liked to meet them, but Hale lived far enough away that it was inconvenient for weekend trips, and he always turned Hale down when he offered him a place to stay for longer than that, refusing to be an inconvenience.

"How's everyone doing?" Ren asked.

Hale gave a long groan in response. "They're exhausting. My cousins don't live here but I can never get away from them, and my mom is being insufferable."

"Your mom?" This was the first time Hale had complained to him about his mother this break. "What'd your mom do?"

There was another noise of distress, this one heavier than the last. "She found me my dream job and is pestering me to apply."

Ren had been scrolling through social media on his laptop as they spoke, and he paused at this. "Huh?"

"She knows someone whose wife works at a publishing company, and they're looking for a junior editor."

The job sounded exactly like what Hale was looking for, and Ren let out a happy laugh. "Well, shit. And your mom has an in? That's amazing. You have to apply. Why *wouldn't* you apply?"

For a long moment, Hale was silent. By the time he spoke, Ren had put it together on his own. "It's in the city here, Ren. I'd be ten hours away from you and Logan. I don't think that's what I want."

It wasn't what Ren wanted, either. "You can't move back home," he told him, though when he said it, he knew it wasn't right. "Fuck. You have to apply."

"I know I do. I will. I just need a little more time to wrap my head around it, and my mom is pressuring me to get it done as soon as possible."

"Is there a deadline?"

"No. They'll take down the job once they find someone."

"Then you should apply as soon as you can," Ren said. "God, I can't believe you're going to be moving back home."

Hale laughed. "I'm just applying. There's no guarantee I'll get the job."

"Why wouldn't you? They're stupid if they don't want you." He was happy for Hale but sad for himself, unable to imagine them living so far apart. Ren was sure that someone else felt the same way. "Have you talked to Logan about this?"

The groan Hale let out answered the question for him. "I don't know how to bring it up," he said. "I will. If I apply, I'll talk to him about it."

"*When* you apply," Ren corrected.

There was a pause. "Yeah. When I apply. I just … I don't want to worry him for no reason, you know?"

"You don't think he'll take it well?"

"I don't know how he'll take it." Hale sighed. "I don't want to talk about this anymore. I came to hide in my room because I wanted to avoid talking about this."

"Okay." Ren resumed scrolling on his laptop. "What do you want to talk about, then?"

Without pause, Hale asked, "Have you been in contact with Miles?"

The question was unexpected. Hale had been laying off the Miles topic lately.

"Um … no? I haven't had a reason to reach out."

"You know that's not why he gave you his number. You don't have to have a reason," said Hale. "Have you wanted to reach out to him?"

Ren had. More than once, he'd taken out his phone and held his thumb over Miles's contact. He had yet to press down.

"We'll talk when break is over," Ren said. "I want to have more figured out when I see him again."

"How are you going to do that?"

"Just being home is helping, I think. Before I got here, the idea of being in this house was suffocating, but the longer I spend here and I'm fine, the better I feel about all that's happened here." Ren grimaced. "I don't know if that makes any sense—"

Hale cut in. "If it's how you feel, it's how you feel. It doesn't need to make sense."

"Thanks." Ren pushed his laptop off his lap and rolled over to lie on his side. "I think I want to have a conversation with my dad before I leave. I think I need to know how he feels about me, once and for all."

There was a pause. "Are you prepared for that?"

Ren hated that he hesitated. "I am," he forced out. "I mean … it's going to hurt, but I'm used to that and I can handle it."

"I'm sorry that's a conversation you even feel you need to have."

"It's alright," he assured. "Now, let's stop talking about serious stuff."

Hale hummed in agreement. "Did Noah tell you his mom forced him to go on a blind date with her coworker's son because she thought the reason he's never had a girlfriend is because he's gay?"

This wasn't something Ren had heard, and it made him laugh for a full minute.

Despite telling Hale he didn't need to call him every day, Ren was happy Hale did call. These lively conversations with his friend kept him sane in that quiet house.

The house was empty that afternoon, so Ren ventured into the living room. He sat on the couch with a book, but it took him a long time to start reading.

Ren tried to recall the last time he'd sat on this couch. It wasn't important, but he still wished he could remember. It was called a *living* room for a reason, but he'd never been comfortable enough in this house to consider any place but his bedroom his living room.

By the time his brother came home, Ren had read only a few pages of his novel. When the door opened, Ren didn't raise his gaze, though he could tell it was his brother by the way all sounds abruptly stopped. Ren's whole body felt tense.

"What are you doing?" his brother asked.

Ren let out a breath he didn't know he had been holding in, and lifted his head. "Reading."

"Did you at least clean up around here or something when we were gone?"

"I don't know where the cleaning supplies are." *This is not my home*, Ren wanted to remind.

There was a loud huff, as if Ren was truly exasperating, and then a mumbled accusation that Ren was useless. His brother crossed the room toward the kitchen.

Ren spoke again before he'd determined whether it was a good idea to. "When was the last time I sat on this couch, do you think?"

His brother slowed to a stop. His expression asked, *What the fuck?* But he said, "Probably never? It's a new fucking couch and you haven't been here in years."

Surprised, Ren glanced down at the cushions once more. He couldn't keep himself from laughing. If it was a new couch, he couldn't tell, and that in itself was funny. The house somehow felt even more removed from him. He didn't know that was possible.

His brother called him crazy before walking off, and Ren closed his book. He didn't want to be there anymore. It was a stranger's home, and he was an intruder.

The diner that Ren would go to often when he was younger, before he went to live with his grandmother, was a few blocks from his father's house.

Without telling his brother, Ren left and walked there from memory.

He had considered driving the old car his grandmother had gifted him when he'd visited her at the nursing home for Christmas, but his brother's car was in the way and he didn't want to ask him to move it.

It wasn't a long walk, but Ren's nose and ears were cold by the time he was pushing open the diner's door. He welcomed the wave of heat that hit him. Curious, he glanced around. Not much had changed over the years. It still smelled of coffee and bacon, and he took a deep breath before going to sit in a booth along the front windows.

Before long, a familiar man approached his table with a menu. They had gone to school together, and he was part of the reason Ren hadn't been to the diner in many years.

"Lucas Gardner," Ren greeted, lowering his gaze when the menu dropped onto the table in front of him. "Thanks."

"You're in town for the holidays?" Lucas asked. "You're never in town."

"Yeah, well." Ren shrugged. "Life happens. I'm glad to see your parents kept this place open. You working here over break?"

Lucas's eyes averted. "I dropped out about two years ago. I'm just working here as I figure some things out."

They were not close enough to discuss it further, so Ren asked for a water and focused on his menu.

It only bought him about a minute free of small talk, but it was enough for him to decide on what he wanted so he could send Lucas away again. When Lucas returned with his drink, Ren ordered the lunch special and handed him the menu.

"Oh," Lucas said, as if taking his order wasn't his job. "Right, sure." He accepted the menu but didn't leave like Ren had been hoping. "Hey, does Rhett know you're in town?"

At the sound of his ex's name, Ren's fingers curled around his water glass. He thought Lucas would know better than to bring him up. As Ren's replacement as Rhett's best friend, he figured Lucas knew everything that had happened between the two of them.

"Why would he?" Ren asked.

Lucas's hazel eyes widened, and Ren thought there was something familiar about them. "Well, I just know he'd like to see you."

This seemed doubtful, and Ren opened his mouth to say as much, but the words froze in his throat with shock as a red-haired man pushed through the saloon doors from the kitchen. At first Ren thought it was just someone who looked like Miles, because there was no reason for him to be there. He realized how wrong he was when the redhead smiled at a person across the counter. Ren knew that smile. It was his polite customer service smile, and he'd seen it at the bar countless times.

"Miles?" Ren asked, more to himself than the man across the diner. It wasn't a large place, and Miles looked up from the mug he was filling with coffee. They made eye contact.

There was a moment in which Ren could see Miles going through the same thought process he had, his expression first confused before shifting into something warm. A look of pain took it over as he poured hot coffee over his knuckles. He dropped the mug, and a loud crack sounded as it broke against the floor.

Ren laughed and tried to cover the sound with his hand.

Lucas seemed confused. "You know my cousin?"

"Your cousin?" Ren asked. He remembered Miles telling him of his plans to stay with his aunt for break. "Oh." When he glanced back toward the counter, he realized Miles was already halfway to him, the customer he had been with watching him leave with a frown.

"You know Warren?" Lucas asked as he approached.

Miles made a face, as if the use of Ren's given name was bothersome. "I do." Grinning at Ren, he slid into the booth across from him. "Lucas, go clean up the mug I broke."

"Why should I—" Lucas began to question.

Miles cut him off. "Oh! And please give the girl at the counter some coffee."

Lucas just stood there for a long moment. When Miles didn't give him any attention, he huffed and went to do as told.

Ren watched him leave. He found it hard to look at Miles right then. The way Miles was staring made him feel very warm, and he was nervous to meet the other man's gaze. "I don't think he wrote down my order."

"Ren." The sound was gentle, and Ren forced himself to look across the table. He was sure his cheeks were red.

"What are you doing here?" Miles asked, sounding completely delighted.

"I live here," Ren responded. "Well, I grew up here is probably a better thing to say."

Laughing, Miles leaned back in the booth and braced his hands on the edge of the table. The hand he had burned with coffee was red. Ren thought it must hurt.

"How have I not seen you before?" Miles asked. "I've been coming here since I was a kid."

"I don't eat here very often," Ren admitted. He curled his fingers into fists in his lap. "I used to eat here a lot in middle school, though, so maybe we saw each other at some point."

Miles rested his chin in his palm. "I think I would have remembered."

Sighing in defeat to his desires, Ren reached out and grabbed Miles's wrist, pulling his hand out from under his chin and holding the back of it against his glass of cold water, hoping to soothe his burn.

With an expression Ren could only describe as fond, Miles looked down at their hands. "They call you Warren at home?"

"I don't go by anything at home," Ren responded. He released Miles's wrist, but before he could pull his hand back, Miles caught it and laced their fingers together. "People don't really talk to me around here."

"So, does that mean you're free for New Year's?"

Miles was grinning. Ren was so happy he had come home for break.

Chapter Thirty-Two

Miles and Ren went out for a late dinner.

Miles picked him up outside the Cleckner house and drove to the restaurant without guidance. It almost felt like they were in Miles's hometown, not Ren's, and Ren wondered how often Miles had visited. He wasn't going to say anything about it, but then Miles pulled into the parking lot of a place he didn't recognize and Ren couldn't help but laugh.

"Is this not a good choice?" asked Miles.

"No, it's fine," Ren assured. "I'm laughing because I didn't even know this place existed and it's funny to me that you know more about where I grew up than I do."

"They opened about a year ago. You said you haven't visited in a while, right? I've probably spent more time here than you these past few years."

"Probably," Ren agreed. "Do you think we would have run into each other sooner if I had been coming home this whole time?"

Miles shut off his car. "I do, but I'm not sure that would have been a good thing."

Ren raised his eyebrows.

"You weren't exactly my biggest fan," Miles reminded.

It was strange to think about. "I could have never imagined we'd end up here." Ren gazed out the windshield at the restaurant. "Is this a date?"

"That's supposed to be my question. You're the one opposed to us dating."

For a long moment, Ren considered it. Did he want it to be a date?

That probably wasn't the right question, because yes, he did, but it was still giving him pause.

Am I in the right space to be dating?

"Should we go in?" asked Miles.

"This is a date," Ren declared, ignoring the question. He looked at the man in the driver's seat. "I don't think I'm fixed or all my issues are solved, but they probably never will be, and I think I've been doing a lot better since returning home. I wanted to be even better before I saw you again, but it feels like us running into each other here is…" He trailed off, not wanting to say something that would make him sound silly, like it had been fate or a sign. "It's good. And so I want to go on a date."

Miles crossed his arms on top of his steering wheel and leaned into them, head still turned toward him.

"Is that cool?" Ren asked, feeling self-conscious.

"It can be whatever you want it to be, Ren."

Nodding, Ren unbuckled his seat belt. "Let's get to our date, then."

After dinner, there still were three hours left in the year, and Ren had no desire to spend them with anyone else.

They drove around town for a while and then parked in an empty lot when it became clear there was nothing else either of them was interested in doing. It was already late, and the only places still open were bars and restaurants, all of which were bound to be packed. While Ren typically didn't mind crowded places, the chances of him running into his old classmates while out were too great for him to risk it.

He and Miles spent the time talking about a lot of things.

Hale and Logan, both of their Christmases, how Ren was doing at his father's house and how Miles was doing at his aunt and uncle's.

It is nice. Besides talking to Hale every day, he hadn't been able to have a proper conversation with anyone since break started.

They were discussing how much time Miles spent in the area over the past few years when Ren asked, "Have you ever dated someone from around here?" He was curious to know whether he had met one of Miles's exes.

"Ahh," Miles said. The look on his face was sheepish. "Not really? I mean, in middle school I had my first kiss with some girl named Mindy Lienburg, and we texted for the rest of the summer, but nothing came of it."

When Ren tried to place the name and wasn't able to, he was actually a little relieved. He imagined he'd compare himself to her and end up feeling bad. "When did you realize you were attracted to men?"

"I don't know. Forever ago? It wasn't like something happened and I realized. It's just how it always was. I've only dated girls before, though. All of my exes approached me first. Before you, there was no one I was interested in pursuing."

He could have just said that to flatter him. It worked.

"Have you kissed other men?" Ren asked.

Miles cringed. "I've kissed one other guy," he admitted, not sounding too happy about it. "He frequented the bar and would flirt with me a lot. One day he got bold, and I just went with it."

Ren's chest got unpleasantly tight. "Does he still come to see you?"

"Are you jealous?" The smile Miles wore was mischievous.

Ren thought he was so hot.

He scoffed, but he was jealous, so he said nothing. Miles reached over to take his hand. "Don't be jealous. I've never felt this way about anyone before. Ex-girlfriends included."

"I hate how easy it is for you to manipulate my emotions."

"I'm not manipulating you."

"I know," Ren told him. "It scares me, how sincere you are."

Sighing, Miles pressed his forehead into their clasped hands and closed his eyes. "Want to talk about something different, then?"

"Yeah."

Miles raised his head. "Okay. Can I ask you about your short story?"

"You actually read it?" Ren felt his cheeks getting hot. "That's kind of embarrassing."

"You're the one who gave it to me to read."

"You can ask me about it … Did you like it?"

"I did," Miles assured. "It's well written. I was just wondering why you'd end it like that?"

Ren didn't need clarification. At the end of his short story, the couple parted ways. "I told you it had to be about something bittersweet. Right person, wrong time. Love isn't always easy."

"It was sad. I think you should write an epilogue where they meet again when they're older and it's the right time."

Ren smiled, pleased that Miles cared so much about something he created. "You know they're fictional, right? They don't have a future."

"I don't know why, but it feels important."

"I'll consider it," Ren offered, though he didn't think he'd be spending any more time on something he had written for a class. Over the past two weeks, he'd finally written for himself again and had already drafted part of a novel he was looking forward to continuing.

He noticed the time on the dashboard. "Oh, hey. We're almost there."

"That went by fast." Miles sounded bummed. "Shall we do some year-end reflection?"

"Why not?" Ren was trying to seem unphased even though his heart was pounding. He wondered whether Miles would kiss him at midnight. "There's not much to talk about. I think it's been a good year, despite some of the shitty things that have happened. Hale got a boyfriend, and I feel like I've gotten at least some of my shit together. I hope next year is even better."

"I'm sure it will be," Miles said. "I mean, you have graduation and your new job to look forward to. You get to be a proper adult."

"That's not really all that exciting when you take taxes into account." Ren glanced at the dashboard again, just as the time switched to 11:58. "What about you? What are some good things that happened to you this year?"

"Well, there was the photography exhibition, and I took a trip this past summer to the Pacific Northwest and got to take some good photos. Hale and Logan got together, and I've gotten to see my best friend happier than he's ever been before. I feel like I've gotten closer to you, which is something I've wanted for years, so it feels good to have made some progress. It was a great year."

When Miles met his eyes again, Ren bit his lip. "That's one of mine too," he added. "This … Us doing whatever it is we're doing. I think you've motivated me to be a better version of myself."

Miles reached out to cup his face. "Don't worry about that too much," he said. "I like all versions of you, you know."

"I can't say the same about myself."

"Do you like who you are now?"

"Right this minute?" He glanced at the time again. 11:59. *How long until it changes?* "These days, I usually like who I am around you."

Miles grinned. "I'm glad." He turned his face to the dashboard. "Happy New Year."

Not looking at the clock, Ren mumbled the words back to him. *This is where he kisses me,* he thought, the anticipation making his lips tingle.

Miles didn't kiss him, though. Instead, he smiled when their eyes met and let his hand fall away from Ren's cheek. "I should get you home," he said.

When Ren swallowed, his throat ached. "Sure," he agreed, trying not to let his disappointment show.

It wasn't the start to the year he had wanted.

Miles pulled into the driveway of Ren's father's house and told him to have a good night. Ren didn't move. He looked at the man in the driver's seat with raised eyebrows. *That's it?*

The question must have been obvious, but Miles only smiled.

It was frustrating, and Ren considered snapping at him like he would have in the past. Instead, he swallowed the bitterness and mumbled, "Thanks for tonight."

He left the car and started up the driveway toward the side door. *I can't believe he's not going to kiss me.* It occurred to him that maybe this was unfair. He couldn't expect Miles to make a move after he'd put up the boundaries he had. Actually, he should be thankful Miles had respected him enough to not go against his wishes—or what he had said were his wishes.

Ren's feet stalled. For a moment longer, he considered it, then turned around and walked back to Miles's car. When he stopped by the driver's side door, Miles rolled down the window.

He was going to ask if he could kiss him, not wanting to catch him off guard, but then the younger man grinned knowingly. "Yes?"

"God," Ren groaned. "You're so fucking annoying."

Ducking his head into Miles's window, Ren kissed him hard on the mouth.

He could feel Miles smiling against him before a hand came to the back of his head to hold him in place.

They kissed for long enough that Ren's neck ached from the angle and his lips felt raw. He pulled away, breathing heavily, and asked, "Why didn't you just say I had to be the one to kiss you? What if I didn't figure it out?"

Miles made a thoughtful noise and swiped his thumb over Ren's lower lip. "I think it was good for you to figure out on your own. Sometimes I wonder if you're truly thinking through the things you say to me. You want me to wait for you, but you also expect me to be the one to make a move, but only when you want me to."

"I always want you to, stupid. Just operate under that assumption."

"What's that mean for us?"

"It means I'm getting there," Ren told him. Miles met his gaze, and Ren had an idea. "Hey, you want to come inside?"

"Isn't your dad home?"

Ren shrugged. "It's late. He's probably asleep already." He shifted back, so he wasn't leaning into the car anymore, giving Miles space.

After following to kiss him again, Miles settled back against his seat. "You're only willing to sleep with me because I'm in love with you, but I won't sleep with you again until you're in love with me too."

There were many things Ren wanted to say about this. It was upsetting, though he supposed it was only fair. It was his own rule, after all. What surprised him the most was that Miles knew this about him. "Why do you know that?"

"Ah." Miles lowered his gaze. "Well … Hale—"

"Hale told you!" The betrayal ran deep.

"Not directly," Miles corrected. "He told Logan, and Logan told me. He probably isn't even aware it got back to me."

Groaning, Ren covered his face with his hand. "This is the problem with our best friends dating."

Miles chuckled. When Ren peeked at him through his fingers, Miles was smiling. Sighing, he dropped his hand.

"Okay then," he said. "I respect your decision not to have sex with me, though I must admit it's a little disappointing."

"Trust me, I know."

Ren laughed. "It's cold, so I'm going to go inside. Thank you for tonight. I had a nice year."

"Me too." Miles reached out the window to touch his wrist. "I'll text you, if that's alright. I'll be in the area for a little while longer, and I'd like to see you again."

"I'd love that. Don't make me wait long, okay?"

Grinning, Miles started to roll up his window. "I don't plan on it."

Chapter Thirty-Three

Ren's vacation was a lot more exciting once he learned Miles was in the area. He ended up visiting the diner every afternoon, reading and snacking until Miles took his break and then keeping him company for half an hour.

It was disappointing that Miles worked so much, and Ren thought how nice it would be to hang out elsewhere every once in a while. After their date on New Year's Eve, Ren recalled their kiss often, and he was itching to do it again sometime soon.

Something similar must have been on Miles's mind, because when he slid into the booth across from Ren for his lunch break five days into the new year, he asked, "You got plans tomorrow night?"

Hopeful, Ren glanced up from his book. "No, why?"

Miles smiled and looked down at his plate. He was eating a bagel breakfast sandwich with a side of fries that Ren suspected were for him. "We're closed Thursday nights," he explained. "I thought you'd maybe want to hang out. We could go ice-skating at the park."

"Ice-skating?" Ren echoed. "I haven't gone since I was in middle school. I'm not very good at it."

"That's okay," Miles assured. "I'll do my best to catch you if you fall. You in?"

This outing had the potential to be embarrassing for him, but it was Miles, so Ren wasn't worried. "Yeah, let's do it. I'm pretty sure my brother has a pair of skates in the basement I can borrow."

The idea of borrowing anything from his brother made Ren want to cringe, but he'd do it if it meant he got to spend time with Miles.

"You sure it's okay to spend your time off with me?" Ren asked. "I don't want to pull you away from your family when you're visiting."

Miles scoffed. "Luke and I have been spending way too much time together. Besides, when he has time off, he hangs out with his friends, and I know I'm welcome, but I'd much rather be with you."

Ren considered asking Miles whether he knew Rhett, but he figured the answer was yes. It didn't matter. Whether Miles knew his ex or not wouldn't ruin his excitement over their relationship or upcoming date.

Ren was just as bad at ice-skating as he thought he'd be. Thankfully, they were the only ones at the park, and Miles was—mostly—telling the truth when he said he'd catch him. Sometimes Ren tripped so quickly that Miles didn't have time to react.

It was obvious that Miles was trying not to laugh, probably afraid he'd upset Ren after years of being constantly snapped at. It was only when Ren laughed at himself after slipping and falling on his butt that Miles chuckled. He offered him a hand.

"Ow," Ren whined as Miles pulled him to his feet.

"Here," Miles said, offering his forearms. "Grab on. I better not let you go far on your own."

When Ren gripped Miles's arms, Miles spotted his bare hands. "You don't have gloves?"

Ren had been keeping his hands tucked into the sleeves of his jacket, so it didn't surprise him that Miles had failed to notice earlier. "Don't have any here."

"Take mine," Miles demanded.

"I'm fine. I'm not that cold."

Miles groaned but let it go. He skated backwards, pulling Ren along with him.

"How are you so graceful?" Ren asked.

"I'm not, really. I've just done this a few times already, so I can manage not falling. My mom is big on family outings and stuff, so she forced me to skate throughout my childhood."

"Forced?"

"I was not pleased. I was one of those kids who wanted to hang out at home and play video games."

"That shocks me," Ren said. "Given your passion for taking photos, I thought you would have spent a lot of time outside."

"Ah." Miles stumbled but caught himself before they could both fall. "I started taking photos after my parents took me on a road trip in high school."

Ren felt as he usually did when he heard people talking about fun things they had done with their family. Despite the ache in his chest, he smiled. "They sound like good parents."

"They are."

"I've never really traveled before. My family was never one to spend quality time together."

There was a moment of silence. Then, sounding unsure, Miles said, "I'll take you on trips."

It was a sweet thing to say, and Ren felt his cheeks warm at the implication along with it, that Miles was promising to be with him for a long time.

"Hey, stop moving," Ren instructed. When Miles did, Ren tightened his hands on his forearms to steady himself as he shifted onto his toes to kiss him.

He was only intending for it to be a quick kiss to show his appreciation, but Miles slipped his arms around his waist. Ren reached his hands up to Miles's face, but as soon as his fingertips made contact, Miles jerked away from him.

"Oh my god," he said, taking Ren's hands in his own. "You're freezing."

Ren shook his head. "I'm fine."

"You're not fine." Miles pulled off his gloves and held them out. "Wear these."

"They're too big."

"That doesn't matter."

Ren jerked his hands away. "Here, give me those," he said. When Miles handed them over, Ren shoved them in his coat pocket. Then he knitted his fingers with Miles's and guided their hands into the pockets of the younger man's coat. He had to close the distance between them to avoid straining his wrists, so they were standing chest to chest. The proximity didn't bother him. "There we go."

Huffing out a breathless laugh, Miles squeezed Ren's hands. "You're very lovable."

"It's only you who thinks that," Ren promised, lowering his gaze.

"If only that were true." Miles rested his forehead against Ren's. "I could rest easy then."

"I have no other pursuers, and even if I did, it's not like it would matter."

It was probably a good time for them to discuss their relationship, but instead Miles ducked to kiss his cheek.

Ren smiled. "When do you go home?"

"Looking to get rid of me already?"

"I want to know how much longer I have you for."

Warm lips pressed to the corner of his mouth. "I go home in a few days."

Ren had spent most of his break without Miles, but now that he had him for the past week, he couldn't imagine reverting to hiding in his room and only speaking to Hale on the phone.

"I don't want you to," he admitted.

Pleased, Miles lowered his head to kiss him. Ren melted, his hands squeezing Miles's within his pockets. When he was kissing Miles, he felt so warm. The cold was a distant memory. He'd never felt this way with anyone else, not even years ago when he had been convinced he'd found the love of his life.

Miles was persistent, and his lips were eager. It took Ren's breath away, but he didn't pull back to catch it, too enamored with the way Miles's mouth felt against his own.

He's way too good at this.

He thought of Miles's ex's and the one other guy he said he'd kissed, but he felt nothing beyond an initial stab of bitterness in his chest. They didn't matter, Ren knew, because Miles was kissing him right then.

It was so easy to get lost in Miles that Ren didn't notice the whooping until it was very close. They were being taunted, he realized, and he pulled away. He was too embarrassed to turn to the group of men who had approached the rink—he couldn't tell how many there were, but it sounded like at least three—so he peeked up at Miles to see his reaction.

Miles was glaring at the interrupters. "Lucas," he snapped.

It took Ren a few seconds to realize what this meant. He recalled what Miles had said at the dinner when they made plans, that when his cousin had free time, he spent it with his friends.

Just as he put it together, he heard, "Warren?" come from one of the men.

Surprised, Ren jerked back from Miles, eyes searching the group to find Rhett. Before he could, the world turned sideways, and he found himself on his back with Miles on top of him.

"Ouch," Ren groaned, because Miles was heavy. That was the only thing that hurt, and he realized Miles had somehow gotten a hand beneath his head before it could smack against the ice.

Miles laughed, rolling off him. "You okay?"

"Yeah." When he saw the back of Miles's hand, he grimaced at the sight of bloody knuckles. "You shouldn't have—"

"You would have hit your head if I didn't."

"That's fine—"

Miles shook his head and sat up. "It's not."

There was a pause, and Ren felt incredibly aware of the people still watching them. Nervously, he shot a look off to the side. He noticed Lucas and Rhett, and a few other kids from his high school whose names he'd forgotten.

Miles got back on his feet and held his hands out to help Ren up. "Are you satisfied, or do you want to stick around?"

With one last glance toward the edge of the rink, Ren shook his head. "Let's go somewhere else to warm up." He eyed the cuts on Miles's knuckles. "We should get something to clean this up."

Nodding, Miles guided him toward the edge of the ice. Thankfully, their shoes were across the rink from Rhett and his friends. The group of guys seemed to ignore them, preparing for the ice while talking amongst themselves, but Ren still felt paranoid having them there. He couldn't keep his eyes away for long.

"Are you okay?" Miles asked.

When Ren looked up, he realized Miles had finished changing into his shoes.

"I'm fine," he promised, hurrying to tie his sneakers. When he was done, he stood, appreciating the stability of his flat shoes to help him get out of there quickly. "Let's go."

Miles nodded but was staring past him toward his cousin's group with narrowed eyes. Slowly, he raised a hand to wave at someone. Ren didn't turn to see who. "Yeah," Miles agreed. "Let's."

They sat in Miles's car outside of the gas station drinking hot chocolate as Ren wrapped Miles's hand in cheap gauze.

They were making small talk as he was doing this, so Ren was caught off guard when Miles suddenly sighed and asked, "Should we talk about it?"

"Talk about what?"

"The look on your face before you fell," Miles said. Surprised, Ren glanced up from Miles's hand to meet his eyes. "It was like you saw a ghost."

Ren let out a laugh. "I pretty much did," he said. "One of your cousin's friends used to be my best friend."

"Oh." It took Miles a moment to process this. "*Oh*. So he's the one who ..."

"Yeah," Ren confirmed. He finished wrapping Miles's hand and pressed his lips to the gauze. "All good."

Miles released a shaky laugh. "You're cute," he told him. "Still not done with the previous conversation, though. Which one was he? Your best friend."

"You know them all, don't you? Which one would you guess it is? Of Lucas's friends, which do you think broke my heart?"

Miles shook his head. "I don't know them that well."

"It's Rhett," Ren admitted, removing his hot chocolate from the cup holder and taking a sip. "He's the one who said my name."

"Warren," Miles echoed.

"I fucking hate that name."

"Because of him?"

Ren shrugged. "Maybe. Maybe because of him, or maybe because of my brother, or maybe because I don't feel like *Warren*. Warren was pathetic."

"Is Warren not Ren?"

"Are you trying to tell me I'm still pathetic?"

Miles laughed. "No. No, I'm not. I'm just saying … you're you. You might not feel like the person you were when you went by Warren anymore, but that's not because you're a different person. It's because that was a long time ago and you've grown. It's still your past, and it's still you. That name … it's *yours*. Don't get rid of it because of things other people did."

"I'm afraid of becoming that person again," Ren admitted. "When I was Warren, I was quick to trust and slow to stand up for myself. I let Rhett walk all over me and took the fall for everything."

"You're never going to be that person again," Miles said. "That doesn't mean that part of you is gone. As you heal, I'm sure you'll come to find things like trusting easier again. At least, I hope you do."

Ren considered telling Miles he already trusted him, but fear froze the words in his throat. He hoped what Miles was saying was true.

He hoped that one day, he could once again be completely honest about his feelings with the person he loved.

Chapter Thirty-Four

Two days after his date with Miles, Ren woke up feeling down. It wasn't as bad as it had been months ago when he would consider hurting himself to chase the numbness away, but it was enough to make him roll over in bed without silencing his alarm.

He wondered whether it was because he'd seen Rhett, or just the usual uncontrollable highs and lows of his depression.

He considered texting Hale to tell him how he was feeling, but it would mean he'd have to reach out of his warm bundle of blankets for his phone, and he wasn't even willing to do that to shut off the annoying alarm.

It rang for a couple of minutes, and his brother came to pound on his door. Only then did Ren shut it off, thinking of a time when his brother would have broken down his door and hit him out of anger. Even though they were older now, he still wouldn't put it past him.

He'd been lying there for a long time when the text from Miles came in: *Should I come pick you up soon?*

The high school employees would be staffing the diner that weekend, so Miles had asked Ren if he wanted to hang out. Eager to spend as much time with him as he could before Miles returned to his hometown, Ren had agreed. He wasn't sure what the plan was, but if it was anything more athletic than what he was doing, he wasn't sure he could handle it.

The response he sent was short. *I don't know if I can get out of bed.*

Within a minute, his phone was ringing. He answered and let it fall to the pillow beside his face. "Hi."

"You okay?" Miles asked.

"I'm alive."

There was a pause. "Want me to come over?"

This seemed like a great idea. There was only one problem. "My brother's home."

Miles sighed. "I'm coming to get you," he declared. "We can go back to my aunt's and hang out. Lucas and his friends are here, but we'll stay in my bedroom."

Thoughts of Rhett had Ren pressing his face into his pillow. "All Lucas's friends?" It was so muffled he had to repeat himself.

"Rhett is here," Miles confirmed. "I'll make sure you don't have to see him. … If it's too much for you, we can do something tomorrow instead if you feel better."

"I want to see you tomorrow," Ren said. "I want to see you today too."

When Mile's spoke, his voice was soft, and Ren thought he was probably smiling. "I'm on my way."

Ren still wasn't out of bed by the time Miles got to his house, and it took a few minutes after having received his arrival text for him to leave the comfort of his blankets. He was wearing a pair of cloth shorts and a T-shirt, and he didn't bother putting on anything other than shoes before leaving the house. On his way out, his brother asked him what the fuck he was doing. The question was left unanswered.

The second he stepped outside, his muscles tensed in response to the cold. He considered grabbing his coat, but Miles's car was close, so he ignored the thought and went straight to it.

When he pulled open the passenger side door, Miles's voice reached him. "What are you *doing*? It's freezing outside."

Ren slid into the passenger seat and shut the door. The heat was on in the car, but Miles still removed his coat and draped it over Ren's bare legs. "Aren't you cold?"

Lowering his gaze, Ren grabbed a fistful of the coat in his lap. "I am," he admitted. "I'm dissociating right now, so it doesn't hurt or anything."

"You don't *feel* hurt," Miles corrected. "It doesn't mean it isn't hurting your body."

Ren pulled his feet up onto his seat and hid his face against his knees. This was a mistake. He didn't want Miles to see him when he was like this. It wasn't the first time, but it was the first time without Hale around as well, and that made him feel more vulnerable. He thought of going back into his house, but he felt Miles pull his seatbelt over him before a decision could be made.

"I can take care of myself," Ren insisted, not lifting his head.

"Yes," Miles agreed. There was the sound of the gear shift. "Just hang on for a few minutes, okay?"

The few minutes were silent. Miles probably didn't know what to say to him. He thought of Noah their freshman year, the first time he'd come home from class and realized Ren hadn't left bed all day. Noah hadn't brought it up until it happened multiple times, and even then it had taken him a few weeks to come up with how he would address it. Maybe Miles would become awkward and unsure of him.

When the car came to a stop and Miles announced their arrival, Ren lifted his head. They were parked on the street behind a familiar blue car that made his chest ache. He'd had his first kiss in that car. "I don't want to see him."

"You won't have to," Miles promised, reaching over to brush his hair behind his ear.

"I don't want him to see me."

Nodding, Miles pulled off the hoodie he was wearing and held it out to Ren. "Put this on."

When Ren made no move to do so, Miles unbuckled his seat belt for him. "Want help?" he offered.

The idea of being helped into clothing like a child by the man he had feelings for was enough to motivate him to do it himself. Given their size difference, the hoodie was large on him and easy to slip into.

"You're very cute," Miles told him, reaching over to pull the hood over Ren's head. He then slipped back into his coat.

He left the car, rounded it, and opened the passenger side door. "I'll carry you in."

"I can walk."

"You'll see them if you walk," Miles said.

Ren considered this, then turned on the seat and wrapped his arms around Miles's neck so he wouldn't fall. As if he weighed nothing, Miles lifted him out of the car and supported his weight with his hands on the backs of his thighs. The touch was burning against his bare skin. He wrapped his legs around Miles's waist and tucked his face against his shoulder.

He wasn't sure how Miles closed the car door, but his hands never left him to do so. Briskly, he walked them up the front walkway to the house. Only then did one of his hands leave to open the front door, and a wave of warm air and sound hit Ren.

He couldn't see anything, but he didn't need to see to tell how different this place was from his own home. There was the smell of bacon and the sound of laughter. Ren tightened his arms around Miles's neck. He didn't belong there.

"Miles?" someone called. He did not stop or respond. "What are you—"

There was a split second of silence, and then someone said, "You're going to push that off the table." Glass broke, and more laughter followed.

Ren felt them going upstairs. Only when he heard the click of a door did he raise his head from Miles's shoulder to look at their destination. They were in what looked like a guest room, though there was a suitcase filled with clothes on the floor, and when Miles lowered him to the mattress, the sheets smelled like him.

Quickly, Miles slipped out of his winter coat, kicked off his shoes and helped Ren out of his, and then crawled into bed beside him. He pulled Ren on top of him, then yanked the blankets to cover them both. "Warm enough?"

Ren closed his eyes. "Thanks."

He thought about Miles's hands, one on his back and the other on his left thigh. It wasn't sexual, but the intimacy of it made his heart pound.

Miles pushed the hood of the hoodie off Ren's head and pressed his face into Ren's hair. "How are you feeling?"

"A little numb," Ren answered, seeing no reason to lie. "It's not awful. If I was at school, I'd still go to class like this, but it's easier when I have nothing going on to lie in bed for the day."

"We can do that."

"This is nothing," he said, turning to press his lips against Miles's collarbone. "Really. This whole year, it's been nothing compared with what it was like at the end of high school and the beginning of college." He took a shaky breath, surprised he was even willing to talk about this. "I'm shocked I even got into college with how my last year of high school went. I told myself I was gonna do better in college, but for the first few months, I was just as bad. I'd stay in bed for days and I wouldn't do homework or go to class."

"What changed?" Miles asked. His hand trailed up and down Ren's spine, the touch soothing.

"Noah and Hale happened," Ren admitted. "I went on medication after I tried to kill myself, but I wasn't taking it regularly. At first, we weren't close enough, and they thought it wasn't any of their business, but ..."

"But what?"

"I would still hurt myself sometimes freshman year, and Noah and Hale found me once, and that's when they started to be more involved. Noah would drag me out of bed some days, and every morning he'd serve me my medication and force me to take it if I didn't want to. Some days, Noah would go to all my classes with me, even the ones he wasn't taking, just so I was with someone."

Miles's hand paused on Ren's back. "He's a great friend, huh?"

"They both are. I couldn't have done it without them." Ren swallowed and closed his eyes. "I don't think I could have gotten to this point without you either."

"I've done nothing."

"That's not true," Ren insisted. "You give me a reason to want to get better. There's only so much I can do for the sake of my friends and them not worrying about me, but you made me want to get better for me … for the first time in a long time, I feel like I might actually be able to be happy."

Miles didn't respond, but his hand began to move again, rubbing up and down Ren's back soothingly. After a only minute, Ren felt himself drifting back asleep, feeling a little less empty than he had before Miles came to get him.

When he woke up, he wasn't sure how long he'd been out. It must have been at least an hour or two, because he felt significantly more well rested.

At some point, Miles had rolled onto his side, but he was still holding Ren tight around the waist. It was warm and safe, and Ren felt very lucky to have him, but he felt guilty at the same time. Miles deserved someone who could spend the day doing something fun. He deserved someone who would make the most of their time together, not sleep through it.

I want to be that person, he thought, pressing his face into Miles's neck. Then, *I'm worried I never will be. Not completely.*

He felt Miles stir, and when he pulled back, hazel eyes were blinking. "Hi," Ren said.

It seemed to wake Miles quicker, because his gaze became more focused. "Sleep well?" he asked.

"Yeah."

"Feel any better?"

"I think so."

With a content sound, Miles pushed Ren's hair off his forehead. He looked at him so tenderly that Ren felt overwhelmed with emotion. He blinked quickly in case tears came to his eyes. "Why did you start to have feelings for me?" he asked.

Miles's eyebrows raised. "*Why?* You want to hear the things I like about you?"

"No," Ren refused, lowering his gaze. "That's not what I'm asking. I mean … how did it come about?"

Fingers finding the back of Ren's neck, Miles began to trace circles there. He didn't respond for long enough that Ren looked up at him again. "You don't want to tell me?"

"That's not it. I don't really know exactly when I developed feelings for you, but I remember when I realized I had."

"And?" Ren prompted when he didn't continue right away.

"Freshman year, I knew you were dating someone, and I realized I was jealous of whoever it was. Kind of weird now that I know it was Julian."

Unsure of what he was implying, Ren was quick to say, "Julian is a great guy."

Miles grimaced. "I know he is. He was my mentor for the whole freshman experience thing. That's why it's so strange. I saw him multiple times a week, and I didn't know he was the guy I envied."

This was the first Ren was hearing of this, and he wanted to know why Julian had failed to mention it.

"How did you not know we were dating?" Ren asked. "Didn't you ever see him come out of the apartment?"

"Yeah, but no more than Noah," Miles claimed. "I thought you two were friends. I guess I didn't want to put it together, since I liked Julian and I hated the idea of your boyfriend, so I just never considered the possibility of them being the same person."

Ren shifted, unsure of what to say. The situation with Julian was weird, since they didn't part on the usual terms. He didn't want to give Miles the wrong idea, but it was also a part of his past, and he didn't want to keep it a secret. "Julian was too good," he mumbled. "He didn't deserve what I put him through. I wonder whether we would still be friends if I had said no when he asked me out."

"Can I ask how you two got together?"

Surprised, Ren rolled onto his back and sat up. He did it without thinking, and it occurred to him how therapeutic his nap with Miles had been. "You want to talk about my history with my ex?"

"Does that make you uncomfortable?"

It didn't. "Not really." Ren paused. "Can I ask about your ex?"

The look on Miles's face suggested he'd tasted something sour. "You can," he accepted. "She cheated on me, and there's not much else to it. It was high school, and we had the typical, boring high school relationship."

"She cheated?"

"Yeah. With some college guy she met at a party. She cried when I found out. The whole thing was very dramatic." His voice sounded tired.

Ren lay back down. "I'm sorry. I was hurt when I found out Sawyer had someone else, and I didn't even like him that much. I can't imagine—"

"You don't have to," Miles assured. He slipped an arm around Ren's waist.

"Did you love her?" Ren was afraid of the answer.

"No," Miles said. "At least, not this much."

It was amazing to Ren that words could have such an effect on him.

I'm not empty after all, he thought.

"I'll tell you about Jules later," he promised. "I want to focus on this right now."

He felt a kiss on his forehead, and Miles's knee pushed between his so they were even closer to each other. "Okay," Miles mumbled. "Focus only on me."

Chapter Thirty-Five

Miles had to work the day before he left, so Ren went to the diner for coffee. He had a novel and his laptop with him, since he planned on staying for far longer than it took him to finish a single cup.

He was the first customer there, so he claimed his favorite booth. Lucas was behind the counter when he entered, and he raised a hand to wave before stepping back into the kitchen to fetch Miles.

He was just logging into his laptop when Miles approached with a coffeepot and a mug.

"Hey," Miles greeted, smiling. "How are you today?"

Ren watched as he filled the mug with steaming coffee. "I'm alright," he answered. "Better than I was yesterday. Each day is a little easier." Three days had passed since his day spent in Miles's bed, and Miles had asked him how he was doing every day since. The answer hadn't changed at all. Each day, he felt a little less like that empty version of himself. "What time do you leave tomorrow?"

"Not sure," Miles answered. "My aunt has the day planned with family things, so I don't know when I'll be able to get away."

"So, today will be the last day I see you before school starts?"

"I'll come to your house and say goodbye before I go," Miles promised. He pushed the coffee mug in front of Ren. "Are you here to eat as well?"

"Not right away." Ren took a sip of the coffee and hummed in delight. "I'll order something in a bit, if that's alright."

"Of course."

When Ren lowered the mug to the table, Miles reached out to brush across his knuckles. "I'll stop back soon."

"Thanks."

As Miles went back to the kitchen, Ren huffed out a sigh. He wondered whether he should call Hale later and tell him everything that was going on. They still spoke frequently, and Ren had told him a bit about the time he spent with Miles, but he had talked little about his feelings and the change in their relationship. He was worried how Hale would react if Ren admitted he and Miles were practically dating. Undoubtedly, he'd be happy, though Ren thought he might ask questions about why they weren't official yet, and he didn't know how he'd answer.

Ren took another sip of his drink and opened the document on his computer where he'd written the draft to a short story. His goal was to finish it before the end of break so he could share it with his advisor when he returned to school. He created a new document to start on the next draft.

The diner was a good place to work, with the perfect amount of background noise and endless access to coffee. He got through three pages before Miles returned to take his order and another two before his food was delivered.

As he ate, he read his novel, so his gaze was down when Rhett and his friends entered the diner. At the sound of them, Ren glanced up from his book. Their eyes met.

This was the first time they ran into each other at the diner. Ren was surprised it had taken this long with how often he'd visited

Not wishing to stare, he focused on his book again. Before he could even find his spot, a question was pulling his attention elsewhere.

"Can I sit here?"

Quickly, Ren lifted his head to look at his ex. If he was being honest, he didn't want to talk to him. There were so many memories that could come back if they spoke, and he worried it would ruin his day. Still, he couldn't bring himself to say no, so Rhett sat after a moment of silence.

Slowly, Ren closed his book.

"You can keep eating," Rhett claimed, gesturing to the half-finished plate of pancakes. There was a small, awkward smile on his face. "I won't be here long."

"Why *are* you here?" Ren asked, taking a sip of his coffee and frowning at how cold it had become. Thinking of waving Miles over, he glanced toward the counter. Miles was already watching them.

"I thought it was about time I apologize to you," Rhett claimed.

The words were unexpected. "I don't need an apology from you." Rhett raised his eyebrows. "I don't care anymore."

Rhett grimaced. "That's fair. I still want to say sorry, even if it's just for me. I feel guilty about what I did to you back then. I knew I was your main support, but I wasn't ready to come out to my parents, and that was more important to me at the time."

More important than me? Ren thought of asking, but he already knew the answer.

"It's okay," he said instead. "It fucked me up a bit, but I'm doing better now."

Rhett grinned, and Ren remembered other times he'd smiled at him like that. To his surprise, the memories didn't hurt. It felt like nothing. "I'm glad you're doing better," Rhett said. "I was shocked to see you back in the area."

"Yeah, well. I can't run from my father forever." Ren eyed Rhett curiously. "Are you done running from your parents?"

"I am," Rhett admitted. "They didn't really care. I came out about two years ago."

"Because you were seeing someone?" Ren realized only after he'd asked that he sounded as if he cared.

Rhett shook his head. "No. I was just sick of hiding." He propped his chin up on his palm. "I haven't dated much since you. Senior year, I had a fling with Jacob Johnson, but we broke up once we went to college and I've been single since then."

This name was familiar to Ren. "I didn't realize Jacob was gay."

"He's bi, and you wouldn't know because we kept it a secret."

Ren couldn't imagine being in a secret relationship. He liked it when the person he was with was unafraid to show others they were together. He wondered whether this was because of what Rhett had done to him in the past, more willing to destroy their relationship than act as a couple with him.

"What about you?" Rhett asked, looking in Miles's direction. "Are you two dating?"

Ren glanced that way as well. His lips curled up when he noticed Miles still watching them. "Not officially."

"So you're available then."

Laughing, Ren shook his head. "No."

"Ah." To Ren's shock, Rhett seemed disappointed. He was curious if Rhett had been planning on asking him out, but Ren decided against asking. It didn't matter.

"I should get back," Rhett announced, sliding from the booth. "I came with the guys and I don't want to keep them waiting." He glanced at Miles again. "Your guard dog also doesn't seem to like me very much."

"He's fine," Ren dismissed. "See you around."

His ex nodded. "Yeah," he agreed. "It was nice to see you, Warren."

The pleasantry was not returned, and Rhett left the table. Ren watched him cross the diner until Miles blocked his view.

"Were you worried?" Ren asked.

Huffing, Miles slid into the booth across from him. "I feel I'm allowed to be worried. You've given me no reassurance whatsoever."

Ren supposed this was fair. He reached across the table toward Miles. "You know you're really important to me, right?"

Taking his hand, Miles asked, "Was that so hard to say?"

With a laugh, Ren squeezed his fingers. "You know, I kind of like it when you actually act younger than me," he said. "It's cute."

Miles shook his head. "What'd you guys talk about?"

"What if I don't want to tell you?" Ren teased. He pulled his hand free to resume eating.

"You don't have to do anything you don't want to."

Of course Ren knew this, just as he knew Miles wouldn't be upset with him if he decided to keep it to himself. It was because Miles was so respectful that he didn't mind sharing. "He apologized to me," he admitted. "Then he asked me if I was seeing anyone."

"What'd you tell him?"

"I said no." Ren took a sip of his cold coffee, observing Miles's expression over the rim. The younger man lowered his gaze and pulled his lips into a frown. Ren didn't enjoy being the one to make Miles look like that, so he added, "I also said I wasn't available."

Hazel eyes lifted to regard him. "You're not interested in him?"

Ren made his *Are you serious* face. "No. I'm interested in you, stupid."

Miles shrugged. "You could be interested in multiple people."

"Are you?"

It was Miles's turn to laugh. "Absolutely not."

"Good," Ren said, feeling warm. "Me neither."

They were going to have to talk about their relationship at some point, but for the time being, Ren thought it was enough to know that they were only like this with each other.

Chapter Thirty-Six

Ren waited all day to hear from Miles. As it got later and later, he worried that when Miles reached out, it would be to tell him he couldn't make it.

This was why Ren sounded so dejected when the call finally came at eight p.m.

"What's wrong?" asked Miles upon hearing his voice. "Is it another bad day?"

"It's not," Ren assured, not wanting to worry him. "Have you left for home already?"

Miles chuckled. "Would you be upset with me if I said yes?"

"No. I know you're busy, and you've spent a lot of your free time with me, so I'm happy you're also spending time with your family."

"Well, I haven't left yet. I'm going to leave soon, but I can't go without seeing you beforehand."

Ren perked up. "Want me to meet you somewhere?"

There was a pause. "I'm outside of your house."

Quickly, Ren sat up in bed. "I'll come out now."

"I'm ringing the doorbell."

"What?" he asked, though Miles had hung up. A second later, the doorbell echoed through the house.

Ren scrambled to get out of bed, dashing to the door. His father and brother were both home, and he didn't want to deal with either of them.

When he saw the front door, he realized he'd been too slow. His father must have been in the living room when the bell rang, and it was too late for Ren to call out to him.

There was a moment of silence in which Miles and Ren's father looked at each other. Ren came to a stop at his father's elbow. "Who are you?" his dad asked.

Miles didn't hesitate. "Hi. I'm Miles. I go to school with your son, and I'm interested in dating him."

Shocked, Ren's mouth dropped open. "Did you really just say that?"

"I wanted to be honest. It's also your father, so I thought I should express my intentions with you."

"We're not getting married."

Miles shrugged. "We might."

Ren's father pushed the door open a little wider. "Come in," he instructed. "Would you like something to drink?"

Miles stepped inside, and it amazed Ren this situation was actually happening. "Want me to make you coffee?" Ren asked.

"If you don't mind, that'd be amazing," Miles answered, reaching out to touch his hip.

It was strange. The only person he'd been involved with who had met his father was Rhett, and he had been sure to keep his distance so no one got the wrong idea. "Let's go to the kitchen," Ren said, reaching for Miles's hand.

Much to his distaste, his dad followed, taking a seat at the counter alongside Miles when Ren went to the coffeepot.

They made small talk as if what was happening wasn't weird. Ren's father asked how they knew each other, and Miles explained they were neighbors.

"He's a year behind me in school, but they moved in around the same time as us," Ren explained, not because it was necessary but because he felt he should take part in the conversation.

"So, you've known each other for a while then. You moved into your apartment the beginning of your sophomore year, right?"

As Ren poured grounds into the coffeemaker, he raised his eyebrows, surprised his father remembered this about him. Maybe it was because he was paying the rent. "Yeah."

"And what is your major?" his dad asked Miles.

"I'm an art major with a focus on photography."

As Miles spoke, Ren observed his father. The older man's eyes lit up, and he looked at Miles with an interest he'd never had for his son. "Photography?"

Clearly sensing his excitement, Miles's eyebrows raised. "Yeah."

"That's wonderful. What do you take pictures of?"

Miles made a face that his father kindly laughed at.

"I know that can be a hard question to answer. Perhaps it's better to ask what you wish to do with photography after you graduate?"

"I'm not sure yet," Miles said. "I like taking photos of nature, but I don't know if I'd want to do that as a career. I know you have to travel a lot and be away from home, and I don't like the idea of living out of a suitcase for a portion of the year. I enjoy taking photos of people and expressions, so maybe I'll try to find something for a magazine or brand."

The coffee brewed, filling the kitchen with the delightful scent. "Dad likes photography. There's a gallery in town he goes to sometimes," Ren said.

"I'm familiar with it," Miles admitted. "I've actually had my photos displayed there before."

Now Ren's father appeared impressed. Ren felt something like pride stir within him over Miles's accomplishments.

"Do you have some photos that you've taken? I'd love to see your work," his father said.

Miles seemed pleased, though slightly overwhelmed. "Uh, yeah. Let me go grab my laptop from my car quick. I could show you what I've taken on my phone, but I don't feel that is a good representation of what I do." Miles stood from the stool, gaze landing on Ren again. "You don't mind, do you?"

"Why would I mind?"

"You're weird," Miles reminded.

It startled a laugh out of Ren and he shook his head. "Go get your computer. The coffee will be ready by the time you're back."

Grinning, Miles left the room. With a deep breath, Ren forced himself to look at his father. The man was already staring back, his eyebrows drawn together. "Sorry for not giving you warning he was coming," Ren said. "I didn't realize he would come to the door."

"I don't mind." The silence they fell into was awkward. "You know …" Trailing off, his father lowered his gaze. "Your mother was a photographer."

The words shocked Ren for two reasons. The first was that his father never talked to him about his mother. The little he knew of her came from his grandmother. The second reason was that this was not something he had known, and it explained his father's interest in photography.

"Oh," Ren voiced. "Really?"

His dad nodded. "Yeah. She was a nature photographer, so she traveled frequently. Your brother and I were used to her not being around, so when she died, the biggest change was you."

Ren winced and took a half step backward.

"It's not your fault," his father assured. "You were just a baby. Even if your mother hadn't passed, we would have had to figure out how you fit into our lives like every family does when they get a new member. We just had to fit you in alongside the grief."

It was too much to look at his father then, so Ren turned toward the counter to grab a mug. "You did a shit job," he declared. "I don't fit in here. You guys despise me and I just try to exist out of your way."

"Warren, I—" his dad began, only to be cut off when Miles came back into the room with his laptop tucked under his arm.

The slight furrow of Miles's brow made Ren wonder how much he had heard. "Your coffee is ready," Ren announced, filling the mug and putting it in front of Miles's spot on the peninsula.

Miles took his stool again. "Thanks."

There seemed to be an implied *Are you okay?* The concern made Ren smile and he lowered his gaze to Miles's laptop. "You have your pictures?"

"Yeah." Miles moved his attention to his computer. "Let me pull some up."

While he did that, Ren poured his dad a cup of coffee.

"Here," Miles said, sliding his laptop down the counter so it sat in front of Ren's father. "You can look through that folder. It's the photos that made up my portfolio for the class I took last semester."

As his father began to look, Miles raised his chin to meet Ren's eyes. "Do you want to sit down?" he asked. "I don't mind standing."

"I'm alright right now," Ren assured, leaning against the counter. "Thanks for coming."

"Of course. I told you I'd see you before I left. It's still a couple of weeks before we can see each other again."

A couple of weeks seemed like far too much time. "Will you call me?"

Miles's lips pulled up. "I was planning on it. I'm glad you said something, because now I know you'll pick up."

"Why wouldn't I pick up?"

Shrugging, Miles raised his coffee to his mouth to take a sip. "This is good, thank you. I'm glad you learned how to make it properly."

Ren recalled their trip with Hale and Logan and the coffee grounds on the floor. "Ah, right. *This* is why I wouldn't pick up." It earned him a chuckle from Miles, and that made him grin. "Seriously though, I'll answer. It would be weird not to talk to you after seeing you every day."

"I'm glad you think that," Miles said, hazel eyes shifting to his laptop screen. "I think you missing me would mean progress."

Ren opened his mouth to respond, because they *were* making progress, but before he could, Miles was addressing his father. "Would you like to see more of him?"

"You have more?"

"More what?" Ren asked. He leaned forward to see the screen and noticed a photo of himself. He couldn't recall when it had been taken, but he was leaning against the railing of the balcony at his apartment with a cigarette pinched between his fingers. "Oh. Me. How many pictures of me have you taken?"

Miles shrugged and pulled his laptop back in front of himself so Ren couldn't see the screen. "Not that many," he claimed. "More recently, since I'm less worried about you being angry if you catch me."

"You smoke?" Ren's dad asked. "That's not very good for you, you know."

Miles laughed, and Ren rolled his eyes. "I quit."

"I take credit for that," Miles claimed.

"So you're a good influence?" his dad asked.

This was embarrassing. Miles chuckled and slid his laptop back over to Ren's father. "Here are the pictures I have of him."

It didn't take his father long to go through them—true to his word, there weren't many—and Ren stood beside Miles so he could see as well. He wasn't smiling in the photos, though he figured that was an accurate representation of him from the past few years. There were very few pictures Ren remembered being taken, and he realized how closely Miles had been watching him all this time.

The last photo of him was the only one he was smiling in. It was from a few days ago, taken during a walk over Miles's lunch break. It had been snowing, and when Ren turned to find Miles's lens on him, he'd smiled without restraint.

His father appeared most affected by this photo. Ren didn't know why until the older man softly mumbled, "You look so much like your mother when you smile."

The words were unexpected, and he looked at his dad with large eyes.

He didn't seem to notice. "You're very talented," he said to Miles.

Miles grinned, his cheeks slightly flushed. "Thank you. He's an excellent subject, so it makes it easy."

Embarrassed, Ren turned away. Miles chuckled at the reaction, then downed his coffee. "Okay," he said, closing his laptop. "I should actually get going. I just stopped to say goodbye on my way out of town."

"You're not from the area?" Ren's dad asked.

"No. I live near our campus. I was just visiting family here while my parents were on vacation. I'll be spending the rest of break in my hometown."

Ren's father thanked him for stopping by and introducing himself. As they shook hands, Ren wished he could tell how his father really felt about meeting a man who was interested in him. He'd always gotten the impression his sexuality was just another disappointment.

When Miles dropped his father's hand, he reached down to link his fingers with Ren's. "Walk me out?" he suggested.

He's really leaving, Ren thought, squeezing the hand holding his.

"Yeah," Ren said, shooting a glance in his father's direction. "I'll be back."

"Sure," he said. "Take your time. I'd like to talk with you when you return."

While Ren didn't really want to talk to his father, it was still something he needed to do before break ended, so he mumbled an agreement before leading Miles to the door.

He stopped to get his jacket from the closet, smiling when his hand was grabbed again as soon as it was on.

"Your dad is cool," Miles said once they were outside. "Most people from that generation are judgmental when they hear I'm going into art."

Ren tucked his face into his collar to hide from the cold. "He's alright," he mumbled. "That's actually the most we've talked all break."

"Really?" They were at Miles's car. He dropped Ren's hand to open the back door and pack his laptop into his backpack. "That makes me want to leave even less."

When Miles shut the car door, he leaned back against it and raised his hands to hold Ren's face. "I'm going to miss you."

"Me too." Ren took a small step forward so they were pressed together. "Thanks for making my break fun."

Humming, Miles leaned down to close some of the distance between them. Ren was expecting to be kissed, so he closed his eyes, but he opened them again when Miles said, "I love you."

His heart squeezed. "You shouldn't."

Miles shook his head.

"Really, Miles. You can do so much better than me. I'm a mess, and even though I'm trying to get better, I'll still always be a mess. I'll always be impulsive and irrational and I don't think I can be the person you deserve."

Sighing, Miles pulled him into a hug. "You're not a mess. You're human. And you're impulsive and irrational, but you're also thoughtful and loyal and loving. You deserve love, and I love you."

They were the words Ren had always wanted to hear, and he felt his eyes get hot.

"Please go on a date with me once we're back on campus. A date as a couple, not just friends or whatever we are now. A date where you're my boyfriend or partner or whatever you want to call it," Miles said.

There was no longer any reason for him to reject. "Okay," Ren agreed. "We can go on a date."

When Miles pulled away, he was beaming. "I can't wait for school to start now."

He ducked to kiss Ren, mouth a hot contrast to the weather. It was a short kiss, not nearly enough, but Ren supposed he had reassurance it wouldn't be the last, so he let Miles pull away. "I'm going to call you," Miles promised.

"You better."

"Every day, I'll call."

"No less than that."

Smiling, Miles kissed his cheek. "I'm going to make you very happy," he declared.

Ren said nothing, but he hoped Miles was right. Judging off the warmth in his chest, Ren was sure he was.

Chapter Thirty-Seven

True to his word, Miles called at least once a day. This was more than welcome, and Ren always smiled when he saw the name pop up on his phone, happy to retreat to his bedroom for their usual hour-long conversation.

They talked about a lot of things, so they only got to the topic of Ren's father a couple of days after Miles had returned home.

They were discussing Miles's photography, which morphed into talking about Miles's interaction with his father, and then the younger man got quiet for a handful of seconds before asking, "Did the two of you talk that night?"

"Huh?"

"You and your dad," Miles elaborated. "Did you guys talk at all after I left?"

"A little. He just said he regrets letting me leave after what happened in high school. He said it was his responsibility as a parent to take care of me, but he thought he'd failed badly enough at that point that it would be better for me to be with my grandma."

"Do you agree with him?"

It didn't surprise Ren that Miles was comfortable asking such a question. He'd always asked the questions Ren didn't want to answer.

He groaned. "You always make me think about things."

"Sorry," Miles offered, and he sounded sincere. "You don't have to answer if you don't want to. I just thought it might be nice for you to get it off your chest if it's something you'd been thinking about."

"I don't *not* agree with him," Ren admitted after a pause. "I also don't regret going to live with my grandma. I really needed to get away from my brother, and she was the only one in my family I felt any warmth from in my childhood."

It seemed like a good time to shift the subject to something lighter. "Dad likes you, though."

"He told you that?"

"Yeah." It was cute how delighted Miles sounded over this. Whether Ren's father liked him didn't matter in the grand scheme of things, but it made Ren happy that Miles seemed to care. "Said it was sweet you have a folder of photos of me."

"Logan says it's creepy."

Chuckling, Ren rolled over onto his back. "I'm sure Logan has a folder full of photos of Hale as well. They're just not as high quality."

"Comparing us to a couple who have been together for months?" Miles teased.

"They're our best friends, so it's easy." Ren thought of Hale and his predicament. "I haven't heard from Hale in a couple of days, now that I think of it. Have you talked to Logan?"

There was the sound of rustling on Miles's end, and Ren smiled at the idea of him also curled up in bed. "I've seen Logan."

Right. He had the luxury of living near his best friend. "Has he said anything about him and Hale? Are they doing okay?"

"Why wouldn't they be?"

Ren resisted the urge to sigh. This meant Hale had yet to talk to Logan about the job he'd interviewed for. He'd have to tell him soon. Last Ren had heard, Hale had gone through two interviews with the company and he had a third coming up the following week.

"I don't know," Ren lied. It wasn't his place to tell anyone, especially not Logan's best friend. "I mean, this is their first time doing long distance, and I know that can be tricky."

"I'm sure they're fine," Miles assured. "I mean ... it's Hale and Logan.

I can't imagine them being anything other than fine."

He understood what Miles was saying. Even though Hale and Logan hadn't been together for long, they were so well suited that it was hard to imagine them having any serious problems. Ren was sure they'd be able to figure something out if Hale got this job.

"Me either," he agreed.

"Every time I say something to Logan that even suggests I miss you, he's been telling me off, since he hasn't seen Hale since we all left for break," Miles said.

The words *I miss you* stuck out more than anything else Miles had said, but Ren didn't draw attention to it. Instead, he let the feeling of being missed warm his chest as he said, "Hale and I are gonna have a call while we drive back to campus at the end of next week, and I'm sure he'll complain about their time apart."

"The end of next week already," Miles commented. "Break went by so fast."

"Are you complaining?"

"Of course not." Even over the phone, he could hear the happiness in Miles's voice. "You know, for the first time, I can't wait to get back."

Ren pulled a pillow over his face to hide his smile. He couldn't wait to see Miles. His excitement for their date was making the remaining days of break feel long, and whenever he thought of what came after their date— *their relationship*—the time almost felt unbearable.

Ren's father prepared breakfast his last morning in town. It was a little awkward, but he appreciated the effort and could admit he felt better about their relationship than he had when he first came home.

That day they had talked, his father had said more to him than he revealed to Miles. He had also denied Ren's accusation that he despised him, and for the first time claimed to love Ren just as much as he loved his brother. This was embarrassing, and Ren wasn't entirely sure he believed it, which was why he'd left it out when talking to Miles. Still, he and his father were going in the right direction.

He told Hale as much over the phone as he drove away from his childhood home in his grandmother's old car. Unfortunately, the car was too old for Bluetooth, so he had Hale on speaker and his phone in the cup holder to amplify the sound.

"So, going home for break was worth it?" Hale asked, his voice echoey but audible.

"I suppose it wasn't a complete waste of my time," Ren answered, though he said it with a smile.

Hale laughed. "You're just smitten with Miles."

This was true, so Ren didn't deny it.

"Honestly, I'm just glad you came to this conclusion on your own. I'd have to spend the next few months nudging you in the right direction if you hadn't."

"Or you could have just not meddled."

"That's no fun."

Shaking his head, Ren checked his blind spot as he merged onto the highway. "So how was your break, then?" He wanted to ask about Hale's most recent job interview but was refraining in case it caused his friend anxiety. "Miss Logan terribly?"

"You have no idea," Hale groaned. "We called every day, but it's just not the same, you know?"

You'll have to do long distance if you move, Ren considered reminding, but of course Hale already knew this.

"He's been great, though," Hale said. "I think I'll bring him home with me sometime to meet everyone. I bet I can convince all the cousins to come if I tell them I'm bringing him."

"That sounds like it'll be crazy." Ren tried to think of how Logan would react.

"Well, that's my family, so if he's going to be a part of it someday, he has to get used to it."

"So you're thinking long term, then?" This didn't surprise Ren. Logan was the first person he'd ever seen Hale date, and he knew his friend wouldn't have gotten into a relationship if he wasn't serious about it.

Hale sighed. "I am, so I'm going to tell him about this job soon."

"I take it the last interview went well?"

"It was amazing," Hale admitted, and Ren's throat tightened. He was happy for him, but the idea of Hale moving away hurt. "They're going to call me in the next week."

After a heavy swallow to push down his sadness, he asked, "You think you'll get an offer?"

Hale groaned.

"Do you want them to give you an offer?"

"I do, but I also feel like it would be best if they didn't. If they don't give me an offer, then I can cry it off and go back to my happy life with my boyfriend. I bet I'd find a job in the area eventually, and if I can't, I can try to get work with one of those online publishing companies. I'd be more stressed about money, but I wouldn't have to move and leave you."

"But you also wouldn't have your dream job," Ren added.

Hale was quiet for a long moment. "Tell me Logan and I will be fine doing long distance for a year."

Ren smiled. "Deep breaths, babe," he urged. "You guys will work it out."

"Thanks." The worry hadn't left Hale's voice.

"How about you, me, and Noah go out for drinks once you find out about the job? If you get it, we can celebrate, and if you don't, we can celebrate."

Hale laughed. "Yes, please."

In the cup holder to his right, Ren's phone buzzed with a message and he lowered his gaze to see who it was from.

He wasn't looking away from the road for long, but Miles's message was short, so it was enough time for him to read it off his lock screen.

I can't wait to see you.

Ren was sure that he'd done nothing in his life that made him deserving of this happiness, but still, he was thankful he was finally feeling it.

"I wish I was back already," he told Hale.

"Me too," his friend agreed. "And not just because I'm already sick of this god-awful drive. This is just how it feels when there's someone waiting for you."

Someone waiting for me. Ren's eyes felt warm from unshed tears of happiness. *How wonderful.*

Chapter Thirty-Eight

Hale woke Ren with a knock on his bedroom door.

As Ren cracked open his eyes, Hale approached the side of his bed. "Good morning."

When Ren had lain down to rest, Hale had still been on his way back. "I thought you'd be hanging out with Logan," Ren said as he sat up to hug his friend.

"He and I have plans for dinner," Hale explained. "We'll be leaving soon, but Miles just got back, so I thought I'd let you know."

Ren rubbed the sleep from his eyes. "Is he next door?"

"Yeah. Noah has also been here for a while, but I didn't think he was important enough to wake you."

A displeased "Hey!" was called from the living room. Both Ren and Hale laughed.

"Thanks," Ren said, climbing out of bed. "I'll go next door and say hello quick."

"Quick?" Hale echoed. "Take your time. You missed him."

"It hasn't been that long."

"Still." Hale followed Ren out of his bedroom.

Sitting on the couch was Noah. He glanced up from his phone when they emerged from the room. "Hey," he said, watching as Ren went to the door and slipped into his shoes. "Don't take too long. I've been waiting forever for you to wake up. Why'd you invite me over to order food if you were just going to fall asleep?"

Playfully, Hale hit the back of Noah's head.

"I'm not gonna be too long," Ren promised. "I'm just going to say hi and see when he plans on taking me out."

Noah's eyebrows raised. He and Ren had talked over break, but not much about what was going on with Miles beyond a brief summary. "You agreed to go on a date with him? I thought you'd be way more stubborn about it."

"I guess I realized happiness is more valuable than pride."

His friend's eyebrows shot up even farther. "Who even are you?"

Laughing, Ren shook his head and grabbed his keys. "I'll be right back and we can order."

"You can invite Miles over if you want," Noah offered. "I won't be upset."

This last bit needed to be spoken. When Ren was dating Jules, Noah had often gotten angry when Ren brought him along places. This probably was because Noah lived with Julian and was a constant witness to their relationship. It made sense he didn't feel the same way with Miles, but Ren wouldn't have asked to find out.

"Thanks," Ren said. "I'll invite him."

"Send Logan over, will you?" Hale asked. "We should leave soon if we're going to make our reservation."

Ren went next door. He only had to knock on the door once before Logan opened it.

"Oh, hi," Logan greeted, glancing over his shoulder. "He's in his room unpacking. Come on in."

"Thanks." Ren stepped into the apartment. "Hale's ready to go."

"I was just about to leave." As Logan stepped into his shoes, he kept a hand on the door to prop it open.

"Have a good time," Ren offered, glancing toward Miles's bedroom.

"I will," Logan said. He hesitated then. "Hey …"

Ren was alarmed by the uncertainty in Logan's voice. "What?"

His unease must have been obvious, because Logan's lips quirked. "It's nothing bad. I just wanted to say thank you."

Confusion pulled Ren's lips down. "Thank you?"

Logan stepped out into the hall, still holding the door open. "For making him happy," he explained.

Ren felt his face heat. He opened his mouth to respond, but closed it when his thoughts were too jumbled to be put into words.

Logan smiled. "I'll see you later, Ren."

The door closed between them.

Well, shit, he thought. He was so overjoyed that it felt fake. He wondered if he would wake up from this dream at any second and go back to being numb and irritable all the time.

"Hey."

At the sound of Miles's voice, Ren turned. He was standing in the doorway of his bedroom, his arms crossed over his chest.

Something akin to fear struck Ren. Everything felt too good right then. He didn't know what losing this would do to him, and he found himself terrified Miles would someday leave or change his mind.

"I thought it would be you," Miles said, coming closer. "Are you alright?"

Nodding, Ren took a deep breath, forcing the negativity out on the exhale. The anxiety was still there, but it wasn't in the foreground any longer. "Yeah," he said, reaching out once Miles was close enough to hug him.

A hand slid down Ren's back. "How have you been?"

"We've talked every day."

"Yeah," Miles agreed. "But this is different."

With a nod, Ren answered, "I'm good. Happy. How about you?"

"I'm also happy," Miles admitted. "I'm looking forward to our date."

Humming in agreement, Ren tilted his head to gaze up at the younger man. "When do you want to go?"

Miles shrugged. "Anytime. As soon as possible."

The feeling was mutual. "I don't start work for another week, and my only class finishes at five on Tuesdays and Thursdays, so any day works for me."

"How about Tuesday?"

"Okay," Ren agreed. "I'm looking forward to it." He pulled away from the hug but kept his hands fisted in the fabric of Miles's sweater. "Want to come over?"

"Logan said Noah was there."

"He is. We're ordering take out if you want to join."

"I won't be interrupting?"

Ren shook his head. "I don't know what you think there is to interrupt. Come over."

"Okay," Miles agreed, smiling. "I'll come over once I'm done unpacking. Give the two of you some time to catch up."

This was sweet. It had been a while since Ren had dated someone who gave a shit about his relationship with his friends.

You're not dating yet, he thought, but it didn't dampen his mood any. He knew that wouldn't be true for long.

When Hale came home two hours later, Ren, Miles, and Noah were playing a drinking game with a deck of cards on the coffee table. Ren was drinking a soda, committed to staying away from alcohol for the time being. At the sound of the door, they all turned.

"You look so guilty," Hale said with a laugh.

"I wasn't expecting you to be home so soon," Ren said, checking the time on his phone. "The other apartment is empty. Go fuck."

Miles huffed out a surprised laugh.

"I wanted to come hang out," Hale explained, kicking off his shoes and crossing the living room to collapse in the chair. "We had sex this afternoon when you were sleeping."

Ren laughed, and Noah handed Hale his drink. He wasn't empty-handed for long. Miles offered him his can. "I'll go hang out with Logan then," he said.

"You're leaving?" Ren asked, pouting as Miles stood.

"We haven't finished our game," Noah protested. He accepted the rest of Miles's seltzer anyway.

"Hale can take my place," Miles said. He ducked to kiss the top of Ren's head. "I'll see you Tuesday."

"Not before that?"

"Probably before that."

When he left, Ren flopped down to stretch out across the couch. "He's so perfect," he groaned.

"Fucking told you," Hale mumbled into his can.

"I've never seen you this happy with someone before," Noah commented, tossing his cards onto the coffee table.

Ren hid his smile behind his hand.

"Hale, did you finally get the balls to tell Logan about your job?" Noah asked.

Also interested in the answer, Ren sat up. His best friend groaned and downed the rest of Noah's drink.

"No," he said once he'd finished.

"Putting it off is only gonna make it harder," Ren told him. Hale fixed him with an *I've already thought about that* expression.

"I'll tell him soon," Hale assured. "I just don't know how to say it."

Noah raised his eyebrows. "Just tell him."

"You don't get it," Hale said. "You're chronically single. You don't know what it's like to have tough conversations."

Noah laughed and took a sip of the seltzer. "Fuck you."

"Enough of this," Hale dismissed, going to the fridge to get another drink. "Let's talk about something else. I want to enjoy the stress-free time before classes start and everything goes to hell."

Chapter Thirty-Nine

Ren was excited as he walked to class on Tuesday. Usually, he dreaded his first class of the semester, but his date with Miles was right after, so he couldn't stop the skip in his step as he made his way across campus.

Noah did not appreciate his attitude, and he made it known pretty much immediately after Ren took the seat beside him. "You look far too happy," he accused. "It's a three-to-five class. No one's thrilled." He glanced to his left, then gestured at the man beside him. "Except Luca, probably. He likes classes at all hours."

Luca, who had been busy writing the date on the first page of his notebook, glanced up at the sound of his name.

"Hi, Luca," Ren greeted, smiling politely at Julian's best friend. "I didn't see you at all last semester. How have you been?"

The brunette frowned, eyeing Ren suspiciously through the lenses of his glasses. He had never warmed to Ren much. "I'm fine," he answered after a pause. "Thanks for asking."

For some reason, this seemed to exasperate Noah, because his eyes rolled. "This is going to be *such* a fun class," he mumbled sarcastically.

Ren shrugged. "As long as it goes fast and I can get on with my date, I don't care."

Groaning, Noah stretched his legs out long in front of him. They were in one of the older classrooms that still had small desks for seating, and the whole thing creaked under his weight. "I can't believe you're in an actual relationship too. Jules has Rita, Hale has Logan, you have Miles. Who am I supposed to hang out with?"

"Luca," Ren said.

The blank look Noah gave him told Ren exactly how he felt about this suggestion. "Luca doesn't want to hang out with anyone but Jules." Luca didn't seem to be paying attention to them, but Noah still lowered his voice to add, "He's also hung up on Julian, and that's just uncomfortable."

"Luca only loves Julian because it's easy to."

"Wasn't easy for you," Noah commented, and Ren hit him on the arm. "I'm just saying."

Class was about to start, so Ren removed his notebook from his backpack. When he lifted his gaze, a familiar dark-haired man was standing in front of his desk, waiting to be noticed.

"Hi, Jason," he greeted. "I didn't know you'd be in this class."

"I didn't know you guys would be here either," Jason said. The only available seat near them was on the other side of Luca, so he went to take it.

"What even is this group of people?" Noah mumbled. He then said, "You're not allowed to harass me to go out with you all semester. I don't have any money," to Jason, who waved a dismissive hand in response.

His eyes landed on Luca. "Who are you?"

"Who are *you*?" Luca shot back.

It shocked Ren to learn not everyone knew Jason already.

"He's Luca," Noah introduced for him. It reminded Ren of a parent and their child, and he resisted the urge to laugh.

"Ah! Julian's elusive best friend."

Luca did not appreciate being called this, if his sour expression was anything to go by.

Noah turned to Ren again. "This class is going to be actual hell."

It was, but Ren couldn't find it in him to care right then. He just laughed, shook his head, and wished for class to start so it could be over sooner.

***

Miles parked in the lot outside the building, so Ren dismissed himself as soon as class was done and ran out to meet him. Noah gave him a *Do not leave me with these two* look—Jason had tried to flirt with Luca throughout the lecture only to get ignored or scolded—but Ren only laughed and went on his way.

When he got in the car, Miles asked him how dinner and ice cream afterward sounded. Miles looked nervous, as if the suggestion wouldn't please Ren, so he leaned over to kiss the man in the driver's seat.

"That sounds perfect."

They went to a Thai restaurant that was twenty minutes away. Ren was more than content to watch Miles drive while an album he wasn't familiar with played on the stereo. He told Miles about his class and who was in it, and Miles talked about his schedule. When Ren asked how many classes he had with Clarisse, Miles smiled and answered, "Only two."

Ren had asked out of jealousy, but he was surprised to not feel any at the answer. "Oh," he said. "Okay."

"Does it bother you?" Miles asked. "She's one of my best friends."

"It doesn't bother me. I'm shocked that it doesn't, but it doesn't." The song on the stereo changed, and he glanced at the track number. "I must be really confident in your feelings for me."

"You should be," Miles said. "I'm in love with you."

Ren doubted he'd ever tire of hearing it. "You're gonna be my boyfriend after tonight, right?" he asked.

"Yeah. As long as you'll have me."

To hide his smile, Ren sunk his teeth into his lower lip. "You're a real upgrade from my last boyfriend."

Scoffing, Miles shook his head. "You've had shit taste in men. I'd hope I'm an upgrade from most of your boyfriends."

"It feels kind of funny now. I was dating around in hopes I would come across the right person, and you were right next door the entire time."

"Maybe I should have confessed sooner," Miles mumbled. "Saved us both some pain."

Humming, Ren watched out the window. "I think we needed to get to know each other through Hale and Logan first. I was so stubborn that something like that needed to happen for me to give you the time of day."

"Probably," Miles agreed. "Thank god our best friends are perfect for each other, right?"

Ren smiled. "Yeah. I'm happy everything worked out the way it did."

Miles's right hand left the steering wheel so he could lace their fingers together.

Ren had never felt so content. "Do you think we ever would have worked it out without Hale and Logan?"

"I was going to confess to you before you graduated no matter what, but like you said, I'm not sure you would have given me the time of day."

"I would have for sure thought about it," Ren said. "Maybe I would have told you off right away, but if we ever ran into each other later in life, I think I would have given you a chance. I mean, I was totally into you the first time we met before you were so short with me."

Miles's eyebrows shot up. "Really?"

"Yeah," Ren confirmed with a gentle laugh. "I think you're super hot, so I was interested pretty much immediately. Then you embarrassed me and shut the door in my face, and I decided you were a prick."

With a smile, Miles shook his head. "You should have said something."

"You gave me no room to," Ren defended. "Also, Hale had told me there was a cute guy moving in next door, so I was actually planning on scoping it out for him. When you, a cute guy, answered the door, I just assumed he was talking about you, so hitting on you was off limits."

Miles laughed at this, and Ren raised his eyebrows. "What's so funny?"

"Nothing, it's just …" Miles squeezed Ren's hand. "You know, when you knocked on the door, I was already very annoyed because I was unpacking our living room by myself because Logan was too busy daydreaming about the guy he met next door. I thought you were cute as shit, but then, when you said you were our neighbor, I thought you were Logan's guy and I didn't want you to distract him more, so I got you out of there quickly."

This was all so stupid, and Ren joined in on the laughter. "I was going to ask if you remembered meeting Hale in the hall."

"I realize that now."

"So if you had let me get out a few more words, you would have realized I wasn't Logan's guy and I would have realized you weren't Hale's guy, and our entire relationship could have gone completely different."

"Unbelievable, isn't it?" Miles asked, shaking his head. "Once I realized you weren't the guy Logan was hung up on, I tried to apologize to you and explain, but you were so unwilling to listen to me."

Ren raised Miles's hand to his lips and kissed his knuckles. "Assumptions fucked us over, didn't they? You assumed Logan had dibs, and I assumed you were an asshole."

"I think we should just blame it on Hale and Logan for not being clear in their descriptions of each other. I mean, it's not like Logan and I look alike. All Hale had to say was that *cute neighbor* was a black guy, and there would have been no misunderstandings."

"Can you imagine how horrified Hale would be to hear that? He wanted us together so bad. I can't wait to see the look on his face when I tell him it was his fault we weren't together sooner."

"Let's tell him together," Miles suggested.

Together. The use of the word pleased Ren. They'd have a lot more *together*s in the future, he was sure.

Ren kissed Miles's hand again. He couldn't believe how unbelievably easy it felt to be with him like this. Even if they had delayed the start of a relationship because of miscommunication, he was happy they were finally there.

When they got back to the apartment, they held hands and went up together.

Outside of Ren's apartment, they faced each other. "Thank you for tonight," Miles said.

"You're the one who planned everything and paid. I'll have to make it up to you next time."

"So there will be a next time," Miles said, though Ren didn't believe for a second that had been a concern of his. The night had been so perfect it couldn't have felt that way to only him.

"Yeah," Ren confirmed. "You're my boyfriend, right?"

Miles was hiding a smile as he forced an unsure expression. "Am I? I don't recall you ever asking me …"

Huffing, Ren pulled Miles's hand until he stepped forward and closed the distance between them. "I like you a lot. Wanna be my boyfriend?"

"I'd like nothing more," Miles responded, now full-out grinning.

Ren snaked an arm around his neck and pulled him down for a kiss. Miles tasted like the chocolate ice cream he had just eaten, and Ren sighed in content before pulling away. "I don't want the night to be over," he declared. He met Miles's eyes, his lip pulled between his teeth. "Wanna come in?"

Miles groaned. "I meant it when I said I wouldn't have sex with you until you were in love with me."

"So we don't have sex," Ren said, even though that was exactly what he had in mind. "We can just hang out and kiss some more."

Miles considered it for a moment, then sighed. "I can't even imagine saying no, even though having self-restraint will be incredibly difficult."

Laughing, Ren dropped his arm from around his neck to free his key from his pocket. "You don't have to restrain yourself for my sake."

"Believe me, I know," Miles grumbled. "I have no doubt you won't make it easy for me."

As Ren unlocked his door, he looked over his shoulder at the younger man. "That's half the fun, isn't it?"

When he opened the door, the only thing on his mind was how to best tease his boyfriend as soon as they got to his bedroom.

The thought left him at the sight of Hale on the couch, crying.

A switch flipped in him, and he dropped Miles's hand to go to his roommate. "What's wrong?" He took in Hale's puffy eyes and the abundance of tissues scattered about. Clearly he had been crying for a while.

"Hale—"

"We broke up," Hale choked out before sobs wracked his body again. "Logan broke up with me."

Ren and Miles shared a look. With a nod from Ren, Miles left the doorway to go check on Logan. Shocked, Ren took the seat on the couch beside Hale and pulled him into a hug.

He didn't think there was anything he could say to fix this, so he just let his friend sob on his shoulder.

This was not how the semester was supposed to begin.

www.ingramcontent.com/pod-product-compliance
Lightning Source LLC
Chambersburg PA
CBHW032352310726
48973CB00007B/1982